GREAT IRISH DETECTIVE STORIES

Edited by Peter Haining

BARNES
&NOBLE
BOOKS
NEW YORK

For
Philippa, Richard, Wendy
Ray and Kari
and unforgettable memories
of Dunmore East

1997 Barnes & Noble Books

ISBN 0-7607-0662-X *casebound*
ISBN 0-7607-1388-X *paperback*

Printed and bound in the United States of America

97 99 00 01 02 MC 9 8 7 6 5 4 3 2 1
99 00 01 02 03 MP 9 8 7 6 5 4 3 2 1

QF

CONTENTS

INTRODUCTION

A columnist writing in the *Irish Post* has declared, 'It would be fair to say that Ireland has not produced much in the way of crime fiction over the years.'

This statement is both surprising and puzzling. Not only has Ireland produced a considerable number of outstanding crime writers during the one hundred and fifty or so years that the genre has been a part of literature, but some of its leading names have been pioneers in the field, introducing entirely new developments into stories of murder, mystery and detection. For example, the first crime story to feature a tell-tale clue found clutched in the hand of a murder victim was by an Irish writer, as was the first in which a photograph helped to solve the mystery of a missing person. Indeed, a little further investigation soon reveals that the Irish influence has actually been at work in the field since its very beginning . . .

Edgar Allan Poe, the 'Father of the Detective Story', as crime historians refer to him, came from Irish stock. The Poes were, apparently, tenant farmers in County Cavan until John Poe, grandfather of the famous writer, collected together his meagre possessions and, with high hopes of a better life, sailed for the New World in 1750. Poe himself never visited Ireland, although he did live for a time in England and also travelled to Scotland, but his fame as the man who founded the detective story genre with three stories featuring the sleuth C. Auguste Dupin, which anticipated virtually every possible type of detective-mystery-crime story, might be said to owe *something* to the resolute and inquisitive Irish bloodline from which he sprang.

Wilkie Collins, author of *The Moonstone* (1868) which has been described by T.S. Eliot as 'the first, the longest, and the best of modern English detective novels', also had Irish roots, with a grand-

7

father, Willliam Collins (1740-1812), who was a well-known Irish author in his own right.

Then there is the greatest of all fictional detectives, Sherlock Holmes, who visited Ireland several times on cases that took him to places as far apart as Belfast, Maynooth, Dublin, Waterford and Skibbereen, where he 'gave serious trouble to the constabulary', according to Doctor Watson in the case of 'The Cardboard Box'. Holmes's creator, Sir Arthur Conan Doyle, was born in Scotland of Irish parents: his mother was Mary Foley, while his father was the eldest child of the Irish political cartoonist, John Doyle.

Other famous names come readily to mind. Sax Rohmer, whose inscrutable villain Fu Manchu has almost as many fans as Sherlock Holmes, had Irish parents, although he was actually born in Birmingham. His real name was Arthur Sarsfield Ward—Sarsfield after a great seventeenth-century Irish General, and Ward being the anglicised version of Mac and Bhaird, 'son of the bard'. Equally familiar are the names of Alfred Hitchcock and Raymond Chandler, in both of whose veins Irish blood flowed.

Hitchcock, the master of the cinema thriller, had a Catholic Irish-London background. His East End grandfather had converted to Catholicism when he married Ann Mahoney from Ireland, and his father also took an Irish bride, Emma Jane Whelan, a matriachal Catholic lady who, a number of the film-maker's biographers believe, was responsible for her son's problems in his later relationships with women.

Raymond Chandler's mother was Florence Dart Thornton, a member of an old Irish Quaker family, and Chandler was always proud of his ancestry, writing in 1940, 'I have a great many Irish relatives, some poor, some not poor, and all Protestants, and some of them Sinn Feiners (republicans), and some entirely pro-British.'

Among more recent crime and thriller novelists there are further eminent names to be found. Francis Clifford, author of *The Naked Runner,* filmed with Frank Sinatra, came from Cork; Leonard Holton, creator of the Los Angeles crime fighter Father Joseph Bredder, and author of the famous Peter Sellers movie, *The Mouse That Roared,* was a Waterford man; Bill Naughton, creator of the irrepressible *Alfie,* was born in County Mayo; and Frank Ryan, continuing the Conan Doyle tradition of being both doctor and crime writer, came from Dublin. On the female side there are the prolific Dublin-born Sheila Pim and Ruth Dudley Edwards, the distinguished biographer and author of four highly praised crime novels in the tradition of Dorothy L. Sayers, Margery Alllingham and Ngaio Marsh.

The list of the 'Irish Crime Connection' is full of short story writers, too, and the evidence of their contributions will be found in the following pages. Among the familiar names such as Frank O'Connor, Sean O'Faolain, Liam O'Flaherty and William Trevor—all of whom confessed to being admirers of the mystery story and produced several outstanding examples of the genre—the reader will find some surprises. The hugely successful Peter Cheyney, for instance, who introduced the hard-boiled style of American crime fiction into a British setting, came from County Clare; while Cecil Day Lewis, the Poet Laureate who wrote crime stories under the pseudonym Nicholas Blake, was born in Ballintubber. Everyone is surely aware of Brendan Behan's Irish ancestry, but few may realise that the notorious drinker and celebrated playwright also wrote crime fiction under the pen name 'Emmet Street'; or that Flann O'Brien, master of the comic tale, supplemented his earnings by anonymously writing some of the adventures of Sexton Blake.

On the evidence of names such as these I think I can disprove the assertion that Ireland has 'not produced much in the way of crime fiction'. Indeed, the stories that make up this volume are merely a representative cross-section of a much larger number in which the particularly Irish approach to the writing of mystery and mayhem will be found at its thrilling and ingenious best. I only regret that space has made it impossible to include them all.

Nevertheless, the evidence is here that Ireland has produced a rich vein of crime and detective fiction for at least a century and a half. The cases now await your judgement.

PETER HAINING
March, 1993

1

FOUL PLAY
Stories of Murder and Death

EVENTS AT DRIMAGHLEEN

William Trevor

Few present-day Irish short story writers are more steeped in the lore of the detective story than William Trevor (1928-) whose first recollection of being introduced to the 'staid, adult occupation of reading' was via the pages of Agatha Christie's Ten Little Indians. *The experience was to have a profound effect on his interests and his eventual decision to become a writer. The orange-jacketed edition of the Christie classic had been obtained for him by his mother, a dedicated borrower from the Argosy Library, a book-lending service available at most sweet shops in County Cork where the family lived in the 1930s and '40s. Trevor was so enthralled by the ingenious murder story that he went straight on to read all Christie's other novels, as well as those by such popular crime writers as Sapper and Edgar Wallace. 'For years I read nothing else,' he admits, 'and am a considerable expert on the detective fiction of that period, even to this day.'*

He had an early real-life encounter with death which further excited his interest. 'In Youghal there was a man who shot himself in a henhouse,' he recalled in an interview in 1992. 'Life had been hell for this man, the voices whispered, and the henhouse, quite near the back of our garden, developed an eeriness that the chatter of birds made even more sinister. The henhouse isn't there any more, but even so as I stand where it was I shudder, and remember other deaths.'

William Trevor is widely respected as one of the best short story authors, Irish or otherwise, and it is small wonder that crime and detection should be the theme of a number of his tales, which are the envy of many specialist thriller writers. In my estimation there are few better examples of his work in this genre than 'Events at Drimaghleen' (written in 1990), which exploits another of his fascinations — small town Irish life — in a story of foul play at its most foul . . .

13

Nothing as appalling had happened before at Drimaghleen; its people had never been as shocked. They'd had their share of distress, like any people; there were memories of dramatic occurrences; stories from a more distant past were told. In the 1880s a woman known as the Captain's wife had run away with a hunch-backed pedlar. In 1798 there'd been resistance in the hills and fighting in Drimaghleen itself. During the Troubles a local man had been executed in a field by the Black and Tans. But no story, and no long memory, could match the horror of the tragedy that awaited the people of Drimaghleen on May 22nd, 1985, a Wednesday morning.

The McDowds, that morning, awoke in their farmhouse and began the day as they always did, McDowd pulling on his shirt and trousers and lifting down a black overcoat from the pegs beside the kitchen door. He fastened it with a length of string which he kept in one of its pockets, and found his socks in his gumboots and went out with his two sheepdogs to drive the cows in for milking. His wife washed herself, put the kettle on the stove, and knocked on her daughter's door. 'Maureen!' she called. 'Come on now, Maureen!'

It was not unusual that Maureen failed to reply. Mrs McDowd re-entered her bedroom, stepped out of her nightdress and dressed herself. 'Get up out of that, Maureen!' she shouted, banging again on her daughter's door. 'Are you sick?' she enquired, puzzled now by the lack of movement from within the room: always at this second rousing Maureen yawned or spoke. 'Maureen!' she shouted again, and then opened the door.

McDowd, calling in the cattle, was aware that there had been something wrong in the yard, as he'd passed through it, but an early-morning torpor hindered the progression of his thoughts when he endeavoured to establish what it was. His wife's voice shouting across the field at him and his daughter's name used repeatedly in the information that was being inadequately conveyed to him, jolted him into an awareness that what had been wrong was that Maureen's bicycle had not been leaning against the kitchen window-sill. 'Maureen hasn't come back,' his wife repeated again when he was close enough to hear her. 'She's not been in her bed.'

The cows were milked because no matter what the reason for Maureen's absence they had to be. The breakfast was placed on the kitchen table because no good would come of not taking food. McDowd, in silence, ate with an appetite that was unaffected; his wife consumed less than usual. 'We will drive over,' he said when they had finished, anger thickening his voice.

She nodded. She'd known as soon as she'd seen the unused bed that they would have to do something. They could not just wait for a letter to arrive, or a telegram, or whatever it was their daughter had planned. They would drive over to the house where Lancy Butler lived with his mother, the house to which their daughter had cycled the evening before. They did not share the thought that possessed both of them: that their daughter had taken the law into her own hands and gone off with Lancy Butler, a spoilt and useless man.

McDowd was a tallish, spare man of sixty-two, his face almost gaunt, grey hair ragged on his head. His wife, two years younger, was thin also, with gnarled features and the hands of a woman who all her life had worked in the fields. They did not say much to one another, and never had; but they did not quarrel either. On the farm, discussion was rarely apt, there being no profit in it; it followed naturally that grounds for disagreement were limited. Five children had been born to the McDowds; Maureen was the youngest and the only one who had remained at home. Without a show of celebration, for that was not the family way, her twenty-fifth birthday had passed by a month ago.

'Put your decent trousers on,' Mrs McDowd urged. 'You can't go like that.'

'I'm all right the way I am.'

She knew he would not be persuaded and did not try, but instead hurried back to her bedroom to change her shoes. At least he wouldn't drive over in the overcoat with the string round it; that was only for getting the cows in from the field when the mornings were cold. He'd taken it off before he'd sat down to his breakfast and there would be no cause to put it on again. She covered up her own old skirt and jumper with her waterproof.

'The little bitch,' he said in the car, and she said nothing.

They both felt the same, anxious and cross at the same time, not wanting to believe the apparent truth. Their daughter had ungratefully deceived them: again in silence the thought was shared while he drove the four miles to the Butlers' house. When they turned off the tarred road into a lane, already passing between the Butlers' fields, they heard the dog barking. The window of the Volkswagen on Mrs McDowd's side wouldn't wind up, due to a defect that had developed a month ago: the shrill barking easily carried above the rattle of the engine.

That was that, they thought, listening to the dog. Maureen and Lancy had gone the night before, and Mrs Butler couldn't manage the cows on her own. No wonder the old dog was beside himself. Bitterly, McDowd called his daughter a bitch again, though only to himself. Lancy Butler, he thought, my God! Lancy Butler would lead her a dance, and lead her astray, and lead her down into the gutters of some town. He'd warned her a thousand times about Lancy Butler. He'd told her the kind of fool he was.

'His father was a decent man,' he said, breaking at last the long silence. 'Never touched a drop.'

'The old mother ruined him.'

It wouldn't last long, they both thought. Lancy Butler might marry her, or he might wriggle out of it. But however it turned out she'd be back in six months' time or at any rate a year's. There'd probably be a baby to bring up.

The car turned into the yard, and neither McDowd nor his wife immediately saw their daughter lying beside the pump. For the first few moments of their arrival their attention was claimed by the distressed dog, a black and white sheepdog like their own two. Dust had risen from beneath the Volkswagen's wheels and was still thick in the air as they stepped from the car. The dog was running wildly across a corner of the yard, back and forth, and back and forth again. The dog's gone mad, Mrs McDowd thought, something's after affecting it. Then she saw her daughter's body lying by the pump, and a yard or so away her daughter's bicycle lying on its side, as if she had fallen from it. Beside the bicycle were two dead rabbits.

'My God,' McDowd said, and his wife knew from his voice that he hadn't seen his daughter yet but was looking at something else. He had walked to another part of the yard, where the dog was. He had gone there instinctively, to try to calm the animal.

She knelt down, whispering to Maureen, thinking in her confusion that her daughter had just this minute fallen off her bicycle. But Maureen's face was cold as stone, and her flesh had already stiffened. Mrs McDowd screamed, and then she was aware that she was lying down herself, clasping Maureen's dead body. A moment later she was aware that her husband was weeping piteously, unable to control himself, that he was kneeling down, his hands on the body also.

Mrs McDowd did not remember rising to her feet, or finding the energy and the will to do so. 'Don't go over there,' she heard her husband saying to her, and saw him wiping at his eyes with the arm of his jersey. But he didn't try to stop her when she went to where the dog was; he remained on his knees beside his daughter, calling out to her between his sobs, asking her not to be dead.

The dog was crouched in a doorway, not barking any more. A yard or so away Mrs Butler lay with one of her legs twisted under her, blood on the ground already turned brown, a pool of it still scarlet. Looking down at her, Mrs McDowd thought with abrupt lucidity: Maureen did not fall off her bicycle. She went back to where her daughter lay and behind the two tin barrels that stood by the pump she saw the body of Lancy Butler, and on the ground not far from it the shotgun that must have blown off Mrs Butler's face.

*   *   *

O'Kelly of the Garda arrived at a swift conclusion. Old Mrs Butler had been as adamant as the McDowds in her opposition to the match that her son and Maureen McDowd had planned for themselves. And there was more to it than that: Mrs Butler had been obsessively possessive, hiding from no one her determination that no other woman should ever take her son away from her. Lancy was her only child, the single one to survive years of miscarrying. His father had died when Lancy was only two years old, leaving mother and child to lead a lonely life on a farm that was remote. O'Kelly knew that Mrs Butler had been reputed to be strange in the head, and given to furious jealousies where Lancy was concerned. In the kind of rage that people who'd known her were familiar with she had shot her son's sweetheart rather than suffer the theft of him. He had wrenched the shotgun from her and by accident or otherwise it had exploded. A weak man at the best of times, he had turned it upon himself rather than face the reality of what had happened. This deduction, borne out by the details in the yard, satisfied O'Kelly of the Garda; the people of Drimaghleen arrived themselves at the same conclusion. 'It was always trouble,' McDowd said on the day of the funerals. 'The minute she went out with Lancy Butler it was trouble written down for poor Maureen.'

Drimaghleen was a townland, with nothing to mark it except a crossroads that was known as Drimaghleen Crossroads. The modest farms that comprised it, each of thirty or so acres, were scattered among bogland, one separated from the next by several miles, as the

McDowds' and the Butlers' were. The village of Kilmona was where the people of Drimaghleen went to mass, and where they confessed to Father Sallins. The children of the farms went to school in the small town of Mountcroe, driven each morning in a yellow bus that drove them back to the end of their lanes or farm tracks in the afternoon. Milk churns were collected in much the same way by the creamery lorry. Bread and groceries were bought in the village; fresh meat in Mountcroe. When the men of Drimaghleen got drunk they did so at Mountcroe, never in the village, although often they took a few bottles of stout there, in the bar beside the grocery counter. Hardware and clothes were bought in Mountcroe, which had had a cinema called the Abbey Picture House until the advent of television closed it in the early 1960s. Drimaghleen, Kilmona and Mountcroe formed a world that bounded the lives of the people of the Drimaghleen farms. Rarely was there occasion to venture beyond it to the facilities of a town that was larger—unless the purpose happened to be a search for work or the first step on the way to exile.

The children of the McDowds, whose search for such work had taken them far from the townland, returned heartbroken for their sister's mass. All four of them came, two with husbands, one with a wife, one on her own. The weddings which had taken place had been the last family occasions, two of them in Kilmona, the third in distant Skibbereen, the home of the girl whom the McDowds' son had married a year ago. That wedding was on their minds at Maureen's mass—the long journey there had been in the Volkswagen, the night they had spent in Eldon's Hotel, the farewells the next day. Not in the wildest horror of a nightmare could any of the McDowds have guessed the nature of the occasion destined to bring them together next.

After the funeral the family returned to the farm. The younger McDowds had known of Maureen's and Lancy Butler's attachment, and of their parents' opposition to it. They had known as well of Mrs Butler's possessive affection for her son, having grown up with stories of this maternal eccentricity, and having witnessed Lancy himself, as a child and as a boy, affected by her indulgence. 'Oh, it can wait, Lancy, it can wait,' she would say a dozen times an hour, referring to some necessary chore on the farm. 'Ah, sure, we won't bother with school today,' she had said before that, when Lancy had complained of a difficulty he was experiencing with the seven times table or Brother Martin's twenty weekend spellings. The people of Drimaghleen used to wonder whether the farm or Lancy would suffer more in the end.

'What did she see in him?' Mrs McDowd mused sadly at the funeral meal. 'Will anyone ever tell me what she saw in him?'

They shook their heads. The cheeks of all of them were still smeared with the tears they had shed at the service. Conversation was difficult.

'We will never recover from it,' the father said, with finality in his voice. It was all that could be said, it was all they knew with certainty: for as long as the older McDowds remained in this farmhouse—which would be until their own deaths—the vicious, ugly tragedy would haunt them. They knew that if Maureen had been knocked from her bicycle by a passing motorcar they could have borne her death with greater fortitude; or if she had died of an illness, or been the victim of incurable disease. The knife that turned in their pain was their memory of the Butlers' farmyard, the barking dog running back and forth, the three still bodies. There was nothing but the waste of a life to contemplate, and the cruelty of chance—for why should it have been simple, pretty Maureen whose fate it was to become mixed up with so peculiar a couple as that mother and son? There were other girls in the neighbourhood—underhand girls and girls of doubtful character—who somehow more readily belonged with the Butlers: anyone would tell you that.

'Why don't you drive over and see us?' one of the daughters invited. 'Can't we persuade you?'

Her father stared into the table without trying to reply. It was unnecessary to say that a drive of such a distance could only be contemplated when there was a wedding or a funeral. Such journeys had not been undertaken during Maureen's lifetime, when she might have looked after the farm for a day; in no way could they be considered now. Mrs McDowd tried to smile, making an effort to acknowledge the concern that had inspired the suggestion, but no smile came.

*   *   *

Being of a nature that might interest strangers, the deaths were reported in the newspapers. They were mentioned on the radio, and on the television news. Then everything became quiet again at

Drimaghleen, and in the village and in the town. People wrote letters to the McDowds, expressing their sorrow. People came to see them but did not stay long. 'I am always there,' Father Sillans said. 'Kilmona 23. You have only to summon me. Or call up at the rectory.'

The McDowds didn't. They watched the summer going by, taking in their hay during the warm spell in June, keeping an eye on the field of potatoes and the ripening barley. It began to rain more than usual; they worried about the barley.

'Excuse me,' a man said in the yard one afternoon in October. 'Are you Mr McDowd?'

McDowd said he was, shouting at the dogs to behave themselves. The stranger would be a traveller in fertilisers, he said to himself, a replacement for Donoghue, who had been coming to the farm for years. Then he realised that it was the wrong time of year for Donoghue.

'Would it be possible to have a word, Mr McDowd?'

McDowd's scrawny features slowly puckered; slowly he frowned. He lifted a hand and scratched at his grey, ragged hair, which was a way he had when he wished to disguise bewilderment. Part of his countryman's wiliness was that he preferred outsiders not to know, or deduce, what was occurring in his mind.

'A word?' he said.

'Could we maybe step inside, sir?'

McDowd saw no reason to step inside his own house with this man. The visitor was florid-faced, untidily dressed in dark corduroy trousers and a garbardine jacket. His hair was long and black, and grew coarsely down the sides of his face in two brushlike panels. He had a city voice; it wasn't difficult to guess he came from Dublin.

'What d'you want with me?'

'I was sorry to hear that thing about your daughter, Mr McDowd. That was a terrible business.'

'It's over and done with.'

'It is, sir. Over and done with.'

The red bonnet of a car edged its way into the yard. McDowd watched it, reminded of some cautious animal by the slow creeping movement, the engine purring so lightly you could hardly hear it. When the car stopped by the milking shed nobody got out of it, but McDowd could see a figure wearing sunglasses at the wheel. This was a woman, with black hair also, smoking a cigarette.

'It could be to your advantage, Mr McDowd.'

'What could be? Does that car belong to you?'

'We drove down to see you, sir. That lady's a friend of mine, a colleague by the name of Hetty Fortune.'

The woman stepped out of the car. She was taller than the man, with a sombre face and blue trousers that matched her blue shirt. She dropped her cigarette on to the ground and carefully stubbed it out with the toe of her shoe. As slowly as she had driven the car she walked across the yard to where the two men were standing. The dogs growled at her, but she took no notice. 'I'm Hetty Fortune,' she said in an English accent.

'I didn't tell you my own name, Mr McDowd,' the man said. 'It's Jeremiah Tyler.'

'I hope Jeremiah has offered you our condolences, Mr McDowd. I hope both you and your wife will accept our deepest sympathy.'

'What do you want here?'

'We've been over at the Butlers' place, Mr McDowd. We spent a long time there. We've been talking to a few people. Could we talk to you, d'you think?'

'Are you the newspapers?'

'In a manner of speaking. Yes, in a manner of speaking we represent the media. And I'm perfectly sure,' the woman added hastily, 'you've had more than enough of all that. I believe you'll find what we have to say to you is different, Mr McDowd.'

'The wife and myself have nothing to say to the newspapers. We didn't say anything at the time, and we have nothing to say since. I have things to do about the place.'

'Mr McDowd, would you be good enough to give us five minutes of your time? Five minues in your kitchen, talking to yourself and your wife? Would you give us an opportunity to explain?'

Attracted by the sound of voices, Mrs McDowd came out of the house. She stood in the doorway, not quite emerging from the kitchen porch, regarding the strangers even more distrustfully than her husband had. She didn't say anything when the woman approached her and held out a hand which she was obliged to shake.

'We are sorry to obtrude on your grief, Mrs McDowd. Mr Tyler and I have been keen to make that clear to your husband.'

Mrs McDowd did not acknowledge this. She didn't like the look of the sombre-faced woman or her unkempt companion. There was a seediness about him, a quality that city people seemed often to exude if they weren't smartly attired. The woman wasn't seedy but you could see she was insincere from the way her mouth was. You could hear the insincerity when she spoke.

'The full truth has not been established, Mrs McDowd. It is that that we would like to discuss with you.'

'I've told you no,' McDowd said. 'I've told them to go away,' he said to his wife.

Mrs McDowd's eyes stared at the woman's sunglasses. She remained where she was, not quite coming into the yard. The man said:

'Would it break the ice if I took a snap? Would you mind that, sir? If I was to take a few snaps of yourself and the wife?'

He had spoken out of turn. A shadow of anger passed over the woman's face. The fingers of her left hand moved in an irritated wriggle. She said quickly:

'That's not necessary at this stage.'

'We've got to get the pictures, Hetty,' the man mumbled, hushing the words beneath his breath so that the McDowds wouldn't hear. But they guessed the nature of his protest, for it showed in his pink face. The woman snapped something at him.

'If you don't leave us alone we'll have to get the Guards,' McDowd said. 'you're trespassing on this land.'

'Is it fair on your daughter's memory that the truth should be hidden, Mr McDowd?'

'Another thing is, those dogs can be fierce if they want to be.'

'It isn't hidden,' Mrs McDowd said. 'We all know what happened. Detectives worked it out, but sure anyone could have told them.'

'No, Mrs McDowd, nothing was properly worked out at all. That's what I'm saying to you. The surface was scarcely disturbed. What seemed to be the truth wasn't.'

McDowd told his wife to lock the door. They would drive over to Mountroe and get a Guard to come back with them. 'We don't want any truck with you,' he harshly informed their visitors. 'If the dogs eat the limbs off you after we've gone don't say it wasn't mentioned.'

Unmoved by these threats, her voice losing none of its confidence, the woman said that what was available was something in the region of three thousand pounds. 'For a conversation of brief duration you would naturally have to be correctly reimbursed. Already we have taken up your working time, and of course we're not happy about that. The photograph mentioned by Mr Tyler would naturally have the attachment of a fee. We're talking at the end of the day of something above a round three thousand.'

Afterwards the McDowds remembered that moment. They remembered the feeling they shared, that this was no kind of trick, that the money spoken of would be honestly paid. They remembered thinking that the sum was large, that they could do with thirty pounds never mind three thousand. Rain had destroyed the barley; they missed their daughter's help on the farm; the tragedy had aged and weakened them. If three thousand pounds could come out of it, they'd maybe think of selling up and buying a bungalow.

'Let them in,' McDowd said, and his wife led the way into the kitchen.

*   *   *

The scene of the mystery is repeated all over rural Ireland. From Cork to Cavan, from Roscommon to Rosslare you will come across small, tucked-away farms like the Butlers' and the McDowds'. Maureen McDowd had been gentle-natured and gentle-tempered. The sins of sloth and greed had not been hers; her parents called her a perfect daughter, close to a saint. A photograph, taken when Maureen McDowd was five, showed a smiling, freckled child; another showed her in her First Communion dress; a third, taken at the wedding of her brother, was of a healthy-looking girl, her face creased up in laughter, a cup of tea in her right hand. There was a photograph of her mother and father, standing in their kitchen. Italicised beneath it was the information that it had been taken by Jeremiah Tyler. *The Saint of Drimaghleen*, Hetty Fortune had written, *never once missed mass in all her twenty-five years.*

The story was told in fashionably faded pictures. 'You know our Sunday supplement?' Hetty Fortune had said in the McDowds' kitchen, but they hadn't: newspapers from England had never played a part in their lives. They read the *Sunday Independent* themselves.

The Butlers' yard was brownly bleak in the pages of the supplement; the pump had acquired a quality not ordinarily noticed. A bicycle similar to Maureen's had been placed on the ground, a sheepdog similar to the Butlers' nosed about the doors of the cowshed. But the absence of the three bodies in the photographed yard, the dust still rising where the bicycle had fallen, the sniffing dog, lent the composition an eerie quality—horror conveyed without horror's presence. 'You used a local man?' the supplement's assistant editor enquired, and when informed that Jeremiah Tyler was a Dublin man he requested that a note be kept of the photographer's particulars.

The Gardai—in particular Superintendent O'Kelly—saw only what was convenient to see. Of the three bodies that lay that morning in the May sunshine they chose that of Lancy Butler to become the victim of their sluggish imagination. Mrs Butler, answering her notoriously uncontrollable jealousy, shot her son's sweetheart rather than have him marry her. Her son, so Superintendent O'Kelly infers from no circumstantial evidence whatsover, wrenched the shotgun out of her hands and fired on her in furious confusion. He then, within seconds, took his own life. The shotgun bore the fingerprints of all three victims: what O'Kelly has signally failed to explain is why this should be so. Why should the Butlers' shotgun bear the fingerprints of Maureen McDowd? O'Kelly declares that 'in the natural course of events' Maureen McDowd would have handled the shotgun, being a frequent visitor to the farm. Frequent visitors, in our experience, do not, 'in the natural course of events' or otherwise, meddle with a household's firearms. The Superintendent hedges the issue because he is himself bewildered. The shotgun was used for keeping down rabbits, he states, knowing that the shotgun's previous deployment by the Butlers is neither here nor there. He mentions rabbits because he still can offer no reasonable explanation why Maureen McDowd should ever have handled the death weapon. The fingerprints of all three victims were blurred and 'difficult', and had been found on several different areas of the weapon. Take it or leave it is what the Superintendent is saying. And wearily he is saying: Does it matter?

We maintain it does matter. We maintain that this extraordinary crime—following, as it does, hard on the heels of the renowned Kerry Babies mystery, and the Flynn case—has not been investigated, but callously shelved. The people of Drimaghleen will tell you everything that O'Kelly laboured over in his reports: the two accounts are identical. Everyone knows that Lancy Butler's mother was a sharp-tongued, possessive woman. Everyone knows that Lancy was a ne'er-do-well. Everyone knows that Maureen McDowd was a deeply religious girl. Naturally it was the mother who sought to end an intrusion she could not bear. Naturally it was slow, stupid Lancy who didn't pause

*to think what the consequences would be after he'd turned the gun on
his mother. Naturally it was he who could think of no more imaginative way out of his dilemma than to join the two women who had
dominated his life.*

*The scenario that neither O'Kelly nor the Butlers' neighbours
paused to consider is a vastly different one. A letter, apparently—and
astonishingly—overlooked by the police, was discovered behind the
drawer of a table which was once part of the furniture of Lancy
Butler's bedroom and which was sold in the general auction after the
tragedy—land, farmhouse and contents having by this time become
the property of Allied Irish Banks, who held the mortgage on the Butlers' possessions. This letter, written by Maureen McDowd a week
before the tragedy, reads:*

'Dear Lancy, Unless she stops I can't see any chance of marrying
you. I want to, Lancy, but she never can let us alone. What would it
be like for me in your place, and if I didn't come to you where would
we be able to go because you know my father wouldn't accept you
here. She has ruined the chance we had, Lancy, she'll never let go of
you. I am always cycling over to face her insults and the way she has
of looking at me. I think we have reached the end of it.'

*This being a direct admission by Maureen McDowd that conclu-
sion in the romance had been arrived at, why would the perceptive
Mrs Butler—a woman who was said to 'know your thoughts before
you knew them yourself'—decide to kill Lancy's girl? And the more
the mental make-up of that old woman is dwelt upon the more absurd
it seems that she would have destroyed everything she had by committing a wholly unnecessary murder. Mrs Butler was not the kind to act
blindly, in the fury of the moment. Her jealousy and the anger that
protected it smouldered cruelly within her, always present, never
varying.*

*But Maureen McDowd—young, impetuous, bitterly deprived of
the man she loved—a saint by nature and possessing a saint's fervour,
on that fatal evening made up for all the sins she had ever resisted.
Hell hath no fury like a woman scorned—except perhaps a woman
unfairly defeated. The old woman turned the screw, aware that victory was in sight. The insults and 'the way of looking' became more
open and more arrogant; Mrs Butler wanted Maureen McDowd out,
she wanted her gone for ever, never to dare to return.*

It is known that Lancy Butler found two rabbits in his snares that night: It is known that he and Maureen often made the rounds of the snares when she visited him in the evenings. He would ride her bicycle to the field where they were, Maureen sitting side-saddle on the carrier at the back. Lancy had no bicycle of his own. It is our deduction that the reason the shotgun bore Maureen's fingerprints is because they had gone on a shooting expedition as well and when they returned to the yard she was carrying both the shotgun and the snared rabbits. It is known that Maureen McDowd wept shortly before her death. In the fields, as they stalked their prey, Lancy comforted her but Maureen knew that never again would they walk here together, that never again would she come over to see him in the evening. The hatred his mother bore her, and Lancy's weakness, had combined to destroy what most of all she wanted. Mrs Butler was standing in the yard shouting her usual abuse and Maureen shot her. The rabbits fell to the ground as she jumped off the bicycle, and her unexpectedly sudden movement caused the bicycle itself, and Lancy on it, to turn over. He called out to her when it was too late, and she realised she could never have him now. She blamed him for never once standing up to his mother, for never making it easier. If she couldn't have this weak man whom she so passionately loved no one else would either. She shot her lover, knowing that within seconds she must take her own life too. And that, of course, she did.

There was more about Maureen. In the pages of the colour supplement Mrs McDowd said her daughter had been a helpful child. Her father said she'd been his special child. When she was small she used to go out with him to the fields, watching how he planted the seed-potatoes. Later on, she would carry out his tea to him, and later still she would assist with whatever task he was engaged in. Father Sallins gave it as his opinion that she had been specially chosen. A nun at the convent in Mountcroe remembered her with lasting affection.

O'Kelly fell prey to this local feeling. Whether they knew what they were doing or not, the people of Drimaghleen were protecting the memory of Maureen McDowd, and the Superintendent went along with the tide. She was a local girl of unblemished virtue, who had been 'specially chosen'. Had he publicly arrived at any other conclusion Superintendent O'Kelly might never safely have set foot in the neighbourhood of Drimaghleen again, nor the village of Kilmona, nor the town of Mountcroe. The Irish do not easily forgive the purloining of their latter-day saints.

*   *   *

'I wanted to tell you this stuff had been written,' Father Sallins said. 'I wanted it to be myself that informed you before you'd get a shock from hearing it elsewhere.'

He'd driven over specially. As soon as the story in the paper had been brought to his own notice he'd felt it his duty to sit down with the McDowds. In his own opinion, what had been printed was nearly as bad as the tragedy itself, his whole parish maligned, a police superintendent made out to be no better than the criminals he daily pursued. He'd read the thing through twice; he'd looked at the photographs in astonishment. Hetty Fortune and Jeremiah Tyler had come to see him, but he'd advised them against poking about in what was over and done with. He'd explained that people wanted to try to forget the explosion of violence that had so suddenly occurred in their midst, that he himself still prayed for the souls of the Butlers and Maureen McDowd. The woman had nodded her head, as though persuaded by what he said. 'I have the camera here, Father,' the man had remarked as they were leaving. 'Will I take a snap of you?' Father Sallins had stood by the hydrangeas, seeing no harm in having his photograph taken. 'I'll send it down to you when it's developed,' the man said, but the photograph had never arrived. The first he saw of it was in the Sunday magazine, a poor likeness of himself, eyelids drooped as though he had taken drink, dark stubble on his chin.

'This is a terrible thing,' he said in the McDowds' kitchen, remembering the photograph of that also: the cream-enamelled electric cooker, the Holy Child on the green-painted dresser, beside the alarm clock and the stack of clothes pegs, the floor carpeted for cosiness, the blue formica-topped table, the radio, the television set. In the photograph the kitchen had acquired an extraneous quality, just as the photograph of the Butlers' yard had. The harsh, ordinary colours, the soiled edges of the curtains, the chipped paintwork, seemed like part of a meticulous composition: the photograph was so much a picture that it invited questioning as a record.

'We never thought she was going to say that about Maureen,' Mrs McDowd said. 'It's lies, Father.'

'Of course it is, Mrs McDowd.'

'We all know what happened that night.'

'Of course we do.'

McDowd said nothing. They had taken the money. It was he who had said that the people should be allowed into the house. Three thousand, one hundred and fifty pounds was the sum the woman had written the cheque for, insisting that the extra money was owed.

'You never said she'd been specially chosen, Father?'

'Of course I didn't, Mrs McDowd.'

He'd heard that Superintendent O'Kelly had gone to see a solicitor to enquire if he'd been libelled, and although he was told he probably had been he was advised that recourse in the courts would be costly and might not be successful. The simple explanation of what had happened at the Butlers' farm had been easy for the people of Drimaghleen and for the police to accept because they had known Mrs Butler and they had known her son. There'd been no mystery, there'd been no doubt.

'Will we say a prayer together?' the priest suggested.

They knelt, and when they rose again Mrs McDowd began to cry. Everyone would know about it, she said, as if the priest had neither prayed nor spoken. The story would get about and people would believe it. '*Disadvantaged people,*' she quoted from the newspaper. She frowned, still sobbing, over the words. 'It says the Butlers were disadvantaged people. It says we are disadvantaged ourselves.'

'That's only the way that woman has of writing it down, Mrs McDowd. It doesn't mean much.'

'*These simple farm folk,*' Mrs McDowd read, '*of Europe's most western island form limited rural communities that all too often turn in on themselves.*'

'Don't pay attention,' Father Sallins advised.

'Does disadvantaged mean we're poor?'

'The way that woman would see it, Mrs McDowd.'

There was confusion now in Drimaghleen, in Kilmona and Mountcroe; and confusion, Father Sallins believed was insidious. People had been separated from their instinct, and other newspaper articles would follow upon this one. More strangers would come. Father Sallins imagined a film being made about Maureen McDowd, and the mystery that had been created becoming a legend. The nature of Maureen McDowd would be argued over, books would be written because all of it was fascinating. For ever until they died her mother and her father would blame themselves for taking the money their poverty had been unable to turn away.

'The family'll see the pictures.'

'Don't upset yourself, Mrs McDowd.'

'No one ever said she was close to being a saint. That was never said, Father.'

'I know, I know.'

Mrs McDowd covered her face with her hands. Her thin shoulders heaved beneath the pain of her distress; sobs wrenched at her body. Too much had happened to her, the priest thought; it was too much for any mother that her murdered daughter should be accused of murder herself in order to give newspaper readers something to think about. Her husband had turned away from the table she sat at. He stood with his back to her, looking out into the yard. In a low, exhausted voice he said:

'What kind of people are they?'

The priest slowly shook his head, unable to answer that, and in the kitchen that looked different in Jeremiah Tyler's photograph Mrs McDowd screamed. She sat at the blue-topped table with her lips drawn back from her teeth, one short, shrill scream following fast upon another. Father Sallins did not again attempt to comfort her. McDowd remained by the window.

THE HAND AND THE WORD

Gerald Griffin

*The crime story tradition which William Trevor exploited so skilfully
in his tale has a long history in Ireland: what is almost certainly the
very first tale of detection was created more than a hundred and sixty
years earlier by a fellow countryman. Although the American writer
Edgar Allan Poe is credited with being the 'Father of the Detective
Story', Gerald Griffin's tale 'The Hand and the Word', written in
1827, fourteen years before Poe's 'The Murders in the Rue Morgue',
is a story of foul play in which the murderer is revealed in the courtroom by a sharp-eyed witness who spots a vital clue clutched in the
dead man's hand. It is a theme that has since been used by numerous
detective story writers, in particular another famous American
author, Ellery Queen.*

*There are interesting similarities between the brief and tragic lives
of Poe and Gerald Griffin (1803-1840) who was born in Limerick and
initially made his living as a hack writer. Like Poe, Griffin suffered
from poor health which led to a nervous breakdown, and he too nur-
tured an ill-fated love for a married woman. He died in a typhus
epidemic just when his calibre as a writer was beginning to be
appreciated. 'The Hand and the Word' is a classic tale of crime about
a beautiful girl, her lover and the black-hearted criminal determined
to ruin their happiness. The climactic court scene, in which the
parishioners of Kilkee meet to determine the cause of death of the
young man and each in turn lays a hand on the corpse displayed to
public view in order to prove their innocence, is as dramatic as anything to be found in present-day detective writing.*

The village of Kilkee, on the southwestern coast of Ireland, has
been for many years to the city of Limerick, (on a small scale) that

which Brighton is to London. At the time, however, when the events which form the subject of the following little history took place, it had not yet begun to take precedence of a watering place somewhat farther to the north, on the same coast, called Miltown Malbay, which had been for a long time, and still was a favourite summer resort with the fashionables of the county, such as they were. The village itself consists merely of six to eight streets, or straggling rows of houses, scattered irregularly enough over those waste banks of sand in which the land terminates as it approaches the Atlantic.

Those banks, or sandhills, as they are called, do not, in this place, slope gradually to the marge of the sea, but form a kind of abrupt barrier or natural terrace around the little bay; descending with such a suddenness that the lodges on the extreme verge completely overhang the water, and with their snow-white fronts, and neat green lattices, produce a sufficiently picturesque effect when the tide is at the full.

The little inlet which has been dignified by the title of a bay, opens to the north-west by a narrow mouth, rendered yet narrower in appearance by the Duggara rocks, which stretch more than halfway across from the southern extremity. A bed of fine hard sand reaches as far as low water mark, and when the retiring waves have left it visible, affords a pleasant promenade to the bathers. Winding on either side toward the opening of the bay, and along the line of coast, are seen a number of broken cliffs which, gradually rising to a considerable height, form to the north a precipituous headland called Corballagh; and to the southward they stretch away behind Duggara, in a thousand fantastic shapes. Close to the mouth or opening, on this side, is the Amphitheatre, which has been so named in later years, from the resemblance which instantly suggests itself to the beholder. Here the rocks lift themselves above the level of the sea in regular grades, bearing a kind of rude similitude to the benches of such a theatre as that above-named, to the height of two or three hundred feet. In the bathing season this place is seldom without a few groups or straggling figures, being turned to account in a great many different ways, whether as a resting place to the wanderers on the cliffs, or a point of rendezvous to the numerous picnic parties who come here to enjoy a dinner *al fresco*, and luxuriate on the grand and boundless ocean prospect which lies beneath and beyond them.

A waggish host of the village with whom I had the honour to

domiciliate during a brief sojourn on the place a few years since, informed me that a number of serious accidents had rendered the visitors to the amphitheatre somewhat more cautious of suffering themselves to become entangled among the perils of the shelving and disjointed crags of which it was composed. Among many anecdotes of warning he mentioned one which occurred to a meditative guest of his own, for which I at first gave him credit for a poetical imagination, though I afterwards found he had spoken nothing more than a real fact:

'To take out his book,' he said in answer to a question from me, as to the manner of the occurrence, 'and to sit down as it might be this way on a shelving rock, and the sea to be roaring, and he to be thinking of nothing, only what he was reading, when a swell riz and took him out a distins, as it might be to give him a good sea view of the cliffs, and the place, and turning again the same way it came, laid him up on the same stone, where, I'll be your bail, he was mighty scarce in less than no time.'

Beyond the Amphitheatre, the cliff rises to a still greater height, forming an eminence called the Lookout. Shocking as the tale may appear to modern readers, it has been asserted, and but too many evidences remain to give weight and colour to the supposition, that in those barbarous (though not very distant) times, this place was employed as an observatory by the wild fishermen of the coast and neighbouring hamlets, the principal portion of whose livelihood was derived from the plunder of the unfortunate men who happened to be wrecked on this inhospitable shore; and it is even recorded, and generally believed, that fires were, on tempestuous nights, frequently lighted here, and in other dangerous parts of the coast, in order to allure the labouring vessel, already hardly set by the war of winds and waves, to a more certain and immediate destruction on the rocks and shoals beneath, a practice, it is said, which was often successful to a fearful extent.

The most remarkable point of scenery about the place, and one with which we shall close our perhaps not unneedful sketch of the little district, is the Puffing-hole, a cavern near the base of the cliff last-mentioned, which vaults the enormous mass of crag to a considerable distance inland, where it has a narrow opening, appearing to the eyes of a stranger like a deep natural well. When the tremendous sea from abroad rolls into this cavern, the effect is precisely the same as if water were forced into an inverted funnel, its impetus of course increasing as it ascends through the narrow neck, until at length reaching the perpendicular opening, or Puffing-hole, it jets frequently to an immense height into the air, and falls in rain on the mossy fields behind.

At a little distance from this singular phenomenon stood a rude cottage. It was tenanted by an aged woman of the place, the relict of one of the most daring plunderers of the coast, who was suspected to have been murdered by one of his own comrades a good many years before. The interior of the little building bore sufficient testimony to the unlawful habits of its former master. All, even the greater proportion of the domestic utensils, were formed of ship timbers: a rudder had been awkwardly hacked and hewed up into something bearing a resemblance to a table, which stood in the middle of the principal apartment, the rafters were made from the spars of boom, peek, and yard; a *settle-bed* at the further end had been constructed from the ruins of a gallant ship, and the little boarded parlour inside was furnished in part from the same materials. A number of planks, carelessly fastened together by way of a dresser, stood against the wall, shining forth in all the glory of burnished pewter, wooden platter, and gaudily painted earthenware, the heirlooms of the house of Moran.

Terrified and shocked to the soul by the sudden fate of her late spouse, Mrs Moran, the proprietress of the cottage, resolved that their boy, an only child, should not follow the dangerous courses of his father. In this she happened to be seconded by the youth's own disposition, which inclined to quietude and gentleness of character. He was, at his sixteenth year, far beyond his compeers of the village in point of education, and not behind in beauty of person, and dexterity at all the manual exercises of *goal*, single-stick and so on, accomplishments, however, which were doomed not to be wasted in the obscurity of his native wilderness, for before he had completed his seventeenth year, he was laid by the heels, one morning as he sat at breakfast, and pressed to sea.

One day was allowed him to take leave of old friends, and prepare to bid a long adieu to his native home. This day was a painful one, for more reasons than one.

Of course it is not to be supposed that so smart, handsome, clever, and well-disposed a lad as Charlie Moran, should be unappreciated among the maidens of the district in which he vegetated. He had in short a lover; a fine flaxen-haired girl, with whom he had been intimate from infancy up to youth, when the wars (into the service of which he suspected he was betrayed by the agency of the girl's parent, a comfortable *Palatine* in the neighbourhood) called him away from his boyish sports to the exercise of a premature manhood. Their parting was by no means more agreeable to little Ellen Sparling than to himself, seeing that they were more fondly and deeply attached to one another, than is frequently the case with persons of their age and rank in life, and moreover that it would not have been the easiest matter possible to find a pair so well matched in temper and habits, as well as in personal loveliness, (just then unfolding itself in each with a promise of perfect maturity) anywhere about the countryside.

The father of the girl, however, who, to say a truth, was indeed the contriver of Moran's impressment, looked forward to his absence with a great deal of joy. The old Palatine, who possessed all the prudence of parents in every soil and season, and all the natural obstinacy of disposition, inherent in the national character of the land of his forefathers, had on this occasion his prejudices doubly strengthened, and rendered at last inveterate, by the differences of religion and education, as well as by that external, reciprocal, and indomitable hatred which invariably divides the usurping and favoured emigrant from the oppressed, indigenous, disinherited inheritor of the soil. Fond of his little girl, yet hating her friend, he took the part of wearing them asunder by long absence, a common mistake among more enlightened parents than Mr Sparling.

On the day preceding that of young Moran's departure, when the weeping girl was hanging on his neck, and overwhelming him with conjurations to 'prove true', an advice, to follow which he assured her over and over again in his own way, he needed no exhortations, her lover proposed to her to walk (as it might be for the last time) towards a spot which had been the usual limit of their rambles, and their general rendezvous whenever her father thought proper to forbid their communing in his house, which was only done at intervals, his vigilance being a sort of chronic affection, sometimes rising to a height which seemed dangerous to their hopes, sometimes relapsing into a state of almost perfect indifference. To this spot the lovers now repaired.

It was a recess in the cliffs that bedded over the caverns, and was so formed as to hold no more than three or four persons; who, when they occupied the rude seats naturally formed in the rock, were invisible to any human eye which might be directed otherwhere than from the sea. The approach to it was by a narrow footway, in ascending or descending which, one seemed almost to hang in air, so far did the cliff-head project over the waters, and so scanty was the path of the descent on either side; custom however had rendered it a secure footing to the inhabitants of the village, and the lovers speedily found themselves within the little nook, secluded from every mortal eye. It was a still autumn evening, there was no sunshine, but the fixed splendour of the sky above and around them, on which the lines, or rather waves of thin vapour extending from the northwest, and tinged on one side by the red light of the sun, which had just gone down, presented the similitude of a sea frozen into a brilliant mass, in the act of undulation. Beyond them lay Bishop's Island, a little spot of land, shooting up from the waves in the form of a gigantic column, about three hundred feet in height, the sides barren and perpendicular, and the plain above covered with verdure to the marge itself. Immediately above their heads was a blighted elder tree, (one of the most remarkable phenomena of this woodless district) which now hung, like a single grey hair, over the bare and barren brow of the aged cliff.

The wanderers sat here in perfect security, although by a step forward they might look upon a tremendous in-slanting precipice beneath, against the base of which, at times, the sea lashed itself with such fury, as to bound in huge masses over the very summit, and to make the cliff itself shake and tremble to a considerable distance inland.

'I have asked you to come here, Ellen,' said her lover, as he held her hand in one of his, while the other was passed round her waist, 'for a very solemn purpose. It is a belief amongst us, and many have seen it come to pass, that those who pledge themselves to any promise, whether of hate or love, and who, with their hands clasped together as ours are now, plight their faith and troth to perform that promise to one another—it is our belief, I say, that whether in the land of the living, or the dead, they can never enjoy a quiet soul until that promise is made good. I must serve five years before I obtain my discharge; when I get that, Ellen, I will return to this place, and let you know, by a token, that I am in the neighbourhood. Pledge me your hand and word, that when you receive that token, whether you are married or unmarried, whether it be dark, moonlight, or stormy, you will come out alone to meet me where I shall appoint, on the night when I shall send it.'

Without much hesitation the young girl solemnly pledged herself to what he required. He then unbound from her hair a ribbon by which it was confined, kissed it, and placed it in his bosom, after which they ascended the cliff and separated.

After the departure of young Moran, his mother, to relieve her loneliness, opened a little place of entertainment for the *fish-jolters*, whose trade it was (and is) to carry the fish taken on the coast to the nearest market town for sale, as also for the fishermen of the village, and chance passengers. By this means she had accomplished a very considerable sum of money in a few years. Ellen Sparling observed this with the more satisfaction, as she felt it might remove the greatest bar that had hitherto opposed itself to her union with Charles Moran.

Five years and some months had rolled away since his departure, and he had not been heard of during that time in his native village. All things remained very nearly in the same state in which he had left them, with the exception of the increased prosperity of his mother's circumstances, and the matured beauty of Ellen, who was grown into a blooming woman, the admiration of all the men, and it is said, though I don't vouch for the fact, of all the women too, of her neighbourhood. There are limits of superiority beyond which envy cannot reach, and it might be said, perhaps, that Ellen was placed in this position of advantage above all her female acquaintances. It is not to be supposed that she was left untempted all this while, or at least unsought. On the contrary, a number of suitors had directly or indirectly presented themselves, with one of whom only, however, I have any business at present.

He was a young fisherman, and one of the most constant visitors at the elegant *soirées* of the widow Moran, where, however, he was by no means a very welcome guest, either to the good woman or her customers. He held, nevertheless, high place at the board, and seemed to exercise a kind of dominion over the revellers, perhaps as much the consequence of his outward appearance, as of his life and habits. He was powerfully made, tall, and of a countenance which, even in his hours of comparative calmness and inaction, exhibited in the mere arrangement of its features a brutal violence of expression which was exceedingly repugnant. The middle portion of his physiognomy was rather flat and sunken, and his mouth and forehead projecting much, rendered this deformity disgustingly apparent. Deep black, large glistening eyes glanced from beneath a pair of brows, which so nearly approached each other, as, on every movement of passion, or impulse of suspicion, to form in all appearance one thick shaggy line across, and the unamiable effect of the countenance altogether was not improved by the temper of the man, who was feared throughout the neighbourhood, as well for his enormous strength, as for the violence, the suspicious tetchiness, and the habitual gloominess of his character, which was never more visible than when, as now, he affected the display of jollity and hearted good fellowship. It was whispered, moreover, that he was visited, after some unusual excitement, with fits of wildness approaching to insanity, at the accession of which he was wont to conceal himself from all human intercourse for a period, until the evil influence (originating, as it was asserted privately among his old associates, in the remorse with which the recollection his manifold crimes was accompanied) had passed away—a circumstance which seemed to augur a consciousness of this mental infirmity. At the end of those periods of retirement, he was wont to return to his companions with a haggard and jaded countenance, a dejected demeanour, and a sense of shame manifested in his address, which, for a short space only, served to temper the violence of his conduct. Robbers and murderers, as all of his associates were, this evil-conditioned man had gone so far beyond them in his total recklessness of crime, that he had obtained for himself the distinguishing appellative (like most nicknames in Irish low life, ironically applied) of Yamon Macauntha, or Honest Ned; occasionally varied (after he had reached the estate of manhood, and distinguished himself among the smugglers, over whom he acquired a speedy mastery, by his daring spirit, and almost invariable success in whatever he undertook) with that of Yamon Dhiu, or Black Ned, a name which applied as well to his dark complexion, long, matted, coal-black hair and beard, as to the fierce and relentless energy of his disposition.

One anecdote, which was told with suppressed breath, and involuntary shuddering, even among those who were by his side in all his deeds of blood, may serve to illustrate the terrific and savage cruelty of the man. A Dutch vessel had gone to pieces on the rocks beneath the Lookout. The waves rolled in like mountains, and lashed themselves with such fury against the cliffs, that very speedily nearly all those among the crew who clung to the drifting fragments of the wreck, were dashed to atoms on the projecting granite. A few only, among whom was the captain of the vessel, who struggled with desperate vigour against the dreadful element, succeeded in securing themselves on a projecting rock, from whence, feeble and exhausted as they were, the poor mariners endeavoured to hail a number of people, who were looking out on the wreck from the cliff-head above them. They succeeded in attracting attention, and the spectators prepared to lower a rope for their relief, which, as they were always provided against such accidents, they were not long in bringing to pass. It was first girded around the waist of the captain, and then fastened around that of his two companions, who, on giving a signal, were drawn into the air, the former holding in one hand a little casket, and with the other defending himself against the pointed projections of the cliff as he ascended. When very near the summit, which completely overhung the waves, he begged, in a faint tone, that someone would take the casket from his hands, as he feared it might be lost in the attempt to secure his own hold. Yamon was but too alert in acceding to the wretched man's request; he threw himself forward on the sand, with his breast across the rope, and took the casket from his uplifted hand.

'God's blessing on your souls, my believers,' cried the poor man, wringing his clasped hands, with a gesture and look of fervent gratitude, 'the casket is safe, thank God! thank God! and my faith to my employers——' he was yet speaking, when the rope severed under Black Yamon's breast, and the three men were precipitated into the yawning waters beneath. They were hurried out by the retiring waves, and the next moment their mangling bodies were left in the recesses of the cliff.

A cry of horror and of compassion burst even from the savage hearts of the crew of smugglers, who had been touched by the courage and constancy which was displayed by the brave unfortunates. Yamon alone remained unmoved, (and hard must the heart have been which even the voice of gratitude, unmerited though it was, could not soften or penetrate) he gave utterance to a burst of hoarse, grumbling laughter, as he waved the casket in triumph before the eyes of his comrades:

'Huh! huh!' he exclaimed, 'she was a muthaun—why didn't she keep her casket till she drew her painther ashore?'

One of the men, as if doubting the possibility of the inhuman action, advanced to the edge of the cliff. He found the rope had been evidently divided by some sharp instrument; and observing something glittering where Yamon lay, he stooped forward and picked up an open clasp knife, which was presently claimed by the unblushing monster. However shocked they might have been at the occurrence, it was no difficult matter for Yamon to persuade his companions that it would be nowise convenient to let the manner of it transpire in the neighbourhood; and in a very few minutes the fate of the Dutchmen seemed completely banished from their recollection, (never very retentive of benevolent emotions) and the only question held regarded the division of the booty. They were disappointed, however, in their hopes of spoil, for the casket which the faithful shipman was so anxious to preserve, and to obtain which his murderer had made sacrifice of so many lives, contained nothing more than a few papers of bottomry and insurance, valueless to all but the owners of the vessel. This circumstance seemed to touch the villain more nearly than the wanton cruelty of which he had been guilty; and his gang, who were superstitious exactly in proportion to their want of honesty and of all moral principle, looked upon it as a supernatural occurrence, in which the judgment of an offended Deity was made manifest.

This amiable person had a sufficiently good opinion of himself to make one among the admirers of Ellen Sparling. It is scarcely necessary to say his suit was unsuccessful. Indeed the maiden was heard privately to declare her conviction that it was impossible there could be found anywhere a more ugly and disagreeable man, in every sense.

One fine frosty evening, the widow Moran's was more than usually crowded. The fire blazed cheerfully on the hearth, so as to render any other light unnecessary, although the night had already begun to close in. The mistress of the establishment was busily occupied in replenishing the wooden *noggins*, or drinking vessels, with which the board was covered; her glossy white hair turned up under a clean kerchief, and a general gala-gladness spreading an unusual light over her shrivelled and attenuated features, as by various courtesies, addressed to the company around her, she endeavoured to make the gracious in her own house. Near the chimney corner sat Dora Keys, a dark-featured bright-eyed girl, who, on account of her skill on the bagpipe, a rather unfeminine accomplishment, and a rare one in this district, (where, however, as in most parts of Ireland, music of some kind or another was constantly in high request) filled a place of high consideration among the merrymakers. The remainder of the scene was filled up with the fishermen, smugglers, and fish-jolters; the latter wrapt in their blue friezecoats, and occupying a more unobtrusive corner of the apartment, while Yamon, as noisy and imperious as usual, sat at the head of the rude table, giving the word to the whole assembly.

A knocking was heard at the slight hurdle-door. The good woman went to open it, and a young man entered. He was well formed, though rather thin and dark skinned, and a profusion of black curled hair clustered about his temples, corresponding finely with his glancing, dark, fiery eye. An air of sadness, or of pensiveness, too, hung about him, which gave an additional interest to his appearance, and impressed the spectator with an involuntary respect. Mrs Moran drew back with one of her lowest curtsies. The stranger smiled sadly, and extended his hand. 'Don't you know me, mother?' he asked. The poor woman sprung to his neck with a cry of joy.

All was confusion in an instant. 'Charles'—'Charlie'—'Mr Moran'—was echoed from lip to lip in proportion to the scale of intimacy which was enjoyed by the several speakers. Many a rough hand grasped his, and many a good-humoured buffet and malediction had he to endure before the tumultuous joy of his old friends had subsided. At length, after all questions had been answered, and all old friends, the dead, the living, and the absent, had been tenderly inquired for, young Moran took his place among the guests; the amusements of the evening were renewed, and Yamon, who had felt his importance considerably diminished by the entrance of the young traveller, began to reassume his self-constituted sovereignty.

Gambling, the great curse of society in all climes, classes, ages, and states of civilization, was not unknown or unpractised in this wild region. Neither was it here unattended with its usual effects upon the mind, heart, and happiness of its votaries. The eager manifestation of assent which passed round the circle, when the proposition of just 'a hand o'five-and-forty' was made, showed that it was by no means an unusual or unacceptable resource to any person present. The young exile, in particular, seemed to catch at it with peculiar readiness; and, in a few minutes, places and partners being arranged, the old woman deposited in the middle of the table a pack of cards, approaching in shape more to the oval than the oblong square, and in colour scarcely distinguishable from the black oaken board on which they lay. Custom, however, had rendered the players particularly expert at their use, and they were dealt round with as much flippancy as the newest pack in the hands of a demon of St James's, in our own time. One advantage, certainly, the fashionable gamesters possessed over these primitive gamblers: the latter were perfectly ignorant of the useful niceties of play, so much in request among the former. *Old gentlemen, stags, bridges,* and so on, were matters totally unknown among our coast friends, and the only necessary consequences of play, in which they (perhaps) excelled, were the outrageous violence, good mouth-filling oaths, and the ferocious triumph which followed the winnings or the losses of the several parties.

After he had become so far acquainted with the dingy pieces of pasteboard in his hand, as to distinguish the almost obliterated impressions upon them, the superior skill of the seafarer became apparent. Yamon, who played against him, soon began to show symptoms of turbulence, which the other treated with the most perfect coolness and indifference, still persevering in his good play, until his opponent, after lavishing abundance of abuse on everybody around him, especially on his unfortunate partner in the game, acknowledged that he had no more to lose. The night had now grown late, and the guests dropping off one by one, Moran and his mother were left alone in the cottage.

'Mother,' said the young man, as he threw the little window-shutter open, and admitted a gush of moonlight which illumined the whole room, 'will you keep the fire stirring till I return, the night is fine, and I must go over the cliffs?'

'The cliffs! tonight, child!' ejaculated the old woman. 'You don't think of it, my heart?'

'I must go,' was the reply, 'I have given a pledge that I dare not be false to.'

'The cliffs!' continued the old woman. 'The way is uncertain even to the feet that know it best, and sure you wouldn't try it in the night, and after being away till you don't know maybe, a foot o' the way.'

'When I left Ellen Sparling, mother,' said the young man, 'I pledged her my faith, that I would meet her on the night on which she should receive from me a token she gave me. She, in like manner, gave me hers. That token I sent to her before I entered your doors this evening, and I appointed her father's old house, where he lived in his poor days, and where I first saw her, to meet me. I must keep my word on all hazards.' And he flung the cottage door open as he spoke.

'Then take care, take care,' said the old woman, clasping her hands and extending them towards him, while she spoke in her native tongue. 'The night, thank God! is a fine night, and the sea is still at the bottom of the cliffs, but it is an unsure path. I know the eyes that will be red, and the cheeks that will be white, and the young and the fair ones, too, if anything *contrary* should come to you this holy evening.'

'I have given her my hand and word,' was Moran's reply as he closed the door, and took the path over the sandhills.

The moon was shining brightly when he reached the cliffs, and entered on the path leading to the old rendezvous of the lovers, and from thence to the ruined building, where he expected to meet Ellen. He trudged along in the light-heartedness of feeling inspired by the conviction he felt, that the happiness of the times, which every object he beheld brought to his recollection, had not passed away with those days, and that a fair and pleasant future yet lay before him. He turned off the sandhills while luxuriating in those visions of unchecked delight.

Passing the rocks of Duggara, he heard the plashing of oars, and the rushing of a canoe through the water. It seemed to make towards a landing place further down, and lying almost on his path. He pursued his course, supposing, as in fact to be the case, that it was one of the fishermen drawing his canoe nearer to the caverns which were to be made the scene of a seal hunt on the following day. As the little vessel glided through the water beneath him, a wild song, in the language of the country, rose to the broken crag on which he now rested, chaunted by a powerful masculine voice, with all the monotonous and melancholy intonation to which the construction of the music is peculiarly favourable.

Before Moran had descended much further on his way, he perceived that the canoe had reached a point of the rock close upon his route. The fisherman jumped to land, made fast the painter, and turning up the path by which Moran was descending, soon encountered him. It was Yamon Macauntha.

'Ho! Mr Moran! Out on the cliffs this hour o' the night, sir?'

'Yes, I have a good way to go. Goodbye to you.'

'Easy a while, sir,' said Yamon, 'that is the same way I'm going myself, and I'll be with you.'

Moran had no objection to this arrangement, although it was not altogether pleasing to him. He knew enough of the temper and habits of the smuggler to believe him capable of any design, and although he had been a stronger built man than he was, yet the odds, in case of any hostile attempt, would be fearfully in Yamon's favour. He remembered too certain rumours which had reached him of the latter being occasionaly subject to fits of gloom, approaching in their strength and intensity to actual derangement, and began to hesitate as to the more advisable course to be pursued. However, not to mention the pusillanimity of anything having the appearance of retreat, such a step would in all probability have been attempted in vain, for Yamon stood directly behind him, and the path was too narrow to admit the possibility of a successful struggle. He had only to obey the motion of the fisherman and move on.

'You don't know,' said the latter, 'or may be you never heard of what I'm going to tell you now; but easy, and you'll know all in a minute. Do you see that sloping rock down by the sea, which the horsegull is standing at this minute, the same we passed a while ago. When my mother was little *better* than seven months married, being living hard by on the sandhills, she went many's the time down to that rock, to fetch home some of the salt-water for pickle and things, and never made any work of going down there late and early, and at all hours. Well, it was as it might be this way, on a fine bright night, that she took her can in her hand, and down with her to the rock. The tide was full in, and when she turned off o' the path, what should she see fronting her, out, and sitting quite erect intirely upon the rock, only a woman, and she having the tail of her gown turned up over her head, and she sitting quite still, and never speaking a word, and her back towards my mother. *"Dieu uth,"* says my mother, careless and civil, thinking of nothing, and wanting her to move; but she took no notice. "Would it be troubling you if I'd just step down to get a drop o' the saltwater?" says my mother. Still no answer. So thinking it might be one of the neighbours that was funning, or else that it might be asleep she was, she asked her very plain and loud to move out o' the way. When there wasn't ere a word come after this, my mother stooped forward a little, and lifted the *gownd* from the woman's forehead, and peeped under—and what do you think she seen in the dark, within? Two eyes as red as fire, and a shrively old face without any lips hardly, and they drawn back, and teeth longer than lobster's claws, and as white as the bleached bones. Her heart was down on her brogue when *it* started up from her, and with a screech that made two halves of my mother's brains, *it* flew out over the wide sea.

'My mother went home and took to her bed, from which she never stirred till 'twas to be taken to Kilfiehera churchyard. It was in that week I was born. I never pass that place at night alone, if I can help it—and that is partly the reason why I made so free to ask you to bear me company.'

Moran had his confidence fully re-established by these words. He thought he saw in Yamon a wretch so preyed upon by remorse and supersition, as to be incapable of contemplating any deep crime, to which he had not a very great temptation. As Yamon still looked toward the rock beneath, the enormous horsegull by which he had first indicated its position to Moran, took flight, and winged its way slowly to the elevation on which they stood. The bird rose above, wheeled round them, and with a shrill cry, that was repeated by a hundred echoes, dived again into the darkness underneath. Moran, at this instant, had his thoughts turned in another direction altogether, by the sight of the little recess in which Ellen and he had held their last conversation. He entered, followed by Yamon, who threw himself on the rude stone seat, observing that it was a place 'for the phuka to make her bed in.'

The young traveller folded his arms, and gazed around for a few minutes in silence, his heart striving beneath the load of recollections which came upon him at every glance and motion. On a sudden, a murmured sound of voices was heard underneath, and Moran stooped down, and overlooked the brink of the tremendous precipice. There was a flashing of lights on the calm waters beneath, and in a few minutes a canoe emerged from the great cavern, bearing three or four men, with lighted torches, which, however, they extinguished as soon as they came into the clear moonlight. He continued to mark them until they were lost behind a projecting crag. He then turned, and in removing his hand from the verge, detached a pebble, which, falling after a long pause into the sea, formed what is called by the peasant children, who practise it in sport, 'a dead man's skull.' It is formed when a stone is cast into the water so as to emit no spray, but cutting rapidly and keenly through, in its descent, produces a gurgling evolution, bearing a momentary resemblance to the tables of a human skull. The sound ceased, and all again was still and silent, with the exception of the sound, which the stirring of the waters made in the mighty caverns beneath.

'I remember the time when that would have won a button for me,' said Moran, turning round. He at the same instant felt his shoulder grasped with a tremendous force. He looked quickly up, and beheld Yamon, his eyes staring and wild with some frantic purpose, bending over him. A half-uttered exclamation of terror escaped him, and he endeavoured to spring towards the path which led from the place. The giant arm of Yamon, however, intercepted him.

'Give me, cheat and plunderer that you are,' cried the fisherman, while his limbs trembled with emotion, 'give me the money you robbed me of this night, or by the great light that's looking down on us, I'll shake you to pieces.'

'There, Yamon, there, you have my life in your power—there is your money, and now—' He felt the grasp of the fisherman tightening upon his throat. He struggled, as a wretch might be expected to do, to whom, life was new and dear; but he was as a child in the gripe of his enemy. There was a smothering shriek of entreaty—a wild attempt to twine himself in the limbs and frame of the murderer—and in the next instant he was hurled over the brow of the cliff.

'Another! another life!' said Yamon Dhu, as with hands stretched out, and fingers spread, as though yet in act to grasp, he looked out over the precipice. 'The water is still again—Ha! who calls me?—From the caverns?—No.—Above?—Another life!—A deal of Christian's blood upon one man's soul!' and he rushed from the place.

*   *   *

About eleven o'clock on the following morning (as fine a day as could be), a young lad named Terry Mick, (Terry, the son of Mick, a species of patronymic very usual in Ireland), entered, with considerable haste, the kitchen of Mr Morty Shannon, a gentleman farmer, besides being coroner of the county, and as jolly a man as any in the neighbourhood. Terry addressed a brief tale in the ear of Aby Galaghar, Mr Shannon's steward and factotum, which induced the said Sandy to stretch his long, well-seasoned neck, from the chimney corner, and directing his voice towards the door of an inner room, which was complimented with the appellation of a parlour, exclaim, 'Mr Morty! you're *calling*, sir.'

'Who am I *calling*?' asked a rich, waggish voice, from within.

'Mr Sparling, the Palatine's boy, sir,' replied Aby, quite unconscious of the *quid pro quo*.

'Indeed! More than I knew myself. Walk in, Terry.'

'Go in to him, Terry dear,' said Aby, resuming his comfortable position in the chimney corner, and fixing a musing, contented eye upon a great cauldron of potatoes that hung over the turf fire, and on which the first simmering froth, or *white horse* (as it is called in Irish cottages), had begun to appear.

'The master sent me to you, sir,' said Terry, opening the door, and protruding an eye, and half a face into the sanctum sanctorum, 'to know—with his compliments——'

But first, I should let you have the glimpse that Terry got of the company within. The person to whom he immediately addressed himself sat at one end of a small deal table, on which were placed a jug of cold water, a broken bowl, half filled with coarse brown sugar, and a little jar, which, by the frequent changes of position it underwent, seemed to contain the favourite article of the three. Imagine to yourself a middle-sized man, with stout, well-set limbs, a short and thick head of hair, an indented forehead, eyes of a piercing grey, bright and sparkling, with an expression between leer and satire, and a nose running in a curvilineal direction towards the mouth. Nature had, in the first instance, given it a *sinister inclination*, and chance, wishing to rectify the *morals* of the feature, had, by the agency of a blackthorn stick, in the hands of a rebellious tenant, sent it again to the right. 'Twas kindly meant, as Mr Morty himself used to say, though not so dexterously executed.

'*The* master's compliments, sir,' continued Terry, 'to know if your honour would just step over to Kilkee, where there has been a bad business this morning—Charlie Moran being lying dead, on the broad of his back, at the house, over.'

When I say that an expression of involuntary satisfaction, which he in vain endeavoured to conceal, diffused itself over the tortuous countenance of the listener, at this intelligence, it is necessary I should save his character by reminding the reader that he was a county coroner, and that in addition to the four pounds which he was to receive for the inquest, there was the chance of an invitation to stay and dine with the Sparlings, people whose mode of living Mr Morty had before now tried and approved.

'Come here, Terry, and take your morning,' said he, filling a glass of ardent spirits, which the youth immediately disposed of, with a speed that showed a sufficient familiarity with its use, although some affectation of mincing decency induced him to colour the delicious relish with a grimace and shrug of comical dislike, as he replaced the glass on the table.

'E'then, that's good stuff, please your honour. Sure I'd know the master's any where over the world. This is some of the two year old, sir. 'Twas made the time Mr Grady, the gauger, was stationed below there, at the white house—and faix, many a drop he tasted of it himself, in the master's barn.'

'And is the still so long at work, Terry?'

'Oh, long life to you, sir—aye is it, and longer too. The master has *sech* a 'cute way with him in managing the still-hunters. 'Tis in vain for people to inform—to be sure, two or three tried it, but got nothing by it, barring a good lacing at the next fair day. Mr Grady used regularly to send notice when he got an information, to have him on his guard against he'd come with *the army*—and they never found anything there, I'll be your bail for it, more than what served to send 'em home as drunk as pipers, every mother's son. To be sure, that Mr Grady was a pleasant man, and well liked wherever he came, among high and low, rich and poor, although being a gauger and a protestant. I remember making him laugh hearty enough once. He asked me, says he, as it might be funning, "Terry", says he, "I'm very bad inwardly. How would you like to be walking after a gauger's funeral this morning?" "Why thin, Mr Grady," says I, "I'd rather see a thousand of your *religion* dead than yourself, and maneing no love for *you*, neither." And poor man, he did laugh hearty, to be sure. He had no pride in him—no pride, more than a child, hadn't Mr Grady. God's peace be with him, wherever he is, this day.'

In a few minutes Mr Shannon's blind mare was saddled, and the head of the animal being directed towards Kilkee, away went Terry, trotting by the coroner's side, and shortening the road with his quaint talk. On arriving at the Palatine's house, they found it crowded with the inhabitants of the village. The fairy doctor of the district sat near the door; his brown and weather-beaten face wrapped in an extraordinary degree of mystery, and his eyes fixed with the assumption of deep thought on his twirling thumbs: in another part of the outer room was the schoolmaster of the parish, discussing the 'coroner's quest law,' to a circle of admiring listeners. In the chimney corner, on stools which were ranged for the purpose, were congregated the 'knowledgeable' women of the district. Two soldiers, detached from the nearest guard, were stationed at the door, and at a little distance from them, seated at at table, and basking in the morning sunshine, might be seen a number of the fishermen and others, all deeply engaged in converse upon the occurrence which had summoned them together. One of them was in the act of speaking when the coroner arrived:

'We had been drawing the little canoe up hard by the cavern, seeing would we be the first to be in upon the seals when the hunt would begin, when I see a black thing lying on the shore among the seaweed, about forty yards or upwards from the rock where I stood; and 'tisn't itself I see first, either, only two seagulls, and one of 'em perched up on it, while the other *kep* wheeling round above it, and screaming as nait'rel as a christen; and so I ran down to Phil, here, and says I, "there's murder down upon the rocks, let us have it in for the fishes." So we brought it ashore. 'Twas pale and stiff, but there was no great harm done to it, strange to say, in regard of the great rocks, and the place. We knew poor Moran's face, and we said nothing to one another, only wrapped the spritsail about it, and had it up here to Mr Sparling's, (being handier to us than his own mothers) where we told our story.'

Passing into the house, Mr Morty Shannon was received with all the respect due to his exalted station. The women curtsied low, and the men raised their hands to their foreheads with that courteous action which is familiar to all, even the most unenlightened of the peasantry of the south of Ireland. The master of the mansion, a comfortable looking farmerlike sort of person, rose from his seat near the hearth, and greeted the man of office with an air of greater familiarity, yet with a reserve becoming the occasion. As the door of an inner apartment stood open, Mr Shannon could see the corpse of the murdered man laid out on a table near the window. Close to the head stood the mother of the dead, hanging over the corpse in silent grief, swaying herself backward and forward with a gentle motion, and wringing her hands; yet with so noiseless an action, that the profound silence of the room was never broken. On the opposite side, her fine head resting against the bier—her white, wan fingers wreathed together in earnest prayer about the body, while a half-stifled sob occasionally shook her delicate frame—and her long curling tresses fell in flaxen masses over the boson of the murdered, knelt Moran's betrothed love, Ellen Sparling. As she prayed, a sudden thought seemed to rush upon her, she raised her head, took from her bosom a light green ribbon, and kissing it fervently and repeatedly, she folded and placed it in that of the murdered youth, after which she resumed her kneeling posture. There are few, I believe, who have lived among scenes of human suffering to so little purpose as not to be aware, that it is not the heaviness of a particular calamity, nor the violence of the sorrow which it produces, that is at any time most powerful in awakening the commiseration of an uninterested spectator. The capability of deep feeling may be more or less a property of all hearts, but the power of communicating it is a gift possessed by few. The murmur of a bruised heart, the faint sigh of a broken spirit, will often stir and thrill through all the strings of sympathy, while the frantic ravings of a wilder, though not less real woe, shall fail to excite any other sensation than that of pain and uneasiness. Perhaps it may be, that the selfishness of our nature is such, that we are alarmed and put on our guard, in proportion to the violence of the appeal which is made to us; and must be taken by surprise, before our benevolent emotions can be awakened. However all this might be, being no philosopher, I can only state the fact, that Mr Morty Shannon, who had witnessed many a scene of frantic agony, without experiencing any other feeling than that of impatience, was moved, even to a forgetfulness of his office, by the quiet, unobtrusive grief, which he witnessed on entering this apartment.

It was the custom in those days, and is still the custom in most parts of Ireland, where any person is supposed to have 'come by his end' unfairly, that all the inhabitants of his parish, or district, particularly those who, from any previous circumstances, may be rendered at all liable to suspicion, shall meet together and undergo a kind of ordeal, by touching the corpse, each in his turn. Among a superstitious people, such a regulation as this, simple though it was, had been frequently successful in betraying the guilty conscience; and it was a current belief among the peasantry, that in many instances where the perpetrator of the horrid deed possessed strength of mind, or callousness of heart sufficient to subdue all appearance of emotion in the moment of trial, some miraculous change in the corpse itself had been known to indicate the evil doer. At all events, there was a degree of solemnity and importance attached to the test, which invested it with a strong interest in the minds of the multitude.

Suspicion was not idle on this occasion. The occurrences of the previous evening at the widow's house, and the loss there sustained by Yamon, contributed in no slight degree to fix the attention of the majority upon him. It did not pass without remark, neither, that he had not yet made his appearance at Mr Sparling's house. Many wild tales, moreover, were afloat respecting Ellen Sparling, who had, on that morning, before sunrise, been seen by a fish-jolter, who was driving his mule loaded with fish along the road towards Kilrush, returning across the hills toward her father's house, more like a mad-woman than a sober Christian. Before we proceed further in our tale, it is necessary we should say something of the circumstances which led to this appearance.

When Ellen received the token on the previous evening from young Moran's messenger, she tied her light chequered straw bonnet under her chin, and stole out by a back entrance, with a beating and anxious heart, to the appointed rendezvous. The old ruined house which had been named to her, was situated at the distance of a mile from her father's, and was at present tenanted only by an aged herdsman in his employment. Not finding Moran yet arrived, although the sun was already in the west, she sent the old man away on some pretext, and took his place in the little rush-bottomed chair by the fireside. Two hours of a calm and silent evening had already passed away, and yet be came not. Wearied with the long expectation, and by the tumult of thoughts and feelings which agitated her, she arose, walked to a short distance from the cottage, and sitting on a little knoll in the vicinity, which commanded a wide prospect to the sea, she continued to await his arrival, now and then gazing in the direction of the cliffs by which the messenger told her he was to pass. No object, however, met her eye on that path, and no sound came to her ear but the loud, full-toned, and plaintive whistle of the ploughman, as he guided his horses over a solitary piece of stubble-ground, lightening his own and their labour by the wild modulations of the *Keen-the-cawn*, or death-wail; the effect of which, though it had often delighted her under other circumstances, fell now with an an oppressive influence upon her spirits.

Night fell at length, and she returned to the old house. As she reached the neglected *haggart* on the approach, a light breeze sprang up inland, and rustling in the thatch of the ruined outhouses, startled her by its suddenness, almost as much as if it had been a living voice. She looked up an instant, drew her handkerchief closer around her neck, and hurried on towards the door. It might be he had arrived by another path during her absence! High as her heart bounded at the suggestion, it sunk in proportion as she lifted the latch, and entered the deserted room. The turf embers were almost aspiring on the hearth, and all was dark, cold, saddening, and comfortless. She felt vexed at the absence of the old servant, and regretted the caution which induced her to get rid of him. Amid all the intensity of her fondness too, she could not check a feeling of displeasure at the apparent want of ardour on the part of her lover. It had an almost slighting look; she determined she would make it evident in her manner on his arrival. In the next moment the fancied sound of a footstep made her spring from her seat, and extend her arms in a perfect oblivion of all her stern resolutions. Quite beaten down in heart by constant disappointments, and made nervous and feverish by anxiety, the most fearful suggestions began now to take the place of her pettishness and ill-humour. She was alarmed for his safety. It was a long time since he had trod the path over the cliffs. The possibility that here rushed upon her, made her cover her face with her hands, and bend forward in her chair in an agony of terror.

Midnight now came on. A short and heavy breathing at the door, as she supposed, startled her as she bent over the flame which she kept alive by placing fresh *sods* on the embers. She rose and went to the door. A large Newfoundland dog of her father's bounded by her as she opened it, and testified by the wildest gambols about the kitchen, the delight he felt in meeting her so unexpectedly, at such an hour, and so far from her home. She patted the faithful animal on the head, and felt restored in spirits by the presence, even, of this uncommunicative acquaintance. The sagacious servant had evidently traced her to the ruin by the fineness of its sense, and seemed overjoyed at the verification of his diagnostic. At length, after having sufficiently indulged the excitement of the moment, he took post before the fire, and after diverse, indecisive evolutions, he coiled himself up at her feet and slept. The maiden herself in a short time imitated the example.

The startling suggestions that had been crowding on her in her waking moments, now began to shape themselves in vivid and fearful visions to her sleeping fancy. As she lay back in her chair, her eyes not so entirely closed as to exclude the 'lengthening rays' of the decaying fire before them, she became unaccountably oppressed by the sense of a person sitting close at her side. There was a hissing, as if of water falling on the embers just before the figure, and after a great effort she fancied that she could turn so far round as to recognise the face of her lover, pale, cold, with the long dark hair hanging drearily at each side, and as she supposed, dripping with moisture.

She strove to move, but was perfectly unable to do so, and the figure continued to approach her, until at length placing his chilling face so close to her cheek, that she thought she felt the damp upon her neck, he said gently, 'Ellen, I have kept my hand and word: living I would have done it; dead, I am permitted.' At this moment a low grumbling bark from the dog Minos, awoke her, and she started from her seat, in a state of nervousness which for a short time prevented a full conviction of the nonexistence of the vision that had oppressed her slumber. The dog was sitting erect, and gazing, with crouched head, fixed eyes, and lips upturned in the expression of canine fear, toward the door. Ellen listened attentively for a few minutes, and a gentle knocking was heard. She recognised too, or thought she recognised, a voice precisely similar to that of the figure in her dream, which pronounced her name with the gentlest tone in the world. What surprised her most, was that Minos, instead of starting fiercely up as was his wont, on hearing an unusual sound at night, cowed, whimpered, and slunk back into the chimney corner. Not in the least doubting that it was her lover, she rose and opened the door. The vividness of her dream, being yet fresh upon her, and perhaps the certainty she felt of seeing him, made her imagine for the instant that she beheld the same figure standing before her. It was but for an instant, however; on looking a second time, there was no person to be seen. An overwhelming sensation of terror now rushed upon her, and she fled from the place with the rapidity of madness. In a state half-frantic, half-fainting, she reached her father's house, and flung herself on her bed, where the news of Moran's death reached her next morning.

To return, however, to the present position of our tale. A certain number of the guests were now summoned into the room where the body lay, and all things were prepared for the ordeal. At a table near the window, with writing materials before him, was placed the worthy coroner, together with the lieutenant of the guard at the lighthouse, who had arrived a few minutes before. Mr Sparling stood close by them, his face made up into an expression of wise abstraction, his hands thrust into his breeches pockets, and jungling some halfpence which they contained. The betrothed lover of the murdered man had risen from her knees, and put on a completely altered manner. She now stood in silence, and with tearless eyes, at the head of the bier, gazing with an earnestness of purpose, which might have troubled the carriage even of diffident innocence itself, into the face of everyone who approached to touch the body. Having been made aware of the suspicions afloat against Yamon, and the grounds for those suspicions, she expected with impatience the arrival of that person.

He entered at length. All eyes were instantly turned on him. There was nothing unusual in the manner or appearance of the man. He glanced round the room, nodded to a few, touched his forehead to the coroner and the lieutenant, and then walking firmly and coolly to the centre of the apartment, awaited his turn for the trial. A very close observer might have detected a quivering and wincing of the eyelid, as he looked toward Ellen Sparling, but it was only momentary, and he did not glance in that direction a second time.

'Isn't that droll, Shawn?' whispered Terry in the ear of the fairy doctor, who stood near him. The latter did not deem it convenient to answer in words, but he compressed his lips, contracted his brows, and threw an additional portion of empty wisdom into his physiognomy.

'E'then,' continued Terry, 'only mark Tim Fouloo going to touch the dead corpse all a' one anybody would sispect *him* to be taking the life of a chicken, the *lahu-muthawn*,' (half-natural); as a foolish-looking, open-mouthed, open-eyed young booby advanced in his turn in a slow waddling gait to the corpse, and passing his hand over the face, retired with a stare of comic stupidity, which, notwithstanding the awful occasion, provoked a smile from many of the spectators.

Yamon was the last person who approached the corpse. From the moment he entered, the eye of Ellen Sparling had never been withdrawn from him for an instant, and its expression now became vivid and intense. He walked to the place, however, with much indifference, and passed his hand slowly and repeatedly over the cheek and brow of the dead man. Many a head was thrust forward, as if in expectation that the inanimate lump of clay might stir beneath the feeler's touch. But no miracle took place, and they gazed on one another in silence as he slowly turned away, and folding his arms, resumed his place in the centre of the apartment.

'Well, Mr Sparling,' said his worship the coroner, 'here is so much time lost: had we began to take evidence at once, the business would be nearly at an end by this time.'

The old Palatine was about to reply, when their conversation was interrupted by an exclamation of surprise from Ellen Sparling.

Turning quickly round, they beheld her with one of the clenched hands of the corpse between hers gazing on it in stirless amazement. Between the dead-stiff fingers, appeared something of a bluish colour slightly protruded. Using the utmost strength of which she was mistress, Ellen forced open the hand, and took from it a small part of the lapel of a coat, with a button attached. And letting the hand fall, she rushed through the crowd, putting all aside without looking at one, until she stood before Yamon. A glance was sufficient. In the death-struggle, the unhappy Moran had torn away this portion of his murderer's dress, and the rent was visible at the moment.

'The murderer! blood for blood!' shrieked the frantic girl, grasping his garment, and looking almost delirious with passion. All was confusion and uproar. Yamon darted one fierce glance around, and sprung toward the open door, but Ellen Sparling still clung as with a drowning grasp to her hold. He put forth the utmost of his giant strength to detach himself from her, but in vain. All his efforts seemed only to increase her strength, while they diminished his own. At last he bethought him of his fishing knife, he plucked it from his belt, and buried it in her bosom. The unfortunate girl relaxed her hold, reeled, and fell on the corpse of her lover, while Yamon bounded to the door. Poor Terry crossed his way, but one blow laid him sprawling senseless on the earth, and no one cared to tempt a second. The rifles of the guard were discharged after him, as he darted over the sandhills, but just before the triggers were pulled, his foot tripped against a loose stone, he fell, and the circumstance perhaps saved his life, (at least the marksmen said so). He was again in rapid flight before the smoke cleared away.

'*Shuil! Shuil!* The sandhills! the cliffs!' was now the general shout, and the chase immediately commenced. Many minutes elapsed ere they arrived at the cliffs, and half a dozen only of the most nimble-footed just reached the spot in time to witness the last desperate resource of the murderer. He stood and looked over his shoulder for an instant, then rushing to the verge of the cliff, where it walled in the land to a height of forty feet, he waved his hand to his pursuers, and cast himself into the sea.

The general opinion was that he had perished, but there was no trace ever seen that could make such a consummation certain. The body was never found, and it was suspected by a few, that, incredible as the story might appear, he had survived the leap, and gained the little rocky island opposite.

The few who returned at dusk to Mr Sparling's house, found it the abode of sorrow, of silence, and of death. Even the voice of the hired keener was not called in on this occasion to mock the real grief that sat on every brow, and in every heart. The lovers were waked together, and buried in the same grave at Kilfiehera.

THE HANGING OF MYLES JOYCE

James Joyce

Surprising as it may seem, James Joyce (1882-1941) took a keen interest in the subject of crime and lawlessness and wrote several articles on this theme, first for the Irish newspapers and later for the Italian and French press when he was living abroad. His strongest words were reserved for the Belfast riots and a series of attacks on cattle in Clare, Galway, Leitrim and Roscommon, all prompted by the appalling suffering inflicted on country people by the large landholders. He frequently attacked the way English law was used to punish Irish offences, declaring in September 1907, 'The English public conceives of the Irish as highwaymen with distorted faces, roaming the night with the object of taking the hide of every Unionist.'

Joyce introduced several elements of crime into his short stories, such as 'An Encounter' and 'A Painful Case' in Dubliners *(1914), and into his great novel,* Ulysses *(1922). In 'The Hanging of Myles Joyce' he employs his typically caustic style to write of the terrible injustice suffered by a family named Joyce who, it has been suggested, may well have been related to him . . .*

There is less crime in Ireland than in any other country in Europe. In Ireland there is no organised underworld, and when one of those events which the journalists, with atrocious irony, call 'red idylls' occurs, the whole country is shaken by it.

Five years ago an innocent man, now at liberty, was condemned to forced labour to appease public indignation. But even while he was in prison the crimes continued.

Some years before this a sensational trial was held in Ireland concerning a family bearing the same name as my own. The case had its origins in a lonely place in a western province called Maamtrasna where a terrible murder was committed.

The facts were these. A man named Joyce, his wife and three of his four children, had been murdered in County Galway by a party of men who believed they were informers. Four or five townsmen, all belonging to the ancient tribe of the Joyces, were arrested and charged with the crime and brought before the court.

The oldest of these men, a seventy-year-old named Myles Joyce, was the prime suspect of the outrage. Public opinion at the time, though, thought him innocent and today considers him a martyr.

Neither the old man nor the others accused knew any English. The court had to resort to the services of an interpreter to hear their evidence. The questioning, conducted through the interpreter, was at times comic and at times tragic.

On one side of the courtroom was the excessively ceremonious interpreter, while on the other stood the patriarch of a miserable tribe unused to civilised customs, who seemed stupefied by all the judicial ceremony.

At one point, the magistrate said to the interpreter, 'Ask the accused if he saw the lady that night?'

The question was referred to him in Irish, and the old man broke out into an involved explanation, gesticulating, appealing to the others accused, and to heaven. Then he quietened down, worn out by his effort.

At this the interpreter turned to the magistrate and said, 'He says, "No, your worship".'

'Ask him if he was in that neighbourhood at that hour?' the magistrate went on.

The old man again began to talk, to protest, to shout, almost beside himself with the anguish of being unable to understand or to make himself understood, weeping in anger and terror. At last he fell silent once more.

And again the interpreter said, 'He says, "No, your worship".'

When the questioning was over, the guilt of the poor old man was declared proved by that court. He was remanded to a superior court, where, with two others, he was condemned to the noose.

On the day the sentence was executed, the square in front of the prison in Galway was jammed full of kneeling people shouting prayers in Irish for the repose of Myles Joyce's soul.

The story was told that the executioner, also unable to make the victim understand him, kicked at the miserable man's head in anger to shove it into the noose.

TELLING

Elizabeth Bowen

The harsh economic conditions in Ireland during the early 1900s were responsible for making a writer of Elizabeth Bowen (1899-1973), who was born in County Cork. The illness of her father and death of her mother when she was still in her teens compelled her to seek a way of earning her living away from Ireland, and so she turned to writing. Her sheer will to succeed resulted in novels and short stories which, through their understanding of human emotions, soon made her a household name. In time her achievements enabled her to refurbish the family's ancestral home in Cork, Bowen's Court, and she would frequently retreat there to write.

Elizabeth Bowen confessed early in her career that detective stories were her favourite reading matter. In 'Telling' she presents the experience of murder as relived in the mind of an abnormal human being. The effect is so realistic that many readers have wondered just where and how she got the inspiration to create such a morbid and compelling tale.

Terry looked up; Josephine lay still. He felt shy, embarrassed all at once at the idea of anyone coming here. His brain was ticking like a watch: he looked up warily.

But there was nobody. Outside the high cold walls, beyond the ragged arch of the chapel, delphiniums crowded in sunshine—straining with brightness, burning each other up—bars of colour that, while one watched them, seemed to turn round slowly. But there was nobody there.

The chapel was a ruin, roofed by daylight, floored with lawn. In a corner the gardener had tipped out a heap of cut grass from the lawn-mower. The daisy-heads wilted, the cut grass smelt stuffy and sweet. Everywhere, cigarette ends, scattered last night by the couples who'd come here to kiss. First the dance, thought Terry, then this: the servants will never get straight. The cigarette ends would lie here for days, till after the rain, and go brown and rotten.

Then he noticed a charred cigarette stump in Josephine's hair. The short wavy ends of her hair fell back—still in lines of perfection—from temples and ears; by her left ear the charred stump showed through. For that, he thought, she would never forgive him; fastidiousness was her sensibility, always tormented. ('If you must know,' she had said, 'well, you've got dirty nails, haven't you? Look.') He bent down and picked the cigarette end out of her hair; the fine ends fluttered under his breath. As he threw it away, he noticed his nails were still dirty. His hands were stained now—naturally—but his nails must have been dirty before. Had she noticed again?

But had she, perhaps, for a moment been proud of him? Had she had just a glimpse of the something he'd told her about? He wanted to ask her: 'What do you feel now? Do you believe in me?' He felt sure of himself, certain, justified. For nobody else would have done this to Josephine.

Himself they had all—always—deprecated. He felt a shrug in this attitude, a thinly disguised kind of hopelessness. 'Oh, *Terry*, . . .' they'd say, and break off. He was no good: he couldn't even put up a tennis-net. He never could see properly (whisky helped that at first, then it didn't), his hands wouldn't serve him, things he wanted them to hold slipped away from them. He was no good; the younger ones laughed at him till they, like their brothers and sisters, grew up and were schooled into bitter kindliness. Again and again he'd been sent back to them all (and repetition never blunted the bleak edge of these home-comings) from school, from Cambridge, now—a month ago—from Ceylon. 'The bad penny!' he would remark, very jocular. 'If I could just think things out,' he had tried to explain to his father, 'I know I could do *something*.' And once he had said to Josephine: 'I know there is Something I could do.'

'And they will know now,' he said, looking round (for the strange new pleasure of clearly and sharply seeing) from Josephine's face to her stained breast (her heavy blue beads slipped sideways over her shoulder and coiled on the grass—touched, surrounded now by the unhesitant trickle); from her breast up the walls to her top, the top crumbling, the tufts of valerian trembling against the sky. It was as though the dark-paned window through which he had so long looked out had swung open suddenly. He saw (clear as the walls and the sky) Right and Wrong, the old childish fixities. I have done right, he thought (but his brain was still ticking). *She ought not to live* with this flaw in her. Josephine ought not to live, and to die.

All night he had thought this out, walking alone in the shrubberies, helped by the dance-music, dodging the others. His mind had been kindled, like a dull coal suddenly blazing. He was not angry; he kept saying: 'I must not be angry, I must be just.' He was in a blaze (it seemed to himself) of justice. The couples who came face to face with him down the paths started away. Someone spoke of a minor prophet, someone breathed 'Caliban.' . . . He kept saying: 'That flaw right through her. She damages truth. She kills souls; she's killed mine.' So he had come to see, before morning, his purpose as God's purpose.

She had laughed, you see. She had been pretending. There was a tender and lovely thing he kept hidden, a spark in him; she had touched it and made it the whole of him, made him a man. She had said: 'Yes, *I* believe, Terry. I understand.' That had been everything. He had thrown off the old dull armour . . . Then she had laughed.

Then he had understood what other men meant when they spoke of her. He had seen at once what he was meant to do. 'This is for me,' he said. 'No one but I can do it.'

All night he walked alone in the garden. Then he watched the french windows and when they were open again stepped in quickly and took down the African knife from the dining-room wall. He had always wanted that African knife. Then he had gone upstairs (remembering, on the way, all those meetings with Josephine, shaving, tying of ties), shaved, changed into flannels, put the knife into his blazer pocket (it was too long, more than an inch of the blade came out through the inside lining) and sat on his window-sill, watching sunlight brighten and broaden from a yellow agitation behind the trees into swathes of colour across the lawn. He did not think; his mind was like somebody singing, somebody able to sing.

And, later, it had all been arranged for him. He fell into, had his part in, some kind of design. Josephine had come down in her pleated white dress (when she turned the pleats whirled). He had said, 'Come out!' and she gave that light distant look, still with a laugh at the back of it, and said, 'Oh—right-o, little Terry.' And she had walked down the garden ahead of him, past the delphiniums into the chapel. Here, to make justice perfect, he had asked once more: '*Do* you believe in me?' She had laughed again.

She lay now with her feet and body in sunshine (the sun was just high enough), her arms flung out wide at him, desperately, generously: her head rolling sideways in shadow on the enclosed, silky grass. On her face was a dazzled look (eyes half closed, lips drawn back), an expression almost of diffidence. Her blood quietly soaked through the grass, sinking through to the roots of it.

He crouched a moment and, touching her eyelids—still warm—tried to shut her eyes. But he didn't know how. Then he got up and wiped the blade of the African knife with a handful of grass, then scattered the handful away. All the time he was listening; he felt shy, embarrassed at the thought of anyone finding him here. And his brain, like a watch, was still ticking.

On the way to the house he stooped down and dipped his hands in the garden tank. Someone might scream; he felt embarrassed at the thought of somebody screaming. The red curled away through the water and melted.

He stepped in at the morning-room window. The blinds were half down—he stooped his head to avoid them—and the room was in dark yellow shadow. (He had waited here for them all to come in, that afternoon he arrived back from Ceylon.) The smell of pinks came in, and two or three blue-bottles bumbled and bounced on the ceiling. His sister Catherine sat with her back to him, playing the piano. (He had heard her as he came up the path.) He looked at her pink pointed elbows—she was playing a waltz and the music ran through them in jerky ripples.

'Hullo, Catherine,' he said, and listened in admiration. So his new voice sounded like this!

'Hullo, Terry,' She went on playing, worrying at the waltz. She had an anxious, methodical mind, but loved gossip. He thought: Here is a bit of gossip for you—Josephine's down in the chapel, covered with blood. Her dress is spoilt, but I think her blue beads are all right. I should go and see.

'I say, Catherine——'

'Oh, Terry, they're putting the furniture back in the drawing-room. I wish you'd go and help. It's getting those big sofas through the door . . . and the cabinets.' She laughed: 'I'm just puting the music away,' and went on playing.

He thought: I don't suppose she'll be able to marry now. No one will marry her. He said: 'Do you know where Josephine is?'

'No, I haven't'—rum-tum-tum, rum-tum-*tum*—'the slightest idea. Go on, Terry.'

He thought: She never liked Josephine. He went away.

He stood in the door of the drawing-room. His brothers and Beatrice were punting the big arm-chairs, chintz-skirted, over the waxy floor. They all felt him there: for as long as possible didn't notice him. Charles—fifteen, with his pink scrubbed ears—considered a moment, shoving against the cabinet, thought it was rather a shame, turned with an honest, kindly look of distaste, said, 'Come on Terry.' He can't go back to school now, thought Terry, can't go anywhere, really: wonder what they'll do with him—send him out to the Colonies? Charles had perfect manners: square, bluff, perfect. He never thought about anybody, never felt anybody—just classified them. Josephine was 'a girl staying in the house', 'a friend of my sisters.' He would think at once (in a moment when Terry had told him), 'A girl staying in the house . . . it's . . . well, I mean, if it hadn't been *a girl staying in the house . . .*'

Terry went over to him; they pushed the cabinet. But Terry pushed too hard, crooked; the further corner grated against the wall. 'Oh, I say, we've scratched the paint,' said Charles. And indeed they had; on the wall was a grey scar. Charles went scarlet: he hated things to be done badly. It was nice of him to say: '*We've* scratched the paint.' Would he say later: 'We've killed Josephine'?

'I think perhaps you'd better help with the sofas,' said Charles civilly.

'You should have seen the blood on my hands just now,' said Terry.

'Bad luck!' Charles said quickly and went away.

Beatrice, Josephine's friend, stood with her elbows on the mantelpiece looking at herself in the glass above. Last night a man had kissed her down in the chapel (Terry had watched them). This must seem to Beatrice to be written all over her face—what else could she be looking at? Her eyes in the looking-glass were dark, beseeching. As she saw Terry come up behind her she frowned angrily and turned away.

'I say, Beatrice, do you know what happened down in the chapel?'

'Does it interest you?' She stooped quickly and pulled down the sofa loose-cover where it had 'runkled' up, as though the sofa legs were indecent.

'Beatrice, what would you do if I'd killed somebody?'

'Laugh,' said she, wearily.

'If I'd killed a woman?'

'Laugh harder. Do you know any women?'

She was a lovely thing, really: he'd ruined her, he supposed. He was all in a panic. 'Beatrice, swear you won't go down to the chapel.' Because she might, well—of course she'd go down: as soon as she was alone and they didn't notice she'd go creeping down to the chapel. It had been *that* kind of kiss.

'Oh, be quiet about that old chapel!' Already he'd spoilt last night for her. How she hated him! He looked round for John. John had gone away.

On the hall table were two letters, come by the second post, waiting for Josephine. No one, he thought, ought to read them—he must protect Josephine; he took them up and slipped them into his pocket.

'I say,' called John from the stairs, 'what are you doing with those letters?' John didn't mean to be sharp but they had taken each other unawares. They none of them wanted Terry to *feel* how his movements were sneaking movements; when they met him creeping about by himself they would either ignore him or say: 'Where are *you* off to?' jocosely and loudly, to hide the fact of their knowing he didn't know. John was Terry's elder brother, but hated to sound like one. But he couldn't help knowing those letters were for Josephine, and Josephine was 'staying in the house.'

'I'm taking them for Josephine.'

'Know where she is?'

'Yes, in the chapel . . . I killed her there.'

But John—hating this business with Terry—had turned away. Terry followed him upstairs, repeating: 'I killed her there, John . . . John, I've killed Josephine in the chapel.' John hurried ahead, not listening, not turning round. 'Oh yes.' he called over his shoulder. 'Right you are, take them along.' He disappeared into the smoking room, banging the door. It had been John's idea that, from the day after Terry's return from Ceylon, the sideboard cupboard in the dining-room should be kept locked up. But he'd never said anything; oh no. What interest could the sideboard cupboard have for a brother of his? he pretended to think.

Oh yes, thought Terry, you're a fine man with a muscular back, but you couldn't have done what I've done. There had, after all, been Something in Terry. He *was* abler than John (they'd soon know). John had never kissed Josephine.

Terry sat down on the stairs saying: 'Josephine, Josephine!' He sat there gripping a baluster, shaking with exaltation.

The study door-panels had always looked solemn; they bulged with solemnity. Terry had to get past to his father; he chose the top left-hand panel to tap on. The patient voice said: 'Come in!'

Here and now, thought Terry. He had a great audience; he looked at the books round the dark walls and thought of all those thinkers. His father jerked up a contracted, strained look at him. Terry felt that hacking with his news into this silence was like hacking into a great grave chest. The desk was a havoc of papers.

'What exactly do you want?' said his father, rubbing the edge of the desk.

Terry stood there silently: everything ebbed. 'I want,' he said at last, 'to talk about my future.'

His father sighed and slid a hand forward, rumpling the papers. 'I suppose, Terry,' he said as gently as possible, 'you really *have* got a future?' Then he reproached himself. 'Well, sit down a minute . . . I'll just . . .'

Terry sat down. The clock on the mantelpiece echoed the ticking in his brain. He waited.

'Yes?' said his father.

'Well, there must be some kind of future for me, mustn't there?'

'Oh, certainly . . .'

'Look here, father, I have something to show you. That African knife——'

'What about it?'

'That African knife. It's here. I've got it to show you.'

'What about it?'

'Wait just a minute.' He put a hand into either pocket: his father waited.

'It *was* here—I did have it. I brought it to show you. I must have it somewhere—that African knife.'

But it wasn't there, he hadn't got it; he had lost it; left it, dropped it—on the grass, by the tank, anywhere. He remembered wiping it . . . Then?

Now his support was all gone; he was terrified now; he wept.

'I've lost it,' he quavered, 'I've lost it.'

'What do you mean?' said his father, sitting blankly there like a tombstone, with his white, square face. 'What are you trying to tell me?'

'Nothing,' said Terry weeping and shaking. 'Nothing, nothing, nothing.'

A STUDY IN WHITE

Nicholas Blake

The device of presenting all the facts relating to a case of foul play and then inviting the reader to solve the mystery has rarely been used more effectively than it has in this next story. Nicholas Blake, whose real name was Cecil Day Lewis (1904-1975), was the son of an Irish Protestant clergyman in Ballintubber. Descended from Oliver Goldsmith on his mother's side and related to W.B. Yeats through his paternal grandmother, he was surely destined to become a writer, and indeed, by the age of six he was already writing 'serious poetry'. His achievements through his verse, novels and literary criticism were recognised in 1968 when he was made Poet Laureate by the Queen. As early as 1935 he had also begun to utilise his interest in detective fiction, and produced the first of a string of successful crime thrillers under the pen-name Nicholas Blake, many of them featuring an erudite private investigator named Nigel Strangeways. Although written unashamedly to supplement his meagre income from poetry, Day Lewis believed the detective story to be 'the folk myth of the 20th Century', offering a harmless release for the cruelty he believed was present in everyone.

Among Nicholas Blake's most acclaimed works have been The Beast Must Die *(1938), about a small boy killed by a hit-and-run driver and his father's unrelenting quest to find the culprit (the story was filmed as* This Man Must Die *in 1969), and* The Private Wound *(1968), featuring the problems that have divided his native Ireland. The theme of murder in the snow was one that haunted him and he uses it with stunning effect in 'A Study in White', challenging the reader to solve the mystery. For those who remain perplexed, the solution will be found at the end of the book.*

'Seasonable weather for the time of year,' remarked the Expansive Man in a voice succulent as the breast of a roast goose.

The Deep Chap, sitting next to him in the railway compartment, glanced out at the snow, swarming and swirling past the window-pane. He replied: 'You really like it? Oh well, it's an ill blizzard that blows nobody no good. Depends what you mean by seasonable, though. Statistics for the last fifty years would show——'

'Name of Joad, sir?' asked the Expansive Man, treating the compartment to a wholesale wink.

'No, Stansfield, Henry Stansfield.' The Deep Chap, a ruddy-faced man who sat with hands firmly planted on the knees of his brown tweed suit, might have been a prosperous farmer but for the long, steady, meditative scrutiny which he now bent upon each of his fellow-travellers in turn.

What he saw was not particularly rewarding. On the opposite seat from left to right, were a Forward Piece, who had taken the Expansive Man's wink wholly to herself and contrived to wriggle her tight skirt farther up from her knee; a dessicated, sandy, lawyerish little man who fumed and fussed like an angry kettle, consulting every five minutes his gold watch, then shaking out his *Times* with the crackle of a legal parchment; and a Flash Card, dressed up to the nines of spivdom, with the bold yet uneasy stare of the young delinquent.

'Mine's Percy Dukes,' said the Expansive Man. 'P.D. to my friends. General Dealer. At your service. Well, we'll be across the border in an hour and a half, and then hey for the bluebells of bonny Scotland!'

'Bluebells in January? You're hopeful,' remarked the Forward Piece.

'Are you Scots, master?' asked the Comfortable Body sitting on Stansfield's left.

'English outside'—Percy Dukes patted the front of his grey suit, slid a flask from his hip pocket, and took a swig—'and Scotch within.' His loud laugh, or the blizzard, shook the railway carriage. The Forward Piece giggled.

'You'll need that if we run into a drift and get stuck for the night,' said Henry Stansfield.

'Name of Jonah, sir?' The compartment reverberated again.

'I do not apprehend such an eventuality,' said the Fusspot. 'The stationmaster at Lancaster assured me that the train would get through. We are scandalously late already, though.' Once again the gold watch was consulted.

'It's a curious thing,' remarked the Deep Chap meditatively, 'the way we imagine we can make Time amble withal or gallop withal, just by keeping an eye on the hands of a watch. You travel frequently by this train, Mr——?'

'Kilmington. Arthur J. Kilmington. No, I've only used it once before.' The Fusspot spoke in a dry Edinburgh accent.

'Ah, yes, that would have been on the 17th of last month. I remember seeing you on it.'

'No, sir, you are mistaken. It was the 20th.' Mr Kilmington's thin mouth snapped tight again, like a rubber band round a sheaf of legal documents.

'The 20th? Indeed? That was the day of the train robbery. A big haul they got, it seems. Off this very train. It was carrying some of the extra Christmas mail. Bags just disappeared, somewhere between Lancaster and Carlisle.'

'Och, deary me,' sighed the Comfortable Body. 'I don't know what we're coming to, really, nowadays.'

'We're coming to the scene of the crime, ma'am,' said the expansive Mr Dukes. The train, almost deadbeat, was panting up the last pitch towards Shap Summit.

'I didn't see anything in the papers about where the robbery took place,' Henry Stansfield murmured. Dukes fastened a somewhat bleary eye upon him.

'You read all the newspapers?'

'Yes.'

The atmosphere in the compartment had grown suddenly tense. Only the Flash Card, idly examining his fingernails, seemed unaffected by it.

'Which paper did you see it in?' pursued Stansfield.

'I didn't.' Dukes tapped Stansfield on the knee. 'But I can use my loaf. Stands to reason. You want to tip a mail-bag out of a train—get me? Train must be moving slowly, or the bag'll burst when it hits the ground. Only one place between Lancaster and Carlisle where you'd *know* the train would be crawling. Shap Bank. And it goes slowest on the last bit of the bank, just about where we are now. Follow?'

Henry Stansfield nodded.

'OK. But you'd be balmy to tip it off just anywhere on this Godforsaken moorland,' went on Mr Dukes. 'Now, if you'd travelled this line as much as I have, you'd have noticed it goes over a bridge about a mile short of the summit. Under the bridge runs a road: a nice, lonely road, see? The only road hereabouts that touches the railway. You tip out the bag there. Your chums collect it, run down the embankment, dump it in the car they've waiting by the bridge, and Bob's your uncle!'

'You oughta been a detective, mister,' exclaimed the Forward Piece languishingly.

Mr Dukes inserted his thumbs in his armpits, looking gratified. 'Maybe I am,' he said with a wheezy laugh. 'And maybe I'm just little old P.D., who knows how to use his loaf.'

'Och, well now, the things people will do?' said the Comfortable Body. 'There's a terrible lot of dishonesty today.'

The Flash Card glanced up contemptuously from his fingernails. Mr Kilmington was heard to mutter that the system of surveillance on railways was disgraceful, and the Guard of the train should have been severely censured.

'The Guard can't be everywhere,' said Stansfield. 'Presumably he has to patrol the train from time to time, and——'

'Let him do so, then, and not lock himself up in his van and go to sleep,' interrupted Mr Kilmington, somewhat unreasonably.

'Are you speaking from personal experience, sir?' asked Stansfield.

The Flash Card lifted up his voice and said, in a Charing-Cross-Road American accent, 'Hey, fellas! If the gang was gonna tip out the mail-bags by the bridge, like this guy says—what I mean is, how could they rely on the Guard being out of his van just at that point?' He hitched up the trousers of his loud check suit.

'You've got something there,' said Percy Dukes. 'What I reckon is, there must have been two accomplices on the train—one to get the Guard out of his van on some pretext, and the other to chuck off the bags.' He turned to Mr Kilmington. 'You were saying something about the Guard locking himself up in his van. Now if I was of a suspicious turn of mind, if I was little old Sherlock H. in person'—he bestowed another prodigious wink upon Kilmington's fellow-travellers—'I'd begin to wonder about you, sir. You were travelling on this train when the robbery took place. You went to the Guard's van. You *say* you found him asleep. You didn't by any chance call the Guard out, so as to——?'

'Your suggestion is outrageous! I advise you to be very careful, sir, very careful indeed,' enunciated Mr Kilmington, his precise voice crackling with indignation, 'or you may find you have said something actionable. I would have you know that, when I——'

But what he would have them know was to remain undivulged. The train, which for some little time had been running cautiously down from Shap Summit, suddenly began to chatter and shudder, like a fever patient in high delirium, as the vacuum brakes were applied: then, with the dull impact of a fist driving into a feather pillow, the engine buried itself in a drift which had gathered just beyond the bend of a deep cutting.

It was just five minutes past seven.

'What's this?' asked the Forward Piece, rather shrilly, as a hysterical outburst of huffing and puffing came from the engine.

'Run into a drift, I reckon.'

'He's trying to back us out. No good. The wheels are slipping every time. What a lark!' Percy Dukes had his head out of the window on the lee side of the train. 'Coom to Coomberland for your winter sports!'

'Guard! Guard, I say!' called Mr Kilmington. But the blue-clad figure, after one glance into the compartment, hurried on his way up the corridor. 'Really! I *shall* report that man.'

Henry Stansfield, going out into the corridor, opened a window. Though the coach was theoretically sheltered by the cutting on this windward side, the blizzard stunned his face like a knuckleduster of ice. He joined the herd of passengers who had climbed down and were stumbling towards the engine. As they reached it, the Guard emerged from the cab: no cause for alarm, he said; if they couldn't get through, there'd be a relief engine sent down to take the train back to Penrith; he was just off to set fog-signals on the line behind them.

The driver renewed his attempts to back the train out. But what with its weight, the up-gradient in its rear, the icy rails, and the clinging grip of the drift on the engine, he could not budge her.

'We'll have to dig out the bogeys, mate,' he said to his fireman. 'Fetch them shovels from the forward van. It'll keep the perishers from freezing, anyhow.' He jerked his finger at the knot of passengers who, lit up by the glare of the furnace, were capering and beating their arms like savages amid the swirling snow-wreaths.

Percy Dukes, who had now joined them, quickly established him-

self as the life and soul of the party, referring to the grimy-faced fireman as "Snowball", adjuring his companions to "Dig for Victory",
affecting to spy the approach of a herd of St Bernards, each with a
keg of brandy slung round its neck. But after ten minutes of hard
digging, when the leading wheels of the bogey were cleared, it could
be seen that they had been derailed by the impact with the drift.

'That's torn it, Charlie. You'll have to walk back to the box and get
'em to telephone through for help,' said the driver.

'*If* the wires aren't down already,' replied the fireman lugubri-
ously. 'It's above a mile to that box, and uphill. Who d'you think I
am. Captain Scott?'

'You'll have the wind behind you, mate, anyhow. So long.'

A buzz of dismay had risen from the passengers at this. One or
two, who began to get querulous, were silenced by the driver's offering to take them anywhere they liked if they would just lift his engine
back onto the metals first. When the rest had dispersed to their carriages, Henry Stansfield asked the driver's permission to go up into
the cab for a few minutes and dry his coat.

'You're welcome.' The driver snorted: 'Would you believe it?
"Must get to Glasgow tonight." Damn ridiculous! Now Bert—that's
my Guard—it's different for him: he's entitled to fret a bit. Missus
been very poorly. Thought she was going to peg out before Christmas; but he got the best surgeon in Glasgow to operate on her, and
she's mending now, he says. He reckons to look in every night at the
nursing home, when he goes off work.'

Stansfield chatted with the man for five minutes. Then the Guard
returned, blowing upon his hands—a smallish, leathery-faced chap,
with an anxious look in his eye.

'We'll not get through tonight, Bert. Charlie told you?'

'Aye. I doubt some of the passengers are going to create a rumpus,' said the Guard dolefully.

Henry Stansfield went back to his compartment. It was stuffy, but
with a sinister hint of chilliness, too: he wondered how long the
steam heating would last: depended upon the amount of water in
the engine boiler, he supposed. Among the wide variety of fates he
had imagined for himself, freezing to death in an English train was
not included.

Arthur J. Kilmington fidgeted more than ever. When the Guard
came along the corridor, he asked him where the nearest village
was, saying he must get a telephone call through to Edinburgh—

most urgent appointment—must let his client know, if he was going to miss it. The Guard said there was a village two miles to the northeast; you could see the lights from the top of the cutting; but he warned Mr Kilmington against trying to get there in the teeth of this blizzard—better wait for the relief engine, which should reach them before 9 p.m.

Silence fell upon the compartment for a while; the incredulous silence of civilised people who find themselves in the predicament of castaways. Then the expansive Mr Dukes proposed that, since they were to be stuck here for an hour of two, they should get acquainted. The Comfortable Body now introduced herself as Mrs Grant, the Forward Piece as Inez Blake; the Flash Card, with the over-negligent air of one handing a dud half-crown over a counter, gave his name as Macdonald—I. Macdonald.

The talk reverted to the train robbery and the criminals who had perpetrated it.

'They must be awfu' clever,' remarked Mrs Grant, in her singsong Lowland accent.

'No criminals are clever, ma'am,' said Stansfield quietly. His ruminative eye passed, without haste, from Macdonald to Dukes. 'Neither the small fry nor the big operators. They're pretty well subhuman, the whole lot of 'em. A dash of cunning, a thick streak of cowardice, and the rest is made up of stupidity and boastfulness. They're too stupid for anything but crime, and so riddled with inferiority that they always give themselves away, sooner or later, by boasting about their crimes. They like to think of themselves as the wide boys, but they're as narrow as starved eels—why, they haven't even the wits to alter their professional methods: that's how the police pick 'em up.'

'I entirely agree, sir,' Mr Kilmington snapped. 'In my profession I see a good deal of the criminal classes. And I flatter myself none of them has ever got the better of me. They're transparent, sir, transparent.'

'No doubt you gentlemen are right,' said Percy Dukes comfortably. 'But the police haven't picked up the chaps who did this train robbery yet.'

'They will. And the Countess of Axminster's emerald bracelet. Bet the gang didn't reckon to find that in the mail-bag. Worth all of £25,000.'

Percy Dukes' mouth fell open. The Flash Card whistled. Over-

come, either by the stuffiness of the carriage or the thought of
£25,000-worth of emeralds, Inez Blake gave a little moan and
fainted all over Mr Kilmington's lap.

'Really! Upon my soul! My dear young lady!' exclaimed that
worthy. There was a flutter of solicitude, shared by all except the
cold-eyed young Macdonald who, after stooping over her a
moment, his back to the others, said, 'Here you—stop pawing the
young lady and let her stretch out on the seat. Yes, I'm talking to
you, Kilmington.'

'How dare you! This is an outrage!' The little man stood up so
abruptly that the girl was almost rolled onto the floor. 'I was merely
trying to——'

'I know your sort. Nasty old men. Now, keep your hands off her.
I'm telling you.'

In the shocked silence that ensued, Kilmington gobbled
speechlessly at Macdonald for a moment; then, seeing razors in the
youth's cold-steel eye, snatched his black hat and brief-case from
the rack and bolted out of the compartment. Henry Stansfield made
as if to stop him, then changed his mind. Mrs Grant followed the little
man out, returning presently, her handkerchief soaked in water,
to dab Miss Blake's forehead. The time was just 8.30.

When things were restored to normal, Mr Dukes turned to
Stansfield. 'You were saying this necklace of—who was it?—the
Countess of Axminster, it's worth £25,000? Fancy sending a thing of
that value through the post! Are you sure of it?'

'The value? Oh, yes.' Henry Stansfield spoke out of the corner of
his mouth, in the manner of a stupid man imparting a confidence.
'Don't let this go any further. But I've a friend who works in the Cosmopolitan—the Company where it's insured. That's another thing
that didn't get into the papers. Silly woman. She wanted it for some
big family-do in Scotland at Christmas, forgot to bring it with her,
and wrote home for it to be posted to her in a registered packet.'

'£25,000,' said Percy Dukes thoughtfully. 'Well, stone me down!'

'Yes. Some people don't know when they're lucky, do they?'

Dukes' fat face wobbled on his shoulders like a globe of lard.
Young Macdonald polished his nails. Inez Blake read her magazine.
After a while Percy Dukes remarked that the blizzard was slacken-
ing; he'd take an airing and see if there was any sign of the relief
engine yet. He left the compartment.

At the window the snowflakes danced in their tens now, not their thousands. The time was 8.55. Shortly afterwards Inez Blake went out; and ten minutes later Mrs Grant remarked to Stansfield that it had stopped snowing altogether. Neither Inez nor Dukes had returned when, at 9.30, Henry Stansfield decided to ask what had happened about the relief. The Guard was not in his van, which adjoined Stansfield's coach, towards the rear of the train. So he turned back, walked up the corridor to the front coach, clambered out, and hailed the engine cab.

'She must have been held up,' said the Guard, leaning out. 'Charlie here got through from the box, and they promised her by nine o'clock. But it'll no' be long now, sir.'

'Have you seen anything of a Mr Kilmington—small, sandy chap—black hat and overcoat, blue suit—was in my compartment? I've walked right up the train and he doesn't seem to be in it.'

The Guard pondered a moment. 'Och aye, you wee fellow? Him that asked me about telephoning from the village. Aye, he's awa' then.'

'He did set off to walk there, you mean?'

'Nae doot he did, if he's no' on the train. He spoke to me again— juist on nine, it'd be—and said he was awa' if the relief didna turn up in five minutes.'

'You've not seen him since?'

'No, sir. I've been talking to my mates here this half-hour, ever syne the wee fellow spoke to me.'

Henry Stansfield walked thoughtfully back down the permanent way. When he had passed out of the glare shed by the carriage lights on the snow, he switched on his electric torch. Just beyond the last coach the eastern wall of the cutting sloped sharply down and merged into moorland level with the track. Although the snow had stopped altogether, an icy wind from the northeast still blew, raking and numbing his face. Twenty yards further on his torch lit up a track, already half filled in with snow, made by several pairs of feet, pointing away over the moor, towards the northeast. Several passengers, it seemed, had set off for the village, whose lights twinkled like frost in the far distance. Stansfield was about to follow this track when he heard footsteps scrunching the snow farther up the line. He switched off the torch; at once it was as if a sack had been thrown over his head, so close and blinding was the darkness. The steps came nearer. Stansfield switched on his torch, at the last minute, pinpointing the squat figure of Percy Dukes. The man gave a muffled oath.

'What the devil! Here, what's the idea, keeping me waiting half an hour in that blasted——?'

'Have you seen Kilmington?'

'Oh, it's you. No, how the hell should I have seen him? Isn't he on the train? I've just been walking up the line, to look for the relief. No sign yet. Damn parky, it is—I'm moving on.'

Presently Stansfield moved on, too, but along the track towards the village. The circle of his torchlight wavered and bounced on the deep snow. The wind, right in his teeth, was killing. No wonder, he thought, as after a few hundred yards he approached the end of the trail, those passengers turned back. Then he realised they had not all turned back. What he had supposed to be a hummock of snow bearing a crude resemblance to a recumbent human figure, he now saw to be a human figure covered with snow. He scraped some of the snow off it, turned it gently over on its back.

Arthur J. Kilmington would fuss no more in this world. His brief-case was buried beneath him: his black hat was lying where it had fallen, lightly covered with snow, near the head. There seemed, to Stansfield's cursory examination, no mark of violence on him. But the eyeballs started, the face was suffused with a pinkish-blue colour. So men look who have been strangled, thought Stansfield, or asphyxiated. Quickly he knelt down again, shining his torch in the dead face. A qualm of horror shook him. Mr Kilmington's nostrils were caked thick with snow, which had frozen solid in them, and snow had been rammed tight into his mouth also.

And here he would have stayed, reflected Stansfield, in this desolate spot, for days or weeks, perhaps, if the snow lay or deepened. And when the thaw at last came (as it did that year, in fact, only after two months), the snow would thaw out from his mouth and nostrils, too, and there would be no vestige of murder left—only the corpse of an impatient little lawyer who had tried to walk to the village in a blizzard and died for his pains. It might even be that no one would ask how such a precise, pernickety little chap had ventured the two-mile walk in these shoes and without a torch to light his way through the pitchy blackness; for Stansfield, going through the man's pockets, had found the following articles—and nothing more: pocket-book, fountain pen, handkerchief, cigarette case, gold lighter, two letters, and some loose change.

Stansfield started to return for help. But only twenty yards back he noticed another trail of footprints, leading off the main track to the left. This trail seemed a fresher one—the snow lay less thickly in the indentations—and to have been made by one pair of feet only. He followed it up, walking beside it. Whoever made this track had walked in a slight right-handed curve back to the railway line, joining it about one hundred and fifty yards up the line from where the main trail came out. At this point there was a platelayers' shack. Finding the door unlocked, Stansfield entered. There was nothing inside but a coke-brazier, stone cold, and a smell of cigar smoke. . . .

Half an hour later, Stansfield returned to his compartment. In the meanwhile, he had helped the train crew to carry back the body of Kilmington, which was now locked in the Guard's van. He had also made an interesting discovery as to Kilmington's movements. It was to be presumed that, after the altercation with Macdonald, and the brief conversation already reported by the Guard, the lawyer must have gone to sit in another compartment. The last coach, to the rear of the Guard's van, was a first-class one, almost empty. But in one of its compartments Stansfield found a passenger asleep. He woke him up, gave a description of Kilmington, and asked if he had seen him earlier.

The passenger grumpily informed Stansfield that a smallish man, in a dark overcoat, with the trousers of a blue suit showing beneath it, had come to the door and had a word with him. No, the passenger had not noticed his face particularly, because he'd been very drowsy himself, and besides, the chap had politely taken off his black Homburg hat to address him, and the hat screened as much of the head as was not cut off from his view by the top of the door. No, the chap had not come into his compartment: he had just stood outside, enquired the time (the passenger had looked at his watch and told him it was 8.50); then the chap had said that, if the relief didn't turn up by nine, he intended to walk to the nearest village.

Stansfield had then walked along to the engine cab. The Guard, whom he found there, told him that he'd gone up the track about 8.45 to meet the fireman on his way back from the signal-box. He had gone as far as the place where he'd put down his fog-signals earlier; here, just before nine, he and the fireman met, as the latter corroborated. Returning to the train, the Guard had climbed into the last coach, noticed Kilmington sitting alone in a first-class apartment (it was then that the lawyer announced to the Guard his intention of walking if the relief engine had not arrived within five minutes). The Guard then got out of the train again, and proceeded down the track to talk to his mates in the engine cab.

This evidence would seem to point incontrovertibly at Kilmington's having been murdered shortly after 9 p.m., Stansfield reflected as he went back to his own compartment. His fellow-passengers were all present now.

'Well, did you find him?' asked Percy Dukes.

'Kilmington? Oh, yes, I found him. In the snow over there. He was dead.'

Inez Blake gave a little, affected scream. The permanent sneer was wiped, as if by magic, off young Macdonald's face, which turned a sickly white. Mr Dukes sucked in his fat lips.

'The puir wee man,' said Mrs Grant. 'He tried to walk it then? Died of exposure, was it?'

'No,' announced Stansfield flatly, 'he was murdered.'

This time, Inez Blake screamed in earnest; and, like an echo, a hooting shriek came from far up the line: the relief engine was approaching at last.

'The police will be awaiting us back at Penrith, so we'd better all have our stories ready.' Stansfield turned to Percy Dukes. 'You, for instance, sir. Where were you between 8.55, when you left the carriage, and 9.35 when I met you returning? Are you sure you didn't see Kilmington?'

Dukes, expansive no longer, his piggy eyes sunk deep in the fat of his face, asked Stansfield who the hell he thought he was.

'I am an enquiry agent, employed by the Cosmopolitan Insurance Company. Before that, I was a Detective Inspector in the CID. Here is my card.'

Dukes barely glanced at it. 'That's all right, old man. Only wanted to make sure. Can't trust anyone nowadays.' His voice had taken on the ingratiating, oleaginous heartiness of the small business man trying to clinch a deal with a bigger one. 'Just went for a stroll, y'know—stretch the old legs. Didn't see a soul.'

'Who were you expecting to see? Didn't you wait for someone in the platelayers' shack along there, and smoke a cigar while you were waiting? Who did you mistake me for when you said "What's the idea, keeping me waiting half an hour?" '

'Here, draw it mild, old man.' Percy Dukes sounded injured. 'I certainly looked in at the huts: smoked a cigar for a bit. Then I toddled back to the train, and met up with your good self on the way. I didn't make no appointment to meet——'

'Oo! Well I *must* say,' interrupted Miss Blake virtuously. She could hardly wait to tell Stansfield that, on leaving the compartment shortly after Dukes, she'd overheard voices on the track below the lavatory window. 'I recognised this gentleman's voice,' she went on, tossing her head at Dukes. 'He said something like: "You're going to helps us again, chum, so you'd better get used to the idea. You're in it up to the neck—can't back out now." And another voice, sort of mumbling, might have been Mr Kilmington's—I dunno—sounded Scotch anyway—said, "All right. Meet you in five minutes: platelayers' hut a few hundred yards up the line. Talk it over." '

'And what did you do then, young lady?' asked Stansfield.

'I happened to meet a gentleman friend, farther up the train, and sat with him for a bit.'

'Is that so?' remarked Macdonald menacingly. 'Why, you four-flushing little——!'

'Shut up!' commanded Stansfield.

'Honest I did,' the girl said, ignoring Macdonald. 'I'll introduce you to him, if you like. He'll tell you I was with him for, oh, half an hour or more.'

'And what about Mr Macdonald?'

'I'm not talking,' said the youth sullenly.

'Mr Macdonald isn't talking. Mrs Grant?'

'I've been in this compartment ever since, sir.'

'Ever since——?'

'Since I went out to damp my hankie for this young lady, when she'd fainted. Mr Kilmington was just before me, you'll mind. I saw him go through into the Guard's van.'

'Did you hear him say anything about walking to the village?'

'No, sir. He just hurried into the van, and then there was some havers about its no' being lockit this time, and how he was going to report the Guard for it.'

'I see. And you've been sitting here with Mr Macdonald all the time?'

'Yes, sir. Except for ten minutes or so he was out of the compartment, just after you'd left.'

'What did you go out for?' Stansfield asked the young man.

'Just taking the air, brother.'

'You weren't taking Mr Kilmimgton's gold watch, as well as the air, by any chance?' Stansfield's keen eyes were fastened like a hook into Macdonald's, whose insolent expression visibly crumbled beneath them.

'I don't know what you mean,' he tried to bluster. 'You can't do this to me.'

'I mean that a man has been murdered, and when the police search you, they will find his gold watch in your possession. Won't look too healthy for you, my young friend.'

'Naow! Give us a chance! It was only a joke, see?' The wretched Macdonald was whining now, in his native cockney. 'He got me riled—the stuck-up way he said nobody'd ever got the better of him. So I thought I'd just show him—I'd have given it back, straight I would, only I couldn't find him afterwards. It was just a joke, I tell you. Anyway, it was Inez who lifted the ticker.'

'You dirty little rotter!' screeched the girl.

'Shut up, both of you. You can explain your joke to the Penrith police. Let's hope they don't die of laughing.'

At this moment the train gave a lurch, and started back up the gradient. It halted at the signal-box, for Stansfield to telephone to Penrith, then clattered south again.

On Penrith platform Stansfield was met by an Inspector and a Sergeant of the County Constabulary, with the Police Surgeon. Then, after a brief pause in the Guard's van, where the Police Surgeon drew aside the Guard's black off-duty overcoat that has been laid over the body, and began his preliminary examination, they marched along to Stansfield's compartment. The Guard who, at his request, had locked this as the train was drawing up at the platform and was keeping an eye on its occupants, now unlocked it. The Inspector entered.

His first action was to search Macdonald. Finding the watch concealed on his person, he then charged Macdonald and Inez Blake with the theft. The Inspector next proceeded to make an arrest on the charge of wilful murder . . .

The solution to this mystery will be found on p. 364

RATS

Rearden Connor

The problems of divided Ireland which absorbed Cecil Day Lewis also featured in a number of the novels and short stories of the prolific Rearden Connor (1907-). Connor, who was born in Belfast, served as the fiction critic on the Fortnightly Review *until the advent of World War Two, during which he worked for the Ministry of Defence. He thereafter combined his duties as a scientific officer with writing both fact and fiction, as well as a series of thrillers under the name of Peter Malin. His novel* Shake Hands with the Devil (1933) *was made into a classic movie in 1960, starring James Cagney, Michael Redgrave and Richard Harris. His native Northern Ireland also featured in* Wife of Colum *(1939) and* House of Cain *(1952).*

Rearden Connor's story 'Rats', which completes this section, might have made another film vehicle for the same trio of talented actors, with its authentic and dramatic portrait of a group of criminals who have carried out a robbery and then been cornered by a group of soldiers. Forced to fight for their lives, the men find themselves in a situation of mounting violence which culminates in a brutally apposite finale . . .

Since early morning the soldiers had been peppering the heavily shuttered house. They had erected barricades on the opposite side of the street, and here several riflemen and a machine-gunner crouched. The wooden shutters of the house were as full of holes as a sponge. But still revolvers barked from hidden loopholes.

The soldiers knew that the four men trapped in the house would fight to the last shot before surrendering. They were murderers, men who had been surprised in the act of robbing a safe by a member of the Civic Guard.

They had shot the guard down in cold blood and had later been tracked to this house on the outskirts of the town. The military had come down from the barracks to rout them out.

Mickey-dad Riley was the leader of the men. From earliest boyhood he had been called 'Mickey-dad' because of his solemn dominant manner, which made his playmates, and later his associates in crime look for leadership from him. It was his proud boast that he had never done a day's work in his life. This old house in which he and his mates were now cornered was the 'hang-out' of his little gang.

Mickey-dad had been a gunman in the war against the Black-and-Tans, and his business had solely a 'stick-up' basis. He and his disciples haunted racecourses and sports meetings up and down the country and made a pleasant income from 'sticking-up' bookies and game-merchants on their way home from the meets. But lately Buck Maloney had joined up with the gang. Buck could crack a safe like a nut, and indeed had 'done time' in England for his activities. Mickey-dad immediately opened a new branch of business, so to speak, and cast his eyes towards the by-no-means up-to-date safes owned by the traders in the town.

Buck Maloney was now dead. He lay on his back in the front bedroom of the house. His beautifully cut navy suit was crushed (Buck had been a bit of a dandy); his perfectly shaved face and silk shirt were stained with his life's blood. In his hand he still clutched a revolver. He sprawled under the window like a stuck frog, his long pointed brown shoes lending an air of incongruity to his appearance as they jutted up below his trouser-ends.

The machine-gunner had spotted him peering through a half-open shutter and had promptly torn away the side of his head. Mickey-dad had cursed him roundly after he had fallen. 'To hell with ye!' he had cried out.

He could not afford to lose a man just then. A few minutes later Tommy Gallagher had been shot in the back as he stood in the middle of the room. He had not been standing in front of one of the windows either, but directly between them. A rifle bullet from a sharp angle had spat in at the side of the window and had broken Tommy's spine. Now he lay on a horse-hair sofa, powerless, useless, whining like a young animal.

There remained only Mickey-dad and Bill Cogan. Bill was a good fellow, Mickey-dad reflected. He would fight to the very last, although there did not seem to be much hope of holding off the soldiers until nightfall, when there might be some chance of a getaway. But even escape by night would be difficult, for Mickey-dad knew that behind the high wall which backed on to the rear of the house a dozen soldiers lurked, waiting.

He was nervous lest the soldiers would realise that two of his men had been picked off. He sent Cogan rushing all over the house, firing from this and that room to give the illusion that the four were still going strong. It was an old trick, and he hoped fervently that it would work.

Gallagher's perpetual whine was beginning to get on his nerves. It pierced his brain like an endless needle. Then, suddenly, it ceased. Mickey-dad walked over to the sofa. Gallagher opened his eyes and looked up at him with the innocent gaze of a child. It was a reproachful look. His body heaved. A last spasm of pain crossed his features. Then he relaxed and lay as though he were quietly sleeping. One foot slipped gently over the edge of the sofa and then crashed on to the floor.

Mickey-dad went in search of Cogan. He found him in the attic. Cogan had succeeded in making a loop-hole in the wall at the floor level just under the window by scrabbling out two bricks. The soldiers could not see his manoeuvre because the wall at that point was screened by a row of chimney-pots.

'Tommy's kicked out,' Mickey-dad told Cogan.

'Lord have mercy on him!' muttered Cogan. ''Twas better for him that he did.'

Mickey-dad sent Cogan down to the parlour. He lay flat on his stomach with his eyes at the loop-hole. A little draught blew around the chimney and wafted some of the mortar-dust into his face. He swore profusely and spent some minutes on his knees cleaning his eyes with a handkerchief. Then he brushed away the dust from the hole with the thoroughness of a housewife.

For a long time he lay as still as a log watching the soldiers behind the barricade. They were very intent on their job. After all, it was not every day that they had an opportunity to test their markmanship on living targets. Behind the barricade there was an archway, and now and again one or other of them crept in or out on hands and knees.

Mickey-dad had about thirty rounds of ammunition belted to his person. He decided to use each one to full advantage. With his first bullet he knocked away one of the chimney-pots. Now he had a clearer view. The falling pieces of the pot attracted the soldiers, and he saw two of them look up at the attic window. His second bullet accounted for the machine-gunner.

The gun was immediately manned by another, but before he had time to point the muzzle at the attic window Mickey-dad's third bullet had crashed into his head. Mickey-dad crowed with delight as he saw the soldier give a sudden spring, throw out his arms, and fall back on his dead comrade. He saw an officer crawling out from the archway. In his smooth-faced uniform he looked like a huge green dog as he edged his way towards the machine-gun on all fours.

Rifle bullets smashed through the attic window. Broken glass showered down on Mickey-dad's back. Men came running out from the archway and hastily heightened the barricade in front of the machine-gun. The muzzle of the gun was trained on the attic window. A stream of lead whistled into the room above Mickey-dad's head and buried itself in the plaster ceiling. But even the high barricade could not save the soldiers from his bullets. One by one the gunners fell over the weapon until at last the soldiers withdrew into the archway.

A quarter of an hour elapsed and Mickey-dad waited impatiently. There was not even the sound of a footfall in the street below. The dead soldiers lay there like so many discarded bolsters. In death they had no individuality. They were just corpses dressed alike. Then Bill Cogan started to snap at something with his revolver down below in the parlour. Mickey-dad had almost forgotten him in his excitement. He wondered for a moment if Cogan were fool enough to waste ammunition, and was about to run downstairs and curse him for an omadhaun. But then he remembered that Cogan was the least impetuous of all his boys and he concluded that something was happening in the archway.

The next moment a spray of machine-gun bullets swept through the shattered window over his head. He thanked his stars that he had not stood up to go downstairs. The bullets flitted across the room with sounds like a fluttering of thrushes' wings at the height of a man's chest. The soldiers were now firing from the attic window of the house opposite. They had the window heavily sandbagged, leaving themselves only a peep-hole from which a red tongue of flame darted spitefully.

Mickey-dad could not fire at the sandbagged window from his

peep-hole. That was a physical impossibility, and, anyway, the brickwork of the chimney was in his way. He saw now that it was futile to remain there any longer. He lay for some time, thinking hard. This fight was hopeless from every point of view. There were soldiers in the front, soldiers at the back. If he held out much longer they would surely bomb the place.

He was fed up with the whole business. The soldiers were determined to get him, dead or alive. He had certainly no intention of surrendering and being in due course hanged by the neck. He had started this fight in the first place because he knew what fate lay in store for him, having shot the guard who had discovered Buck Maloney rifling the safe.

In his pocket he had a large envelope. In that envelope there were £200 in notes—not crisp notes fresh from the bank which would be a trap for any man, but old creased notes paid to Sam Moynihan, the grain dealer, on the previous day by his various customers. Sam was not a methodical man. He would not have kept a list of the numbers. Mickey-dad thought how easy it would be to get away to Liverpool if he could only escape from the house.

Suddenly he had an inspiration. His eyes shone with joy. The solution was simple. He would hide in the cavity under the kitchen floor which the gang had made to conceal their loot, weapons and ammunition. But then there was Cogan to consider. Mickey-dad had once again almost forgotten his partner.

Cogan would naturally want to escape, too. Two men would not fit in the cavity under the floor. And, besides, Cogan would be sure to demand a goodly portion of the £200, perhaps even half of it. Two hundred pounds was such a nice round sum that Mickey-dad was grieved to think of it being wilfuly divided into two odd sums.

He began to crawl along by the skirting of the wall. The machine-gun bullets still flicked through the window and ripped up the end wall of the room.

He reached the door and worked his way on all-fours to the landing outside. Then he clattered down the stairs. Cogan came out of the parlour into the little hall at the foot of the stairs and said: 'They're firin' from the house over the street.' He looked pale and scared.

'I know that,' said Mickey-dad shortly.

'Can't we get out of here?' Cogan cried. 'We'll be caught in a trap of we stick on.'

'We'll be caught, anyway,' Mickey-dad retorted. 'The place is surrounded.'

'Oh, Mother of God!' groaned Cogan. 'Why did I ever get into this mess?'

'That's what many a man has said to hisself with the rope round his neck. But it was too late then.'

'I'm not goin' to let them sojers get me!' Cogan said fiercely. 'I'll blow me brains out first!'

'Where's your gun?' asked Mickey-dad.

'In the room. I haven't a round left. Give us a few if ye have any to spare?'

'Ye can have this one,' said Mickey-dad, lifting his revolver and pointing it at Cogan's head. Horror was registered instantly on Cogan's face. His lips writhed.

'What's the matter with ye, man?' he shouted. 'Have ye taken leave of your senses?'

'Just savin' ye the trouble of blowin' out yer own brains,' Mickey-dad told him. He pressed the trigger. The gun roared in the narrow confines of the hall. Cogan swayed and slumped down, his fingers twitching as though he sought to grasp at his already departed life.

Mickey-dad pocketed the revolver and went into the kitchen. He lifted back the faded red linoleum and revealed a long slit in the floor. By inserting a knife blade in the slit he was able to lift up a section of the floor which swung like a door on concealed hinges. Underneath there was a cavity about six feet in length, not quite two feet in depth, and three feet in width. For over a year this had been the 'strong room' of the gang.

'Now,' thought Mickey-dad, 'I'll sit tight until they come. Then I'll pop in there an' after they've searched the house and gone I'll slip out.'

He sat down on a bentwood chair. He had a few cigarettes in his jacket pocket and a box of matches. He lit a cigarette and puffed heartily. The machine-gun was still stuttering, and an occasional rifle shot rang out. He smoked through all his cigarettes, and still the soldiers did not come. One by one he dropped the butts into the cavity.

Then came a pregnant silence. He listened so hard that he was positive he had no more than a suggestion of an ache in his ear drums.

He sat as still as a Buddha in an eastern temple for a full hour.

Then he heard loud voices outside the front door. Men shouted. A rain of blows fell on the stout oak panels. He rose from his chair and lay down in the cavity. He lowered the camouflaged lid after him, but so shallow was his hiding-place that the lid did not fall into position until he had stretched his arms down by his side.

He heard the sounds of smashing timber, of feet running, of men calling to one another. All were muffled so that they seemed very far away. Then feet tramped above his head. The soldiers were in the kitchen now. He had been desperately afraid that the lid had not fitted properly into place, that some bulge in the linoleum would betray his presence under the floor. But now those heavy-booted feet were making sure that the lid was properly pressed home. The footsteps boomed in Mickey-dad's ears.

He visualised the soldiers poking and prodding and searching everywhere for the fourth man.

Eventually they would conclude that he had escaped before they had surrounded the house. After the bodies were removed to the mortuary they would clear off and he would creep out of this wretched hole for a breather and escape at nightfall.

But the soldiers seemed to be a long time searching and Mickey-dad was growing more and more uncomfortable. The rough concrete which had been laid on the bottom of the cavity to protect the loot from vermin was racking his flesh. His whole body was cramped. A stale clayey smell assailed his nostrils. The air was foul. He could find scarcely enough to breathe. He knew that if he did not get out it would be but a matter of hours until he would suffocate.

Now there was less running about overhead. But the men were still in the kitchen. They talked a lot, talked and talked and talked.

Two hours passed. Mickey-dad was in agony. He was gasping for breath. His limbs ached. His wrists and even his collar-bone ached. A pain not dissimilar to the 'growing-pains' of his youth throbbed down to his big toes. Still the men talked in the kitchen. Mickey-dad was using up more air in his agitation than he need have done if he had kept calm.

But a man who is slowly, very slowly, suffocating can scarcely remain calm. He hoped desperately that every sound overhead was an indication of the departure of the soldiers. This hope sustained him, and only for it he would have cried out long before through sheer physical discomfort.

He felt his face clammy with cold perspiration. To keep his nerve he tried to think of what he could do with the two hundred pounds in his pocket. The minutes dragged on till another hour had been ticked off. Mickey-dad's lungs were so starved of air that he croaked faintly at every gasp. He tried to put his hand to his chest, but he could not move his arms. He was held there between wood and concrete like a garment in a presser. Still the men talked on. 'What the hell do they keep talkin' about, anyway!' Mickey-dad thought. 'Why don't they clear out!'

The men, however, had no intention of clearing out. Only four soldiers were left in charge of the house. The others had gone back on the barracks. One of the soldiers was on guard at the battered front door and another at the back door. A corporal and a private were seated at the kitchen table, playing cards. These two men were doing all the talking.

Mickey-dad lifted his body so as to raise the section of the flooring just a half-inch to let in some fresh air. But it did not budge because the corporal (who was stout and jolly) had placed his chair exactly on top of it. Mickey-dad became desperate. The urge to live overwhelmed him. He beat at the floor with his head.

The corporal paused in his diatribe against his run of ill luck with the cards that day. He listened for a moment. Then he whispered across the table to the private: 'A bloomin' rat! Just under me chair it is!' He drew his revolver gently from its holster, pointed the muzzle at the floor and fired twice. He listened again. There was not a sound.

'That's put the kybosh on that poor baste!' he said heartily, and went on with his game.

2

LAW BREAKING
Cases of Theft and Robbery

THE CURSE OF KISHOGUE

Samuel Lover

This is another example of a story of detection when the genre was still very much in its infancy. Samuel Lover (1797-1868), born in Dublin, was a novelist and dramatist who drew much of the material for his stories from the folklore of his native land, making his name with a collection entitled Legends and Stories of Ireland *which he published in 1831. Among these stories is 'The Curse of Kishogue', in which a light-fingered young Irishman is apparently caught by the police red-handed while stealing a horse. Taken into custody and charged, he is then tried—in a superbly described courtroom scene—and, convicted, finds himself on that fatal journey to the gallows. The tale provides an interesting picture of law and order in Ireland in the early years of the nineteenth century not long after the establishment of the 'Peelers' by Sir Robert Peel—as well as containing a typically Irish macabre twist in the tail.*

You see there was wanst a mighty dacent boy, called Kishogue—and not a complater chap was in the siven parishes nor himself—and for dhrinkin' or coortin' (and by the same token he was a darlint among the girls, he was so bowld), or cudgellin', or runnin', or wrastlin', or the like o' that, none could come near him; and at patthern, or fair, or the dance, or the wake, Kishogue was the flower o' the flock.

Well, to be sure, the gintlemen iv the counthry did not belove him so well as his own sort—that is, the *eldherly* gintlemen; for as to the young 'squires, by gor they loved him like one of themselves, and betther a'most, for they knew well, that Kishogue was the boy to put them up to all sorts and sizes of divilment and divarshin, and that was all they wanted—but the owld, studdy (steady) gintlemen—the responsible people like, didn't give into his ways at all—and, in

throth, they used to be thinkin' that if Kishogue was out of the counthry, body and bones, that the counthry would not be the worse iv
it, in the laste, and that the deer, and the hares, and the partheridges
wouldn't be scarcer in the laste, and that the throut and the salmon
would lade an aisier life—but they could get no howlt of him good
or bad, for he was as cute as a fox, and there was no sitch thing as getting him at an amplush, at all, for he was like a weasel, a'most—
asleep wid his eyes open.

Well, that's the way it was for many a long day, and Kishogue was
as happy as the day was long, until, as bad luck id have it, he made
a mistake one night, as the story goes, and by dad how he could
make the same mistake was never cleared up yet, barrin' that the
night was dark, or that Kishogue had a dhrop o' drink in; but the
mistake *was* made, and *this* was the mistake, you see; that he con-
saived he seen his own mare threspassin' an the man's field, by the
road side, and so, with that, he cotched the mare—that is, the mare,
to all appearance, but it was not his own mare, but the squire's
horse, which he tuk for his own mare—all in a mistake, and he
thought that she had sthrayed away, and not likin' to see *his* baste
threspassin' an another man's field, what does he do, but he dhrives
home the horse *in a mistake*, you see, and how he could do the like
is hard to say, excep'n that the night was dark, as I said before, or
that he had a dhrop too much in; but howsomever the mistake was
made, and a sore mistake it was for poor Kishogue, for he never per-
saived it at all, until three days afther, when the polisman kem to
him and towld him he should go along with him.

'For what?' says Kishogue.

'Oh, you're mighty innocent,' says the polisman.

'Thrue for you, sir,' says Kishogue, as quite (quiet) as a child.
'And where are you goin' to take me, may I make bowld to ax, sir?'
says he.

'To jail,' says the Peeler.

'For what?' says Kishogue.

'For staalin' the 'squire's horse ,' says the Peeler.

'It's the first I heerd of it,' says Kishogue.

'Throth then, 'twon't be the last you'll hear of it,' says the other.

'Why, tare an ouns, sure it's no housebrakin' for a man to dhrive
home his own mare,' says Kishogue.

'No,' says the Peeler, 'but it is *burglaarious* to sarcumvint
another's man's horse,' says he.

'But supposin' 'twas a mistake,' says Kishogue.

'By gor, it'll be the *dear* mistake to you,' says the polisman.

'That's a *poor* case,' says Kishogue.

But there was no use in talkin'—he might as well have been whistlin' jigs to a milestone as sthrivin' to invaigle the polisman, and the ind of it was, that he was obleeged to march off to jail, and there he lay in lavendher, like Paddy Ward's pig, antil the 'sizes kem an, and Kishogue you see, bein' of a high sperrit, did not like the iday at all of bein' undher a compliment to the King for his lodgin'. Besides, to a chap like him, that was all his life used to goin' round the world for sports, the thoughts o' confinement was altogether contagious, though indeed his friends endayvoured for to make it as agreeable to him as they could, for he was mightily beloved in the counthry, and they wor goin' to see him mornin', noon, and night—throth, they led the turnkey a busy life lettin' them in and out, for they wor comin' and goin' evermore, like Mulligan's blanket.

Well, at last the 'sizes kem an, and down kem the sheriffs and the judge, and the jury, and the witnesses, all book-sworn to tell nothin' but the born truth: and with that, Kishogue was the first that was put an his thrial for not knowin' the differ between his own mare and another man's horse, for they wished to give an example to the counthry, and he was bid to howld up his hand at the bar (and a fine big fist he had of his own, by the same token), and up he held it—no ways daunted at all, but as bowld as a ram. Well, then, a chap in a black coat and a frizzled wig and spectacles gets up, and he reads and reads, and you'd think he'd never have done readin'; and it was all about Kishogue—as we heard afther—but could not make out at the time—and no wondher: and in throth, Kishogue never done the half of what the dirty little ottomy was readin' about him—barrin' he knew lies iv him; and Kishogue himself, poor fellow, got frekened at last, when he heerd him goin' an at that rate about him, but afther a bit, he tuk heart and said:

'By this and by that, I never done the half o' that any how.'

'Silence in the coort!' says the crier—puttin' him down that-a-way. Oh, there's no justice for a poor boy at all!

'Oh, murther!' says Kishogue, 'is a man's life to be sworn away afther this manner, and mustn't spake a word.'

'Howl' your tongue!' says my lord the judge. And so afther some more jabberin' and gibberish, the little man in the spectacles threw down the paper and asked Kishogue if he were guilty or not guilty.

'I never done it, my lord,' says Kishogue.

'Answer as you are bid, sir,' says the spectacle man.

'I'm innocent, my lord!' says Kishogue.

'Bad cess to you, can't you say what you're bid,' says my lord the judge—'*Guilty* or *not* guilty.'

'*Not* guilty,' says Kishogue.

'I don't believe you,' says the judge.

'Small blame to you,' says Kishogue, 'you're ped for hangin' people, and you must do something for your wages.'

'You've too much prate, sir,' says my lord.

'Faix then, I'm thinkin' it's yourself and your friend the hangman will cure me o' that very soon,' says Kishogue.

And thrue for him, faith, he wasn't far out in sayin' that same, for they murthered him intirely. They brought a terrible sight o' witnesses agin him, that swore away his life an the cross examination; and indeed sure enough, it *was* the crossest examination altogether I ever seen. Oh, they wor the bowld witnesses, that would *sware a hole in an iron pot* any day in the year. Not but that Kishogue's friends done their duty by him. Oh, they stud to him like men and swore a power for him, and sthrove to make out a *lullaby* for him; maynin', by that same, that he was asleep in another place, at the time—but it wouldn't do, they could not make it *plazin'* to the judge and the jury; and my poor Kishogue was condimned for to die; and the judge put an his black cap, and indeed it's not becomin', and discoorsed the hoighth of fine language, and gev Kishogue a power o' good advice, *that it was a mortial pity Kishogue didn't get sooner;* and the last words the judge said was, 'The Lord have marcy an your sowl!'

'Thank'ee, my lord,' says Kishogue; 'though indeed it is few has luck or grace afther your prayers.'

And sure enough faith; for the next Sathurday Kishogue was ordhered out to be hanged, and the sthreets through which he was to pass was mighty throng; for in them days, you see the people used to be hanged outside o' the town, not all as one as now, when we're hanged genteelly out o' the front o' the jail; but in them days they did not attind to the comforts o' the people at all, but put them into a cart, all as one as a conthrairy pig goin' to market, and stravaiged them through the town to the gallows, that was full half a mile beyant it; but to be sure, whin they kem to the corner of the crass-streets, where the Widdy Houlaghan's public-house was then, afore them dirty swaddlers (methodists) knocked it down and built a meetin'-house there, bad cess to them, sure they're spylin' divarshin wherever they go—when they kem there, as I was tellin' you, the purcesshin was always stopped, and they had a fiddler and mulled wine for the divarshin of the pres'ner, for to rise his heart for what he was to go through; for, by all accounts, it is not plasin' to be goin' to be hanged, supposin' you die in a good cause itself, as my uncle Jim towld me whin he suffered for killin' the gauger. Well, you see, they always stopped tin minutes at the public-house, not to hurry a man with his drink, and, besides, to give the pres'ner an opportunity for sayin' an odd word or so to a frind in the crowd, to say nothin' of its bein' mighty improvin' to the throng, to see the man lookin' pale at the thought o' death, and maybe an idification and warnin' to thim that was inclined to sthray. But however, it happened, and the like never happened afore nor sence; but, as bad luck would have it, that day, the divil a fiddler was there whin Kishogue dhruv up in the cart, no ways danted at all; but the minit the cart stopped rowlin', he came out as stout as a ram, 'Sind me out Tim Riley here,'— Tim Riley was the fiddler's name—'sind me out Tim Riley here,' says he, 'that he may rise my heart wid the tune, The Rakes o' Mallow'; for he was a Mallow man, by all accounts, and mighty proud of his town. Well, av coorse the tune was not to be had, bekase Tim Riley was not there, but was lyin' dhrunk in a ditch at the same time comin' home from confission, and when poor Kishogue heerd that he could not have his favourite tune, it wint to his heart to that degree, that he'd hear of no comfort in life, and he bid them dhrive him an, and put him out o' pain at wanst.

'Oh take the dhrink any how, aroon,' says the Widdy Houlaghan, who was mighty tinderhearted, and always attinded the man that was goin' to be hanged with the dhrink herself, if he was ever so grate a sthranger; but if he was a friend of her own, she'd go every fut to the gallows wid him and see him suffer: Oh she was a darlint! 'Well, take the dhrink, Kishogue my jewel,' says she, handin' him up a brave big mug o' mulled wine, fit for a lord:—but he wouldn't touch it:—'Take it out o' my sight,' says he, 'for my heart is low bekase Tim Riley desaived me, whin I expected to die game, like one of the Rakes o' Mallow! Take it out o' my sight,' says he, puttin' it away wid his hand, and sure 'twas the first time Kishogue was ever known to refuse the dhrop o' dhrink, and many remarked that it was *the change before death* was comin' over him.

Well, away they rowled to the gallows, where there was no delay in life for the pres'ner, and the sheriff asked him if he had any thing to say to him before he suffered; but Kishogue hadn't a word to throw to a dog, and av coorse he said nothin' to the sheriff, and wouldn't say a word that might be improvin' even to the crowd, by way of an idification; and indeed a sore disappointment it was to the throng, for they thought he could make an iligant dyin' speech; and the prenthers there, and the ballad-singers all ready to take it down complate, and thought it was a dirty turn of Kishogue to chate them out o' their honest penny, like; but they owed him no spite, for all that, for they considhered his heart was low an account of the disappointment, and he was lookin' mighty pale while they wor makin' matthers tidy for him; and indeed, the last words he said to himself was, 'Put me out o' pain at wanst, for my heart is low bekast Tim Riley desaived me, whin I thought he would rise it, that I might die like a rale Rake o' Mallow!' And so, to make a long story short, my jew'l, they done the business for him: it was soon over wid him; it was just one step wid him, aff o' the laddher into glory; and to do him justice, though he was lookin' pale, he died bowld, and put his best leg foremost.

Well, what would you think, but just as all was over wid him, there was a shout o' the crowd, and a shilloo that you'd think would split the sky; and what should we see gallopin' up to the gallows, but a man covered with dust an a white horse, to all appearance, but it wasn't a white horse but a black horse, only white wid the foam, he was dhruv to that degree, and the man hadn't a breath to dhraw, and couldn't spake, but dhrew a piece o' paper out of the breast of his coat and handed it up to the sheriff; and, my jew'l, the sheriff grew as white as the paper itself, when he clapt his eyes an it; and, says he. 'Cut him down—cut him down this minute!' says he; and the dhragoons made a slash at the messenger, but he ducked his head and sarcumvinted them. And then the sheriff shouted out, 'Stop, you villains, and bad luck to yiz, you murtherin' vagabones,' says he to the sojers; 'is it goin' to murther the man you wor?—It isn't him at all I mane, but the man that's hangin'. Cut *him* down,' says he: and they cut him down; but it was no use. It was all over wid poor Kishogue; he was dead as small-beer, and as stiff as a crutch.

'Oh, tare an ouns,' says the sheriff, tarin' the hair aff his head at the same time, with the fair rage, 'Isn't it a poor case that he's dead, and here is a reprieve that is come for him; but, bad cess to him,' says he, 'it's his own fault, he wouldn't take it aisy.'

'Oh millia, murther, millia murther!' cried out the Widdy Houlaghan, in the crowd. 'Oh, Kishogue, my darlint, why did you refuse my mull'd wine? Oh, if you stopped wid me to take your dhrop o' dhrink, you'd be alive and merry now!'

So that is the maynin' of the curse o' Kishogue; for you see, Kishogue was hanged *for lavin' his liquor behind him.*

NEGATIVE EVIDENCE

Richard Dowling

This story also represents a 'first' for Irish detective fiction—the first use in a story of photographic evidence to solve the whereabouts of a missing person. I have found no acknowledgement of this landmark achievement in any history of crime fiction, nor, indeed, more than a passing mention of its author Richard Dowling (1846-1898), who was actually responsible for writing a number of excellent thrillers during the late Victorian era, including The Mystery of Killard *(1879),* A Dark Intruder (1895) *and* When London Sleeps *(1896). Dowling was born in Clonmel and educated in Limerick, after which he worked on* The Nation, *a republican journal. He was also for a time the editor of the Dublin comic paper* Zozimus, *modelled on similar lines to* Punch.

'Negative Evidence', published in East and West *magazine in 1888, is a tale strong in atmosphere and tension enhanced by the ingenious use of a camera—then still very much a novelty used only by experts— in helping to resolve the mystery.*

John Hastings of Barford had, as a matter of course, promised to dine at Charcombe House that evening. The next morning he was to be married to Maud Bathurst, the only child of Mr Frank Bathurst, who owned Charcombe House. John had seen Maud the day before, and it had been arranged he was to come over in the afternoon of this day. He had some business to transact in Dunfield, the nearest town, and as soon as he had made an end of it, he told Maud he should walk over Charcombe Hill, so that they might have a few hours together before dinner. She was not to come to meet him, as he did not know how long his business would detain him in Dunfield. After dinner he would drive back to his own place, The Oaks. It would take less time to walk from Dunfield to Charcombe over the hill, than to drive round the hill from the town to the House. Hence he had decided upon walking. Maud might expect him at any time between four and six. Dinner would not be until half-past seven.

The marriage between John Hastings and Maud Bathurst had been arranged by mutual inclination, and with the cordial approval of her parents. Indeed, it seemed as though Nature and Fate had destined them for one another. He was tall and dark and sincere, she small and fair and light-hearted and affectionate. He was alone in the world, and in choosing a wife need consult no one but the girl upon whom he had set his heart, and her relations or guardians. The lands of Charcombe, which in time would be hers, adjoined the lands of Barford, which now were his. The families had been friendly neighbours for generations. Both in London and in the neighbourhood of their own homes Maud and he had met continually for years, and successive heads of the families had wished that the two races might be joined in one, the two properties go down to a common heir. But somehow this hope had never seemed likely to be realised until now. Formerly there had never been a marriageable heir when there happened to be a marriageable heiress, and Mr and Mrs Bathurst rejoiced that a traditional aspiration was about to be fulfilled at last.

As for the two young people themselves, they cared nothing for traditional aspirations. They were simply in love with one another, and they wanted to get married and live all their lives together, just as do thousands, millions of other people, who have neither ancestors nor acres.

It was bright July weather. As four o'clock struck in the tiny tower that stood over the gate of the coach-house, the sun appeared hardly lower in the heavens than at noon. It seemed tireless, and full of light that could never die. It was king absolute of the pale azure realms, and ruled in lonely despotism, its sway unchallenged by subtlest conspirator cloud.

The pendulum of the clock in the tower swung backward and forward with a dull, mechanical, despairing tick, tick. It had no more interest in its work than a felon at the oar. The sun noiselessly continued its imperceptible, invincible triumph towards the west. It did not move because of any law that bound it, but because of its slowness to remain.

In the sky the only events are clouds; in the tower the only events are hours. But it matters not whether clouds came into the sky or the hammer of the clock struck the hour, the sun and pendulum went on unheeding. The sun might be lost in the clouds, the ticking of the pendulum drowned in the booming of the bell, but the progress of the sun westward and the oscillation of the pendulum over the central point of earth suffered no mutation.

From her own window she could best get sight of John as he came over the brow of the hill. She knew the point of the hill from which his head would strike upwards against the pale sky. She was in her room, and on that point her blue eyes were fixed when the clock struck four.

As soon as she should see him, she would fly on tip-toe out of the room, along the corridor and down the stairs. Should she meet anyone, she would slacken her pace and go demurely—except that someone was her mother. If she met her mother she would kiss hands and flee past without abating her speed, for her mother would know and understand that she was speeding because he was coming over the hill. Once in the open air she would have to go quietly, for many windows looked on the lawn. But as soon as she was round the garden wall she might hasten again until she came to their favourite resting-place, the rustic bench under the great chestnut-tree. There no one could see them meet, and by the time she had reached the chestnut he would be near enough to speak to her—to speak to her! And then they should sit down and rest.

Maud waited minute after minute, and yet that figure did not start up against the sky. She knew he had many things to do in Dunfield that day, and, young and inexperienced as she was, she felt that when a man has many things to do, although he may happen to be a bridegroom-elect, he cannot always calculate to a nicety how long his business may take him, for though he may be a model of punctuality he may meet men who do not estimate that royal virtue at its proper worth.

John had said he would be with her between four and six, and it was not yet five. It would, of course, have been delightful if he had appeared on the top of the hill just as the clock struck four, but then one must not expect in this ordinary climate and time to have things fall out as they do in an Eastern fairy tale of long ago. Even to desire such a miracle would be childish and absurd.

She leaned against the window for support, and kept her wide-open blue eyes fixed on that heather-clad slanting ridge.

Gradually, as minutes of expectancy unfulfilled went by, the brightness and animation faded from her face, until it became almost pensive, and the full rose-red of her cheeks paled to pink. She put one of her hands upon the sash of the window, and leaned her forehead against the glass. This pushed her hat back, and disclosed the rich waves of golden hair that lay over the mantling white forehead. She was physically tired of standing so long in almost the same position, but she was not conscious she was tired. She only thought——

'He will come presently. The moment his head rises above the hill I shall see him, and, oh, then!'

Suddenly she started. The clock struck five. She looked at the sun. It was plainly lower in the heavens than when she looked at it last, as she began her vigil. She looked to the east. A low, slender smoke-coloured cloud lay along the horizon, visible between the house and the precipitous ends of the hills. Still the light was superb.

John had now got half way through the time he had allowed himself. But after all this was the better way; for, while before it struck five there was, let her say, one chance of his appearing each minute, now there were two chances. In the hour gone by luck might keep him away from her for a couple of hours. Now that was impossible. All the rich chances of his coming were packed and crowded into the little space of sixty minutes. Every second that went by brought him nearer to her. She was so easy about him, now that it was less than an hour from the time of his absence to the time of his presence, that she might as well make herself comfortable.

She sat down, leaning her elbow on the high window sill and keeping her eyes still fixed on the brow of the hill.

As minutes went by those between the present moment and six grew thicker and thicker with promises of him, until suppressed excitement took the place of languor, and she fancied she could feel him pressing forward towards the verge of that hill.

Still the hard, sharp line of the distant heather lay flat and unbroken against the darkening blue of the sky. The margin of smoke-colour cloud had advanced far westward, and down in the east lay a sombre shadow under a bank of dun vapour.

The sun passed slowly westward. The pendulum of the clock swung monotonously backward and forward with its slow, unwearying tick, tick.

Once more the girl started. She stood hastily up. The clock had begun to strike six.

Surely before it had finished striking he would appear. He had said six as the last moment which could delay him from her. It could not be that he would tarry beyond the last second of the hour.

The clock ceased striking. The girl sighed, and, sitting down, clasped her hands in her lap. Still no figure rose between her and the sky above the edge of that hill.

It was strange to her that on this, the last evening of her maiden life, he should for the first time be late in keeping his appointment. They had now been engaged six months, and during all that time he had never been one moment late. She had already told herself that one or several of many things might have delayed him beyond all reasonable calculation. But when the heart is anxious or hungry there is small consolation in the reason. She did not want to think he was blameless in being late. What she wanted was his presence, not a knowledge of what caused his absence. In a short time the ordinary common-place guests of the evening would begin to arrive, and she would have to go down and meet them, and talk dull, pointless nothings to them, while her heart and its attendant senses were in expectation on that hill-top.

Half an hour went by. The sun was now getting low in the west. The clock went on impassively. Maud's spirits fell low. A feeling akin to fear had gradually begun to gather in her mind. She resolved upon one thing: Here she would wait till the last moment. Then, when duties to others called, she should go and try to smile as though she had suffered no disappointment.

What!—seven o'clock striking and yet he had not come! The sun was now far down in the west. It would set in about an hour. The last day of her girlhood would come to an end when the clock struck again. Surely, surely it was hard he had not come. There was now no further time for watching or waiting. She should dress and go down. She had put on her hat and gloves in vain. Well, it would not do to be gloomy. It would not do to show she was disappointed. She did not blame him for not coming. She was only sorry he had not come. She knew he had to go to a number of places in Dunfield—his lawyer's and his banker's, and several tradesmen's, and the post-office; but still it was a pity he had not come. There was so much she had to say to him in those two hours she had promised herself with him before dinner. Well, there was no use in fretting now, and perhaps, after all, when he did come, when a little while hence she turned round and unexpectedly saw him, the delight of that moment would recompense her for the disappointment of this.

Dinner came and went, and brought no lover—no message from him, no news of him. A hundred different harmless and blameless reasons were assigned by her father and mother and sympathetic friends for his absence. But they fell idly into her ears. If all was well, why was not he here? If anything were wrong, what was it? If anything had happened to him, then—— She did not finish the thought. She did not weep.

What would happen tomorrow?

Next morning came, and brought no news of John Hastings. The hour for the marriage came, but no bridegroom with it. In the meantime inquiries had been made.

As far as could be discovered, the history of John Hastings's action the previous day was as follows:

At about noon he arrived in Dunfield, put up his horse and dog-cart at 'The Oaks', and went first to his lawyer, with whom he had a long interview. Nothing of any unusual interest occurred at this meeting; it was merely for the purpose of arranging tedious and uninteresting details connected with the missing man's approaching marriage, and with the routine business of the six weeks which Mr Hastings intended passing abroad after the ceremony.

From his lawyer's Mr Hastings went to the bank, out of which he drew, in Bank of England notes, a sum of £300. Mr Hastings did not stay more than ten minutes in the bank. After this he called on three tradesmen, who were concerned in certain alterations and repairs going on at his place, Barford.

When he had finished with the tradesmen, he went to 'The Oaks', the principal inn of the town, and gave orders that his dogcart should be sent for him to Charcombe House, so as to arrive about eleven o'clock. He said he was going to walk over the hill to Charcombe, which he expected to reach at four. He owed the landlord of 'The Oaks' a baiting account, and paid it out of the bundle of notes he had that day got from the bank. He paid the money in the bar. Several people saw him pay the money, and, in honour of his marriage, he left some money with the landlord to be distributed among the servants and hangers-on at the inn. Then he set off in the direction of the House, taking the way that led over the hill. From that time to this he had not been seen by anyone.

What humour did he seem in?

The very best possible. He spoke in a friendly way to everyone, and received congratulations and good wishes with cheerful graciousness.

Was it known if he had any enemies, if there were any people who owed him a grudge?

As far as was known he had no enemy, and no one owed him a grudge. On the contrary, he was popular and universally respected in the neighbourhood. It was the general impression that no one in or near Dunfield would do him harm.

Then, if no one in the district was likely to injure him, and if he had been injured or made away with, in all likelihood a stranger had had something to do with it. Were there any strangers or suspicious-looking people in the town? Particularly was any stranger or suspicious-looking person in the bank when he got the money?

No. Mr Hastings was the only one in the bank, beyond the officials, when he drew the money.

Was any strange or suspicious-looking person in 'The Oaks' when he so injudiciously pulled out that bundle of notes to pay the landlord?

Ah! that was a different matter. Wait a moment. Yes. Now it was recollected, while Mr Hastings was paying his account in the bar, a man named William Laycroft, a photographer he appeared to be, who had been staying at 'The Oaks' a few days, came downstairs with his apparatus in his hand, and passed through. He left the bar before Mr Hastings, taking his apparatus with him, and went in the direction of Charcombe Hill, but not exactly by the same route as the missing man had taken.

Where was the photographer now? Had he left the town?

It was believed not. He had been seen that morning at 'The Oaks', and the impression was that there he might still be staying.

The photographer was sought at 'The Oaks', and found there.

He was a low, wiry, thin man, of swarthy complexion and nervous manner. He was clad in rusty black cloth coat, waistcoat, and trousers, and wore a black silk hat, much the worse for wear. His clothes fitted him ill, and his hat was too big for him, so that he had every now and then to thrust it back off his forehead, or it would have come down on his nose.

When first interrogated as to his movements the day before, he said that was no business of anyone but himself, and that he did not intend giving any answers; but upon having matters explained, and the gravity of the position pointed out to him, he said he would reply to any question. He offered in extenuation of his reluctance to speak when first asked, the statement that he was secretly getting together a certain class of photograph landscapes for a particular purpose, and if this purpose became known, someone else might forestall him, and so render all his labour up to this valueless. His account of his actions after leaving 'The Oaks' the day before was:

He had made up his mind to take a photograph of a piece of broken ground on the Dunfield side of Charcombe Hill. He set off at a brisk pace and soon after gained the place he had selected for placing his camera. The point (which he minutely described, commanded the route by which the missing man would go) was in a little hollow well sheltered from sun and wind, and sight for that matter, because a large stone hung over the camera, and, save by standing directly in front of what he might describe as a cave, no one could see him or his instrument.

The day was most favourable to his purposes, the air being pure and the light full and strong. He had prepared almost everything for his work before setting out from 'The Oaks'. In a few minutes all was ready, and he slipped off the cap. As he had explained, he wanted this photograph for a particular purpose, and one of the essentials for this purpose was that the period of exposure should be long. He lit his pipe and looked around him, although the plate was ready for removal. When he had everything tidy once more he set off back to the inn, encountering no one on the way. He had not seen Mr Hastings or anyone else on the hill, or from the time he began to ascend the hill until he got to the bottom again. He now wished to apologise for his brusqueness of manner when first asked about his experience on the hill yesterday. His temper had been somewhat soured by the ill success of that plate; for, although the day had been everything his heart could wish, the plate turned out defective. There was an unaccountable smudge on the right-hand side of it at the horizon line.

The people who were listening had paid great attention to all his story, until he came to his apology and grievance towards the end. They felt that the apology ought to have come earlier, and that the grievance ought not to have been mentioned at all. It was little short of impertinence to intrude upon so grave and anxious an inquiry as the present, the success or want of success with a paltry photograph negative.

All felt, moreover, that though there was nothing like evidence against William Laycroft, the itinerant photographer, his position was far from being free from suspicion. The informal inquiry was being held by a few friends of both families in the little private parlour of 'The Oaks'.

As soon as Laycroft had finished his story he withdrew. It was desirable that everything should be kept as quiet as possible for the present, and so, as yet, the police had not been communicated with. A couple of men had gone over the road John Hastings had intended following, but they had come back with no tidings of the missing man. The friends were beginning to think of calling in the police at last. It was now past noon, and the wedding could not take place that day. Half a dozen different scouts, besides those who went over the hill, had been sent out, but each returned with no word or clue.

All at once, and without a word of warning, William Laycroft, the itinerant photographer, burst into the room in a state of great excitement. He held a thin film of paper in his hand.

'Quick!' he cried, looking round him and holding up the limp piece of paper. 'Quick, I say! Some men come with me. I know the ground well. I've been over it all before, I think. Quick, I say! Who will follow me?'

The other men stared at one another. They thought him mad.

'I call you no men if you sit there and will not follow me. I'm going up the hill to find the body of the gentleman you are looking for, the gentleman whom, I could see by your looks, you thought a while ago I had murdered. Whoever wants to be at the finding of the body of Mr John Hastings will follow me.'

There was something startling, and at the same time impressive, in the man's manner, and the men in the parlour rose and asked, 'Where? where?'

'Follow me!' he cried, and they could get no other words from him.

He led the way up the hill, but kept more to the east than the way John Hastings had taken. The men told him this.

'Follow me,' was all the reply he would deign.

For some time he held on almost due east, and then made a sharp turn north. This brought him, on a lower level than the hill, to a kind of shelf here running along the whole side of the hill. Over this shelf an almost perpendicular wall of rock rose to the height of forty feet. The shelf or ledge, which was quite level, appeared like a road cut into the side of the hill.

The little party kept on at a quick pace for half an hour. All at once Laycroft stopped and looked eagerly around. Nothing unusual was to be seen. He then looked up the face of the rock. Here, also, was nothing unusual.

He seemed inexpressibly perplexed and confounded. The men who had accompanied him were about to turn and desert him, when all were startled by hearing a strange sound, a moan from some part of the cliff above them.

'He is there! He is there, and alive!' said Laycroft.

Search was instantly made, and at last John Hastings was found jambed between two rocks a few feet below the cliff.

When he was extricated, and had recovered somewhat, he said that everything had gone well with him until, upon reaching a point a little south of where they found him, and a couple of hundred yards further west, he received a tremendous blow on the back of the head, and he remembered nothing till he awoke in the middle of the night where he was found. Here he was helpless, and too weak to call out or give any sufficient sign.

Laycroft's account was that, after his interrogation in the parlour, he printed an impression from the negative taken the evening before, and upon examining the horizon line at the right or left-hand corner he came to the conclusion that this defect was caused by something moving over the heather from west to east in the direction of the horizon. Upon scrutinising the blur carefully with a magnifying glass, he came to the further conclusion that there was a human figure for a brief moment between the lens and the sky. Still further examination showed him that this figure carried another in its arms. At this moment he felt convinced that this would prove to be the photograph of the last scene in a tragedy.

However, although John Hastings got a bad shaking and lost £300, he did not die. The man who robbed him and tried to kill him was never found. The marriage had to be postponed for a month. There is now no further relique of that afternoon's bad work save the negative of a certain photograph hanging in Maud's room, a negative which John says has been, excepting herself, the cause of the greatest mercy ever shown to man.

A LUNATIC AT LARGE

George A. Birmingham

Quite a lot of Irish detective fiction is tinged with humour, both conscious and unconscious, but certainly few writers have written with more wit and sly bathos than George A. Birmingham (1865-1950), the author of 'A Lunatic at Large'. Indeed, many of Birmingham's novels of adventure, the supernatural and crime, such as Spanish Gold *(1908),* The Inviolable Sanctuary *(1912) and* Bindon Parva *(1926), are notable for the comic elements that skilfully enhance the moments of high drama. The author himself was also something of a surprise—for he had been born James Owen Hannay in Belfast, and served for many years in the Church as, first, Rector of Westport, County Mayo, and then Canon of St Patrick's Cathedral, Dublin.*

George Birmingham undoubtedly drew on his wide experience of Irish life for many of his short stories—especially tales like 'A Lunatic at Large' which is set in the little village of Dunailin and chronicles the adventures of Sergeant Rahilly, a local policeman with his own particular way of interpreting the law, and his efforts to assist the cause of a doctor newly arrived from England . . .

It was Tuesday, a Tuesday early in October. Dr Lovaway finished his breakfast quietly, conscious that he had a long morning before him and nothing particular to do. Tuesday is a quiet day in Dunailin; Wednesday is market day and people are busy, the doctor as well as everybody else. Young women who come into town with butter to sell take the opportunity of having their babies vaccinated on Wednesday. Old women, with baskets on their arms, find it convenient on that day to ask the doctor for something to rub into knee-joints where rheumatic pains are troublesome. Old men, who have ridden into town on their donkeys, consult the doctor about chronic coughs, and seek bottles likely to relieve 'an impression on the chest.'

Fridays, when the Petty Sessions' Court sits, are almost as busy. Mr Timothy Flanagan, a magistrate in virtue of the fact that he is Chairman of the Urban District Council, administers justice of a rude and uncertain kind in the Court House. While angry litigants are settling their business there, and repentant drunkards are paying the moderate fines imposed on them, their wives ask the doctor for advice about the treatment of whooping-cough or the best way of treating a child which has incautiously stepped into a fire. Fair days, which occur once a month, are the busiest days of all. Everyone is in town on fair days, and every kind of ailment is brought to the doctor. Towards evening he has to put stitches into one or two cut scalps and sometimes set a broken limb. On Mondays and Thursdays the doctor sits in his office for an hour or two to register births and deaths.

But Tuesdays, unless a fair happens to fall on Tuesday, are quiet days. On this particular Tuesday Dr Lovaway was pleasantly aware that he had nothing whatever to do, and might count on having the whole day to himself. It was raining very heavily, but the weather did not trouble him at all. He had a plan for the day which rain could not mar.

He sat down at his writing-table, took from a drawer a bundle of foolscap paper, fitted a new nib to his pen, and filled his ink bottle. He began to write.

'A study of the Remarkable Increase of Lunacy in Rural Connaught.'

The title looked well. It would, he felt, certainly attract the attention of the editor of *The British Medical Journal*.

But Dr Lovaway did not like it. It was not for the editor of *The British Medical Journal*, or, indeed, for a scientific public that he wanted to write. He started fresh on a new sheet of paper.

'Lunacy in the West of Ireland: Its Cause and Cure.'

That struck him as the kind of title which would appeal to the philanthropist out to effect a social reform of some kind. But Dr Lovaway was not satisfied with it. He respected reformers and was convinced of the value of their work, but his real wish was to write something of a literary kind. With prodigal extravagance he tore up another sheet of foolscap and began again.

'The Passing of the Gael. Ireland's Crowded Madhouses.'

He purred a little over the title and then began the article itself. What he wanted to say was clear in his mind. He had been weeks in Dunailin, and he had spent more time over lunatics than anything else. Almost every day he found himself called upon by Sergeant Rahilly to 'certify' a lunatic, to commit some unfortunate person with diseased intellect to an asylum. Sometimes he signed the required document. Often he hesitated, although he was always supplied by the sergeant and his constables with a wealth of lurid detail about the dangerous and homicidal tendencies of the patient. Dr Lovaway was profoundly impressed.

He gave his whole mind to the consideration of the problem which pressed on him. He balanced theories. He blamed tea, inter-marriage, potatoes, bad whisky, religious enthusiasm, and did not find any of them nor all of them together satisfactory as explanations of the awful facts. He fell back finally on a theory of race decadence. Already fine phrases were forming themselves in his mind: 'The inexpressible beauty of autumnal decay.' 'The exquisiteness of the decadent efflorescence of a passing race.'

He covered a sheet of foolscap with a bare—he called it detached—statement of the facts about Irish lunacy. He had just begun to recount his own experience when there was a knock at the door. The housekeeper, a legacy from Dr Farelly, came in to tell him that Constable Malone wished to speak to him. Dr Lovaway left his MS with a sigh. He found Constable Malone, a tall man of magnifi-cent physique, standing in the hall, the raindrops dripping from the cape he wore.

'The sergeant is after sending me round to you, sir,' said Consta-ble Malone, 'to know would it be convenient for you to attend at Ballygran any time this afternoon to certify a lunatic?'

'Surely not another!' said Dr Lovaway.

'It was myself found him, sir,' said the constable, with an air of pride in his achievement. 'The sergeant bid me say that he'd have Patsy Doolan's car engaged for you, and that him and me would go with you so that you wouldn't have any trouble more than the trou-ble of going to Ballygran, which is an out-of-the-way place sure enough, and it's a terrible day.'

'Is the man violent?' asked Dr Lovaway.

By way of reply Constable Malone gave a short account of the man's position in life.

'He's some kind of a nephew of Mrs Finnegan,' he said, 'and they call him Jimmy Finnegan, though Finnegan might not be his proper name. He does be helping Finnegan himself about the farm, and they say he's middling useful. But, of course, now the harvest's gathered, Finnegan will be able to do well enough without him till the spring.'

This did not seem to Dr Lovaway a sufficient reason for incarcerating Jimmy in an asylum.

'But is he violent?' he repeated. 'Is he dangerous to himself or others?'

'He never was the same as other boys,' said the constable, 'and the way of it with fellows like that is what you wouldn't know. He might be quiet enough today and be slaughtering all before him tomorrow. And what Mrs Finnegan says is that she'd be glad if you'd see the poor boy today, because she's in dread of what he might do tomorrow night.'

'Tomorrow night! Why tomorrow night?'

'There's a change in the moon tomorrow,' said the constable, 'and they do say the moon has terrible power over fellows that's took that way.'

Dr Lovaway, who was young and trained in scientific methods, was at first inclined to argue with Constable Malone about the effect of the moon on the human mind. He refrained, reflecting that it is an impious thing to destroy an innocent superstition. One of the great beauties of Celtic Ireland is that it still clings to faiths forsaken by the rest of the world.

At two o'clock that afternoon Dr Lovaway took his seat on Patsy Doolan's car. It was still raining heavily. Dr Lovaway wore an overcoat of his own, a garment which had offered excellent protection against rainy days in Manchester. In Dunailin, for a drive to Ballygran, the coat was plainly insufficient. Mr Flanagan hurried from his shop with a large oilskin cape taken from a peg in his men's outfitting department. Constable Malone, under orders from the sergeant, went to the priest's house and borrowed a waterproof rug. Johnny Conerney the butcher appeared at the last moment with a sou'wester which he put on the doctor's head and tied under his chin. It would not be the fault of the people of Dunailin if Lovaway, with his weak lungs, 'died on them'.

Patsy Doolan did not contribute anything to the doctor's outfit, but displayed a care for his safety.

'Take a good grip now, doctor,' he said. 'Take a hold of the little rail there beside you. The mare might be a bit wild on account of the rain, and her only clipped yesterday, and the road to Ballygran is jolty in parts.'

Sergeant Rahilly and Constable Malone sat on one side of the car, Dr Lovaway was on the other. Patsy Doolan sat on the driver's seat. Even with what weight behind her the mare proved herself to be 'a bit wild.' She went through the village in a series of bounds, shied at everything she saw in the road, and did not settle down until the car turned into a rough track which led up through the mountains to Ballygran. Dr Lovaway held on tight with both hands. Patsy Doolan, looking back over his left shoulder, spoke words of encouragement.

'It'll be a bit strange to you at first, so it will,' he said. 'But by the time you're six months in Dunailin we'll have you taught to sit a car, the same as it might be an armchair you were on.'

Dr Lovaway, clinging on for his life while the car bumped over the boulders, did not believe that a car would ever become to to him as an armchair.

Ballygran is a remote place, very difficult of access. At the bottom of a steep hill, a stream, which seemed a raging torrent to Dr Lovaway, flowed across the road. The mare objected very strongly to wading through it. Farther on the track along which they drove became precipitous and more stony than ever. Another stream, scorning its properly appointed course, flowed down the road, rolling large stones with it. Patsy Doolan was obliged to get down and lead the mare. After persuading her to advance twenty yards or so he called for the help of the police. Sergeant Rahilly took the other side of the mare's head. Constable Malone pushed at the back of the car. Dr Lovaway, uncomfortable and rather nervous, wanted to get down and wade too. But the sergeant would not hear of this.

'Let you sit still,' he said. 'The water's over the tops of my boots, so it is, and where's the use of you getting a wetting that might be the death of you?'

'Is it much farther?' asked Lovaway.

The sergeant considered the matter.

'It might be a mile and a bit,' he said, 'from where we are this minute.'

The mile was certainly an Irish mile, and Dr Lovaway began to think that there were some things in England, miles for instance, which are better managed than they are in Ireland. 'The bit' which followed the mile belonged to a system of measurement even more generous than Irish miles and acres.

'I suppose now,' said the sergeant, 'that the country you come from is a lot different from this.'

He had taken up his seat again on the car after leading the mare up the river. He spoke in a cheery, conversational tone. Dr Lovaway thought of Manchester and the surrounding district, thought of trams, trains, and paved streets.

'It is different,' he said, 'very different indeed.'

Ballygran appeared at last, dimly visible through the driving rain. It was a miserable-looking hovel, roofed with sodden thatch, surrounded by a sea of mud. A bare-footed woman stood in the doorway. She wore a tattered skirt and a bodice fastened across her breast with a brass safety-pin. Behind her stood a tall man in a soiled flannel jacket and a pair of trousers which hung in a ragged fringe round his ankles.

'Come in,' said Mrs Finnegan, 'come in the whole of yez. It's a terrible day, Sergeant, and I wonder at you bringing the doctor out in the weather that does be it in. Michael'—she turned to her husband who stood behind her—'let Patsy Doolan be putting the mare into the shed, and let you be helping him. Come in now, Doctor, and take an air of the fire. I'll wet a cup of tea for you, so I will.'

Dr Lovaway passed through a low door into the cottage. His eyes gradually became accustomed to the gloom inside and to the turf smoke which filled the room. In a corner, seated on a low stool, he saw a young man crouching over the fire.

'That's him,' said Mrs Finnegan. 'That's the poor boy, Doctor. The sergeant will have been telling you about him.'

The boy rose from his stool at the sound of her voice.

'Speak to the gentleman now,' said Mrs Finnegan. 'Speak to the doctor, Jimmy alannah, and tell him the way you are.'

'Your honour's welcome,' said Jimmy, in a thin, cracked voice. 'Your honour's welcome surely, though I don't mind that ever I set eyes on you before.'

'Whisht now, Jimmy,' said the sergeant. 'It's the doctor that's come to see you, and it's for your own good he's come.'

'I know that,' said Jimmy, 'and I know he'll be wanting to have me put away. Well, what must be, must be, if it's the will of God, and if it's before me it may as well as be now as any other time.'

'You see the way he is,' said the sergeant. 'And I have the papers here ready to be signed.'

Dr Lovaway saw, or believed he saw, exactly how things were. The boy was evidently of weak mind. There was little sign of actual lunacy, no sign at all of violence about him. Mrs Finnegan added a voluble description of the case.

'It might be a whole day,' she said, 'and he wouldn't be speaking a word, nor he wouldn't seem to hear if you speak to him, and he'd just sit there by the fire the way you seen him without he'd be doing little turns about the place, feeding the pig, or mending a gap in the wall or the like. I will say for Jimmy, the poor boy's always willing to do the best he can.'

'Don't be troubling the doctor now, Mrs Finnegan,' said the sergeant. 'He knows the way it is with the boy without your telling him. Just let the doctor sign what has to be signed and get done with it. Aren't we wet enough as it is without standing here talking half the day?'

The mention of the wet condition of the party roused Mrs Finnegan to action. She hung a kettle from a blackened hook in the chimney and piled up turf on the fire. Jimmy was evidently quite intelligent enough to know how to boil water. He took the bellows, went down on his knees, and blew the fire diligently. Mrs Finnegan spread a somewhat dirty tablecloth on a still dirtier table and laid out cups and saucers on it.

Dr Lovaway was puzzled. The boy at the fire might be, probably was, mentally deficient. He was not a case for an asylum. He was certainly not likely to become violent or to do any harm either to himself or anyone else. It was not clear why Mrs Finnegan, who seemed a kindly woman, should wish to have him shut up. It was very difficult to imagine any reason for the action of the police in the matter. Constable Malone had discovered the existence of the boy in this remote place. Sergeant Rahilly had taken a great deal of trouble in preparing papers for his committal to the asylum, and had driven out to Ballygran on a most inclement day. Dr Lovaway wished he understood what was happening.

Finnegan, having left Patsy Doolan's mare, and apparently Patsy Doolan himself in the shed, came into the house.

Dr Lovaway appealed to him.

'It doesn't seem to me,' he said, 'that this boy ought to be sent to an asylum. I shall be glad to hear anything you have to tell me about him.'

'Well now,' said Mr Finnegan, 'he's a good, quiet kind of a boy, and if he hasn't too much sense there's many another has less.'

'That's what I think,' said Dr Lovaway.

Jimmy stopped blowing the fire and looked round suddenly.

'Sure, I know well you're wanting to put me away,' he said.

'It's for your own good,' said the sergeant.

'It'll do him no harm anyway,' said Finnegan, 'if so be he's not kept there.'

'Kept!' said the sergeant. 'Is it likely now that they'd keep a boy like Jimmy? He'll be out again as soon as ever he's in. I'd say now a fortnight is the longest he'll be there.'

'I wouldn't like,' said Finnegan, 'that he'd be kept too long. I'll be wanting him for spring work, but I'm willing to spare him from this till Christmas if you like.'

Dr Lovaway, though a young man and constitutionally timid, was capable of occasional firmness.

'I'm certainly not going to certify that boy as a lunatic,' he said.

'Come now, Doctor,' said the sergeant persuasively, 'after coming so far and the wet day and all. What have you to do only to put your name at the bottom of a piece of paper? And Jimmy's willing to go. Aren't you, Jimmy?'

'I'll go if I'm wanted to go,' said Jimmy.

The water boiled. Mrs Finnegan was spreading butter on long slices cut from a home-baked loaf. It was Jimmy who took the kettle from the hook and filled the teapot.

'Mrs Finnegan,' said Dr Lovaway, 'why do you want the boy put into an asylum?'

'Is it me wanting him put away?' she said. 'I want no such thing. The notion never entered my head, nor Michael's either, who's been like a father to the boy. Only when Constable Malone came to me, and when it was a matter of pleasing him and the sergeant, I didn't want to be disobliging, for the sergeant is always a good friend of mine, and Constable Malone is a young man I've a liking for. But as for wanting to get rid of Jimmy! Why should I? Nobody'd grudge the bit the creature would eat, and there's many a little turn he'd be doing for me about the house.'

Mr Finnegan was hovering in the background, half hidden in the smoke which filled the house. He felt that he ought to support his wife.

'What I said to the sergeant,' he said, 'no longer ago than last Friday when I happened to be in town about a case I had on the Petty Sessions' Court—what I said to the sergeant was this: "So long as the boy isn't kept there too long, and so long as he's willing to go——"'

Jimmy, seated again on his low stool before the fire, looked up. 'Amn't I ready to go wherever I'm wanted?' he said.

'There you are now, Doctor,' said the sergeant. 'You'll not refuse the poor boy when he wants to go?'

'Sergeant,' said Dr Lovaway, 'I can't, I really can't certify that boy as a lunatic. I don't understand why you ask me to. It seems to me——'

Poor Lovaway was much agitated. It seemed to him that he had been drawn into an infamous conspiracy against the liberty of a particularly helpless human being.

'I don't think you ought to have asked me to come here,' he said. 'I don't think you should have suggested——It seems to me, Sergeant, that your conduct has been most reprehensible. I'm inclined to think I ought to report the matter to—to——' Dr Lovaway was not quite sure about the proper place to which to send a report about the conduct of a sergeant of the Irish Police. 'To the proper authorities,' he concluded feebly.

'There, there,' said the sergeant soothingly, 'we'll say no more about the matter. I wouldn't like you to be vexed, Doctor.'

But Dr Lovaway, having once begun to speak his mind, was not inclined to stop.

'This isn't the first time this sort of thing has happened,' he said. 'You've asked me to certify lunacy in some very doubtful cases. I don't understand your motives, but——'

'Well, well,' said the sergeant, 'there's no harm done anyway.'

Mrs Finnegan, like all good women, was anxious to keep the peace among the men under her roof.

'Is the tea to your liking, Doctor,' she said 'or will I give you a taste more sugar in it? I'm a great one for sugar myself, but they tell me there's them that drinks tea with ne'er a grain of sugar in it at all. They must be queer people that do that.'

She held a spoon, heaped up with sugar, over the doctor's cup as she spoke. He was obliged to stop lecturing the sergeant in order to convince her that his tea was already quite sweet enough. It was, indeed, far too sweet for his taste, for he was one of those queer people whose tastes Mrs Finnegan could not understand.

The drive home ought to have been in every way pleasanter than the drive out to Ballygran. Patsy Doolan's mare was subdued in temper; so docile, indeed, that she allowed Jimmy to put her between the shafts. She made no attempt to stand on her hind legs, and did not shy even at a young pig which bolted across the road in front of her. Dr Lovaway could sit on his side of the car without holding on. The rain had ceased, and great wisps of mist were sweeping clear of the hilltops, leaving fine views of grey rock and heather-clad slopes. But Dr Lovaway did not enjoy himself. Being an Englishman he had a strong sense of duty, and was afflicted as no Irishman ever is by a civic conscience. He felt that he ought to bring home some-how to Sergeant Rahilly a sense of the iniquity of trying to shut up sane, or almost sane, people in lunatic asylums. Being of a gentle and friendly nature, he hated making himself unpleasant to anyone, especially to a man like Sergeant Rahilly, who had been very kind to him.

The path of duty was not made any easier to him by the behaviour of the sergeant. Instead of being overwhelmed by a sense of disco-vered guilt, the police, both Rahilly and Constable Malone, were pleasantly chatty, and evidently bent on making the drive home as agreeable as possible for the doctor. They told him the names of the hills and the more distant mountains. They showed the exact bank at the side of the road from behind which certain murderous men had fired at a land agent in 1885. They explained the route of a light railway which a forgotten Chief Secretary had planned but had never built owing to change of Government and his loss of office. Not one word was said about Jimmy, or lunatics, or asylums. It was with great difficulty that Dr Lovaway succeeded at last in breaking in on the smooth flow of chatty reminiscences. But when he did speak he spoke strongly. As with most gentle and timid men, his lan-guage was almost violent when he had screwed himself up to the point of speaking at all.

The two policemen listened to all he said with the utmost good humour. Indeed, the sergeant supported him.

'You hear what the doctor's saying to you, Constable Malone,' he said.

'I do, surely,' said the constable.

'Well, I hope you'll attend to it,' said the sergeant, 'and let there be no more of the sort of work that the doctor's complaining of.'

'But I mean you too, Sergeant,' said Dr Lovaway. 'You're just as much to blame as the constable. Indeed more, for you're his superior officer.'

'I know that,' said the sergeant; 'I know that well. And what's more, I'm thankful to you, Doctor, for speaking out what's in your mind. Many a one wouldn't do it. And I know that every word you've been saying is for my good and for the good of Constable Malone, who's a young man yet and might improve if handled right. That's why I'm thanking you, Doctor, for what you've said.'

When Solomon said that a soft answer turneth away wrath, he understated a great truth. A soft answer, if soft enough, will deflect the stroke of the sword of justice. Dr Lovaway, though his conscience was still uneasy, could say no more. He felt that it was totally impossible to report Sergeant Rahilly's way of dealing with lunatics to the higher authorities.

That night Sergeant Rahilly called on Mr Flanagan, going into the house by the back door, for the hour was late. He chose porter rather than whisky, feeling perhaps that his nerves needed something and that a stronger stimulant might be a little too much for him. After finishing a second bottle and opening a third, he spoke.

'I'm troubled in my mind,' he said, 'over this new doctor. Here am I doing the best I can for him ever since he came to the town, according to what I promised Dr Farelly.'

'No man,' said Flanagan, 'could do more than what you've done. Everyone knows that.'

'I've set the police scouring the country,' said the sergeant, 'searching high and low and in and out for anyone, man or woman, that was the least bit queer in the head. They've worked hard, so they have, and I've worked hard myself.'

'No man harder,' said Flanagan.

'And every one we found,' said the sergeant, 'was a guinea into the doctor's pocket. A guinea, mind you; that's the fee for certifying a lunatic, and devil a penny either I or the constables get out of it.'

'Nor you wouldn't be looking for it, Sergeant. I know that.'

'I would not. And I'm not complaining of getting nothing. But it's damned hard when the doctor won't take what's offered to him, when we've had to work early and late to get it for him. Would you believe it now, Mr Flanagan, he's refused to certify half of the ones we've found for him?'

'Do you tell me that?' said Flanagan.

'Throwing good money away,' said the sergeant; 'and today, when I took him to see that boy that does be living in Finnegan's, which would have been two guineas into his pocket, on account of being outside his own district, instead of saying "Thank you" like any ordinary man would, nothing would do him only to be cursing and swearing. "It's a crime," says he, "and a scandal," says he, "and it's swearing away the liberty of a poor man," says he; and more to that. Now I ask you, Mr Flanagan, where's the crime and where's the scandal?'

'There's none,' said Flanagan. 'What harm would it have done the lad to be put away for a bit?'

'That's what I said to the doctor. What's more, they'd have let the boy out in a fortnight, as soon as they knew what way it was with him. I told the doctor that, but "crime," says he, and "scandal," says he, and "conspiracy," says he. Be damn, but to hear him talk you'd think I was trying to take two guineas out of his pocket, instead of trying to put it in, and there's the thanks I get for going out of my way to do the best I could for him so as he'd rest content in this place and let Dr Farelly stay where he is to be cutting the legs off the Germans.'

'It's hard, so it is,' said Flanagan, 'and I'm sorry for you, Sergeant. But that's the way things is. As I was saying to you once before and maybe oftener, the English is queer people, and the more you'd be trying to please them, the less they like it. It's not easy to deal with them, and that's a fact.'

THE GLASS PANEL

Eimar O'Duffy

Deception is the key to this next story by Eimar Ultan O'Duffy (1893-1935). O'Duffy, who was born in Donegal and became well-known as a satirist and novelist—in particular for his book, The Wasted Island *(1919)—was also a great enthusiast of detective stories and published several books in the genre including* The Secret Enemy *(1932) and* Head of a Girl *(1935). He also wrote a number of crime short stories, of which the following case related by Bradley, 'a capable detective with a record of well-earned success', is generally considered his best.*

A sense of artistic propriety would make my friend Bradley a more interesting companion, and also a more capable detective, as this story will show. Those who are familiar with his record of well-earned successes will smile at this, and, referring to his latest case, demand if there was ever in the history of crime-detection a smarter piece of work than his handling of the Littlecroft Murder. Good! I accept the challenge. The Littlecroft Murder proves my contention to the hilt.

One bitterly cold evening in January, Bradley and I were ensconced in a pair of deep armchairs before a roaring fire in his sitting-cum-consulting-room, when the landlady announced Mr Jonathan Harbottle. I have an abominable habit, due, I suppose, to my occupation as a story-writer, of forming a complete mental picture of a person from his name; and Mr Jonathan Harbottle was at once presented to me as one of those hard-featured men who have done well out of the War, fifty-seven years of age with a full jowl and paunch. Judge of my chagrin when a handsome young fellow made his appearance at the door, tall and spare, with penetrating, observant eyes, and fine, nervous hands. He opened his business abruptly and without ceremony, jerking out the words as if he had held them

120

in constraint longer than he could endure.

'What would you think, Mr Bradley, if in the midst of an absolutely uneventful country life you suddenly received a letter like this?' He gave my friend an envelope which he had held crushed up in his hand.

Motioning the young man to a chair, Bradley extracted the letter and read out its contents.

'"Here we are. Travellers' Rest, Southampton Docks. Don't fail this time, Shell out, or we'll come and see you.'

'Short and to the point. No signature, I see. Cheapest quality paper, and uneducated writing. You don't recognise the hand, I suppose, Mr Harbottle?'

Our visitor shook his head.

'Posted on the fifth,' went on my friend, 'after having spent some time in an excessively dirty pocket. Well, Mr Harbottle, if you don't recognise the handwriting, and have no idea who could have sent it, and have led a perfectly uneventful life, I can't see what there is to worry about. The thing looks to me like a hoax.'

'So I thought myself,' replied our client, 'when the first one came.'

'You have had several?'

'This is the third I have received,' continued Harbottle. 'Unfortunately I destroyed the other two. This is the first I dreamt of taking seriously.'

'Were the others in the same hand?' my friend interrupted.

'Exactly. The first had an American stamp, and was posted in New York. It arrived about a month ago. I couldn't make much meaning out of it. As well as I remember, it said something about "shelling out," with a warning not to double-cross the writer. The second also came from New York, about a fortnight later. It simply repeated the message of the first, but in more threatening terms.'

'Have you informed the police?' asked Bradley.

'Yes: and they insist that it must be a hoax, though they have promised to make inquiries at Southampton. Mr Bradley,' went on the young man earnestly, 'I'm convinced that there's some mysterious but real danger threatening me. I live in the depths of the country, seven miles from the nearest village. You can understand what a difference that makes. My wife, who isn't at all nervous by nature, and treated the first letter as a joke, just as I did, has been thoroughly upset by this last one, and could hardly be persuaded to let me leave the house this morning.'

'You are not long married?' questioned Bradley.

'Only a year.'

'And your wife, I suppose, knows nothing about these letters either?'

'No more than myself.'

Bradley paused a moment, then said: 'Very well, Mr Harbottle, I shall look into this case at once. What is your profession, by the way—or your way of living?'

'I have no profession. I live on a small income derived from investments. If you have nothing more to ask me I'll leave you now. Here is my card. I am staying at the Euston Hotel for the night, and return home by the first train tomorrow.'

'I have nothing more to ask,' replied Bradley; 'but just one word to say. When you employ a doctor or a private detective, it is best to trust him and tell him *everything*. It tends to simplify the case.'

'I do trust you, and have kept back nothing,' protested his client; but I saw that his cheek reddened slightly.

'Very well, then,' said Bradley impassively, and held open the door.

'Our friend, of course, was lying,' observed the detective as he calmly relit his pipe after the young man's departure. 'His story is too thin altogether. You observed, of course, that the senders of the letter never signed their names, showing that they knew themselves to be known to the recipient. Then the allusiveness of their tone shows that they knew that the nature of the business would be familiar to him also. I'm afraid it's only too clear that our friend has been mixed up in some very shady transactions in the past. You must have noticed that they state their requirements and declare their whereabouts with complete faith in his direction—knowing that he cannot betray them without involving himself.'

'He betrayed them to us,' I objected.

'The greater fear sometimes expels the lesser. As I read it, our friend Harbottle has bolted with the spoils of some joint expedition, and his pals have tracked him down. It's none of my business to help him to keep them out of their share; but I shall certainly make some inquiries at Southampton—in the interests of those to whom the spoil originally belonged.'

*   *   *

I stayed at Bradley's rooms that night, and next morning we breakfasted early, with a view to getting to Southampton as soon as possible. We were just putting on our overcoats when we heard the hall doorbell ring: one long ring, then two shorter ones at decreasing intervals.

'Someone's in a hurry,' observed Bradley.

Next minute his landlady came in with an agitated young woman at her very heels.

'Oh, Mr Bradley,' gasped the latter. 'I'm so glad to have found you in,' and she almost collapsed on the nearest chair.

'Wouldn't give any name, sir,' apologised the landlady. 'She was too excited to say anything but just "Mr Bradley."'

'I am Mrs Jonathan Harbottle,' announced the strange young woman.

She was a beautiful creature, not more than twenty-two years of age, with dark hair and pale skin, flushed with the agitation of the moment. Her clothes were obviously of the most expensive kind, but must have been put on in the greatest haste.

'Mr Bradley,' she said, when the landlady had withdrawn, 'did my husband tell you everything yesterday?—I mean literally everything.'

'I regret to say that he did not, madam,' replied Bradley.

'Well,' said Mrs Harbottle, 'I won't keep the secret any longer. His life is more important than any secret, and I believe it's his life those dreadful men are after. There are two of them, Mr Bradley: two of the most dreadful-looking ruffians you ever saw.'

Bradley paid no attention to this. He was taking a cup and saucer from the china cupboard and laying a place at the table. Then, pouring out tea from the pot that had served us, and cutting some slices of bread, he said casually: 'Better have a little breakfast, Mrs Harbottle.'

The lady thanked him for his kindness, and admitted that she had had none before starting. She was steadied by the tea, and made a very good meal: indeed, she was a little shamefaced at her appetite. Bradley chatted with her urbanely as she ate, but as soon as she had finished he asked her for her story.

'But first,' he said, 'let me warn you that you do so of your own free will. My duty may compel me to use it against your husband.'

'It can do him no harm,' she said confidently. 'In the first place, you must know that his name is not Harbottle, but Wetheral—Wal ter Wetheral.'

'Not *the* Walter Wetheral?' I asked.

'Yes.'

Here was a quite unexpected revelation. Wetheral was the coming man in the English dramatic world. Indeed, he had all but arrived. Two of his plays were drawing crowded houses in London at that very moment.

Mrs Wetheral continued her statement.

'You may not know that my husband was years waiting for recognition, struggling along at hack work in Fleet Street, and often on the verge of starvation. It was at that period that I first met him and became engaged to him; and it was on my account that he took the step that so radically altered our lives. We were both eager to get married, and six months after our engagement recognition seemed as far off as ever. Then one day Walter put an SOS advertisement in the Agony Column of *The Times*, asking for work of any kind. To our surprise it received an immediate answer, a letter signed Jonathan Harbottle, asking Walter to come that night to the Carlton Hotel.

'Walter, of course, kept the appointment, and next day told me all that had occurred there. It appeared that this Mr Harbottle was an old bachelor without relatives of any sort, and was looking round for someone to leave his money to when he saw Walter's advertisement. He had previously been struck by some of his work in magazines, and decided that his money could not be better placed than in giving him a start in life. As a sort of preliminary test, Walter was to take over his country house for a year, with sufficient income to run it, while Mr Harbottle went to Madeira for his health. During that time he was to give up journalism, and devote himself entirely to literature. He was also to keep the whole transaction a secret.'

'What sort of man was this Harbottle?' asked Bradley, as the lady paused.

'I met him next day,' said Mrs Wetheral. 'He was one of those jolly old gentlemen, with a white beard and big beaming spectacles, and terribly amusing to talk to. He told us that he had already made his will. "But mind," he said, shaking his finger in comic admonition at Walter, "if you write one word of commercial stuff—one word that isn't real art—I'll cut you off with a shilling." It was on this occasion that he asked Walter to take his name. "Keep your own for literary purposes," he said. "But—well, I'd like to feel as if you were a sort of son to me." When he put it that way, of course, Walter couldn't very well object, and the whole thing was carried out in legal form a few days later.

'Not long after that, Walter and I were married, and Mr Harbottle at once went off to Madeira. When we came back from our honeymoon we took over the house he had lent us in Hertfordshire. It's in a lonely spot, right in the depths of the country, but the house itself is handsome and comfortable. Mr Harbottle had left his old butler in charge, and he had already got in new servants—two maids and a boy—in order to keep our arrangements a secret. The butler is a confidential old man who had been always in his employment, and, of course, knows everything.

'Well,' concluded Mrs Wetheral, 'there we've been living for the past year, ideally happy, until these dreadful letters arrived. And now you know the whole truth, Mr Bradley.'

'Your story certainly puts a very different complexion on the case,' said Bradley. 'Tell me, Mrs Wetheral, has it never occurred to you that these letters have been intended for the genuine Mr Harbottle?'

'Certainly. When the third one came, and we began to be afraid it wasn't a hoax, that solution occurred to us at once, and my husband wrote to him about it before coming to you. But of course it will take a long time for his letter to reach Madeira, and something happened which made me realise that it might be dangerous to keep his secret any longer.'

Long practice has given Bradley a professional impassivity, but at these words I could not help drawing my chair a little closer to our client.

'Yesterday afternoon I happened to be sitting at the drawing-room window, when I saw two men come walking up the avenue. They looked like seamen. One was very tall, the other quite short, but before I could observe any more they were hidden by an angle of the house, and next minute the hall doorbell rang. Instantly the words of the letter flashed into my memory. "Don't fail . . . or we'll come and see you," and I felt very thankful that Walter was away. I waited breathless at the window until, after what seemed like an age, the two men reappeared and retreated down the avenue. I rushed downstairs at once, and found the butler in the hall. He told me that the men had asked for my husband, but wouldn't state their business, so, putting them down as cadgers, he had sent them away.

And what do you think, Mr Bradley?—he said one of them had an ugly-looking knife stuck in his belt.'

'You certainly did well to come to me, Mrs Wetheral,' said Bradley, 'and you may count on my wasting no time in getting on the track of these callers of yours. If you will take my advice, you will go straight home now and tell your husband all that has happened. I know that he intended to take the first train this morning, so you will probably find him there when you arrive. I have a few things to attend to here in town, but I shall follow you as soon as possible, and you may expect to see me at Willowdene either this evening or tomorrow morning.'

*   *   *

As soon as Mrs Wetheral had gone, Bradley caught up a railway guide and quickly ran through its pages.

'Excellent,' he said. 'She will catch the ten forty-five, and we can get another fifty minutes later. It wouldn't do at all if protectors and protected were to arrive on the same train. There may be tough work tonight, so, if you're coming, we'd better slip over to your rooms for your revolver.'

He took his own from a drawer as he spoke, and loaded its six chambers.

A two hours' run in a slow train brought us to Littlecroft, the station named on Wetheral's card. We at once sought out the less reputable of the two inns in the place, and went into the dining-room, where lunch was already being served. There were not many occupants of the room, and two of them caught our attention immediately. Both were obviously seamen, and equally obviously of criminal type. One was more than six feet in height, the other rather less than five. They were, in fact, our quarry, to the last letter of Mrs Wetheral's description.

When they had finished their meal they sauntered out to the bar, where they sat drinking and smoking the whole afternoon. Supper was served at six. Harbottle's dupes ate theirs quickly, then rose and went out. A minute later we heard them leave the inn and take the direction in which, we had learnt, lay Wetheral's house. Bradley waited to give them some start, then sprang to his feet saying: 'Come.'

It was quite dark outside, but we kept in touch with our quarry quite easily by the ring of their feet on the frozen road—the better to hear which, as well as for the concealment of our own movements, we walked on the grass by the wayside. Careful as we were, however, we could not avoid an occasional stumble, with the result that the suspicions of the pursued were aroused, and once they stopped to listen while we stood still and held our breath. We were obliged to keep farther behind after that, and, to make matters worse for us, a mist was beginning to rise. Where exactly we lost our way we never found out, but lost it we did. Alarmed after a while at hearing no sound ahead of us, we put on pace a little; then, as there was no sign of the quarry, we ran. We ran for nearly a mile before we realised that we had been given the slip.

We turned at once in our tracks and went back about a mile and a half to a likely-looking branch road, but after following that for twenty minutes we came to a crossroad that baffled us completely. What we did during the next six hours I cannot accurately remember. There were few houses to inquire at, and the sleepy-eyed inhabitants of one gave us directions that confused us worse than ever. Dread of what those two evil men might do would not, however, let us abandon the search. Yet it was by sheer chance that we finally came upon the house at about one o'clock in the morning.

I almost cried out with relief to make out the name on the gate: *Willowdene*. We walked up the avenue and rang at the hall door. Almost immediately a window overhead was opened, and a voice— Wetheral's—asked who was there. Bradley having announced our identity, Wetheral's head was withdrawn, and a minute later he opened the door. Briefly Bradley explained what had occurred; which Wetheral supplemented with the information that the men had arrived at about nine o'clock, that, on being refused admittance by the butler, they had gone the round of the house as if seeking another entry, and, failing to find one, had gone off after discharging a battery of bad language.

Wetheral offered us beds, and, for his sake as much as for our own, we accepted so far as to take a couple of couches and rugs in the drawing-room. Throughly exhausted by our long tramp, we were fast asleep in an instant.

A crash of breaking glass woke us to broad daylight. Instinctively we sprang from our couches, and rushed from the room and up the stairs. Two frightened-looking domestics stood on the landing above, and an old man, evidently the butler, came out to meet us from one of the rooms.

'I'm Bradley, the detective,' said my friend quickly. 'What has happened?'

'I'm afraid you're too late, sir,' said the butler. 'My master has been murdered in his sleep.'

At that moment a muffled female voice sounded from the room he had just left.

'That will be the mistress, sir,' said the butler. 'They must have locked her up.'

We followed him into the room, and, scarcely pausing to glance at the ghastly thing that lay on the blood-soaked bed, hastened to unlock the door communicating with Mrs Wetheral's room, the key being still in the lock. She knew nothing of what had occurred, having only just wakened, like ourselves; and though we broke the news to her as gently as possible, she immediately fainted. I helped the butler to carry her to another room, where, after applying restoratives, we left her in charge of the very capable maid, and returned to the scene of the crime.

It was now for the first time that I noticed the glass panels that formed the upper part of Wetheral's door. One of them was completely smashed—evidently the cause of our waking—and through it I could see Bradley, not, to my surprise, hunting about for clues, but quietly smoking a cigarette. As soon as we entered he turned to the butler.

'Do you remember, er——?'

'Wingate, sir,' said the old man.

Bradley acknowledged the name.

'Do you remember exactly what sort of knife that seaman was carrying yesterday?'

'Perfectly, sir. It was about as long as a table-knife, with a black leather sheath, and a horn handle.'

'Is that it, do you think?'

Wingate peered closely at the weapon which Bradley held towards him, examining it for quite three minutes before making up his mind. He was one of those ponderous old servants with a double chin and a great sense of personal importance. He took off his blue-tinted glasses twice, and polished them, before he could come to a decision. At last he said: 'It's certainly very like it, sir, but I couldn't swear to it without the sheath.'

'Very good, Wingate. Will you now be so good as to tell us exactly how the discovery of the crime took place?'

'Certainly, sir. It was Jane, the parlourmaid, sir, who discovered it first, indirectly. When she brought the master his shaving water, as usual, at seven o'clock, she could get no answer to her knock. So after a while she just tried the door, and found it locked. After that she came down to me, sir, to know what she should do. Of course I felt anxious at once, with those fellows hanging about yesterday, so I went up with her right away. I knocked at the master's door myself then, and of course there was still no answer, so I took the liberty of looking through the keyhole, and saw that the key was still in the lock. I immediately took off my shoe, sir, and broke the glass. Then I slipped my hand through, unlocked the door, and was just looking at the body when you gentlemen arrived.'

'I suppose you have guessed already, Wingate,' said Bradley, 'that these seamen are after your old master, the real Mr Harbottle.'

Wingate, thoroughly startled, began to stammer denials.

'Oh, that's no use with me, my man,' said Bradley. 'I know everything from Mrs Wetheral's own lips. But perhaps you might tell me if you know of any incidents in Mr Harbottle's life which might have set these fellows against him.'

Wingate drew himself up with dignity.

'Mr Harbottle,' he said, 'may not have been all he might have been. But a good master who pays good wages is entitled to good service, *and* discretion.'

'Excellent, Wingate,' said Bradley. 'I wish all servants were as loyal. Now, would you mind getting someone to take this note to the police station at Littlecroft? The sooner they get on the tracks of those two scoundrels the better.'

'I suppose you're quite satisfied that they are the scoundrels,' I remarked when Wingate had set off on his errand.

'I don't see that there can be any doubt of it,' Bradley replied. 'We know all their movements up to a late hour last night. If you look out of that window you will see a ladder propped against the sill. I understand from the parlourmaid—whose story of the morning's events, by the way, completely confirms Wingate's—that it was kept in a shed in the garden, where they must have found it. You must have already observed the piece cut out of that pane by which they opened the window. Finally, there's the knife.'

'Yes,' I said. 'But don't forget this is a sort of blackmailing case, and it's most unusual for blackmailers to kill their victim—except as a last resort. Of course I grant you that this may have been the last resort, but, then, as you said just now, there's the knife. Did you ever hear of a murderer, not an absolute imbecile, who carried his knife about for days for everybody to identify, and then left it sticking in his victim's body?'

'He didn't, as a matter of fact. I found it near the window, where he might easily have dropped it in climbing out.'

'*Touché*,' I admitted. 'But if I were you I'd make some inquiries at the village whether anyone else than Wingate ever saw that knife.'

'You mean that Wingate——?'

'Wingate,' I said, 'is a most discreet and confidential servant. And while you're about it,' I added, 'just have a look at the footprints round the bottom of the ladder.'

Bradley darted downstairs in an instant, leaving me alone to frame into shape a sudden wild suggestion that had leaped to my mind when first I caught sight of Wetheral's door. I went out now to look at this again, and again the question asked itself: what on earth are those two glass panels for? It was their utter incongruity with their surroundings that had struck me at first and set me wondering. They were of that abominable patterned kind that one associates with city offices and railway stations, and they ruined the harmony of a landing, every door of which was of carved oak. Nobody with the smallest artistic sense would have perpetuated such a piece of vandalism even for a useful purpose: and what useful purpose did these things serve? Certainly they had not been put there for lighting's sake, for the landing was amply lighted without them. Then why?

The jagged hole in the left-hand panel stared at me like an evil interrogation mark; and even as the answer came to my mind, up the stairs came Bradley in the worst of humours.

'There are no footprints,' he admitted. 'But the ground is as hard as rock anyway, and if you think I'm going on a wild-goose chase after that knife, you're mistaken.'

'Quite right,' I said. 'It would be a waste of time. If these men did carry a knife, it proves they didn't mean murder. If they didn't carry one, our business lies with Wingate, who said they did.'

'You seem bent on dragging the most absurd complications into a perfectly simple case,' said Bradley irritably. 'If these two seamen didn't commit the murder, the whole thing becomes chaos. You say that blackmailers don't usually kill their victims. But how do we know they were only blackmailers? Those letters are altogether too vague to build on. Depend upon it, Harbottle knew his life was in danger, and counted on their killing his substitute and putting their own necks in the noose at the same time.'

'What an innocent a detective can be!' I exclaimed. 'I'm afraid, Bradley, you're a long way from having sounded the depth of human wickedness.'

'I think I've painted Harbottle fairly black,' remonstrated Bradley.

'No. Only a dirty grey. You see, he knew quite well that these men would *not* kill his substitute. That's why he had to kill him himself.'

Bradley's expression was one of blank astonishment. I hastened to enlighten him.

'Observe those panels. If you had any artistic sense you'd see that they are entirely out of place in this house; and even without it you must see that they are no earthly use. They were put there for one purpose, and for one purpose only.'

'Yes?'

'They were put there by Harbottle so that while on the landing he could slip his hand through and unlock the door from the inside. You see, he had the key in his hand when he broke the glass.'

'But Wingate——' began Bradley.

'Wingate wears close-cropped iron-grey hair, blue spectacles, and a shaven chin. Harbottle wore bushy white hair and a beard. The Wetherals never saw them together.'

'I do believe you've got it,' cried Bradley in great excitement. 'The astute scoundrel must have murdered his own substitute in order to get those other poor devils hanged. I think that the sooner we get in touch with the police the better.'

At the trial it turned out that this solution was correct. Harbottle had been concerned, years before, in a series of jewel robberies in the United States, with the two seamen as his accomplices—or rather his tools; for he was the brain of the enterprise—and when his catspaws were taken he escaped arrest and got away with the whole of the spoils. The seamen had done seven years in a penitentiary, and when their release became due he began planning to preserve his gains and rid himself of his enemies at one stroke.

Of course Bradley got all the credit for the arrest. Nobody could be expected to believe that it was my sense of artistic propriety that had run so desperate a criminal to earth. But if only Bradley had a touch of it, what a detective he would make!

THE STING

Flann O'Brien

Flann O'Brien (1911-1966), who has been linked with Samuel Beckett as the most important Irish writer to have emerged since the 'Golden Age' of Joyce, Yeats and Synge, enjoyed little financial success during his lifetime and in the 1950s, in order to placate his creditors, wrote some adventures for the famous Sexton Blake detective series under the pen name 'Stephen Blakesley'. He is believed to have used this same pseudonym for a number of thrillers published at this time—including A Case for the Cardinal, The Cardinal and the Corpse *and* The Case of the Alpha Murders.

Born Brian O'Nolan in Strabane, he began writing while a student at University College, Dublin, first displaying his genius for comic storytelling in the pages of a satirical weekly called Blather! *He also began the heavy drinking which was to lead to his premature death. Although his novels such as* At Swim-Two-Birds *(1939) and* The Third Policeman *(1967) are now accepted as classics, during his lifetime he was certainly best known in Ireland for his column,* Cruiskeen Lawn, *written under the pen name Myles na gCopaleen ('Myles of the Ponies' after a character in Dion Boucicault's classic play,* The Colleen Bawn), *which ran in the* Irish Times *from 1940 until his death. O'Brien's interest in crime and mystery frequently surfaced in his column in stories about absurd crimes, ridiculous criminals and fatuous court cases—in a good many of which he himself appeared as the man in the dock! A collection of all these stories about the 'District and Other Courts' is, I believe, long overdue, but here in the meantime is one of my favourite tales about a most outrageous fraud . . .*

Mr Myles na gCopaleen, who gave his address as Westmoreland Street, Dublin, and described himself as 'the grand old Irish man', appeared on 492 currency charges at Bow Street, London, yesterday. He was fined a total of £2,350,000 and ordered to pay £6 5s 6d expenses. A beautiful creature attired in furs, who gave her name as Yvonne Desirée Lebaisir, was bound to the peace for aiding and abetting. She described herself as 'a former member of the Résistance'.

Mr Gerald Cockshott, prosecuting, said that a Treasury agent who was investigating currency transactions on the Continent was accosted by the male accused in the bar of the Hotel Carlton at Cannes and asked whether he would mind cashing in francs a cheque for £500,000. Accused added that he would give the Treasury agent 'a monkey for himself'. When the latter revealed his identity, the accused apologised and gave particulars of over four hundred other cheques he had already cashed. Accused also showed the stub of his cheque book, which indicated that cheques totalling some two million pounds had been drawn in favour of Max Intrator. Accused characterised his own behaviour as 'incredibly naïve and stupid and out of all harmony with the fundamental considerations' and expressed his readiness to return to Britain, by air if necessary, 'to face the music'. He permitted himself to say that possibly Miss Lebaisir was 'not incapable of extravagant attitudes'. Counsel understood that defendant had some standing as a statesman in Ireland but otherwise was not known to have criminal associations. The Treasury was pressing for the most exemplary penalties.

Mr Maurice Maul, for the defendant, said that his client, who was the famous author, could have pleaded diplomatic immunity, but, scorning such a course, actually insisted on the strictest examination of his affairs by the court. The law was the law but each one in court, in whatever interest bound, would have his own opinions as to the merits of a process whereby a gallant fighter pilot of the RAF found himself in the dock for innocently indulging the same selfless impulses which made him answer the call when Britain was in distress. He did not think it would be disputed that defendant had brought down 312 machines during the war.

MAGISTRATE: What sort of machines?
COUNSEL: On that point my brief is silent.
MAGISTRATE: If you wish to present an attested military record by way of character, do so.
COUNSEL: My instructions are to attempt nothing of the kind.

Proceeding, he said defendant had travelled to the Continent on

urgent national business, and it became necessary to have Miss
Lebaisir in his suite. Miss Lebaisir was by profession a nurse.

MAGISTRATE: Whom does this lady nurse?
COUNSEL: The defendant, I understand.

Defendant, in evidence, said he went to France on a secret political mission which would not be 'in anybody's interest to discuss'. It
was true that Miss Lebaisir was a nurse and had on occasions satis-
factorily nursed himself, but her main business was to be seen with
him in public, owing to her costly appearance. It was his experience
that it was impossible for a man to look costly in public by himself.
It was necessary to be accompanied by a costly-looking lady. Then
it was easy.

MAGISTRATE: What was easy?
DEFENDANT: The game I was at.

Continuing, defendant said that the cheques which the Treasury
complained of arose through thoughtlessness on his part. Some
strangers whom he met in the hotel bar told him they had been
unlucky at the tables, and asked for the loan of a million pounds. He
had, foolishly perhaps, given them three-quarters of a million. It
appeared that unfortunately their luck did not turn and he felt that
he had no option but to advance them further monies, possibly
another million. On the instructions of the men he made the
cheques out to Mr Max Intrator, for whose co-operation he was
obliged. The half a million he asked the Treasury officer to get him
was to cover his travelling expenses home. He now realised that he
had acted foolishly and impulsively and was prepared to pay such
monetary penalties as the Treasury might demand. He asked that
there should be no question of jail, as he was not the jail-going type.

The Magistrate imposed the fines stated, without comment.
Defendant immediately paid by cheque and left the court.

(NOTE: Defendant was subsequently re-arrested on the instructions
of the Treasury, who found his cheque was worthless, but was later
quietly released when it was found that all cheques issued in the case
were also worthless and that Mr Max Intrator had probably been
badly stung. Defendant, on reaching Collinstown, was entertained
to a banquet by Aer Lingus.)

THE INFORMERS

Brendan Behan

The life of Brendan Behan (1923-1964) rebel, poet, playwright, author and drinker, is now part of Irish legend and his works part of the nation's literary heritage. Lawlessness and crime were a part of Behan's life virtually from the days of his childhood in Dublin, and certainly during his time on the run after a shooting incident at Glasnevin Cemetery and subsequent years of penal servitude. Though writing gave him a new direction in life, his dedication to drink also doomed him to alcoholism and eventual breakdown. His intimate knowledge of Irish low life, however, was to provide the inspiration for several of his best works, including his plays The Quare Fellow *(1954) and* The Hostage *(1958), and his books* Borstal Boy *(1957) and* Confessions of an Irish Rebel *(1965).*

Some years earlier, in 1953, Behan had written a serial story for the Irish Times *about the Dublin underworld, which he called 'The Scarperer' and published under the pen-name Emmet Street. For years the true authorship of this powerful tale of crime and duplicity was unknown, until Behan happened to admit to a friend who found him reading a detective novel that he had quite an admiration for the genre and had actually written a story of this kind himself. Typically, he did not possess copies of the paper nor could he remember the dates when the story had been published. Only the dedicated research in the archives of the* Irish Times *by his biographer, Rae Jeffs, brought the story to light again. I have here selected an episode from it, complete in itself, in which the Dublin police and their informers attempt to outsmart one another. On the strength of this story alone, I believe Brendan Behan deserves to have the epithet 'crime writer' added to the list of his literary achievements.*

At half-past-seven a new Customline swung out through the Castle gates and down Dame Street.

'Which way now, Sergeant?' asked the driver.

'I suppose Spillane's of Gardiner Street might be worth a visit. Well begun is half done. We can work back from the North Side.'

'Across O'Connell Bridge, down Eden Quay, across Beresford Place and up into Lower Gardiner Street. I suppose that would be the best way.'

'Certainly,' said a middle-aged detective, sitting in the back with the sergeant, 'if you want everyone the whole length and breadth of the district to know that we're on our way there.'

The sergeant clucked his tongue and said to the middle-aged man: 'You're right, Mick. Don't you think he'd have thought of that himself, without you or me having to tell him?'

The middle-aged man and the sergeant hated each other like poison because of the sergeant's promotion and some other squabbles that they would have described as 'politics.' They were, therefore, always very polite to each other and showed it by abusing lesser policemen when they were together, which broke the monotony of their abuse of each other when they were apart.

The car had reached Westmoreland Street and the driver was afraid to make the slightest suggestion in case they would fall on him again.

'Which way, now, ah?' he said nervously, lapsing into his native accent.

'Take it this way, avic,' said the sergeant soothingly. Like Lanna Machree's dog, he liked to go a bit of the road with everyone. 'Go up straight to Dorset Street and we'll turn right, and to the top of Upper Gardiner Street and down on top of them from that direction. Taking them unawares, as you'd say.'

'I see that fellow Cole on the pavement there,' said the middle-aged man. 'There above Findlater's Church. Fellow used to be a warder above there.'

'You've an eye like a hawk,' said the sergeant, admiringly, 'I see him there. Looking in the garage window. That fellow made a right few ha'pence up there, shopping in drink and cigarettes and shopping out letters; and the last night before he was given his notice, bringing the files and dumping the ladder for that other pair to scarper a couple of years ago.'

'Will I go in on the kerb for him?' asked the driver eagerly.

The sergeant and the detective looked at each other hopelessly and clicked their tongues in unison.

'Ah, she's rearing them yet,' said the detective.

'Well, dear knows,' said the sergeant frankly, 'you'll never get your promotion, acting that stupid. Am I right, Mick?'

'I suppose you are,' said Mick, who felt it was a bit of a dig, as the man said, at himself.

'But I mean to say,' said the sergeant. 'That's all right, go right here and wait on the lights. We're no more than anyone else, now, down Dorset Street. If we wanted to tell everyone we're out to find out whatever we can about this fellow breaking out of the 'Joy this morning, not to mention his confederate, we'd pull in someone that had to do with escapes. But we won't do that. If we want ex-Warder Cole, we know where to find him; but just now we're trying to get at this business without anyone being the wiser what we're at. So far as they know, it's only a routine raid; and if we do happen to get some fellow we're looking for on another account altogether—well, so much the better. He'll think it's someone else has shopped him, his china maybe, and he'll shop him in return and we'll take whatever is sent us and be grateful for it.'

'There's Spillane's, down across Summerhill; don't waste any time now—but don't kill us either. Me nor Mick; we mightn't be as well prepared as we should be.'

Mick, the sergeant, and a third, silent detective approached the pub from the two entrances.

'Good evening all,' said the sergeant, putting his head in the doorway.

His greeting was returned in muttered curses and one man made as if to leave, though his pint was barely touched.

He bumped into the silent one at the far door, however, and was called back by the sergeant.

'Sure, what hurry is on you, Billy Boy?'

He came back to the counter. 'I suppose I can finish me scoop, anyway.'

'Of course, you can,' said the sergeant, his voice as soft as butter. 'Far be it from us to get between a decent man and his drop of nourishment. And us with a grand new automobile to take you down as far as College Street with us. Nobody else we're looking to have a bit of a chat with, I suppose? No? Well, I suppose you'd better come along with us, Billy Boy.'

The man drank up his pint and went away with them.

'Not,' said the sergeant, 'that we were looking for you at all.'

'Oh, no, not at all,' said Billy Boy sarcastically. 'I suppose no one gave yous the bend I had an appointment here for this time.'

'Settle yourself comfortably there on the cushions,' said the sergeant. 'College Street, first stop,' he said to the driver. The car moved off. 'Billy Boy, I'd take a solemn oath——'

'That'd come easy to you,' said Billy Boy with bitterness. 'You'd never fail for the want of practice, anyway.'

'Oh, now, now,' said the sergeant, waving his fore-finger reprovingly. 'I was only going to say that we were no more looking for you, that time we went into Spillane's——'

'Of course not. Yous only went in to look at the clock. Don't give me that old stuff. I know who gave yous the bend, but if he shopped me I can double-shop him. He done screwing jobs with me and without me.'

'Now, don't be jumping to hasty conclusions. The Liverpool boat was there every night for the past week, since you did that bit of a hoist down on the Point.'

'And he was fixing me for a collier to Garston, so as I wouldn't have to pass through with the passengers. But I'll fix him. I know who he met in the Shaky Man's the other night.'

'That'll wait, that'll wait. I'll dump you in here now and I'll be back round before twelve to charge you. I'm not taking you to the Bridewell, for I'm letting you go on the rent-book. I suppose she'll come down to bail you out?'

'Oh, she will, Sergeant. You know the address. But you're not codding me, Sergeant, are you?'

'I'd want to eat a few more loaves, Billy Boy, before I'd cod you; but I don't like to see people that I know is worse than the ones they lead into these things getting away with it, because they were first to the super with confessions—their own and every other body's. Even us, though we have to deal with them,' he raised his eyes piously to heaven, 'we don't like an informer. Especially a man to give away on a chap that he practically brought on a job.'

'That's it, Sergeant, that's it. Sure it was him in the first place. He——'

'That's all right, Billy Boy, you can tell me all about it, when I come down with herself and the rent-book. We're there now, hop out, avic.'

'You won't forget, Sergeant, will you?' he said eagerly in through the car window.

'Certainly and I won't and before you go in there, remember this from me. The next time you go out on a screwing job, pick a better china—go with an honest robber.'

He waved to Billy from the car. Billy waved back and was led inside.

'What was he talking about?' asked the sergeant. 'Who's his china?'

'We had him down for some snaking bit of a hoist. Cigarettes down the quay. Nothing much. They lifted them out of the back of a lorry. Just his strength,' said Mick. 'He goes to work sometimes with that fellow that they call Pig's Eye. That's why he mentioned the Shaky Man's. This Pig's Eye drinks there.'

'And he said something about Pig's Eye meeting someone there, the other night.'

'Pig's Eye wasn't down for the cigarette job the other fellow was down for.'

'Well, he's down for it now,' said the sergeant. 'I'd like to know who he was meeting in the Shaky Man's. I'll dump him in the Bridewell and neither will know the other is in. Back and forward I'll go,' his lips opening in ecstasy, 'one telling me one thing and the other telling me another.'

'And,' said the driver eagerly, 'we might pick up someone else be good luck, up in the Shaky Man's.'

'That's right,' said the sergeant graciously, 'the night's only a pup. Drive up there and we'll see.'

'Which way, Sergeant?' asked the driver.

The sergeant and Mick looked at each other and spoke slowly together: 'A Guard that doesn't know where the Shaky Man's is . . .'

'All right,' said the sergeant resignedly, 'you take the first on your right and the——'

The car went up the quays.

*   *   *

Outside the Shaky Man's, Glimmers Gleeson was settling himself preparatory to returning to his place of business on the bridge farther down the Liffey. He adjusted his black spectacles, settled squarely on his breast the sign: 'Blind from birth,' and reached his stick for the pavement.

An approaching car caught his attention and he looked towards it, then turned back and put his head in the doorway of the Shaky Man's and shouted hoarsely: 'Nick nick give the nick there the squad leave a drink for me there one of yous God bless you,' all in one breath. Then he turned the corner and walked quickly away from the quays.

Some of the men at the bar, Pig's Eye O'Donnell in the van, rushed out the back, through a door held open by the Shaky Man, and downstairs to a cellar. They settled themselves in the darkness and cocked their ears towards a grating above them for the sound of the squad-car. It groaned in to the kerb and they heard a door slamming, nodding to each other in the half-light.

'Go in you, Mick,' said the sergeant, 'and myself and the other man will cover the doors.'

He stood on the corner and the silent detective stood at the door in the side street.

Mick looked round the pub, nodding to the Shaky Man, who wished him a good evening. There was no one at the bar and the place was empty but for two women sitting in the snug, taking snuff from a mustard tin.

He looked in at them. 'How are you, Maggie?'

'I'm nothing the better of you,' said the older and snuffier woman.

'Not going to tell us who ran out the back, when Glimmers gave the bend we were coming up in the car?'

'If it's your time for hearing,' said the other old woman, 'it's not ours for confessing.'

He came out on the street and turned to speak to the sergeant. 'There's nobody . . .' but the sergeant was speaking to Nancy Hand and nodded to him to be silent.

'Just met this little girl coming down the street here. Going in here for a message, I suppose, Nancy?'

'I was going in for a drink, to tell you the truth, Sergeant.'

'A wonder a girl like yourself wouldn't get some better place to drink than that. And that old wing,' he rolled his little eyes in sadness, 'is enough to ruin you.'

'What can you do, Sergeant, when you haven't the price of anything better?'

'A few bottles of stout, or drop of whiskey, even. Wouldn't it be better?' He fumbled in his pocket and took out a pound note, fondling it between finger and thumb and speaking casually.

'I suppose you didn't, be any chance, see a sign of Pig's Eye O'Donnell in your travels?'

Nancy looked at the pound note, looked up at him, and moistened her lips.

'I saw him in the shop here, a few nights ago. And do you know who was in the shop?'

The sergeant shook his head slowly.

'Eddie Collins. The fellow got weighed off in London and scarpered from Parkhurst last year. He was doing ten stretch.'

The sergeant nodded.

'You're a good girl, Nancy, and I know you wouldn't mind a man old enough to be your father standing you a drink. Here's the price of one now, and take my advice lay off that old wine. Good-night.'

He shook her hand, pressing a pound note into it.

She shook her head in thanks and went into the shop.

'We'll have a look in a few other places,' said the sergeant. 'Come on, back into the car.'

The car went off down the quay. The sergeant remarked to Mick, 'If we happened to run into that Eddie Collins, we'd be elected.'

'So we would be too, if we won the Sweep.' As he often remarked about the sergeant, he was all right before the films and the wireless and such came in: but now his head was full of all manner of notions of terrible cute detectives that weren't as green as they were cabbage-looking. Why wouldn't he just do his patrols in a straightforward manner and leave whatever bit of mystery there might be to be cleared up by some of the new fellows that were trained up in other things besides handball and cabbage-catching up in the Depot?

'Drive down as far as Townsend Street, avic,' said the sergeant to the driver, leering to himself and chuckling behind his hand in a softly mysterious fashion.

It's a good thing, thought Mick, we haven't the television here yet or that fellow would be finished altogether.

In the cellar they heard the car move off and prepared to move back upstairs. A man at the back muttered something about Nancy Hand and her conversation with the sergeant. They looked at Pig's Eye.

'We'll leave her to Heaven,' said he.

'If she's upstairs when we go up, I'll leave her for Jervis Street,' said the man that had muttered.

'You don't say one dicky-bird to her,' said Pig's Eye, who used Edgware Road English when he wanted to say something important. 'Nor none of yous say nothing to her.'

'You're not going to let her get away with the like of that, are you?'

'Whether I am or not is nobody's business but mine and,' here he smiled, 'there's more ways of killing a cat than dragging it through a keyhole on a bit of string.'

The others chuckled, as it's called, and trooped back up the stairs.

Nancy turned towards them when they came into the bar. Pig's Eye stared at her.

'Hello, Pig's Eye, and Bowser.'

'You too,' said Pig's Eye.

'How's the form, Nan?' said Bowser.

'I'm powerful.'

'More of that to you,' said Pig's Eye, nodding to the Shaky Man. 'Give us back that gargle I left down and I leaving the room.'

'Ah, not at all,' said Nancy Hand, 'give him a fresh pint and a drop of the chat with it. And you, too, Bowser?'

'You must have met an angel,' said Pig's Eye.

'I did,' said Nancy, laughing nervously, 'a two-legged one.'

'I never heard of any other sort,' said Bowser.

'Ah, no,' said Nancy, quickly, 'it's just a few makes I had, you know.'

Bowser rose his glass.

'Good luck, Bosy,' said Nancy.

'May I never see you worse,' said Pig's Eye.

FOXER

Brian Cleeve

Just as Brendan Behan was a mixture of the outrageous and the unre-generate, so too is Foxer O'Reilly, the con-man hero of this story by a master storyteller, Brian Cleeve (1921-　). Born in Dublin and for a time a journalist with Radio Telefís Eireann, Cleeve has written a number of suspense novels with vivid Irish settings drawn from per-sonal experience. His more recent books have featured Sean Ryan, who has been called 'one of the most forceful and convincing secret agents in contemporary fiction.'

Brian Cleeve describes Foxer as a 'detective of opportunities' and says he was inspired to write the story in 1964, after a visit to Mountjoy Prison to make a TV programme. When the reader has met O'Reilly and shared his experiences, he will probably not be surprised to learn that the story is one of its author's favourites and was especially cho-sen by him for this collection . . .

Mr Francis O'Reilly, known to a wide circle of enemies as Foxer, lay on his narrow prison bed, thinking of old age and death. Tomorrow he would be seventy-eight! It had crept up on him unawares. Like a policeman in the night. He had grown old and never realised it. He had known, naturally enough, that he was growing older. But not that he was already old. Very old. Too old. He stroked his beard, soft as white silk, wavy, sumptuous, so convincingly old and virtuous that he had never thought of it as a sign of true old age, but rather as a tool of his trade. His victims believed that a man with a beard like that could not conceivably be telling them a string of expensive lies.

He had had it for twenty years, tended it, loved it, seen it grow from mere pale grey to pure, angelic white, defended it with a terri-ble fury from a series of prison doctors and barbers, stolen the most delicate shampoos for it, kept it in defiance of reason, when its mere appearance in any police distict was enough to get him arrested. In fact, many a poor old bearded clergyman, going about his heavenly business in London or Manchester or Dublin, had suddenly become aware of some large man in plain clothes taking an unnatural interest in his innocent old face, and had felt vaguely guilty, until the detective had realised that it wasn't Foxer and had turned away.

For Foxer specialised in clergymen. Catholic priests, Church of England parsons, Congregational ministers, Unitarians—he was entirely ecumenical. But at home in Ireland he was always a priest. From the foreign missions. It might be Africa. Or South America. Or Formosa. He liked variety, and prided himself on giving spiritual value. Many a gull who had already parted with his five-pound donation to the building fund of the mission church in M'Wanga, or the convent in San Felipe in Venezuela, or the seminary in Pei Pei, somewhere in the north of Ping Ping, had been entertained for an hour afterward with fearsome stories of pagan darkness in Pei Pei, of the awful threat of Communistic atheism in San Felipe, or of the dreadful fate of female orphans among the Abongo. Many a hardheaded commercial traveller had wiped away a tear as he put down his contribution to the M'Wanga mission on his expense sheet, suitably disguised as 'entertainment.'

And it was not all lies on Foxer's part. He had truly been in San Felipe. He had spent a fornight in jail there until he bribed his way out. And once he had actually adopted a female Abongo orphan. At least she was female, and probably an orphan. And if she wasn't an Abongo she was certainly black, and strikingly handsome in a dark and lissome way. He had found her in Liverpool, and spent three months of absolute felicity with her in Manchester, until an interfering policeman raked up an old unpleasantness and saw him off to Strangeways Jail for two and half years. But that was life. His at any rate, and he had few regrets.

Of the past fifty years he might have—indeed, he had—spent thrity-seven in various prisons, from Wandsworth to Sing Sing, but when he considered the way he had spent the remaining thirteen he had no regrets at all. 'Oh, boy,' he might have said, 'the times I've had.' And now he had grown old, and all the times were behind him, and only death in front. It was time to make an end of folly and face the facts.

'You've got to face up to it,' the warden had said. 'You're too old for it.' And, taking him by his elbow, the warden had steered him to the barred window of the warden's office and pointed to the neat row of wooden crosses in the cemetery plot. 'Unless you want to join them out there, you'll have to go straight from here on, old friend. You really will.' And he had looked quite sad.

Although the warden was a comparatively young man, barely sixty, he and Foxer had known each other for a very long time, since the days when Foxer still worked the race trains and the warden was a junior turnkey.

'You don't want to die in here, do you, Foxer?' the warden had said, because he didn't want to die in there himself, and sometimes he was afraid he would. And, indeed, neither did Foxer want to die in prison, although for reasons rather different from the warden's. Foxer had been so long connected with the clergy that he had very little faith in a heavenly life beyond the grave. The grave itself was all a man could be sure of, and he had no wish to spend eternity beside some petty thief or defaulting debtor. For years he had had his mind's eye fixed on a charming little plot in Glasnevin near the poet's corner, where his neighbours were certain to be people of intellect and conversation. All that he needed was the price of it, and his last little escapade had been connected with that very thing.

He had been spending the summer working the tourist resorts of southwest Ireland, modestly but profitably. He hadn't touched the Southwest for twenty-five years, and he hadn't had a beard back then. Between the natural generosity of vacationers, and the profound respect of Irish hotelkeepers for the holy cloth—perhaps they hope that it will be counted to them in heaven against their various little occupational offences, like serving the worst coffee west of Kamchatka—he had done quite well. But collecting donations for non-existent missions, while a very safe way of conning gulls, is also a very slow way, and it is almost impossible, given the cost of living, to accumulate much capital. By the end of the summer Foxer had enough to get him through the winter, or a fair part of it, but not a penny more. And it was then, in Tralee, in late September, that the thought of the little plot in Glasnevin came back to him. A mere hundred pounds would secure it. But it might as well have been a thousand. Nearly all the tourists had gone home.

Which meant the Bishop's Party racket. Just once more. For the plot in Glasnevin. And then, as God was his witness, never again. It had already cost him two years in Sing Sing, three and a half in

Wandsworth, and two stretches in Mountjoy. But, after all, he had never worked it in the Southwest.

The next day, therefore, he went into the local branch of the Bank of Ireland, deposited five pounds, and acquired a cheque book. He then went to the largest hotel, booked a room with a private bath, had the finest dinner that the hotel could provide, ordered a bottle of twelve-year-old whisky, and invited the manager to join him for a nightcap. He had already armed himself with a good deal of local clerical knowledge.

The manager came, and for half an hour was treated to a virtuoso display of conning, the fruit and essence of more than fifty years of experience. Female orphans of the Abongo, heart-rendingly grateful babies in Pei Pei, pathetically devout Indians in San Felipe held out their black and yellow and brown hands to the manager until the tears sprang to his eyes and his hand sprang to his pocketbook. But Foxer merely shook his head reproachfully. 'My dear fellow,' he said, 'do you think I invited you up here to get a subscription for my orphans? Another time perhaps, but tonight allow me to lay aside my shepherd's cares and play host for once. Even a missionary grows tired of begging, you know, even for holy charity,' And he tipped the last of the whisky into the manager's glass with a sly wink of hospitality.

'And talking of playing host, I find that I am an old'— he stroked his beard—'a *very* old friend of your bishop, the good Dr McGurk.' For that was, in fact, the bishop's name. 'We were in Maynooth together—oh, half a century ago. Alas for vanished youth, vanished ambitions, *Tempus fugit*, as our old professor of philosophy would say. Little we knew, ah, little indeed, young skipping lambs of the Good Shepherd's, how it would *fugit*. And now the good Aloysius McGurk wears the purple—may God deal gently with him always— and I, I am what you see, my dear fellow: a humble missionary priest, begging bread for his orphans in the four corners of this generous land. But just for once, for old times' sake, I would dearly love to play host to my old friend, and his cathedral clergy. And indeed'—he winked broadly—'I am not entirely disinterested in this, for the good doctor can, if he wishes, favour my mission field in many ways, such as directing the thoughts of young seminarians toward the spiritual needs of my pagan orphans. Alas, we doves must be wiser than serpents if we are to survive in this world.'

Which, in a way, was very true. And so Foxer planned with the manager a most elaborate feast that would melt any bishop's charitable old heart, beginning with oysters and carrying on through a dozen courses to peaches *flambées* in kirsch *à la maréchale*, God forgive Foxer, accompanied by enough wines of France and Rhineland, not to speak of twelve-year-old whisky and ancient brandy, to reduce the clergy of the entire diocese to a benevolent stupor.

'There will be,' said Foxer, 'about a dozen of us. Say fourteen. I would,' he added roguishly, 'say thirteen, if that did not verge on blasphemy. But there is one thing more. I wish to make this little party a memorable one for my old friend—and *his* old friends—for God knows if we shall meet again this side of paradise. And while he is certain of his entry, I, alas . . .' And he struck his breast.

'No, no,' cried the manager, entirely overcome. 'May God spare you both to us for many years yet. May you give many more such little parties.' As well the manager might wish, for his profit on this one looked like being in the neighbourhood of fifty pounds. He and Foxer were both on the edge of weeping, and Foxer had barely voice enough left to call for another bottle. It came, was opened, sampled, approved.

'You were saying?' prompted the manager. 'You wanted to make this occasion truly memorable for our beloved bishop?'

'Ah, yes,' cried Foxer, striking his forehead. 'I'm glad you reminded me. I wish to buy a few little gifts for my guests. Trifles, of course; a missionary's wallet is seldom filled with anything but crumbs.' A sad smile. 'But trifles of taste. Pray tell me, what is the best establishment for such gifts in this estimable town?'

The manager looked extremely thoughtful, fondled his chin and suggested a local jeweller of excellent stock and standing. The bottle was finished. And both manager and missionary—after his share of two bottles of twelve-year-old Irish whisky Foxer *was* a missionary, heart, soul, and body—toddled off to bed and slept the sleep of the truly satisfied.

Next morning, Foxer strolled down to the recommended jeweller's, told the necessary part of his story, bought a handsome pectoral cross for the bishop, a snuff box of gold and enamel for the canon, a gold cigarette lighter for Monsignor O'Flaherty, and so on through the list of his clerical guests, to the amount of about three hundred pounds. When all was parcelled and added up, he produced his cheque book, gave the Bank of Ireland and the hotel manager as his references—not to speak of the bishop, or his own appearance—paid, if that is the word, for his purchases, and walked blithely out of the shop with loot that, properly fenced in the right quarters in Dublin, would net him a hundred pounds in cold cash. He thought he might even keep the pectoral cross for himself. Ten yards down the street, he was arrested.

When he gave evidence against Foxer at the trial, the hotel manager almost wept again, with unkind laughter. Thirty years before, he said, choking back vengeful mirth, Foxer had caught him and the local jeweller in exactly the same way. He had been assistant manager, then, of a large hotel in Roscommon. And to make it worse, the jeweller had been his cousin. That time Foxer had got clean away with one hundred and fifty pounds' worth of jewellery, a four-day hotel bill, five bottles of whisky, and a set of hotel towels. This time Foxer got two years in Mountjoy, the two years he was just finishing in time for his seventy-eighth birthday.

That was one of the things that had made Foxer realise that he was indeed far too old for the profession, and should retire. A con man who can no longer recognise a client he has already gulled—even thirty years earlier—has no right to stay in the business. And not much chance to, either.

The other element in Foxer's decision to retire, aside from the fear of being buried in the prison cemetery, was family feeling. It was a comparatively new growth, but with roots in an incident of almost forty years before. He had met, in London, an Irish widow, handsome, well set up in flesh and bank account, and, in a weak moment, had married her. The marriage, like her bank account, had lasted about a month. A sporty car, a honeymoon at Antibes, moonlight on the Riviera, Monte Carlo—ah, the delights of marriage. But an angry man in Monte had recognised him, and he had fled with the sporty car and the remains of the bank account, and had never seen his wife again.

And, to tell the truth, hardly ever thought of her until about a year ago when a middle-aged woman with vaguely familiar features had come to visit him in Mountjoy, and introduced herself as his daughter. On a later visit, she brought her husband, who was a doctor of psychology and an amateur criminologist. The doctor fell in love with Foxer at once, seeing in him the material for several papers to learned societies, and even a book on the latent schizophrenia of confidence tricksters. It was the doctor, indeed, who had persuaded his wife to visit her disgraceful old father, once the newspaper publicity resulting from his most recent arrest had reminded them of the relationship. The wife herself, Foxer's daughter, was a dull woman, with none of Foxer's dash and imagination. But she was goodhearted, and when her husband suggested that they should make a home for Foxer, she reluctantly agreed.

'What shall we tell the two boys?' was all she said, meaning her sons, Patrick and Martin, twelve and ten. 'They must never know the truth.' As for little Grace, five and a half, the very thought of her baby ever hearing such words as 'prison' and 'crime' made her blood run cold.

'We will tell them he is your great-uncle from South America,' the doctor said. His mouth twitched. 'He is probably well enough used to supporting such stories with a wealth of circumstantial detail.'

And so Foxer went to live with his daughter, his son-in-law, and his three grandchildren, taking to retirement with something approaching content. It was pleasant to stroll aimlessly in the sun, to greet the neighbours with no ulterior motives, to look young policemen fearlessly and even forbiddingly in the eye, to be no longer the lone wolf, but a belonging sheep. It was a great and oddly pleasant change. He found himself sinking into number 10 Acacia Avenue like a tired athlete sinking into a warm bath.

And there, but for little Grace, he might well have stayed forever. Or, at least, until the cemetery plot in Glasnevin received him. He was clean and quiet about the house. He gave immensely good value to the doctor, helped his daughter with the washing up, and entertained the children at their bedtime with elaborate stories about South America. Not missionary stories, naturally; he found it a relief after so long in 'holy orders' to be a layman. He described lost Inca civilisations that he happened to have found, drawing on years of serious travel reading (mainly for professional purposes) in a dozen well-stocked prison libraries. He told of fantastic alligator hunts in the upper waters of the Amazon, where the piranhas ate the alligators as fast as he shot them, which was why he had failed to bring home an alligator handbag for their mother, or a stuffed baby alligator for little Grace.

But the stories the children liked best were connected with The Treasure. 'You might say,' he told them, 'that I have spent my life searching for that treaure.' And he stroked his beard and described to them the fabled treasure lake of the Incas, high up in the Andes, still as glass, cold as ice, deep as the pit of hell itself, and guarded by monstrous swimming serpents with sabre teeth and horned, scaly heads.

'Now, now, Uncle,' his daughter said, coming briskly in with Grace's cocoa, 'you'll give her bad dreams.' And Foxer was gently but firmly ushered off to the kitchen, where there was a great deal of washing up.

These interruptions began to happen more and more often. Foxer's daughter seemed to dread the effects of fantasy on her precious chicks. Fantasy for boys meant insecurity, losing jobs, going to prison. For girls, it meant bad marriages, the stage, journalism, God knew what. Obedient to her husband, she was still a mother and determined not to see her children ruined. She began to drop little hints to them that their South American great-uncle, while a dear, sweet old man, was sometimes a trifle—well—imaginative.

'You mean he tells lies?' Martin asked scornfully. 'Of course he does.' And for obscure reasons this easy acceptance by the boys worried her still more. Only Grace was both shocked and incredulous.

'Oh, no!' she cried. 'He's true, always. And when his money comes from South America, he says he'll buy me a beautiful gold ring, just like the treasure rings. He promised me.'

Indeed, Foxer had promised exactly that, in a weak moment. And he overheard this particular conversation. It worried him very much. Like two small pebbles in an otherwise very comfortable pair of shoes. Both his daughter's coolness and his granddaughter's expectancy were worrying to an old man whose every comfort depended increasingly on these two females. On his daughter to cook and provide for him, make his bed, mend his shirts, and perform those thousand little functions for which God designed the female creature, and without the proper and willing performance of which a home is not very much better than a prison cell, and much less peaceful. And on Grace for two or three small luxuries which he could get in no honourable way.

He could not ask the boys to steal their father's cigars, because they would have thought it wrong, while Grace thought it great fun. And because they would have eaten all the proceeds themselves, he could not ask the boys to get him chocolate cookies and charge them to their mother's account at the grocer's. Grace got them for him on a fifty-fifty basis, and he paid her in more and more lavish promises. A gold necklace. A doll that said 'Hello' and 'Goo-Goo Mama,' a doll's house. Once, when the boys almost caught the pair of them with a half pound of chocolate wafers, he turned the threatened investigations aside with talk of an electric train.

'When?' asked Patrtick.

And with the biscuits melting stickily under his chair cushion, Foxer said, 'Christmas', without realising that Christmas was less than a month away. From then on, life became increasingly difficult. Patrick reported the promise to his mother. His mother warned him to disregard it. Martin repeated the warning to Foxer with a certain unkind mockery that cut the old man to the quick and sent Grace into hysterics. When Martin was gone, Foxer quieted Grace with more promises, and lay down that night with the realisation that if, by Christmas, he reneged on his promises, he could never face the children again. While the loss of Martin's and Patrick's never very real respect would merely hurt his pride, the loss of Grace's belief in him would be something else again.

Martin and Patrick were entirely their parents' children. But in Grace he could see, dimly, childishly, but yet distinctly, a great deal of himself. He saw it in the casual efficiency with which she robbed her father's cigar cabinet, abstracting the key from his desk almost under his nose, and returning it with one hand while stroking his work-tired brow with the other. He saw it in her mature discretion about the cookies—never too many, never a kind her mother didn't buy for herself, in case the grocer should be suspicious. He had begun to think quite seriously of passing on his immense store of experience to this grandchild of his heart and blood. Even her eyes were like his, round and blue and innocent as cornflowers. And he too had once had golden hair. He stroked his beautiful beard. A woman confidence-trickster. Starting at twenty with the benefit of sixty years' experience behind her. She would be unique.

'Little Grace,' he whispered to her one December evening, over chocolate cookies and warm milk, 'would you like me to teach you how to be a student of human nature?'

She nodded carelessly, dropping chocolate crumbs on her tartan frock. But in spite of her apparent carelessness, a swiftly accurate finger wet its pink tip on her tongue and picked up every last telltale crumb.

'Born to it,' the old man breathed. 'In the blood.' She'd be able to play a missionary sister or a mother superior to perfection. 'We'll begin after Christmas,' he whispered. But for lessons to be of value, the pupil must have faith in the teacher. And it was almost Christmas.

Obviously, he had to keep his promises. And equally obviously, with the three-and-sixpence-a-week pocket money that his daughter allowed him, there was only one way to do it. One last fling, before respectability claimed and tamed him forever. He found, suddenly, that he was feeling ten years younger. Ten? He hadn't felt like this since he was sixty. He went to bed for the whole weekend in order to think, undisturbed by washing up.

Another bishop's party was out of the question. His daughter had burned his clerical gear the night he arrived, and he had no money to get any more. Then what? Again, Grace was the finger pointing the way, tiptoeing into his room with a book of raffle tickets from her school. Three tickets for sixpence, seven for a shilling, with a seventeen-pound turkey as first prize.

'You just give me sixpence and put your full name on that bit of the ticket there'—pointing at the stub. 'Your full name.' Light dawned, and Foxer fell asleep with his plan already perfected. On Monday morning, two days before Christmas, he began to operate.

Ever since he came to the district, he had gathered local gossip of a particular kind, not with any real motive, but simply out of the habit of a lifetime. Know the countryside. And among the snippets he had collected was the information that a certain shopkeeper in the next suburb kept his main supply of working cash not in his shop, which had once been successfully burgled, but at home in a heavy safe to which his wife held the keys during the day. His cash was never left unattended. By day, his wife cared for it; by night, he slept beside it.

His business was antique furniture and expensive bric-a-brac which he occasionally bought from callers to the shop. If he needed cash during the day—more, that is, than the smallish amount he carried to the shop each morning and home each night—he sent a messenger to fetch it from his wife. It was not the wisest system, perhaps, but what system is?

His name was Henry Molloy. His wife's was Margaret. And, at ten thirty on the Monday morning before Christmas, Foxer took Grace out on the pretext of buying her a Christmas present with his weekly three-and-sixpence, and from across the road loosed her, with her raffle tickets, at Mr Molloy's antique shop. 'Whatever you do,' he emphasised, 'sell one to Molloy himself. Just think if one of his assistants won a turkey and he didn't!'

Five minutes later he had Mr Henry Molloy's full signature and handwritten address on a raffle ticket stub and was rewarding Grace with a banana split. It crossed his mind briefly that here was a whole new line to exploit, but he realised sadly in the next minute that there is a limit to the number of raffle tickets which even the most angelic little girl can sell in one day. Even at a shilling a time, the turnover would be minute.

In fact, considering the price of banana splits, one would very likely operate at a considerable loss. As it was, he barely had the bus fare home, because Grace refused to give him Mr Molloy's shilling. But at least he had the ticket. And all that night he practiced the signature and the address. The handwriting was quite a simple, straightforward one.

Next morning, he presented himself to Mr Molloy as an elderly American on a visit with relations. Alas, his visit was about to end, and his age told him that he would not pass this way again—how true! He desired, indeed he aimed, to take back a few little souvenirs of his delightful stay to dear old Joliet—er, Illinois. Like, for example, that silver teapot.

When he began, Foxer intended to be modest. Say twenty pounds. But why be modest on a last fling? A man would have to be pretty mean-spirited to restrain his last fling to twenty pounds. 'And that li'l old silver tray. Is that the real McCoy?'

By the time he was done, the total of his purchases came to one hundred and ninety-seven pounds. He added a little fireside screen, 'for my delightful hostess in this beautiful old city of yours, sir,' to make it a round two hundred guineas.

Stroking his luxuriant beard, he said to Mr Molloy, 'Waal, sir, two hundred guineas is a fair sum of money, such as an old man like me would be afraid to carry through the streets.'

'How wise of you, sir,' said Mr Molloy.

'Equally, I guess, I cannot expect a stranger in a strange town, who happens to be leaving for the United States this very afternoon, to be allowed to pay for such an account by cheque'—Mr M. clucked—'but if you would provide me with a piece of that stationery I see lying there, I would scribble a note to my niece and hostess, who is minding my little supply of cash. And then, if by chance you have a messenger who could save my old shanks a journey . . .'

'Why, yes!' cried Mr M. His never very dormant suspicions had been sharply aroused by the beginning of this long spiel, but they had been happily laid to rest by the promise of cash. 'Pray take this sheet of paper, if you will forgive its being headed by my shop address. In fact, I myself can type the note for you, unless it is of too personal a nature?'

'How kind!' cried Foxer. 'Just say, "Dear Margaret," which is my dear niece's given name—'

'What a coincidence,' said Mr M. 'It's also my wife's name!'

'Then she must be a thoroughly good and delightful woman,' cried Foxer. 'I just know it. But I am keeping you too long,' he whispered, seeing the blue shape of a policeman stroll past the door. 'Just write that I've found a couple of small bargains and need two hundred guineas. Use your own words, sir. I'm no hand at composing letters, being a self-educated mill—I mean man.'

'A millionaire!' breathed Mr M., strictly to himself. 'How could I have suspected this sweet old gentleman?' And hastily, using the formula that he used when writing to his own Margaret, typed:

DEAR MARGARET, I have just been offered some rather interesting items. Please let me have two hundred guineas, by bearer.

Your loving,

and gave it to Foxer, who swiftly signed it, *Henry*, casually shading the flowing signature with his cupped hand. 'And the address?' asked Mr M., producing an envelope.

'Why, this one in my pocket will do,' said Foxer. 'Waste not, want not.' Producing a bundle of old letters, he selected an envelope from among them. Swiftly taking the note to Margaret, he tucked it into the envelope on which he had already written Mrs Molloy's name and address, in Henry Molloy's handwriting. Mr M. called forward a spotty and stupid messenger boy, too stupid to be dishonest or even lazy, which was why Mr M. employed him.

Foxer, who had strolled away to consider an antique Windsor chair, beckoned the boy to him. 'Take this letter to this address,' he said, giving the boy the note, together with a half-crown filched from Grace's piggy bank, 'and if you are back here in ten minutes, why, boy, I'll give you another.'

The boy sped off, not at all surprised to be sent to his master's private house, an errand he ran at least once or twice a week. Foxer stayed, admiring this and that for a minute or two more, than pleaded another errand in the neighbourhood and, promising to be back in two shakes of a donkey's tail, toddled out of the shop.

'A millionaire!' breathed Mr M. again. 'And so unaffected!'

Ten minutes later, Foxer waylaid the returning messenger, fifty yards up the street, and took the thick envelope addressed to Henry Molloy by his loving safe-keeper Margaret. Foxer gave the boy Grace's remaining half-crown and disappeared, at a surprising speed for a man of seventy-eight.

He spent the afternoon shopping, after a long and sumptuous champagne lunch in an excellent restaurant. He bought gold rings and a necklace, electric trains, a doll's house with ten rooms and running water, a doll that danced, and one that said 'Peekaboo' as well as 'Mama'; he bought tea sets, copper saucepans, delicious and exotic foods for his daughter; and two dozen cigars and a pure-silk dressing gown for his son-in-law. He bought himself a gold cigarette lighter, and an ivory brush-and-comb set for his beard. When he got home that night, he had four and elevenpence left. He slipped it unobtrusively into Grace's piggy bank and went to bed.

The next day was Christmas Eve. And from midday on, a succession of respectful messengers delivered a series of richly wrapped parcels to the astonished family in number 10 Acacia Avenue.

'Open them!' cried Foxer. And by six that evening the house was filled with coloured wrappings, squeaking children, speechless parents, and a beaming, benevolent Father Christmas of a Foxer. Water gushed out of the doll's house. One doll cried 'Peekaboo'; the other danced on the table. Electric trains circled the floor at ever-increasing speeds. The air was rich with cigar smoke and the subtle and exotic scents of unusual cooking.

'My life savings,' Foxer said to his daughter, 'but why save them?'

'A little legacy,' he murmured to his son-in-law. 'Totally unexpected.'

'Football pools,' he confided to Patrick and Martin. 'Quite a stroke of luck.'

And to Grace, 'My money from South America.'

At half past six, a large man in plainclothes knocked heavily at the door. Foxer answered it. 'How did you know?' he asked sadly.

'The beard, Foxer,' the detective said, with almost equal sadness. 'You're getting senile, that's what it is. As soon as old Molloy described the beard . . .'

'Be discreet,' pleaded Foxer. He went inside, packed his spare false teeth, his gold cigarette lighter, his ivory brush-and-comb set, his socks, and was ready. To tell the truth, he wasn't entirely brokenhearted. He was thoroughly sick of washing up. And rather tired of respectability.

'Just slipping out with a friend for a moment,' he murmured to the adults. 'A visitor from South America,' he whispered to Grace. 'About the treasure.'

'I have tried my hardest,' the judge said, 'to find extenuating circumstances in your case: your age, the pleas of your daughter'—not very passionate ones, it must be admitted—'the partially generous motives of your crime. But when I consider your truly appalling record . . .'

Everyone thought Foxer was extremely lucky to get off with eighteen months. Mr Molloy wrote an indignant letter to his parliamentary representative about it.

By the end of January, Foxer was lying in his old cell, stroking his beard. A slip of a young turnkey put his head round the door. 'Barber, Foxer?' he asked jokingly.

'Why, yes,' Foxer said. 'I think I will. I find this beard is inclined to irritate my chin at times.'

And as he sat in the barber's chair, submitting to the razor, his mind was already eighteen months ahead.

3

CRIME PASSIONEL
Tales of Jealousy and Revenge

MURDER AT COBBLER'S HULK

Sean O'Faolain

Sean O'Faolain (1900-), born John Whelan in Dublin, has better qualifications than many authors for writing about crime, as his father served in the police force for many years. O'Faolain fought in the Irish Civil War on the Republican side and later embraced with fierce determination the cause of civil liberties and the rights of workers. In the 1930s he transferred some of his passions to writing, and has since become acknowledged as one of the masters of the modern Irish short story. He possesses a profound appreciation of human motivations which he demonstrates to great effect in this story of a promiscuous woman and her mysterious death. It was first published in Playboy *magazine in 1972, where it was judged to be among the best short stories of the year.*

It takes about an hour of driving southward out of Dublin to arrive at the small seaside village of Greystones. (For two months in the summer, it calls itself a resort.) Every day, four commuter trains from the city stop here and turn back, as if dismayed by the sight of the desolate beach of shingle that stretches beyond it for twelve unbroken miles. A single line, rarely used, continues the railway beside this beach, so close to the sea that in bad winters the waves pound in across the track, sometimes blocking it for days on end with heaps of gravel, uprooted sleepers, warped rails. When this happens, the repair gangs have a dreary time of it. No shelter from the wind and spray. Nothing to be seen inland but reedy fields, an occasional farmhouse or abandoned manor, a few leafless trees decaying in the arid soil or fallen sideways. And, always, endless fleets of clouds sailing away towards the zinc-blue horizon.

Once there were three more tiny railway stations along these twelve miles of beach, each approached by a long lane leading from

161

the inland carriage-road to the sea. The best preserved of what remains of them is called Cobbler's Hulk. From a distance, one might still mistake it for a real station. Close up, one finds only a boarded waiting-room whose tin roof lifts and squeaks in the wind, a lofty signal-cabin with every window broken and a still loftier telephone pole whose ten crossbars must once have carried at least twenty lines and now bear only one humming wire. There is a rotting, backless bench. You could scythe the grass on the platform. The liveliest thing here is an advertisement on enamelled sheet metal, high up on the brick wall of the signal cabin. It shows the single white word STEPHEN'S splashed across a crazy blob of black ink. Look where one will, there is not farmhouse nor cottage within sight.

It was down here that I first met Mr Bodkin one Sunday afternoon last July. He was sitting straight up on the bench, bowler-hatted, clad, in spite of the warmth of the day, in a well-brushed blue chesterfield with concealed buttons and a neatly tailored velvet half collar that was the height of fashion in the Twenties. His grey spats were as tight as gloves across his insteps. He was a smallish man. His stiff shirt-collar was as high as the Duke of Wellington's, his bow tie was polka-dotted, his white moustaches were brushed up like a *Junker's*. He could have been seventy-three. His cheeks were as pink as a baby's bottom. His palms lay crossed on the handle of a rolled umbrella, he had a neatly folded newspaper under his arm, his patent-leather shoe tips gleamed like his pince-nez. Normally, I would have given him a polite 'Good day to you,' and passed on, wondering. Coming on him suddenly around the corner of the waiting-room, his head lowered toward his left shoulder as if he was listening for an approaching train, I was so taken by surprise that I said, 'Are you waiting for a train?'

'Good gracious!' he said, in equal surprise. 'A train has not stopped here since the Bronze Age. Didn't you know?'

I gazed at his shining shoes, remembering that when I had halted my Morris Minor beside the level-crossing gates at the end of the lane, there had been no other car parked there. Had he walked here? That brambled lane was a mile long. He peeped at the billycan in my hand, guessed that I was proposing to brew myself a cup of tea after my solitary swim, chirruped in imitation of a parrot, 'Any water?' rose and, in the comic-basso voice of a weary museum guide, said, 'This way, please.' I let him lead me along the platform, past the old brass tap that I had used on my few previous visits to Cobbler's Hulk, toward a black-tarred railway carriage hidden below the marshy side of the track. He pointed the ferrule of his umbrella.

'My chalet,' he said smugly. 'My *wagon-lit*.'

We descended from the platform by three wooden steps, rounded a microscopic gravel path, and he unlocked the door of his carriage. It was still faintly marked FIRST CLASS, but it also bore a crusted brass plate whose shining *rilievo* announced THE VILLA ROSE. He bowed me inward, invited me to take a pew (his word for a upholstered carriage seat), filled my billycan from a white enamelled bucket ('Pure spring water!') and, to expedite matters further, insisted on boiling it for me on his Primus stove. As we waited, he sat opposite me. We both looked out the window at the marshes. I heard a Guard's whistle and felt our carriage jolt away to nowhere. We introduced ourselves.

'I trust you find my beach a pleasant spot for a picnic?' he said, as if he owned the entire Irish Sea.

I told him that I had come here about six times over the past thirty years.

'I came here three years ago. When I retired.'

I asked about his three winters. His fingers dismissed them. 'Our glorious summers amply recompense.' At which exact moment I heard sea-birds dancing on the roof and Mr Bodkin became distressed. His summer and his beach were misbehaving. He declared that the shower would soon pass. I must have my cup of afternoon tea with him, right there. 'In first-class comfort.' I demurred; he insisted. I protested gratefully; he persisted tetchily. I let him have his way, and that was how I formed Mr Bodkin's acquaintance.

It never became any more. I saw him only once again, for five minutes, six weeks later. But, helped by a hint or two from elsewhere—the man who kept the roadside shop at the end of the lane, a gossipy barmaid in the nearest hamlet—it was enough to let me infer, guess at, induce his life. Its fascination was that he had never had any. By comparison, his beach and its slight sand dunes beside the railway track were crowded with incident, as he presently demonstrated by producing the big album of pressed flowers that he had been collecting over the pass three years. His little ear finger stirred them gently on their white pages; milfoil, yarrow, thrift, sea daisies, clover, shepherd's-needle, shepherd's purse, yellow bedstraw, great bedstraw, Our Lady's bedstraw, minute sand roses, different types of lousewort. In the pauses between their naming, the leaves were turned as quietly as the wavelets on the beach.

One December day in 1912, when he was fifteen, Mr Bodkin told me, he had entered his lifelong profession by becoming the messenger boy in Tyrrell's Travel Agency, located at 15 Grafton Street, Dublin. He went into Dublin every morning on the Howth tram, halting it outside the small pink house called The Villa Rose, where he lived with his mother, his father, his two young sisters and his two aunts . . .

The Villa Rose! He made a deprecatory gesture—it had been his mother's idea. The plays and novels of Mr A. E. Mason were popular around 1910. He wrinkled his rosy nose. It was not even what you call a real house. Just two fishermen's cottages, joined front to back, with a dip, or valley, between their adjoining roofs. But what a situation! On fine days, he could see, across the high tide of the bay, gulls blowing about like paper, clouds reflected in the still water, an occasional funnel moving slowly in or out of the city behind the long line of the North Wall; and away beyond it, all the silent drums of the Wicklow Mountains. Except on damp days, of course. The windows of The Villa Rose were always sea-dimmed on damp days. His mother suffered from chronic arthritis. His father's chest was always wheezing. His sisters' noses were always running. His aunts spent half their days in bed.

'I have never in my life had a day's illness! Apart from chilblains. I expect to live to be ninety.'

The great thing, it appeared, about Tyrrell's Travel Agency was that you always knew where you were. The Tyrrell system was of the simplest: everybody was addressed according to his rank. (Mr Bodkin did not seem to realise that this system was, in his boyhood as in mine, universal in every corner of the British Empire.) Whenever old Mr Bob wanted him, he shouted 'Tommy!' at the top of his voice. After shouting at him like that for about five years, Mr Bob suddenly put him behind the counter, addressed him politely as 'Bodkin' and shouted at him no longer. Five years passed and, again without any preliminaries, Mr Bob presented him with a desk of his own in a corner of the office and addressed him as 'Mr Bodkin'. At which everybody in the place smiled, nodded or winked his congratulations. He had arrived at the top of his genealogical tree. He might fall from it. He would never float beyond it. Very satisfactory.

One has to have one's station in life. Yes?

The summer shower stopped but not Mr Bodkin. (In the past three years, I wondered if he had had a single visitor to talk to.) There were, I must understand, certain seeming contradictions in the system. An eager ear and a bit of experience soon solved them all. For example, there was the case of old Clancy, the ex-Enniskillener Dragoon, who opened the office in the morning and polished the egyptian floor tiles. Anybody who wanted him always shouted, 'Jimmy!' Clear as daylight. But whenever old Lady Kilfeather came sweeping into the agency from her grey Jaguar, ruffling scent, chiffon, feather boas and Protestant tracts, she clancied the whole bang lot of them.

'Morning, Tyrrell! Hello, Bodkin! I hope Murphy has that nice little jaunt to Cannes all sewn up for myself and Kilfeather? Clancy, kindly read this leaflet on Mariolatry and do, for heaven's sake, stop saying, "Mother of God!" every time you see me!'

The aristocratic privilege. The stars to their stations; the planets in their stately cycles about the sun; until the lower orders bitch it all up. Meaning old Mrs Clancy, swaying into the office like an inebriated camel, to beg a few bob from Clancy for what she genteelly called her shopping. Never once had that woman, as she might reasonably have done, asked for 'Jim'. Never for 'Mr Clancy'. Never even for 'my husband'. Always for 'Clancy'. Mr Bodkin confessed that he sometimes felt so infuriated with her that he would have to slip around the corner to THE THREE FEATHERS, to calm his gut with a Guinness and be reassured by the barman's 'The usual, Mr B?' Not that he had ever been entirely happy about that same B. He always countered it with a stiff, 'Thank you, Mr Buckley.'

It was the only pub he ever visited. And never for more than one glass of plain. Occasionally, he used to go to the theatre. But only for Shakespeare. Or Gilbert and Sullivan. Only for the classics. Opera? Never! For a time, he had been amused by Shaw. But he soon discarded him as a typical Dublin jackeen mocking his betters. Every Sunday, he went to church to pray for the king. He was nineteen when the Rebellion broke out. He refused to believe in it. Or that the dreadful shootings and killings of the subsequent Troubles could possibly produce any change. And did they? Not a damned thing! Oh, some client might give his name in the so-called Irish language. Mr Bodkin simply wrote down, 'Mr Irish'. Queenstown became Cobh. What nonsense! Kingstown became Dun Laoghaire.

Pfoo! Pillar-boxes were painted green. The police were called Guards. The army's khaki was dyed green. All the whole damned thing boiled down to was that a bit of the House of Commons was moved from London to Dublin.

Until the Second World War broke out. Travel stopped dead. The young fellows in the office joined the army. He remembered how old Mr Bob—they ran the office between them—kept wondering for weeks how the Serbians would behave this time. And what on earth had happened to those gallant little Montenegrins? When the Germans invaded Russia, Mr Bob said that the czar would soon put a stop to that nonsense. Mind you, they had to keep on their toes after 1945. He would never forget the first time a client said he wanted to visit Yugoslavia. He took off his glasses, wiped them carefully, and produced a map. And, by heavens, there it was!

There had been other changes. His mother had died when he was forty-three. His two aunts went when he was in his fifties. To his astonishment, both his sisters married. His father was the last to go, at the age of eighty-one. He went on living, alone, in The Villa Rose, daily mustering thousands of eager travellers around Europe by luxury liners, crowded packet-boats, Blue Trains, Orient Expresses, Settlebellos, Rheingolds, alphabetical-mathematical planes. He had cars waiting for some, arranged hotels for others, confided to a chosen few the best places (according to 'my old friend Lady Kilfeather') to dine, drink and dance, and he never went anywhere himself.

'You mean you *never* wanted to travel?'

'At first, yes. When I could not afford it. Later, I was saving up for my retirement. Besides, in my last ten years there, the whole business began to bore me.'

He paused, frowned and corrected himself. It had not 'begun' to bore. His interest in it had died suddenly. It happened one morning when he was turning back into the office after conducting Lady Kilfeather out to her grey Jaguar. Observing him, young Mr James had beckoned him into his sanctum.

'A word in your ivory ear, Mr Bodkin? I notice that you have been bestowing quite an amount of attention on Lady Kilfeather.'

'Yes, indeed, Mr James! And I may say that she had just told me that she is most pleased with us.'

'As she might well be! Considering that it takes six letters and eight months to get a penny out of the old bitch. That woman, Mr

Bodkin, is known all over Dublin as a first-class scrounger, time-waster and bloodsucker. I would be obliged if you would in future bear in mind three rather harsh facts of life that my aged parent seems never to have explained to you. Time is money. Your time is my money. And no client's money is worth more to me than any other client's money. Take it to heart, Mr Bodkin. Thank you. That will be all for now.'

Mr Bodkin took it to heart so well that from that morning on, all those eager travellers came to mean no more to him than a trainload of tourists to a railway porter after he had banged the last door and turned away through the steam of the departing engine for a quick smoke before the next bunch arrived.

Still, my duty was duty. And he had his plans. He hung on until he was sixty-five and then he resigned. Mr James, with, I could imagine, an immense sense of relief, handed him a bonus of £50—a quid for every year of his service, but no pension—shook his hand and told him to go off to Cannes and live there in sin for a week with a cabaret dancer. Mr Bodkin said that for years he had been dreaming of doing exactly that with Mrs Clancy, accepted the fifty quid, said a warm goodbye to everybody in the office, sold The Villa Rose and bought the tarred railway carriage at Cobbler's Hulk. He had had his eye on it for the past five years.

The night he arrived at Cobbler's Hulk, it was dry and cold. He was sweating from lugging two suitcases down the dark lane. The rest of his worldly belongings stood waiting for him in a packing case on the grass-grown platform. For an hour he sat in his carriage by candlelight, in his blue chesterfield, supping blissfully on the wavelets scraping the shingle every twenty seconds and on certain mysterious noises from the wild-life on the marshes. A snipe? A grebe? A masked badger?

He rose at last, made himself another supper of fried salty bacon and two fried eggs, unwrapped his country bread and butter and boiled himself a brew of tea so strong that his spoon could almost have stood up in it. When he had washed his ware and made his bed, he went out onto his platform to find the sky riveted with stars. Far out to sea, the lights of a fishing smack. Beyond them he thought he detected a faint blink. Not, surely, a lighthouse on the Welsh coast? Then, up the line, he heard the hum of the approaching train. Two such trains, he had foreknown, would roar past Cobbler's Hulk every twenty-four hours. Its head lamps grew larger and brighter and then, with a roar, its carriage windows went flickering past him. He could see only half a dozen passengers in it. When it died away down the line, he addressed the stars:

'"O Spirits, merciful and good! I know that our inheritance is held in store for us by Time. I know there is a sea of Time to rise one day, before which all who wrong us or oppress us will be swept away like leaves. I see it, on the flow! I know that we must trust and hope, and neither doubt ourselves nor doubt the good in one another . . . O Spirits, merciful and good, I am grateful!"'

'That's rather fine. Where did you get that?'

'Dickens. *The Chimes*. I say that prayer every night after supper and a last stroll up the lane.'

'Say it for me again.'

As he repeated those splendid radical words, he looked about as wild as a grasshopper. 'Thinner than Tithonus before he faded into air.'

Had he really felt oppressed? Or wronged? Could it be that, during his three years of solitude, he had been thinking that this world would be a much nicer place if people did not go around shouting at one another or declaring to other people that time is money? Or wondering why Mother should have had to suffer shame and pain for years, whild dreadful old women like Kilfeather went on scrounging, wheedling, bloodsucking, eating and drinking their way around this travelled world of which all he had ever seen was that dubious wink across the night sea? He may have meant that in his youth, he had dreamed of marriage. He may have meant nothing at all.

He leaned forward.

'Are you sure you won't have another cup of tea? Now that I can have afternoon tea any day I like, I can make a ridiculous confession to you. For fifty years, I used to see Mr Bob and Mr James walk across Grafton Street every day at four-thirty precisely to have afternoon tea in Mitchell's Café. And I cannot tell you how bitterly I used to envy them. Wasn't that silly of me?'

'But, surely, one of the girls on the staff could have brewed you all a cup of tea in the office?'

He stared at me.

'But that's not the same thing as afternoon tea in Mitchell's! White tablecloths? Carpets? Silverwear? Waitresses in blue and white?'

We looked at each other silently. I looked at my watch and said that I must get going.

He laughed happily.

'The day I came here, do you know what I did with *my* watch? I pawned it for the sum of two pounds. I have never retrieved it. And I never will. I live by the sun and the stars.'

'You are never lonely?'

'I am used to living alone.'

'You sleep well?'

'Like a dog. And dream like one. Mostly of the old Villa Rose. And my poor, dear mamma. How could I be lonely? I have my beautiful memories, my happy dreams and my good friends.'

'I envy you profoundly,' I said.

On which pleasant little coda we parted. But is it possible never to be lonely? Do beautiful memories encourage us to withdraw from the world? Not even youth can live on dreams.

He had, however, one friend.

*   *   *

One Saturday evening in September, on returning from the wayside shop on the carriage road, he was arrested by a freshly painted sign on a gate about 200 yards from the railway track. It said FRESH EGGS FOR SALE. He knew that there was not a house nor a human being in sight. Who on earth would want to walk a mile down this tunnelled lane to buy eggs? Behind the wooden gate, there was a grassy track, leading, he now presumed, to some distant cottage invisible from the lane. He entered the field and was surprised to see, behind the high hedge, an open shed sheltering a red van bearing, in large white letters:

FLANNERY'S
HEAVENLY BREAD

After a winding quarter of a mile, he came on a small, sunken, freshly whitewashed cottage and knocked. The door was opened by a woman of about thirty-five or forty, midway between plain and good-looking, red-cheeked, buxom, blue-eyed, eagerly welcoming. She spoke with a slight English accent that at once reminded him of his mother's voice. Yes! She had lovely fresh eggs. How many did he want? A dozen? With pleasure! Behind her, a dark, handsome, heavily-built man, of about the same age, rose from his chair beside the open turf fire of the kitchen and silently offered him a seat while 'Mary' was getting the eggs.

Mr Bodkin expected to stay three minutes. He stayed an hour. They were the Condors: Mary, her brother Colm—the dark, silent man—and their bedridden mother lying in the room off the kitchen, her door always open, so that she could not only converse through it but hear all the comforting little noises and movements of her familiar kitchen. Their father, a herdsman, had died three months before. Mary had come back from service in London to look after her mother, and poor Colm (her adjective) had come home with her to support them both. He had just got a job as a roundsman for a bakery in Wicklow, driving all day around the countryside in the red van.

Mr Bodkin felt so much at ease with Mary Condor that he was soon calling on her every evening after supper, to sit by the old woman's bed, to gossip or to read her the day's news from his *Irish Times* or to give her a quiet game of draughts. That Christmas Day, on Mary's insistence, he joined them for supper. He brought a box of chocolates for Mary and her mother, 100 cigarettes for Colm and a bottle of grocer's sherry for them all. He recited one of his favourite party pieces from Dickens. Colm so far unbent as to tell him about the bitter Christmas he had spent in Italy with the Eighth Army near a place called Castel di Sangro. Mary talked with big eyes of the awful traffic of London. The old woman, made tipsy by the sherry, shouted from her room about the wicked sea crossing her husband had made during 'the other war', in December of 1915, with a herd of cattle for the port of Liverpool.

'All travelled people!' Mr Bodkin laughed, and was delighted when Mary said that, thanks be to God, their travelling days were done.

As he walked away from their farewells, the channel of light from their open door showed that the grass was laced with snow. It clung to the edges of his carriage windows as he lay in bed. It gagged the wavelets. He could imagine it falling and melting into the sea. As he clutched the blue hot-water bottle that Mary had given him for a Christmas present, he realised that she was the only woman friend he had made in his whole life. He felt so choked with gratitude that he fell asleep without thanking his spirits, the merciful and the good, for their latest gift.

What follows is four-fifths inference and one-fifth imagination:

both, as the event showed, essentially true.

On the Monday of the last week in July, on returning from the roadside shop with a net bag containing *The Irish Times*, tea, onions and a bar of yellow soap, Mr Bodkin was startled to see a white Jaguar parked beside the level crossing. It was what they would have called in the travel agency a posh car. It bore three plaques, a GB, a CD and a blue-and-white silver RAC. Great Britain. *Corps Diplomatique*. Royal Automobile Club. He walked onto his platform to scan the beach for its owner. He found her seated on his bench, in a miniskirt, knees crossed, wearing a loose suede jacket, smoking a cigarette from a long ivory holder, glaring at the grey sea, tiny, blonde (or was she bleached?), exquisitely made up, still handsome. Her tide on the turn. Say, fifty? He approached her as guardedly as if she were a rabbit. A woven gold bangle hung heavily from the corrugated white glove on her wrist. Or was it her bare wrist? Say, fifty-five. Her cigarette was scented.

'Fog coming up,' he murmured politely when he came abreast of her and gave her his little bobbing bow. 'I do hope you are not waiting for a train.'

She slowly raised her tinted eyelids.

'I was waiting for you, Mr Bodkin,' she smiled. (One of the sharp ones?)

Her teeth were the tiniest and whitest he had ever seen. She could have worn them around her neck. Last month, he saw a field mouse with teeth as tiny as hers, bared in death.

'Won't you sit down? I know all about you from Molly Condor.'

'What a splendid woman she is!' he said and warily sat beside her, placing his net bag on the bench beside her scarlet beach bag. He touched it. 'You have been swimming?'

'I swim,' she laughed, 'like a stone. While I waited for you, I was sun-bathing.' She smiled for him. 'In the nude.'

Hastily, he said, 'Your car is *corps diplomatique*!'

'It is my husband's car. Sir Hilary Dobson. I stole it!' She gurgled what ruder chaps in the agency used to call the Gorgon Gurgle. 'You mustn't take me seriously, Mr Bodkin. I'm Scottish. Hilary says I am fey. He is in the FO. He's gone off on some hush-hush business to Athens for a fortnight, so I borrowed the Jag. Now, if it had been Turkey! But perhaps you don't like Turkey, either? Or do you? Athens is such a crummy dump, don't you agree?'

'I have never travelled, Lady Dobson.'

'But Molly says you once owned a travel agency!'

'She exaggerates my abilities. I was a humble clerk.'

'Eoh?' Her tone changed, her voice became brisk. 'Look, Bodkin, I wanted to ask you something very important. How well do you know Molly Condor?'

He increased his politeness.

'I have had the great pleasure of knowing Miss Mary Condor since last September.'

'I have known her since she was twenty-two. I trained her. She was in my service for twelve years. But I have never looked at Molly as just a lady's maid. Molly is my best friend in the whole world. She is a great loss to me. Of course, as we grow older, the fewer, and the more precious, our friends become.'

He considered the name, Molly. He felt it was patronising. He had never lost a friend—never, before Mary, having had one to lose. He said as much.

'Too bad! Well! I want Molly to come back to us. My nerves have not been the same since she left.'

He looked silently out to sea. He was aware that she was slowly turning her head to look at him. Like a field mouse? He felt a creeping sensation of fear. Her nerves seemed all right to him. He watched her eject her cigarette, produce another from a silver case, insert it, light it smartly with a gold lighter and blow out a narrow jet of smoke.

'And then there is her brother. Condor was our chauffeur for five years. It would be simply wonderful if they both came back to us! I know poor old Hilary is as lost without his Condor as I am without my Molly. It would be a great act of kindness if you could say a word in our favour in that quarter. Hilary would appreciate it no end. Oh, I know, of course about the mother. But that old girl can't need the two of them, can she? Besides, when I saw her this morning, I had the feeling she won't last long. Arthritis? *And* bronchitis? *And* this climate? I had an old aunt just like her in Bexhill-on-Sea. One day, she was in splendid health. The next day, her tubes were wheezing like bagpipes. For six months, I watched her, fading like a sunset. In the seventh month . . .'

As she wheedled on and on, her voice reminded him of a spoon inside a saucepan. He listened to her coldly, with his eyes, rather than his ears, as for so many years he used to listen to old ladies who did not know where exactly they wanted to go nor what they wanted to do, alert only to their shifting lids, their mousy fingers, their bewildered shoulders, their jerking lips. Crepe on her neck. French cigarettes. Sun-bathing nude. Bodkin. Condor. Molly. 'Poor old Hilary.' What did this old girl really want? Coming all this way for a lady's maid? My foot!

'And you know, Bodkin, Molly has a great regard for you. She thinks you are the most marvellous thing she ever met. I can see why.' She laid her hand on his sleeve. 'You have a kind heart. You will help me, if you can, won't you?' She jumped up. 'That is all I wanted to say. Now you must show me your wonderful *wagon-lit*. Molly says it is absolutely fab.'

'I shall be delighted, Lady Dobson,' he said and, unwillingly led her to it.

When she saw the brass plate of THE VILLA ROSE, she guffawed and hastened to admire everything else. Her eyes trotted all over his possessions like two hunting mice. She gushed over his 'clever little arrangements'. She lifted pot-lids, felt the springiness of the bed, penetrated to his water-closet, which she flushed, greatly to his annoyance because he never used it except when the marshes were very wet or very cold, and then he had to refill the cistern with a bucket every time he flushed it.

'I find it all most amusing, Bodkin,' she assured him as she powdered her face before his shaving mirror. 'If you were a young man, it would make a wonderful weekend love-nest, wouldn't it? I must fly. It's nearly lunchtime. And you want to make whatever it is you propose to make with your soap, tea and onions. Won't you see me to my car? And do say a word for me to Molly! If you ever want to find me, I'm staying in the little old hotel down the road. For a week.' She laughed naughtily. 'Laying siege! Do drop in there any afternoon at six o'clock for an aperitif,' and she showed half her white thigh as she looped into her car, started the engine, meshed the gears, beamed at him with all her teeth, cried '*A bientôt, Bodkin*,' and shot recklessly up the lane, defoliating the hedges into a wake of leaves like a speedboat.

Watching her cloud of dust, he remembered something. A chap in the office showing him a postcard of *Mona Lisa*. 'Ever seen her before? Not half! And never one of them under fifty-five!' Indeed! *And* indeed! 'I am afraid, Lady Dobson, we must make up our minds. A cool fortnight in Brittany? Or five lovely hot days in Monte

Carlo? Of course, you *might* win a pot of money in Monte Carlo . . .' How greedily their alligator eyelids used to blink at that one! He returned slowly to his *wagon-lit*, slammed down the windows to let out the smell of her cigarette, washed the dust of yellow powder from his washbasin, refilled his cistern and sat for an hour on the edge of his bed, pondering. By nightfall, he was so bewildered that he had to call on Mary.

She was alone. The old lady was asleep in her room. They sat on either side of the kitchen table, whispering about the hens, the up train that had been three minutes late, the down train last night that was right on the dot, the fog that morning, both of them at their usual friendly ease until he spoke about his visitor. When he finished, she glanced at the open door of the bedroom.

'I must say, she was always very generous to me. Sir Hilary was very kind. He went hard on me to stay. He said, "You are good for her." She had her moods and tenses. I felt awfully sorry for him. He spoiled her.'

'Well, of course, Mary, those titled people,' Mr Bodkin fished cunningly and was filled with admiration for her when she refused to bite.

All she said was, 'Sir Hilary was a real gentleman.'

'They are married a long time?'

'Fifteen years. She is his second wife. She nursed his first wife. But I *had* to come back, Mr Bodkin!'

'You did quite right. And your brother did the right thing, too. I mean, two women in a remote cottage. Your brother is never lonely?'

She covered her face with her hands and he knew that she was crying into them.

'He is dying of the lonesome.'

From the room, the old woman suddenly hammered the floor with her stick.

'Is he back?' she called out fretfully.

Mary went to the bedroom door and leaned against the jamb. It was like listening to a telephone call.

'It's Mr Bodkin . . . He went up to the shop for cigarettes . . . I suppose he forgot them . . . About an hour ago . . . He may be gone for a stroll. It's such a fine night . . . Och, he must be sick of that old van . . .' She turned her head. 'Was the van in the shed, Mr Bodkin?' He shook his head. 'He took the van . . . For God's sake, Mother, stop worrying and go to sleep. He maybe took the notion to drive over to Ashford for a drink and a chat. It's dull for him here . . . I'll give you a game of draughts.'

Mr Bodkin left her.

A nurse? It was dark in the lane, but above the tunnel of the hedges, there was still a flavour of salvaged daylight. He started to walk toward the road, hoping to meet Condor on his way back. The air was heavy with heliotrope and meadow-sweet. A rustle in the ditch beside him. Far away, a horse whinnied. He must be turned forty by now. Behind him, Africa, Italy, London. Before him, nothing but the roads and fields of his boyhood. Every night, that solitary cottage. The swell of the night express made him look back until its last lights had flickered past the end of the lane and its humming died down the line.

But I have lived. An old man, now, twice a child.

By the last of the afterlight above the trees of the carriage road, he saw the red nose of the van protruding from the half-moon entrance to the abandoned manor house. He walked to it, peered into its empty cabin, heard a pigeon throating from a clump of trees behind the chained gates. He walked past it to the shop. It was closed and dark. He guessed at a lighted window at the rear of it, shining out over the stumps of decapitated cabbages. Condor was probably in there, gossiping. He was about to turn back when he saw, about 100 yards farther on, the red tail-lights of a parked car. Any other night, he might have given it no more than an incurious glance. The darkness, the silence, the turmoil of his thoughts finally drew him warily toward it along the grassy verge. Within fifteen yards of it, he recognised the white Jaguar, saw the rear door open, the inner light fall on the two figures clambering out of it. Standing on the road, they embraced in a seething kiss. When he released her, she got into the driver's seat, the two doors banged and everything was silent and dark again. She started her engine, floodlit the road and drove swiftly away around the curve. Crushed back into the hedge, he heard Condor's foot-steps approach, pass and recede. In a few moments, the van's door banged tinnily, its headlamps flowered, whirled into the maw of the lane, waddled drunkenly behind the hedges, down toward the sea.

Before he fell asleep that night, Mr Bodkin heard a thousand wavelets scrape the shingle, as during his long life, other countless waves had scraped elsewhere unheard—sounds, moments, places, people to whose lives he had never given a thought. *The Irish Times* rarely recorded such storms of passion and, when it did, they broke and died far away, like the fables that Shakespeare concocted for his entertainment in the theatre. But he knew the Condors. This adulterous woman could shatter their lives as surely as he knew, when he opened his eyes to the sea sun shimmering on his ceiling, she had already shattered his.

It was his custom, on such summer mornings, to rise, strip off his pyjamas, pull on a bathing slip and walk across the track in his slippers, his towel around his neck, down to the edge of the sea for what he called a dip: which meant that since he, too, swam like a stone, he would advance into the sea up to his knees, sprinkle his shoulders, and then, burring happily at the cold sting of it, race back to the prickly gravel to towel his shivering bones. He did it this morning with the eyes of a saint wakened from dreams of sin.

On Tuesday night, he snooped virtuously up the lane and along the carriage road. The red van was not in its shed. But neither was it on the road. Lascivious imaginings kept him awake for hours. He longed for the thunderbolt of God.

On Wednesday night, it was, at first, the same story; but on arriving back at the foot of the lane, there were the empty van and the empty Jaguar before him, flank to flank at the level crossing. He retired at once to his bench, peering up and down the beach, listening for the sound of their crunching feet, determined to wait for them all night, if necessary. Somewhere, that woman was lying locked in his arms. The bared thigh. The wrinkled arms. The crepey neck.

Daylight had waned around nine o'clock, but it was still bright enough for him to have seen shadows against the glister of the water, if there had been shadows to see. He saw nothing. He heard nothing but the waves. It must have been nearly two hours later when he heard their cars starting. By the time he had flitted down to the end of the platform, her lights were already rolling up the lane and his were turning in through his gateway. Mr Bodkin was at the gate barely in time to see his outline dark against the bars of the western sky. As he looked at the van, empty in its shed, it occurred to him that this was one way in which he could frighten him—a warning message left on the seat of the van. But it was also a way in which they could communicate with each other. Her message for him. His answer left early in the morning at her hotel.

On Thursday night, the van lay in its shed. But where was Condor? He walked up the grass track to the cottage and laid his ear to the door. He heard Mary's voice, his angry voice, the mother's shouting. He breathed happily and returned to his bed.

On Friday morning, the Jaguar stood outside Mary's wooden gate. Laying siege? That night, the scarlet van again lay idle in its pen. Wearied by so much walking and watching, he fell asleep over his supper. He was awakened around eleven o'clock by the sound of a car. Scrambling to his door, he was in time to see her wheeling lights hit the sky. He went up the lane to the van, looked around, heard nothing, shone his torch into the cabin and saw the blue envelope lying on the seat. He ripped it open and read it by torchlight. 'Oh, My Darling, for God's sake, where are you? Last night and tonight, I waited and waited. What has happened? You promised! I have only one more night. You are coming back with me, aren't you? If I do not see you tomorrow night, I will throw myself into the sea. I adore you. Connie.' Mr Bodkin took the letter down to the sea, tore it into tiny pieces and, with his arms wide, scattered them over the receding waves.

That Saturday afternoon, on returning from the shop with his weekend purchases in his net bag, there was the Jaguar beside the level crossing, mud-splattered and dusty, its white flanks scarred by the whipping brambless. Rounding the corner of the waiting-room, he saw her on his bench, smoking, glaring at the sparkling sea. She barely lifted her eyes to him. She looked every year of sixty. He bowed and sat on the bench. She smelled of whisky.

'What an exquisite afternoon we are having, Lady Dobson. May I rest my poor bones for a moment? That lane of mine gets longer and longer every day. Has everything been well with you?'

'Quite well, Bodkin, thank you.'

'And, if I may ask, I should be interested to know, you have, I trust, made some progress in your quest?'

'I could hardly expect to with that old woman around everybody's neck. I have laid the seeds of the idea. Molly now knows that she will always be welcome in my house.'

'Wait and see? My favourite motto. Never say die. Colours nailed to the mast. No surrender. It means, I hope, that you are not going to leave us soon.'

'I leave tonight.'

'I do hope the hotel has not been uncomfortable.'

'It is entirely comfortable. It is full of spinsters. They give me the creeps.'

He beamed at the sea and waited.

'Bodkin! There is one person I have not yet seen. For Hilary's sake, I ought to have a word with Condor. Have you seen him around?'

Her voice had begun to crumble. Eyes like grease under hot water. Cigarette trembling.

'Let me think,' he pondered. 'On Thursday? Yes. And again last night. We both played draughts with his mother. He seemed his usual cheerful self.'

She ejected her cigarette and ground it into the dust under her foot.

'Bodkin! Will you, for Christ's sake, tell me what do young people do with their lives in Godforsaken places like this? That lane must be pitch-dark by four o'clock in the winter!'

He looked at his toes, drew his handkerchief from his breast-pocket, and flicked away their dust.

'I am afraid, Lady Dobson, I no longer meet any young people. And, after all, Condor is not a young man, I suppose you could call him a middle-aged man. Or would you?'

She hooted hoarsely.

'And what does that leave me? An old hag?'

'Or me? As the Good Book says, "The days of our years are threescore years and ten; and if by reason of strength they be fourscore years, yet is their strength labour and sorrow; for it is soon cut off, and we fly away".'

She spat it at him:

'You make me sick.'

From under her blue eyelids, she looked at the clouds crimped along the knife of the horizon. He remembered Mary's twisted face when she said, 'He is dying of the lonesome.' She turned and faced him. Harp strings under her chin. Hands mottled. The creature was as old as sin.

'Do you happen to know, Bodkin, if Condor has a girl in these parts? It concerns me, of course, only insofar as, if he has, I need not ask him to come back to us. Has he?'

Mr Bodkin searched the sea as if looking for a small boat in which to escape his conscience.

'I believe he has,' he said firmly.

'Believe? Do you know? Or do you not know?'

'I saw them twice in the lane. Kissing. I presume that means that they are in love.'

'Thank you, Bodkin,' she said brightly. 'In that case, Hilary must get another chauffeur and I must get another lady's maid.' She jumped up. He rose politely. 'I hope you will have a very pleasant winter.' She stared at him hatefully. 'In love? Have you ever in your life been in love? Do you know what it means to be in love?'

'Life has denied me many things, Lady Dobson.'

'Do you have such a thing as a drink in that black coffin of yours?'

'Alas! Only tea. I am a poor man, Lady Dobson. I read in the paper recently that whisky is now as much as six shillings a glass.'

Her closed eyes riveted her to her age like a worn face on an old coin.

'No love. No drink. No friends. No wife. No children. Happy man! Nothing to betray you.'

She turned and left him.

The events of that Saturday night and Sunday morning became public property at the inquest.

Sergeant Delahunty gave formal evidence of the finding of the body on the rocks at Greystones. Guard Sinnot corroborated. Mr T. J. Bodkin was then called. He stated that he was a retired businessman residing in a chalet beside the disused station of Cobbler's Hulk. He deposed that, as usual, he went to bed on the night in question around ten o'clock and fell asleep. Being subject to arthritis, he slept badly. Around one o'clock, something woke him.

CORONER: What woke you? Did you hear a noise?
WITNESS: I am often awakened by arthritc pains in my legs.
CORONER: Are you quite sure it was not earlier than one o'clock? The reason I ask is because we know that the deceased's watch stopped at a quarter to twelve.
WITNESS: I looked at my watch. It was five minutes past one.

Continuing his evidence, the witness said that the night being warm and dry, he rose, put on his dressing-gown and his slippers and walked up and down on the platform to ease his pains. From where he stood, he observed a white car parked in the lane. He went toward it. He recognised it as the property of Lady Constance Dobson, whom he had met earlier in the week. There was nobody in the car. Asked by a juror if he had seen the car earlier in the night, before he went to bed, the witness said that it was never his practice to emerge from his chalet after his supper. Asked by another juror if he was not surprised to find an empty car there at one o'clock at night, he said he was but thought that it might have run out of petrol and been abandoned by Lady Dobson until the morning. It did not arouse his curiosity. He was not a curious man by nature. The witness deposed that he then returned to his chalet and slept until six o'clock, when he rose, rather earlier than usual, and went for his usual morning swim. On the way to the beach, he again examined the car.

CORONER: It was daylight by then?

WITNESS: Yes, sir.

CORONER: Did you look inside the car?

WITNESS: Yes, sir. I discovered that the door was unlocked and I opened it. I saw a lady's handbag on the front seat and a leather suitcase on the rear seat. I saw that the ignition key was in position. I turned it, found the starter and the engine responded at once. At that stage, I became seriously worried.

CORONER: What did you do?

WITNESS: I went for my swim. It was too early to do anything else.

Mr Bodkin further stated that he then returned to his chalet, dressed, shaved, prepared his breakfast and ate it. At seven o'clock, he walked to the house of his nearest neighbours, the Condors, and aroused them. Mr Colm Condor at once accompanied him back to the car. They examined it and, on Mr Condor's suggestion, they both drove in Mr Condor's van to report the incident to the Guards at Ashford.

CORONER: We have had the Guards' evidence. And that is all you know about the matter?

WITNESS: Yes, sir.

CORONER: You mean, of course, until the body was found fully clothed, on the rocks at Greystones a week later; that is to say, yesterday morning, when, with Sir Hilary Dobson and Miss Mary Condor, you helped identify the remains?

WITNESS: Yes, sir.

CORONER: Did you have any difficulty in doing so?
WITNESS: I had some difficulty.
CORONER: But you are satisfied that it was the body of Lady Constance Dobson and no other.
WITNESS: I was satisfied. I also recognised the woven gold bangle she had worn the day I saw her. The teeth were unmistakable.

Dr Edward Halpin of the sanatorium at Newcastle having given his opinion that death was caused by asphyxiation through drowning, the jury, in accordance with the medical evidence, returned a verdict of suicide while of unsound mind. The coroner said it was a most distressing case, extended his sympathy to Sir Hilary Dobson and said no blame attached to anybody.

*   *   *

It was September before I again met Mr Bodkin. A day of infinite whiteness. The waves falling heavily. Chilly. It would probably be my last swim of the year. Seeing him on his bench—chesterfield, bowler hat, grey spats, rolled umbrella (he would need it from now on), his bulging net bag between his feet, his head bent to one side as if he was listening for a train—I again wondered at a couple of odd things he had said at the inquest: such as his reply to a juror that he never emerged from his railway carriage after supper; his answer to the coroner that he was often wakened at night by his arthritis ('I sleep like a dog'), he had told me; ('I have never in my life had a day's illness, apart from chilblains'); and he had observed by his watch that it was five past one in the morning ('I live by the sun and stars'). Also, he had said that from the platform, he had noticed the white car parked at the end of the lane. I had parked my Morris a few moments before at the end of the lane and, as I looked back toward it now, it was masked by the signal-box.

He did not invite me to sit down and I did not. We spoke of the sunless sky. He smiled when I looked at the sky and said. 'Your watch is clouded over.' I sympathised with him over his recent painful experience.

'Ah, yes!' he agreed. 'It was most distressing. Even if she *was* a foolish poor soul. Flighty, too. Not quite out of the top drawer. That may have had something to do with it. A bit spoiled, I mean. The sort of woman, as my dear mother used to say, who would upset a barracks of soldiers.'

'Why on earth do you suppose she did it? But I shouldn't ask; I am sure you want to forget the whole thing.'

'It is all over now. The wheel turns. All things return to the sea. She was crossed in love.'

I stared at him. 'Some man in London?'

He hesitated, looked at me shiftily, slowly shook his head and turned his eyes along his shoulder toward the fields.

'But nothing was said about this at the inquest! Did other people know about it? Did the Condors know about it?'

His hands moved on his umbrella handle.

'In quiet places like this, they would notice a leaf falling. But where so little happens, every secret becomes a buried treasure that nobody mentions. Even though every daisy on the dunes knows all about it. This very morning, when I called on Mary Condor, a hen passed her door. She said, "That hen is laying out. Its feet are clean. It has been walking through grass." They know everything. I sometimes think,' he said peevishly, 'that they know what I ate for breakfast.'

(Was he becoming disillusioned about his quiet beach?)

'How did you know about it? Or are you just guessing?'

He frowned. He shuffled for the second time. His shoulders straightened. He almost preened himself.

'I have my own powers of observation! I can keep my eyes open, too, you know! Sometimes I see things nobody else sees. I can show you something nobody else has ever seen.'

Watching me watch him, he slowly drew out his pocketbook and let it fall open on a large visiting card. I stooped forward to read the name. LADY CONSTANCE DOBSON. His little finger turned it onto its back. There scrawled apparently in red lipstick, was the word *Judas*. When I looked at him, he was smiling triumphantly.

'Where on earth did you find it?'

'That morning at six o'clock, it was daylight. I saw it stuck inside the windscreen wipers'—he hesitated for the last time—'of the Jaguar'.

My mind became as tumbled as a jigsaw. He was lying. How many many other pieces of the jigsaw were missing? Who was it said the last missing bit of every jigsaw is God?

'You did not mention this at the inquest.'

'Should I have? The thought occurred to me. I decided that it would be more merciful not to. There were other people to think of. Sir Hilary, for one. And others.' He replaced his pocketbook and rose dismissively. 'I perceive that you are going for a swim. Be careful. There are currents. The beach shelves rapidly. Three yards out and the gravel slides from under your feet. And nobody to hear you if you shout for help. I had my usual little dip this morning. Such calm. Such utter silence. The water was very cold.'

He bobbed and walked away. I walked very slowly down to the edge of the beach. I tested the water with my hand. He was right. I looked around me. I might have been marooned on some Baltic reef hung between an infinity of clouds and a lustre of a sea gleaming with their iceberg reflections. Not a fishing smack. Not even a cormorant. Not a soul for miles, north and south. Nobody along the railway track. Or was somebody, as he had suggested always watching? If he were concealing something, why had he admitted that he had come out from his railway carriage at all? Why did he choose to mention one o'clock in the morning? Did he know that she had died around midnight? Was he afraid that somebody besides himself might have seen her lights turn down the lane? A timid liar, offering a half-truth to conceal the whole truth?

Above the dunes, I could just see the black roof of his railway carriage. I measured the distance from where I stood and let out a loud 'Help!' for ten seconds, nothing happened. Then his small, dark figure rose furtively behind the dunes. When he saw me, he disappeared.

TWO BOTTLES OF RELISH

Lord Dunsany

*The eighteenth Baron Dunsany, Edward John Moreton Drax Plun-
kett (1878-1957) ws a colourful and exuberant Irish character:
wounded in the Irish Easter Rising of 1916, he was a skilled big game
hunter, national chess champion, and proud owner of the title 'Worst
Dressed Man in Ireland'. He was also a prodigiously imaginative writer of short stories, ranging from fantasy to crime fiction, and the
creator of a number of unique literary characters, including Jorkens,
the teller of tall stories, and John Ripley, 'the old retired detective'
who loves recounting his successful cases. The story that follows,
about a missing girl who may have been murdered and her body
chopped up or burned, is narrated by a man called Smithers, a rather
simple-minded relish salesman, with a mounting sense of unease.
First published in an anonymous anthology,* Powers of Darkness
*(1934), it has been described by Ellery Queen, in his definitive bib-
liography,* The Detective Short Story *(1969), as 'one of the finest
short stories of detection and horror ever written'. It will take the
reader only a few pages to realise just why . . .*

Smithers is my name. I'm what you might call a small man and in a
small way of business. I travel for Num-numo, a relish for meats and
savouries—the world-famous relish I ought to say. It's really quite
good, no delecterious acids in it, and does not affect the heart; so it
is quite easy to push. I wouldn't have got the job if it weren't. But I
hope some day to get something that's harder to push, as of course
the harder they are to push, the better the pay. At present I can just
make my way, with nothing at all over; but then I live in a very expensive flat. It happened like this, and that brings me to my story. And
it isn't the story you'd expect from a small man like me, yet there's
nobody else to tell it. Those that know anything of it besides me, are

all for hushing it up. Well, I was looking for a room to live in in London when first I got my job. It had to be in London, to be central; and I went to a block of buildings, very gloomy they looked, and saw the man that ran them and asked him for what I wanted. Flats they called them; just a bedroom and a sort of a cupboard. Well, he was showing a man round at the time who was a gent, in fact more than that, so he didn't take much notice of me—the man that ran all those flats didn't, I mean. So I just ran behind for a bit, seeing all sorts of rooms and waiting till I could be shown my class of thing. We came to a very nice flat, a sitting-room, bedroom and bathroom, and a sort of little place that they called a hall. And that's how I came to know Linley. He was the bloke that was being shown round.

'Bit expensive,' he said.

And the man that ran the flats turned away to the window and picked his teeth. It's funny how much you can show by a simple thing like. What he meant to say was that he'd hundreds of flats like that, and thousands of people looking for them, and he didn't care who had them or whether they all went on looking. There was no mistaking him, somehow. And yet he never said a word, only looked away out of the window and picked his teeth. And I ventured to speak to Mr Linley then; and I said, 'How about it, sir, if I paid half, and shared it? I wouldn't be in the way, and I'm out all day, and whatever you said would go, and really I wouldn't be no more in your way than a cat.'

You may be surprised at my doing it; and you'll be much more surprised at him accepting it—at least, you would if you knew me, just a small man in a small way of business. And yet I could see at once that he was taking to me more than he was taking to the man at the window.

'But there's only one bedroom,' he said.

'I could make up my bed easy in that little room there,' I said.

'The Hall,' said the man, looking round from the window, without taking his tooth-pick out.

'And I'd have the bed out of the way and hid in the cupboard by any hour you like,' I said.

He looked thoughtful, and the other man looked out over London; and in the end, do you know, he accepted.

'Friend of yours?' said the flat man.

'Yes,' answered Mr Linley.

It was really very nice of him.

I'll tell you why I did it. Able to afford it? Of course not. But I heard him tell the flat man that he had just come down from Oxford and wanted to live for a few months in London. It turned out he wanted just to be comfortable and do nothing for a bit while he looked things over and chose a job, or probably just as long as he could afford it. Well, I said to myself, what's the Oxford manner worth in business, especially a business like mine? Why, simply everything you've got. If I picked up only a quarter of it from this Mr Linley I'd be able to double my sales, and that would soon mean I'd be given something a lot harder to push, with perhaps treble the pay. Worth it every time. And you can make a quarter of an education go twice as far again, if you're careful with it. I mean you don't have to quote the whole of the Inferno to show that you've read Milton; half a line may do it.

Well, about that story I have to tell. And you mightn't think that a little man like me could make you shudder. Well, I soon forgot about the Oxford manner when we settled down in our flat. I forgot it in the sheer wonder of the man himself. He had a mind like an acrobat's body, like a bird's body. It didn't want education. You didn't notice whether he was educated or not. Ideas were always leaping up in him, things you'd never have thought of. And not only that, but if any ideas were about, he'd sort of catch them. Time and again I've found him knowing just what I was going to say. Not thought-reading, but what they call intuition. I used to try to learn a bit about chess, just to take my thoughts off Num-numo in the evening, when I'd done with it. But problems I never could do. Yet he'd come along and glance at my problem and say, 'You probably move that piece first,' and I'd say, 'But where?' and he'd say, 'Oh, one of those three squares.' And I'd say, 'But it will be taken on all of them.' And the piece a queen all the time, mind you. And he'd say, 'Yes, it's doing no good there: you're probably meant to lose it.'

And, do you know, he'd be right.

You see, he'd been following out what the other man had been thinking. That's what he'd been doing.

Well, one day there was that ghastly murder at Unge. I don't know if you remember it. But Steeger had gone down to live with a girl in a bungalow on the North Downs, and that was the first we had heard of him.

The girl had £200, and he got every penny of it, and she utterly disappeared. And Scotland Yard couldn't find her.

Well, I'd happened to read that Steeger had bought two bottles of Num-numo; for the Otherthorpe police had found out everything about him, except what he did with the girl; and that of course attracted my attention, or I should have never thought again about the case or said a word of it to Linley. Num-numo was always on my mind, as I always spent every day pushing it, and that kept me from forgetting the other thing. And so one day I said to Linley, 'I wonder with all that knack you have for seeing through a chess problem, and thinking of one thing and another, that you don't have a go at that Otherthorpe mystery. It's a problem as much as chess,' I said.

'There's not the mystery in ten murders that there is in one game of chess,' he answered.

'It's beaten Scotland Yard,' I said.

'Has it?' he asked.

'Knocked them end-wise,' I said.

'It shouldn't have done that,' he said. And almost immediately after he said, 'What are the facts?'

We were both sitting at supper, and I told him the facts, as I had them straight from the papers. She was a pretty blonde, she was small, she was called Nancy Elth, she had £200, they lived at the bungalow for five days. After that he stayed there for another fortnight, but nobody ever saw her alive again. Steeger said she had gone to South America, but later said he had never said South America, but South Africa. None of her money remained in the Bank where she had kept it, and Steeger was shown to have come by at least £150 just at that time. Then Steeger turned out to be a vegetarian, getting all his food from the greengrocer, and that made the constable in the village of Unge suspicious of him, for a vegetarian was something new to the constable. He watched Steeger after that, and it's well he did, for there was nothing that Scotland Yard asked him that he couldn't tell them about him, except of course of one thing. And he told the police at Otherthorpe five or six miles away, and they came and took a hand at it too. They were able to say for one thing that he never went outside the bungalow and its tidy garden ever since she disappeared. You see, the more they watched him the more suspicious they got, as you naturally do if you're watching a man; so that very soon they were watching every move he made, but if it hadn't been for his being a vegetarian they'd never have started to suspect him, and there wouldn't have been enough evidence even for Linley. Not that they found out anything much against him, except that £150 dropping in from nowhere, and it was Scotland Yard that found that, not the police of Otherthorpe. No, what the constable of Unge found out was about the larch-trees, and that beat Scotland Yard utterly, and beat Linley up to the very last, and of course it beat me. There were ten larch-trees in the bit of a garden, and he'd made some sort of an arrangement with the landlord, Steeger had, before he took the bungalow, by which he could do what he liked with the larch-trees. And then from about the time that little Nancy Elth must have died he cut every one of them down. Three times a day he went at it for nearly a week, and when they were all down he cut them all up into logs no more than two foot long and laid them all in neat heaps. You never saw such work. And what for? To give an excuse, for the axe was one theory. But the excuse was bigger than the axe; it took him a fortnight, hard work every day. And he could have killed a little thing like Nancy Elth without an axe, and cut her up too. Another theory was that he wanted firewood, to make away with the body. But he never used it. He left it all standing there in those neat stacks. It fairly beat everybody.

Well, those are the facts I told Linley. Oh yes, and he bought a big butcher's knife. Funny thing, they all do. And yet it isn't so funny after all; if you've got to cut a woman up, you've got to cut her up; and you can't do that without a knife. Then, there were some negative facts. He hadn't burned her. Only had a fire in the small stove now and then, and only used it for cooking. They got on to that pretty smartly, the Unge constable did, and the men that were lending him a hand from Otherthorpe. There were some little woody places lying round, shaws they call them in that part of the country, the country people do, and they could climb a tree handy and unobserved and get a sniff at the smoke in almost any direction it might be blowing. They did that now and then, and there was no smell of flesh burning, just ordinary cooking. Pretty smart of the Otherthorpe police that was, though of course it didn't help to hang Steeger. Then later on the Scotland Yard men went down and got another fact—negative, but narrowing things down all the while. And that was that the chalk under the bungalow and under the little garden had none of it been disturbed. And he'd never been outside it since Nancy disappeared. Oh yes, and he had a big file besides the knife. But there was no sign of any ground bones found on the file, or any blood on the knife. He'd washed them of course. I told all that to Linley.

Now I ought to warn you before I go any further. I am a small man myself and you probably don't expect anything horrible from me. But I ought to warn you this man was a murderer, or at any rate somebody was; the woman had been made away with, a nice pretty little girl too, and the man that had done that wasn't necessarily going to stop at things you might think he'd stop at. With the mind to do a thing like that, and with the long thin shadow of the rope to drive him further, you can't say what he'll stop at. Murder tales seem nice things sometimes for a lady to sit and read all by herself by the fire. But murder isn't a nice thing, and when a murderer's desperate and trying to hide his tracks he isn't even as nice as he was before. I'll ask you to bear that in mind. Well, I've warned you.

So I says to Linley, 'And what do you make of it?'

'Drains?' said Linley.

'No,' I says, 'you're wrong there. Scotland Yard has been into that. And the Otherthorpe people before them. They've had a look in the drains, such as they are, a little thing running into a cesspool beyond the garden; and nothing has gone down it—nothing that oughtn't to have, I mean.'

He made one or two other suggestions, but Scotland Yard had been before him in every case. That's really the crab of my story, if you'll excuse the expression. You want a man who sets out to be a detective to take his magnifying glass and go down to the spot; to go to the spot before everything; and then to measure the footmarks and pick up the clues and find the knife that the police have over-looked. But Linley never even went near the place and he hadn't got a magnifying glass, not as I ever saw, and Scotland Yard were before him every time.

In fact they had more clues than anybody could make head or tail of. Every kind of clue to show that he'd murdered the poor little girl; every kind of clue to show that he hadn't disposed of the body; and yet the body wasn't there. It wasn't in South America either, and not much more likely in South Africa. And all the time, mind you, that enormous bunch of chopped larchwood, a clue that was staring everyone in the face and leading nowhere. No, we didn't seem to want any more clues, and Linley never went near the place. The trouble was to deal with the clues we'd got. I was completely mys-tified; so was Scotland Yard; and Linley seemed to be getting no for-warder; and all the while the mystery was hanging on me. I mean if it were not for the trifle I'd chanced to remember, and if it were not for one chance word I said to Linley, that mystery would have gone the way of all the other mysteries that men have made nothing of, a darkness, a little patch of night in history.

Well, the fact was Linley didn't take much interest in it at first, but I was so absolutely sure that he could do it, that I kept him to the idea. 'You can do chess problems,' I said.

'That's ten times harder,' he said, sticking to his point.

'Then why don't you do this?' I said.

'Then go and take a look at the board for me,' said Linley.

That was his way of talking. We'd been a fortnight together, and I knew it by now. He meant me to go down to the bungalow at Unge. I know you'll say why didn't he go himself; but the plain truth of it is, that if he'd been tearing about the countryside he'd never have been thinking, whereas sitting there in his chair by the fire in our flat there was no limit to the ground he could cover, if you follow my meaning. So down I went by train next day, and got out at Unge station. And there were the North Downs rising up before me, somehow like music.

'It's up there, isn't it?' I said to the porter.

'That's right,' he said. 'Up there by the lane; and mind to turn to your right when you get to the old yew-tree, a very big tree, you can't mistake it, and then . . .' and he told me the way so that I couldn't go wrong. I found them all like that, very nice and helpful. You see, it was Unge's day at last. Everyone had heard of Unge now; you could have got a letter there any time just then without putting the country or post town; and this was what Unge had to show. I dare say if you tried to find Unge now . . . well, anyway, they were making hay while the sun shone.

Well, there the hill was, going up into sunlight, going up like a song. You don't want to hear about the spring, and all the may rioting, and the colour that came down over everything later on in the day, and all those birds; but I thought, 'What a nice place to bring a girl to.' And then when I thought that he'd killed her there, well I'm only a small man, as I said, but when I thought of her on that hill with all the birds singing, I said to myself, 'Wouldn't it be odd if it turned out to be me after all that got that man killed, if he did murder her.' So I soon found my way up to the bungalow and began prying about, looking over the hedge into the garden. And I didn't find much, and I found nothing at all that the police hadn't found already, but there were those heaps of larch logs staring me in the face and looking very queer.

I did a lot of thinking, leaning against the hedge, breathing the smell of the may, and looking over the top of it at the larch logs, and the neat little bungalow the other side of the garden. Lots of theories I thought of, till I came to the best thought of all; and that was that if I left the thinking to Linley, with his Oxford-and-Cambridge education, and only brought him the facts, as he had told me, I should be doing more good in my way than if I tried to do any big thinking. I forgot to tell you that I had gone to Scotland Yard in the morning. Well, there wasn't really much to tell. What they asked me was, what I wanted. And, not having an answer exactly ready, I didn't find out very much from them. But it was quite different at Unge; everyone was most obliging; it was their day there, as I said. The constable let me go indoors, so long as I didn't touch anything, and he gave me a look at the garden from the inside. And I saw the stumps of the ten larch-trees, and I noticed one thing that Linley said was very observant of me, not that it turned out to be any use, but anyway I was doing my best: I noticed that the stumps had been all chopped anyhow. And from that I thought that the man that did it didn't know much about chopping. The constable said that was a deduction. So then I said that the axe was blunt when he used it; and that certainly made the constable think, though he didn't actually say I was right this time. Did I tell you that Steeger never went outdoors, except to the little garden to chop wood, ever since Nancy disappeared? I think I did. Well, it was perfectly true. They'd watched him night and day, one or another of them, and the Unge constable told me that himself. That limited things a good deal. The only thing I didn't like about it was that I felt Linley ought to have found all that out instead of ordinary policemen, and I felt that he could have too. There'd have been romance in a story like that. And they'd never have done it if the news hadn't gone round that the man was a vegetarian and only dealt at the greengrocers. Likely as not even that was only started out of pique by the butcher. It's queer what little things may trip a man up. Best to keep straight is my motto. But perhaps I'm straying a bit away from my story. I should like to do that for ever—forget that it ever was; but I can't.

Well, I picked up all sorts of information; clues I suppose I should call it in a story like this, though they none of them seemed to lead anywhere. For instance, I found out everything he ever bought at the village, I could even tell you the kind of salt he bought, quite plain with no phosphates in it, that they sometimes put in to make it tidy. And then he got ice from the fishmongers, and plenty of vegetables, as I said, from the greengrocer, Mergin & Sons. And I had a bit of a talk over it all with the constable. Slugger he said his name was. I wondered why he hadn't come in and searched the place as soon as the girl was missing. 'Well, you can't do that,' he said. 'And besides, we didn't suspect at once, not about the girl, that is. We only suspected there was something wrong about him on account of him being a vegetarian. He stayed a good fortnight after the last that was seen of her. And then we slipped in like a knife. But, you see, no one had been enquiring about her, there was no warrant out.'

'And what did you find?' I asked Slugger, 'when you went in?'

'Just a big file,' he said, 'and the knife and the axe that he must have got to chop her up with.'

'But he got the axe to chop trees with,' I said.

'Well, yes,' he said, but rather grudgingly.

'And what did he chop them for?' I asked.

'Well, of course my superiors has theories about that,' he said, 'that they mightn't tell to everybody.'

You see, it was those logs that were beating them.

'But did he cut her up at all?' I asked.

'Well, he said that she was going to South America,' he answered. Which was really very fair-minded of him.

I don't remember now much else that he told me. Steeger left the plates and dishes all washed up and very neat, he said.

Well, I brought all this back to Linley, going up by the train that started just about sunset. I'd like to tell you about the late spring evening, so calm over that grim bungalow, closing in with a glory all round it as though it were blessing it; but you'll want to hear of the murder. Well, I told Linley everything, though much of it didn't seem to me to be worth the telling. The trouble was that the moment I began to leave anything out, he'd know it, and make me drag it in. 'You can't tell what may be vital,' he'd say. 'A tin-tack swept away by a housemaid might hang a man.'

All very well, but be consistent, even if you are educated at Eton and Harrow, and whenever I mentioned Num-numo, which after all was the beginning of the whole story, because he wouldn't have heard of it if it hadn't been for me, and my noticing that Steeger had bought two bottles of it, why then he said that things like that were trivial and we should keep to the main issues. I naturally talked a bit about Num-Numo, because only that day I had pushed close on fifty bottles of it in Unge. A murder certainly stimulates people's minds, and Steeger's two bottles gave me an opportunity that only a fool could have failed to make something of. But of course all that was nothing at all to Linley.

You can't see a man's thoughts, and you can't look into his mind, so that all the most exciting things in the world can never be told of. But what I think happened all that evening with Linley, while I talked to him before supper, and all through supper, and sitting smoking afterwards in front of our fire, was that his thoughts were stuck at a barrier there was no getting over. And the barrier wasn't the difficulty of finding ways and means by which Steeger might have made away with the body, but the impossibility of finding why he chopped those masses of wood every day for a fortnight, and paid, as I'd just found out, £25 to his landlord to be allowed to do it. That's what was beating Linley. As for the ways by which Steeger might have hidden the body, it seemed to me that every way was blocked by the police. If you said he buried it, they said the chalk was undisturbed; if you said he carried it away, they said he never left the place; if you said he burned it, they said no smell of burning was ever noticed when the smoke blew low, and when it didn't they climbed trees after it. I'd taken to Linley wonderfully, and I didn't have to be educated to see there was something big in a mind like his, and I thought that he could have done it. When I saw the police getting in before him like that, and no way that I could see of getting past them, I felt real sorry.

Did anyone come to the house, he asked me once or twice. Did anyone take anything away from it? But we couldn't account for it that way. Then perhaps I made some suggestion that was no good, or perhaps I started talking of Num-numo again, and he interrupted me rather sharply.

'But what would you do, Smithers?' he said. 'What would you do yourself?'

'If I'd murdered poor Nancy Elth?' I asked.

'Yes,' he said.

'I can't ever imagine doing such a thing,' I told him.

He sighed at that, as though it were something against me.

'I suppose I should never be a detective,' I said. And he just shook his head.

Then he looked broodingly into the fire for what seemed an hour.

And then he shook his head again. We both went to bed after that.

I shall remember the next day all my life. I was till evening, as usual, pushing Num-numo. And we sat down to supper about nine. You couldn't get things cooked at those flats, so of course we had it cold. And Linley began with a salad. I can see it now, every bit of it. Well, I was still a bit full of what I'd done in Unge, pushing Num-numo. Only a fool, I know, would have been unable to push it there; but still, I *had* pushed it; and about fifty bottles, forty-eight to be exact, are something in a small village, whatever the circumstances. So I was talking about it a bit; and then all of a sudden I realised that Num-numo was nothing to Linley, and I pulled myself up with a jerk. It was really very kind of him; do you know what he did? He must have known at once why I stopped talking, and he just stretched out a hand and said, 'Would you give me a little of your Num-numo for my salad.'

I was so touched I nearly gave it him. But of course you don't take Num-numo with salad. Only for meats and savouries. That's on the bottle.

So I just said to him, 'Only for meats and savouries.' Though I don't know what savouries are. Never had any.

I never saw a man's face go like that before.

He seemed still for a whole minute. And nothing speaking about him but that expression. Like a man that's seen a ghost, one is tempted to write. But it wasn't really at all. I'll tell you what he looked like. Like a man that's seen something that no one has ever looked at before, something he thought couldn't be.

And then he said in a voice that was all quite changed, more low and gentle and quiet it seemed, 'No good for vegetables, eh?'

'Not a bit,' I said.

And at that he gave a kind of sob in his throat. I hadn't thought he could feel things like that. Of course I didn't know what it was all about; but, whatever it was, I thought all that sort of thing would have been knocked out of him at Eton and Harrow, an educated man like that. There were no tears in his eyes, but he was feeling something horribly.

And then he began to speak with big spaces between his words, saying, 'A man might make a mistake perhaps, and use Num-numo with vegetables.'

'Not twice,' I said. What else could I say?

And he repeated that after me as though I had told of the end of the world, and adding an awful emphasis to my words, till they seemed all clammy with some frightful significance, and shaking his head as he said it.

Then he was quite silent.

'What is it?' I asked.

'Smithers,' he said.

'Yes,' I said.

'Smithers,' said he.

And I said, 'Well?'

'Look here, Smithers,' he said, 'you must 'phone down to the grocer at Unge and find out from him this.'

'Yes?' I said.

'Whether Steeger bought those two bottles, as I expect he did, on the same day, and not a few days apart. He couldn't have done that.'

I waited to see if any more was coming, and then I ran out and did what I was told. It took me some time, being after nine o'clock, and only then with the help of the police. About six days apart they said; and so I came back and told Linley. He looked up at me so hopefully when I came in, but I saw that it was the wrong answer by his eyes.

You can't take things to heart like that without being ill, and when he didn't speak I said, 'What you want is a good brandy, and go to bed early.'

And he said, 'No. I must see someone from Scotland Yard. 'Phone round to them. Say here at once.'

But I said, 'I can't get an inspector from Scotland Yard to call on us at this hour.'

His eyes were all lit up. He was all there all right.

'Then tell them,' he said, 'they'll never find Nancy Elth. Tell one of them to come here, and I'll tell them why.' And he added, I think only for me, 'They must watch Steeger, till one day they get him over something else.'

And, do you know, he came. Inspector Ulton; he came himself.

While we were waiting I tried to talk to Linley. Partly curiosity, I admit. But I didn't want to leave him to those thoughts of his, brooding away by the fire. I tried to ask him what it was all about. But he wouldn't tell me. 'Murder is horrible,' is all he would say. 'And as a man covers his tracks up it only gets worse.'

He wouldn't tell me. 'There are tales,' he said, 'that one never wants to hear.'

That's true enough. I wish I'd never heard this one. I never did actually. But I guessed it from Linley's last words to Inspector Ulton, the only ones that I overheard. And perhaps this is the point at which to stop reading my story, so that you don't guess it too; even if you think you want murder stories. For don't you rather want a murder story with a bit of a romantic twist, and not a story about real foul murder? Well, just as you like.

In came Inspector Ulton, and Linley shook hands in silence, and pointed the way to his bedroom; and they went in there and talked in low voices, and I never heard a word.

A fairly hearty-looking man was the Inspector when they went into that room.

They walked through our sitting-room in silence when they came out, and together they went into the hall, and there I heard the only words they said to each other. It was the Inspector that first broke that silence.

'But why,' he said, 'did he cut down the trees?'

'Solely,' said Linley, 'in order to get an appetite.'

GIRL OF MY DREAMS

Peter Cheyney

Peter Cheyney (1896-1951), famous for his novels of the London underworld and the pair of tough, wise-cracking detectives, Slim Callaghan and Lemmie Caution, may at first seem an unlikely inclusion in this collection. But Reginald Evelyn Peter Southouse-Cheyney was born in County Clare where his forebears had lived for at least two centuries. It was a place to which he loved to return in later years, after he had won fame and fortune following publication of his first brutal and often violent crime stories in the 1930s. Cheyney brought a considerable amount of practical knowledge to his work: he initially trained as a lawyer, then served in World War One in the second battle of the Somme, and afterwards became a journalist and the owner of a detective agency, Cheyney Research Investigations. Among his short stories, the following tale of Michael O'Shaughnessy and a secret love affair which ends in tragedy and death is as ingenious an example of crime passionel *as any I have encountered . . .*

The time has come, I feel, to relate the rather extraordinary events which led to the death of my friend Michael O'Shaughnessy, whose body—as you will doubtless remember—was found in a coppice in the grounds of Honiton Place on the Somersetshire border. The finest brains of Scotland Yard were unable to trace the murderer. Nothing ever came to light except a one-legged sailor from the Argentine who gave himself up for the murder in order—as he put it—'to get a nice rest from his wife,' and who was promptly sent about his business when it was discovered that he was in an intoxicated condition in Lambeth at the time of the tragedy.

The medical evidence shows that my friend Michael had been murdered with a large-bore pistol, and as he had few friends and such relations as he possessed merely regarded the whole business as rather vexing, the matter was left where it was.

Michael O'Shaughnessy was a very charming and attractive man of thirty-five years of age and the fact that he was rather bored with life had nothing to do with this story except that he believed, and often told me, that there is little romance in these utilitarian days; that life is indeed inclined to be weary, flat, stale and unprofitable. The ideal of beautiful woman, he would say, was falling into desuetude. And he would invite me to observe their lot. They stand all day in queues, he said, and thereby acquire large feet; they lack cosmetics and thereby acquire red noses. They waste their nerves, temper and their sweetness in obeying or evading the hundred and one controls that restrict normal life. And, as their menfolk are much too busy getting into or keeping out of financial trouble to spare any time at all in the consideration, much less the practice, of the finer technique of romance, life, thought O'Shaughnessy, was almost redundant.

His background was interesting. He had been born in England of Irish and French parentage. He was tempermental in a queer way. When war broke out in '39 he had been only twenty-six years of age and was learning to be an architect.

He enjoyed the war. To him, it spelled adventure and romance. That tense atmosphere of excitement, which on occasion could make even a doodle-bug seem interesting, brought with it a certain glamour which appealed to him. Naturally, he fought for his country, and as an officer in a cavalry regiment whose light tanks were famous at the Battle of Alamein, he achieved experience, and a philosophy which stood him in good stead during his life and, I must confess, at the moment of his death.

He was tall. His face was inclined to be thin; his figure elegant. He had the soft eyes and high cheek-bones of his Irish ancestry; the charm of manner and ease in conversation of the French—his mother's—side of the family. He liked to laugh, but was not averse from weeping if it would get him any place. He was attractive because . . . well, he couldn't help being attractive.

So much for my murdered friend. Having introduced him to you, I can now recount the events which took place on the night of his death.

*   *   *

At nine o'clock on the night of the 30th January 1948, Michael O'Shaughnessy, who was spending the weekend at the Moat Farm in a romantic and secluded part of the country, the name of which cannot possibly matter, decided to go for a walk. For some reason he was, on this particular evening, a little affected by some peculiar quality in the moonlight. There was something curiously romantic and attractive about it and, walking down the lane which turned into the road that led towards the county border, he noticed, or fancied he noticed, a strange radiance on fields, trees and hedges cast by this full, brilliant and, as it were, tantalising moon.

He walked for some twenty minutes; decided to smoke a cigarette. But he found, when the time came to light it, that a small breeze had sprung up. So he stepped off the road into the little wood that fringed it and, after a minute or two, found himself in a small clearing, at one end of which was a felled tree. He liked this place, sat down on the tree, lit his cigarette and gave himself up to ruminations on the past, present and future.

Quite suddenly he became aware that he was not alone. Sitting on the other end of the tree was the portly figure of a middle-aged gentleman dressed in a suit of shepherd's plaid check. He was smoking a very small cigar and now and then, for some reason best known to himself, he wiped the corner of his mouth delicately with a lady's fine suède glove which he produced from his waistcoat pocket.

O'Shaughnessy gazed at this apparition; wondered how he had arrived on the scene. And he began to get an odd impression that he *knew* this person; that he had seen him before in several places; that, in fact, he had seen him and talked to him in Alamein on the night before the attack, wearing a battle jacket; and somewhere else, wearing something else.

The newcomer turned his head towards O'Shaughnessy, removed his bowler hat courteously and said: 'Good evening, Sir. My name is Krasinsky. I think you know me.'

'I believe I do.' O'Shaughnessy smiled disarmingly. 'But I cannot for the life of me place you.'

'Men never can,' said the other, 'because I am one of those nebulous kinds of person who get about considerably. Some men think I am their conscience; others apprehend me as a sort of astral body driving about the place warning people. They think a thousand things about me.'

'Exactly,' said O'Shaughnessy. 'But—forgive me—I'm rather

puzzled by your sudden arrival here. I didn't see you come through the wood.'

'I didn't,' said Mr Krasinsky. 'I arrive at any place where I wish to be without appreciable effort. And I wanted to be here because I think I should tell you the story of a young friend of mine who looked somewhat like you. He was staying in this part of the world at one time, and circumstances led him, one evening, to a certain mansion not half a mile from here.'

O'Shaughnessy nodded. 'You mean Honiton Place. I've heard about it. In point of fact I'd intended to walk there tonight.'

'A most interesting house,' said Krasinsky. 'Would you care to listen to my story? I think you ought to.'

A pleasurable feeling of anticipation stole over Michael O'Shaughnessy. He felt, for some quite inexplicable reason, that the story which Krasinsky proposed to tell him was bound up with his— O'Shaughnessy's—life.

He said: 'I should like very much to hear it.'

'I'll tell it to you,' said Krasinsky, 'and I'll make it as short as possible because I observe'—he looked at the moon—'that time is getting on. Well then, my young friend, whom I call Armand Dulac, was staying at the Moat Farm, and one night he decided to go for a walk. He walked down this roadway and half a mile further on found the fork in the road. The right side ran away over the hills and disappeared into the horizon. The other, which he took, led him straight to the entrance gates of Honiton Place.

'When he reached them Armand stood by these antique, wrought-iron gates awhile and contemplated the broad parkland that spread out before him. It was dotted with rhododendron bushes, shrubberies and trees. Beyond these, at the top of some terraces, lay the large, historic building. He found it most attractive in the moonlight, which was as bright as it is tonight . . .

'But,' continued Krasinsky, 'he was struck by one thing. He had heard the house spoken of as uninhabited; yet the darkness was interrupted, in one single corner of the second floor, by three lighted windows. Who, he wondered, could possibly be the occupants of such a place, at such a time.

'Now curiosity was a strong point with him, as it is with most young men, so he followed the carriage drive, mounted the terraces and approached the house. When he got there the entrance doors were, he was amazed to find, open, and he walked through large and imposing portals into the hall. There he received a second surprise, for the moonlight, flooding through high stained glass windows, disclosed that, far from being empty, the wide hall before him was furnished with what seemed to be costly antique furniture. Valuable oil-paintings graced the walls and here and there delightful figures, carved in bronze or marble, looked down at him stonily.

'He stood in the middle of this hall possessed by a strange, and possibly odd, desire to know more about the place. Then he concluded that as he had found the doors open it was his duty to find his way up to the apartment, the windows of which were lighted, and to inform the occupant who might, he thought, be the caretaker, that the entrance doors were unlocked.'

Krasinsky inhaled from his small cigar which, however much he smoked it, never seemed to grow any smaller. He continued: 'Armand then ascended the flight of wide marble stairs on the other side of the hall and presently found himself in the first floor gallery which surrounded the hall. The walls of this gallery were lined from floor to ceiling with mirrors, and it was only after some time and by the aid of the moonlight that he discovered the glass knob on one of the mirrors.

'He turned the knob. The door opened. Armand stepped through and closed the mirror door behind him. He was facing a curving carpeted staircase and, without more ado, began to walk up it. At the top was a small landing and on the other side a translucent glass door. Inside this glass door there was a softly diffused light which intrigued him. He opened the door and went in.

'Now,' said Krasinsky, 'I shall have a little difficulty in describing to you the atmosphere in which my young and enterprising friend found himself. He was in a corridor, thickly carpeted, and furnished with rare furniture and pictures. There was a strange atmosphere about the place—a suggestion of the most delightful perfume—a certain fascinating langour in the air which touched something within him. At the end of the corridor he saw a door ajar. He approached it, knocked, and a voice said: "Come in . . ."'

Krasinsky smiled. 'Are you interested, Mr O'Shaughnessy?'

O'Shaughnessy nodded. 'I'm more than interested. I'm enthralled. Please go on.'

'I should explain to you,' said Krasinsky, 'that the words "Come in" are two very ordinary words. In point of fact they are spoken by millions of people all over the world in all sorts of circumstances every day. But *these* two words were different. I would like to be able to describe to you,' said Krasinsky, stroking the head of a baby white owl which had curved down and settled on his hand, 'the quality of the voice which uttered them; the low and vibrant tone; the superb and complete enunciation of the two words, but I am afraid that I have not sufficient vocabulary. Let it suffice that my young friend was so entirely shattered at hearing these two words so beautifully spoken that he felt a little weak in the knees. It was only after a minute's hesitation that he was able to push open the door and step into the room.'

'And what did he find there?' asked O'Shaughnessy.

'I will tell you,' answered Krasinsky. 'The room was long, with a low ceiling. The walls were of a rather mysterious shade of grey, but the lighting which was concealed above them gave them an even more mysterious colour. Opposite to him, beside a large log fire which glowed brightly, was a lady. It was she who had said "Come in".' Krasinsky sighed heavily. 'Armand gazed at her with eyes that almost popped from their sockets because never in his life had he seen a woman with so much beauty, with so much allure . . . well, so much everything . . .' murmured Krasinsky, spreading his hands, at which the white owl flew away.

'Her face was superbly modelled. Her hair was auburn and fell about her shoulders. Her eyes, which were of an exquisite shade of hazel, regarded him coolly. But it was her mouth which fascinated Armand. It is impossible,' said Krasinsky, '*quite* impossible for me to describe the tremulous beauty of her mouth.' He paused and drew on his cigar; then: 'Armand stood there and eventually was able to speak. He said: "I'm sure you'll forgive me for coming here but I was walking in these parts and, inspecting the house, noticed that the front doors were open. I thought I'd better come in and tell you."

'She said very softly: "How nice of you. Wouldn't you like a drink? And please sit down." Armand sat down. He found it impossible to take his eyes from her. He watched the superb grace with which she moved to a nearby table; poured out the whisky and soda; brought it to him. When she came near him he trembled at her proximity because there came to his nostrils a suggestion of such exquisite perfume that his senses were inclined to reel.

'He took the drink from her. He said hoarsely—and as he spoke the words it was almost as if someone else were speaking—"I don't think I've ever seen anybody quite as lovely as you are. I don't think I've ever seen anyone who speaks or moves as exquisitely as you do. I think I adore you".'

Krasinsky sighed again. 'Don't you think that was rather charming?' he said.

O'Shaughnessy started. 'I think it was utterly charming,' he said in his agreeable voice. 'What happened then?'

Krasinsky continued: 'The lovely lady was not at all surprised at this declaration of love,' he said. 'She returned to her couch, sat down and regarded my young friend Armand with her large, melting hazel eyes. She examined him carefully from top to toe. Then she nodded her head and smiled. She said in the same ravishing voice: "How strange that you should say that, because I have thought about you for a long time. I have sat here night after night hoping that somebody that looked like you would come here and talk to me. That is why I had the front doors left open. I think I shall always love you.".'

Krasinsky exhaled cigar smoke. 'Now what do you think of that?' he asked.

O'Shaughnessy shook his head. 'I can't think,' he said. 'Go on.'

Krasinsky went on: 'Imagine the stupor into which this declaration from the lady threw Armand. He found himself unable to move, to speak or think. He would have sat there, I have no doubt, permanently, but for one thing . . .'

'What?' asked O'Shaughnessy impatiently.

'This,' said Krasinsky. 'The lady moved a little. Then she got up. She stood in front of the fire, looking at him. Then she said softly, and with a most delightful smile: "Come here, my darling".'

Krasinsky regarded his finger-nails. 'He went there,' he said. 'And at this moment, presumably by some occult influence, the lights went out.'

He stopped speaking. From the other end of the tree-trunk came a long sigh.

Krasinsky drew on his small cigar. 'It was just after midnight,' he said quietly, 'when Armand Dulac, having taken a lingering farewell of his most beautiful companion, left the apartment and began to descend the curving staircase that led to the gallery below. As he reached the bend in the stairs he stopped and his jaw sagged a little, for approaching him rapidly, no less than two stairs at a time, was a very large, stalwart, black-bearded and burly gentleman whose normal ferocity of countenance was barely concealed by a frosty smile.

'This person stopped three stairs below Armand and regarded him with undoubted hostility, tinged with curiosity. Armand moved to the side of the stair. He said: "Good evening." The other gentleman, who was immaculately dressed in a dinner suit, said: "I hope it will be, sir." His accent was unmistakably Polish. He went on: "I observe that you are leaving my wife's apartment. I shall be grateful if you will return with me in order that we may indulge in a little talk. Don't you think," he added sternly, "that a little explanation might be in order, having regard to the time, the circumstances, my absence and my wife's predilection for love?"

'Armand shrugged his shoulders. What could he say?' asked Krasinsky, regarding O'Shaughnessy with equanimity. 'So he allowed the Polish gentleman to pass him and followed him docilely into the apartment, along the exotic corridor, past another open door, through which the large gentleman put his head and said politely: "Good evening, my dear". Then to the end of a smaller corridor, through a door and into a comfortable and well-furnished library.

'Armand stood in the middle of the room whilst his host pulled two large armchairs in front of the fire. He accepted one and sat down. The Polish gentleman sat in the other. He beamed. He said: "Sir, my name is Count Alexis Michalovski."

'Armand said: "I'm charmed to meet you. I am Armand Dulac."

'"Excellent," said the Count. "Now having presented ourselves to one another we can indulge in a little conversation. It will be quite obvious to you, sir, that I have brought you back here for the purpose of killing you. I return to my wife's apartment at midnight to find you leaving with an expression of equanimity on your face which can only be likened to that of a cat which has swallowed a canary—the canary being, in this case, the wife of my bosom. It will be obvious to you as a gentleman that this situation is not possible. Therefore you must die. Do you understand?"

'Armand thought that life was sufficiently sweet, having regard to what had happened earlier in the evening, to make some effort to prolong it. So he said: "Sir, I should like to tell you that you are making a very grave error. At ten o'clock this evening I did not know of the existence of your wife; I had barely heard of the existence of this house. I did not imagine it was inhabited. I came out for a walk. I came through the iron gates because in the moonlight I thought that this mansion looked old, romantic and interesting. I saw that there were three lighted windows on the second floor; then I noticed that the front doors were open. I looked into the hall and I saw that there were some valuable pictures, antiques, and so on, there. I concluded that it was my duty to tell the caretaker or whoever occupied the mansion that the front doors were open and that any burglar could have entered and stolen what he wanted."

'The Count fingered his moustache. He said: "I am not certain that some burglar has not done exactly that thing, even if his interest was not in pictures." He paused to regard Armand for a long time. "You know, Mr Dulac," he continued, "I'm rather inclined to believe your story. You have about you an air of innocence and truth. Also, I am reminded of my grandfather."

'"Indeed," said Armand. The more prolonged the conversation, he thought, the more his chances of life.

'"Yes, indeed," said the Count. "My grandfather—Count Alexandrei Michalovski—was exceedingly partial to Englishmen. When I was a little boy he used to talk to me about 'the word of an Englishman'. In those days it was considered to be extremely good."

'The Count got up from his chair; began to walk about the room with long strides. "I am inclined to believe your story, Mr Dulac. In fact, I will go so far as to say that I *do* believe it. I hope my acknowledgment of your veracity pleases you."

'"Yes, indeed," said Armand with a sigh. "I'm most grateful to you, sir. Naturally, I expected to be believed because I was telling the truth." He added under his breath: "May God forgive me".

'The Count said: "Very well then, all that remains is for me to wish you a very good evening." Armand got up. They walked down the corridor into the main passage towards the entrance to the apartment. The Count held the door open. He said: "I wish to tell you this, sir: I have decided that I will believe what you say, mainly because I like the shape of your face and also because in some vague way you remind me of my grandfather. But I should also tell you that if I ever see you inside this house again I shall, with pleasure and with a certain horse-pistol which I possess, without one moment's hesitation, murder you. Do you understand?"

'Armand said: "I understand perfectly."

'"Then, goodnight, Mr Dulac," said the Count. "As you go down the stairs you will observe on the landings, double electric light switches. The upper ones illuminate the floor before you; the lower one on each landing turns out the light above you, so that you will have no difficulty in finding your way out." He turned away, closed the door behind Armand and disappeared.

'Armand sighed. He thought that not only was there a little romance left in life, but also a certain amount of luck. He began to descend the curving staircase but, slightly disturbed, and incoherent in his mind at the events of the evening, as he got to the bottom he switched the wrong switch, so plunging the staircase behind him and the gallery in front of him into darkness. Worse, he found himself unable to find the switch again, and he stood there, on the threshold of the wide gallery surrounded by mirrors, not knowing literally or metaphorically which way to turn. For the moon had disappeared and the place was dark with an inky darkness.

'Armand considered the situation. He thought that if he could find the flight of marble stairs that led to the main hall, he could grope his way down, and once there surely, he concluded, it would be a matter of time before he found the entrance doors.'

Krasinsky exhaled cigar smoke. 'Do you not find this a very interesting story, Captain O'Shaughnessy?' he enquired.

O'Shaughnessy started. 'I am *very* much interested,' he said. 'I don't know why but I've never been quite so much interested in my life.'

'That,' said Krasinsky, 'is comprehensible. I will continue. Our friend Armand then took a few cautious and diffident steps in the direction, as he thought, of the marble stairway. But just at this moment he tripped over some small projection, fell forward, shot over the edge of the balaustrade and pitched head foremost into an immense Grecian urn which stood immediately beneath the gallery almost as if it intended itself as a receptacle for him.'

Krasinsky shrugged his shoulders. 'He must have struck his head slightly against the side as he fell,' he said, 'for at this moment an even inkier darkness engulfed him and he lay in the bottom of the urn unconscious . . .'

O'Shaughnessy experienced a peculiar feeling. He could no longer see the figure of Krasinsky at the other end of the tree-trunk. He could no longer see anything. He thought that the moon must have gone behind a cloud. He felt vaguely bemused and bewildered. His head ached. He found himself for some reason no longer sitting on the tree-trunk but lying in a recumbent position. He put out his hands, to discover that they touched stone walls which were cold. He sat up in amazement. What *had* happened? He felt in his pocket for his cigarette lighter; found it; snapped it on.

With the aid of the light he looked about him. Utter astonishment overcame him because, believe it or not, he found himself sitting in the bottom of what he took to be an immense vase for no earthly reason that he could think of. He got up. With difficulty, in spite of his agility, he managed to scramble out of the vase; to drop down on the other side. Now the moon came out again.

He was standing at the side of just such a large hallway as Krasinsky had described to him a short while before. But what was this? What was he doing in this place? How had he arrived here? Obviously, this was the scene of Armand Dulac's adventure which Krasinsky had recounted. Dreamily, O'Shaughnessy remembered it. But what had *he* to do with this place? *Why should he be here?*

He moved towards the wide flight of marble stairs, sat down and considered the matter. Either he was mad or he was sane. If he was sane he must somehow have dreamed the encounter with Krasinsky; dreamed the whole of the story which Krasinsky had told him—the story of Armand Dulac.

He remembered exactly what had happened. He had been taking a walk; had stepped off the road into the clearing to light a cigarette; had sat down on the tree-trunk where he met Krasinsky. He shrugged his shoulders. There was no use in going over it. Here he was and what was he going to do?

He began to smile. His native curiosity asserted itself. Surely, thought he, if I know this place because Krasinsky or somebody told me of it; if I know it well enough to be here, then the rest of the story must be true. O'Shaughnessy remembered the description of the mirrored gallery on the first floor, the concealed door with the glass knob which led to the curving staircase by which one reached the apartment of the lovely lady. He thought: Why not see if such a gallery exists; if such a door with its attendant glass door-knob exists?

The moon through the stained glass windows was helpful. He ascended the wide marble stairs. At the top he found himself in the mirrored gallery. He walked slowly round, searching the reflecting walls for the door-knob. After ten minutes, with a sigh of relief, he found it. He pulled the knob. The door opened and he stepped through on to the stairway. He ascended the stairs slowly.

At the top he knew he would find a glass door. All he had to do was to push it open. At the end of a corridor, if he remembered rightly, was Madame's drawing-room and next to it her bedroom. He reached the top of the staircase, opened the glass door. He stepped into the corridor. To his nostrils came the vague and exotic perfume that Krasinsky had mentioned.

O'Shaughnessy walked slowly along the passage. He had reached the end; was considering tapping on the door in front of him, when at the end of the shorter passage a door opened and, framed in the doorway, he saw the figure of the Count.

Here was something which he had *not* anticipated. His heart jumped a little; but he regained confidence when he saw that the Count was smiling.

'I am very glad to see you again,' said that gentleman· 'Won't you come in?'

O'Shaughnessy moved slowly down the short passage and into the library. The Count closed the door and indicated the armchair in front of the fire.

'I am extremely surprised to see you back so soon, Mr Dulac,' he said. 'I warned you what would happen, didn't I?'

O'Shaughnessy said: 'I'm afraid you are making a mistake, Count. My name is not Dulac. My name is Michael O'Shaughnessy. I came out for a walk and——'

'Nonsense,' said the Count. 'How did you know the geography of this house? You knew, sir, because you are Armand Dulac and you were here less than an hour ago. In this room you told me a story which I desired to believe. I believed it at that time, although, after you had gone and I had looked into my wife's bedroom and observed the seraphic expression on her face, I decided I had made a mistake in believing you.

'And now, after my warning, you have the effrontery to return. You know exactly what is going to happen to you?'

O'Shaughnessy thought: This really isn't so good. But he was overcome by a sense of the strangest philosophy. He knew what the Count had threatened to Armand Dulac. He knew that the same threat menaced himself—more especially as the Count was certain that he *was* Dulac. And was that to be wondered at?

O'Shaughnessy gave it up. He said: 'I presume you are referring to the horse-pistol, sir?'

The Count nodded amiably. 'Exactly,' he said. 'I should like to show it to you.' He moved to an old carved cupboard in the corner of the room, opened it, produced an immense horse-pistol. 'This pistol, Sir, belonged to my grandfather, of whom I spoke—that one who was so well inclined towards Englishmen. It is a large pistol and takes an extremely large ball. But I assure you you need not fear that. I am a crack shot and death, I believe, is practically instantaneous. Would you care to stand up, as I hate to shoot at sitting targets?'

O'Shaughnessy stood up. He said: 'If you will pardon the interruption, Count, I think you will agree that a man who is about to die has a right to ask one favour.'

'Certainly,' said the Count with a smile. 'If it is possible. What do you want?'

O'Shaughnessy said: 'We have a proverb in this country that one might as well be hanged for a sheep as a lamb. It is quite useless for me to point out to you that I am not Armand Dulac because I quite understand that it would be impossible for you to believe that. If I were you I should not believe it myself, because it seems to me that some rather extraordinary occult forces have been at work. However, to return to the favour I wish you to grant me. In the circumstances, and having regard to what is in your mind, I do not think it would do you any harm to permit me merely to take a farewell glance at your most beautiful wife, who is, I believe, asleep. That is all I ask.'

'But why not?' said the Count with a smile. 'I grant this favour willingly. I will await your return expectantly.'

O'Shaughnessy murmured his thanks, left the library, walked down the passageway and pushed open the door of the bedroom. He looked in.

Lying in the middle of the wide bed, on which was a coverlet of embossed green velvet, lay the most beautiful creature he had ever seen in his life. Her bosom rose and fell with extreme regularity; her slightly parted lips showed exquisite teeth.

O'Shaughnessy gazed at her in wonderment; then, with a slight sense of dread, he realised that he must go. He smiled at her. He said softly: 'Goodnight, my dear.'

She moved a little. She murmured sleepily: 'Goodnight, darling.'

O'Shaughnessy sighed and turned away.

In the library, the Count was standing in front of the fire, a whisky and soda in one hand, the horse-pistol in the other.

He asked: 'How do you think she looked?'

'Unutterably delightful,' said O'Shaughnessy. 'I should like to tell you, sir, that I think it was worth it. I no longer fear death.'

'That,' said the Count, 'is the spirit. Would you care to help your-self to a whisky and soda?' He indicated the sideboard.

O'Shaughnessy went to the sideboard. Turning his back on the Count in the process, he mixed a stiff whisky and soda. He knew that as the glass touched his lips the Count would fire the pistol, and that would be the end of Captain Michael O'Shaughnessy.

He raised the glass slowly towards his mouth. Then several things happened simultaneously. The door opened and the lady, in a lace robe, stood framed in the doorway. She said to the Count: 'Alexis . . . must you do this . . .? It always makes such a noise . . .'

At the same moment O'Shaughnessy heard the report of the pis-tol; dropped the glass; crashed to the floor.

This then was death!

Darkness descended upon him.

*   *   *

O'Shaughnessy opened his eyes. He lay flat on his back looking up at the moon. After a little while he sat up. He found himself leaning against the felled tree-trunk in the clearing. He was alive. He had not been shot.

He began to laugh. The whole thing, of course, was unutterably ridiculous. The whole thing had been a dream. He remembered some time ago coming into the clearing and sitting on the felled tree-trunk to light a cigarette. He had, he supposed, fallen asleep during the few seconds that had elapsed before he had fallen off the log—those few seconds which can be so extended to aeons of time in dreams. He had dreamed the whole thing; had dreamed the meeting with Krasinsky, the gentleman in the check suit who had sat on the other end of the tree; he had dreamed the story of Armand Dulac and the mysterious house and the lighted windows; he had dreamed of finding himself there; of the Count, the horse-pistol and the very lovely lady.

A hell of a dream, thought O'Shaughnessy. It had been so realistic that he had almost lived it.

He got up, brushed some dry leaves from his clothes. He lit a cigarette. Life, he thought, was not so unromantic after all, even if romance only occurred in dreams.

He crossed the clearing; found the road; began to walk up it. It was a fine night and the moonlight was still cold and hard. O'Shaughnessy stepped out manfully. Ten minutes' walking brought him to a fork in the road. The right fork ran away over the hills; disappeared over the horizon.

Dimly, O'Shaughnessy remembered Krasinsky in the dream, telling him about that fork.

He took the left road. In three minutes' time he found himself face to face with old, wrought-iron gates. He walked through. Before him, at the end of the long carriage drive, cleaving a large park, stood a house. It was large and old, and it was in darkness except that, on the second floor, three windows at the corner were lighted.

Slowly, almost in spite of himself, O'Shaughnessy began to walk along the carriage drive towards the house. He mounted the terraces and approached the entrance. He thought: It is quite impossible that I shall find the doors open.

He found the doors open. He went in. The moonlight, flooding through the stained glass windows, showed him a hall which he knew—the hall which Krasinsky had described to him in the dream . . .

Or was it a dream . . .?

Slowly he crossed the hall, began to mount the flight of wide marble stairs that led upwards to the mirrored gallery. If the dream had been true, he thought, somewhere in that mirrored gallery was a door with a glass knob. He looked at the wall.

In front of him was the glass knob.

He put out his hand and pulled the knob towards him. The door opened. He went through. Before him lay the curving staircase leading upwards to the glass door.

He sighed happily. Slowly, smiling to himself, he began to ascend the stairs towards the glass door. . . .

ALL IN THE WAY
YOU LOOK AT IT

Edmund Crispin

Despite a modest output of less than a dozen books, Edmund Crispin (1921-), born Robert Bruce Montgomery, has an 'enviable reputation as a master of detective fiction through his ability to construct baffling puzzles, his sense of humour, and his ability to entertain', according to Chris Steinbrunner and Otto Penzler, the editors of The Encyclopedia of Mystery and Detection *(1976). It was the boy's Irish mother who instilled in him a love of Ireland and a passion for crime stories which he read avidly until entering the genre himself in 1944 with* The Case of the Gilded Fly. *This was to prove the first of several cases solved by Gervase Fen, Professor of English Language and Literature at Oxford, said to be 'the only literary critic turned detective in the whole of fiction'. Although many of Fen's cases take place in England, Crispin drew on a number of Irish communities with which he was familiar for the background to cases such as the one here, in which a murder committed for passion generates a most singular kind of justice.*

Seven o'clock . . . the gathering darkness was accentuated by a fog which had appeared dispiritingly at about tea-time. Looking across the river, you could no longer make out the half-demolished Festival buildings on the far side; and although October was still young, the sooty trees on the Embankment had already surrendered their stoic green to the first spears of the cold, and there were few homekeeping folk hardy enough to resist the temptation of a fire. Presently, to a servile nation-wide juggling with clocks, Summer Time would officially end. In the meanwhile, it seemed that Nature's edict had anticipated Parliament's by a matter of several days; so that more

212

213 ALL IN THE WAY YOU LOOK AT IT   213

than one belated office-worker, scurrying to catch his bus in Whitehall or the Strand, shivered a little, and hunched his shoulders, as he met the cold vapour creeping into London from the Thames . . .

In a room high up in a corner of New Scotland Yard, a room where the lights had had to be turned on more than two hours ago, Detective-Inspector Humbleby produced a sherry decanter and two glasses from a filing cabinet implausibly marked *Jewel Thefts*, and displayed them to his visitor, who said: 'I didn't know you were allowed to keep drink on the premises.'

'We're not.' Humbleby poured the sherry without any special sign of perturbation. 'And I,' he added, 'am the only officer in the entire building who does. There's discipline for you . . . But look here, Gervase, are you sure you wouldn't like to go on to the club, or wherever we're dining, and let me join you as soon as this call has come through?'

'No, no.' And Gervase Fen, Professor of English Language and Literature in the University of Oxford, shook his head emphatically. 'It's perfectly comfortable here. What's more, your sherry'—he sipped experimentally and his face brightened—'your sherry is too good to leave. But what is the call? Anything important?'

'A routine report. From a pleasant enough though rather ponderous colleague called Bolsover, of the Mid-Wessex CID. They dragged me in to work with him on a case,' said Humbleby, without relish, 'arising out of primitive rustic passions. Tuesday and Wednesday I was on the spot where the thing happened, but then yesterday I had to travel back here so as to give evidence this morning at the Elderton trial, and Bolsover promised to telephone me here this evening and let me know if there was anything new.'

'What sort of case?'

'Murder. It makes my twentieth this year. There are times when I wish I'd specialised in art forgeries, or something peaceful and infrequent like that. Lloyd Jones, who's our best man for that kind of thing, has done practically nil for the last six months. . . . However, it's no use moaning, I suppose.'

'Will you have to go back to Wessex?'

'Yes, tomorrow—unless in the meantime Bolsover's solved the thing on his own. I'm rather hoping he has, and that that's why he's late with his call.' Humbleby raised his glass to the light and contemplated its contents with solemn gloom. 'It's been an exasperating business, and the sooner it's done with, the better I shall be pleased. I don't like Wessex, either. I don't like any bucolic place.'

'Well, but what is the problem?'

'An alibi. We know who *did* the killing—we're morally certain, that is—but the wretched fellow has an alibi and I can't for the life of me see the flaw in it.'

A little superciliously, Fen sniffed. His long, lean form was sprawled gracelessly in the office's only tolerable chair, his ruddy clean-shaven face wore an expression of credulity, and his brown hair, ineffectually plastered down with water, stood up, as usual, in mutinous spikes at the crown of his head.

'Perhaps there isn't a flaw in it,' he suggested. 'It wouldn't be the first time a moral certainty had been turned out to be a total delusion. What sort of a moral certainty is it, anyway?'

'It's a question,' said Humbleby, 'of fingerprints. A certain man's fingerprints were found on the weapon with which the murder was committed. The prints were slightly blurred, I'll grant you; someone wearing gloves *could* have used the gun subsequently, and left the prints intact. But then, this man's explanation of how they came to be there is a demonstrable lie—and what's more he has a strong motive for the crime. So you see how it is.'

'I'm not sure that I do,' said Fen. 'Not so far. But since we've got to wait for our dinner, we may as well pass the time usefully: tell me about it.'

Humbleby sighed, glancing first at his wrist-watch and then at the telephone which stood mute by his elbow. Then, abruptly reaching a decision, he got up, pulled the curtains to across the windows, dispensed more sherry, and finally settled himself back into the desk-chair with the air of one who is now prepared to stand a long siege. 'Cassibury Bardwell,' he began suddenly, 'is the scene. I don't know if you've ever been there?' Fen shook his head.

'Well, it's a hybrid sort of place, too big to be a village and too small to be a town. The houses are almost all built of a damp-looking grey stone, and the rainwater pours down the surrounding hill-slopes into the main streets from all points of the compass, all year round. The nearest railway station is miles away, and the people are in every sense inbred. They're chiefly occupied with—well, *farming*, I suppose,' said Humbleby dubiously. 'But it's not, in any event, a very prosperous locality. In the countryside, round about, there are, apart from the farms, a few remote, inaccessible, horrid little cot-

cottages, and in one of these, tended only by a sister of advancing years, lived the protagonist of my tale.'

'More matter,' said Fen, somewhat restively, 'with less art.'

'Unconscious of his doom'—Humbleby had at last found a cheroot, and was applying fire to it from a desk lighter—'unconscious of his doom, the little victim, aged about 30 and by name of Joshua Ledlow, which goes to show the potency of the tradition of Biblical nomenclature in these less accessible rural places—the little victim . . . What was I saying?'

'Really, Humbleby . . .'

'Here is this Joshua, then.' All at once Humbleby abandoned frivolity and became businesslike. 'Thirty years old, unmarried, of a rather sombre and savage temperament, socially a cut above the farm labourer and living modestly on money left him by a farmer father. He is looked after by his sister Cicely, a good ten years older than he is, who shows no particular fondness for him and who would in any case prefer to be looking after a husband, but who remains unwooed and, having no fortune of her own, housekeeps for Joshua as a respectable substitute for earning a living. Joshua, meanwhile, is courting, the object of his fancy being a heavily built girl called Vashti Winterbourne, who appears to have cast herself for the role of Cassibury Bardwell's *femme fatale*. She didn't seem to me, when I met her, to be physically very well suited for this task, but the local standard of female beauty is extraordinarily low, so I suppose . . . Well, anyway, you see what I mean.

'Now, as you'd expect, Joshua isn't alone in his admiration for this rustic charmer. He has a rival, by name Arthur Penge, by vocation the local ironmonger; and it is clear that Vashti will soon have to make up her mind which of these two suitors she is going to marry. In the meantime, relations between the two men degenerate into something like open hostility, the situation being complicated by the fact that Joshua's sister Cicely has fallen in love with Penge, thereby converting the original triangle into a sort of—um—quadrangle. So there you have all the ingredients for a thoroughly explosive mixture—and in due course it does, in fact, explode.

'With that much preliminary,' continued Humbleby rather grandly, 'I can go on to describe what happened last Saturday and Sunday. What happened on *Saturday* was a public quarrel, of epic proportions, between Joshua, Cicely, and Penge. This enormous row took place in the entrance-hall of *The Jolly Ploughboy*, which is by just a fraction the less repellent of Cassibury's two pubs, and consisted of (*a*) Penge telling Joshua to lay off Vashti, (*b*) Cicely telling Penge to lay off Vashti and take her, Cicely, to wife instead, (*c*) Penge telling Cicely that no man not demonstrably insane would ever dream of marrying *her*, and (*d*) Joshua telling Penge that if he didn't keep away from Vashti in the future, he, Joshua, would have much pleasure in slitting his, Penge's, throat for him. Various other issues were raised, apparently, of a supplementary kind, but these were the chief items; and when the quarrellers at last separated and went home, they were all, not unnaturally, in a far from forgiving frame of mind.

'Note, please, that this quarrel was quite certainly genuine. I mention the point because Bolsover and I wasted a good deal of energy investigating the possibility that Penge and Cicely were somehow in cahoots together—that the quarrel so far as they were concerned was a fake. However, the witnesses we questioned weren't having any of that; they told us roundly that if Cicely was acting, they were Hottentots, and we were forced to believe them, the more so as one of them was the local doctor, who had to be called in to deal with Cicely's subsequent fit of hysterics. No chance of collusion in that department, then. Mind you, I not saying that if Penge had visited Cicely afterwards, and abased himself and asked her to marry him, she mightn't have forgiven him; she's not, poor soul, of an age at which you can afford to take too much umbrage at the past behaviour of a repentant suitor. But the established fact is that between the quarrel and the murder next day he definitely didn't visit her or communicate with her in any way. With the exception of a single interlude of one hour (and of the half hour during which he must have been committing the crime), his movements are completely accounted for from the moment of the quarrel up to midnight on the Sunday; and *during* that one hour, when he *might* (for all we know) have gone to make his apologies to the woman, she was occupied with entertaining two visitors who can swear that he never came near her.'

'I take it,' Fen interposed, 'that this hypothesis of Cicely and Penge working together would have solved your alibi problem for you.'

'It would have, certainly, if there'd been evidence for it. But in actual fact, the evidence completely excludes it—and you must just accept that, I'm afraid . . . But now let me get on with the story. The next event of any consequence was on Sunday morning, when Cicely broke her ankle by falling out of a tree.'

'A *tree*?'

'An apple tree. She'd been picking the fruit, it seems. Anyway, the effect of this accident was of course to immobilise her and hence, in the event, to free her from any possible suspicion of having herself murdered her brother Joshua, since his body was found some considerable distance from their cottage.'

'You think the killing was done at the place where the body was found, do you?'

'We're certain of it. The bullet went clean through the wretched man's head and buried itself in a tree trunk behind him—and that's a set-up which you can't fake convincingly, however hard you try: it's no use just firing a second bullet into the tree, because it's got to have traces of human blood and brains on it . . . Cicely, then, is in the clear, unless you feel inclined to postulate her hobbling a couple of miles on crutches with a view to doing her brother in.

'The crime was discovered at about 10 o'clock that evening by several people in a party, one of whom fell over Joshua's corpse in the dark: none of these people features in any other way in the affair, so I needn't specify them at all. The *place* was a little-frequented footpath on the direct route between Joshua's cottage and the centre of Cassibury, approximately two miles from the former and one mile from the latter. And I may as well say at once, to avoid describing the scene in detail, that all the obvious lines of investigation—footprints, position of the body, threads of clothing on brambles, and so forth—led absolutely nowhere. However, there was just one substantial clue: I mean the revolver—a great cannon of a thing, an old .45—which Bolsover found shoved into the hedge a little distance away, with a set of prints on it.

'Now, we haven't, I'm afraid, so far discovered anything about this gun—its ownership and history and all the rest of it. It may belong to the Prime Minister or to the Archbishop of Canterbury, for all we know. But in view of the fingerprints we could afford to defer the problem of the gun's origin for a few days anyway; our immediate plan of action was of course to uncover possible motives for Joshua's death, get by guile the fingerprints of anyone suspicious, and compare them with the prints on the gun—and that led us straight away to Penge, because it was impossible to be in Cassibury five minutes without hearing about the Penge-Vashti-Joshua triangle in all its sumptuous detail. Penge, then, had the motive of jealousy—Vashti isn't the sort of girl I personally would do murder for, but then, I've known a *crime passionel* be committed for possession of a penniless old lady of 68, and statistics show sex to be the motive for quite half the murders committed in this country, so that in that particular department I try not to be surprised at anything—Penge had this motive, then. And a comparison of his fingerprints with those on the revolver showed the two sets to be same.

'When eventually he was asked to explain this circumstance he told, as I've mentioned, a demonstrable lie: saying that he'd hand-led the gun three days previously when Joshua (of all people!) had brought it into his ironmonger's shop to ask if a crack in the butt could be repaired. On its being pointed out to him that Joshua had quite certainly been in Dorchester during the whole of the day men-tioned, and so couldn't have visited the Cassibury ironmonger's, he wavered and started contradicting himself and eventually shut up altogether; in which oyster-like condition he's been ever since—and very wise of him, too.

'However, I'm anticipating: we didn't ask him about the gun until after we'd gone into the problem of the time of Joshua's death. There was delay in getting a doctor to look at the body, so that the medical verdict was too vague to be helpful—between 6 and 10 was the best reckoning we could get. But then two women came forward to tell us they'd seen Joshua alive at 7. They said that on hearing of Cicely's accident they'd visited the cottage to console with her, and had glimpsed Joshua on arrival; though he'd disappeared almost at once (having met the two ladies, I can see why) and they hadn't set eyes on him again. So clearly the next thing to do was to talk to Cicely herself. By early Monday morning—the morning after the murder—Bolsover had taken over, and the local Sergeant, an intel-ligent lad, had the sense to warn him before he set off for Cicely's cottage that she was a hysterical type who'd have to be handled care-fully if her evidence was to be of any use—a diagnosis which the event confirmed. However, it turned out that by a great stroke of luck she hadn't heard of the murder yet; the reasons for this being (*a*) the fact that Joshua had planned to be away from home that night in any case, so that his absence had not alarmed her, and (*b*) the fact that the local Sergeant, a temperamentally secretive person, had sworn everyone who knew of the murder to silence until a higher authority should release them from the vow. Consequently,

Bolsover was able to put his most important questions to Cicely *before* telling her his reason for asking them—and a good thing too, because she had a fit of the horrors as soon as she heard her brother was dead, and the doctor refused to allow her to talk to anyone since. Anyway, her testimony was that Joshua, having seen her settled for the night, had left the cottage at about 8.15 on the Sunday evening (a quarter of an hour or so after her own visitors had gone), with a view to walking into Cassibury and catching a bus to Dorchester, where he was to stay with friends. And that, of course, meant that he could hardly have reached the spot where he was killed much earlier than a quarter to 9.

'So the next thing, naturally enough, was to find out where Penge had been all evening. And what it amounted to was that there were two periods of his time not vouched for by independent witnesses—the period from 7 to 8 (which didn't concern us) and the period from 8.30 to 9. Well, the latter, of course, fitted beautifully; and when we heard that he'd actually been *seen*, at about a quarter to 9, close to the place where the murder was committed, we started getting the warrant.

'And that, my dear Gervase, was the point at which the entire case fell to pieces.

'Penge had lied about his whereabouts between 8.30 and 9: we knew that. What we didn't know was that from twenty past 8 to ten past 9, two couples were making love no more than a few feet away from the place of the murder; and that not one of those four people, during the time they were there, heard a shot.

'It's no use talking about silencers, either; even a silenced report would have been heard, on a quiet night. And so that, as they say, was that. Penge certainly shot Joshua. But he didn't do it between 8.30 and 9. And unless Cicely was lying in order to help him—which is inconceivable; and in any case, Bolsover's ready to swear on the Book that her brother's death was an unspeakable shock to her—unless that, then he didn't do it between 7 and 8, either.'

Humbleby stubbed out his cheroot and leaned forward earnestly. 'But he worked it out somehow, Gervase. His lies alone would make me certain that he's guilty. And the thought that he's invented some ingenious trick or other, which I can't for the life of me see, makes me writhe.'

There was a long silence when he had finished speaking. Presently Fen cleared his throat and said diffidently:

'There are lots of things one wants to ask, of course. But on the evidence you've given me so far the trick looks fairly simple.

'If Penge's alibi is watertight,' Fen went on, 'then it's watertight. But just the same, it's easy to see how he killed Joshua.'

'Indeed,' Humbleby spoke with considerable restraint.

'Yes. It's all in the way you look at it. You've been looking at it upside down, you see. The situation, as I understand it, *must* be that it isn't Penge who has the alibi. It's the corpse.'

'The *corpse?*' Humbleby echoed.

'Why not? If Cicely was lying about the time Joshua left the cottage—if, in fact, he left much earlier—then Penge could have killed him between seven and eight.'

'But I've already explained—'

'That it's inconceivable she'd lie on Penge's behalf. I quite agree. But mightn't she lie on her brother's? Suppose that Joshua, with a revolver in his pocket, is setting out to commit a crime. And suppose he tells Cicely, if any questions are asked, to swear he left her much earlier than he did. And suppose that a policeman questions Cicely on this point *before* she learns that it's her brother, and not the man he set out to kill, who is dead. Wouldn't that account for it?'

'You mean—'

'I mean that Joshua intended to murder Penge, his rival for the young woman's affections; that he arranged for his sister (whom Penge had just humiliated publicly) to give him, if necessary, a simple alibi.

'Well, one can't be sure, of course. But it looks as if Joshua's plan misfired—as if Penge struggled with Joshua, got hold of the gun, and killed his assailant in self-defence. Behold Penge, then, with a watertight alibi created—charming irony—by his enemy! If the lovers hadn't been hanging about, he would have spoiled that alibi by going back afterwards—and one wonders why he *did* go—'

'Morbid attraction,' Humbleby interposed. 'I've seen it happen time and again . . . But good God, Gervase, what a fool! It *is* the only explanation! The one trouble about it is that there's no *proof.*'

'I should think there will be,' said Fen. 'as soon as Cicely ceases to be incommunicado and learns what's happened. If what you say about her dislike of Penge is true, she won't persist in the lie which exonerates him from killing her brother.' All at once Fen was pensive. 'Though come to think of it, if I were *Penge*—'

Shatteringly, the telephone rang, and Humbleby snatched it from its cradle. 'Yes,' he said. 'Yes, put him on . . . Bolsover?' A long pause. 'Oh, you've seen that, have you? So have I—though only just . . . Allowed to talk to people again, yes, so you—*WHAT?*' And with this squeak of mingled rage and astonishment Humbleby fell abruptly silent, listening while the telephone crackled despairingly at his ear. When at last he rang off, his face was gloomy.

'Bolsover thought of it too,' he said sombrely. 'But not soon enough. By the time he got to Cicely's bedside, Penge had been there for hours . . . They're going to get married: Cicely and Penge, I mean. She's forgiven him about the quarrel—I told you she doted on him, didn't I? Bolsover says he's never seen a more obsequious, considerate, dutiful, loving bridegroom-to-be. And, of course, she's sticking to her story about the time Joshua left the house. Very definite about it, Bolsover says.'

Fen got to his feet. 'Well, well,' he said, 'you'll never put him in the dock now. And yet I suppose that if he had the courage to tell the truth he'd probably get away with it.'

'All I can say is'—Humbleby, too, had risen—'that I hope it really was self-defence. In the interests of justice—'

'Justice?' Fen reached for his hat. 'I shouldn't worry too much about that, if I were you. Here's a wife who knows her husband killed her brother. And here's a husband who knows his wife can by saying a word deprive him of his liberty and just possibly—if things didn't go well—of his life. And each knows that the other knows. And the wife is in love with the husband, but one day she won't be any longer, and then he'll begin to be afraid. And the wife thinks her husband is in love with her, but one day she'll find out he isn't, and then she'll begin to hate him and to wonder what she can do to harm him, and he will know this, and she will know that he knows it and will be afraid of what he may do . . .

'Justice? My dear Humbleby, come and have some dinner. Justice has already been done.'

IN THE TRAIN

Frank O'Connor

It is no surprise that Frank O'Connor (1903-1966) 'the Old Master of the Irish Short Story', should have written a handful of stories about crime and detection amongst his outstanding portfolio of work. Examples which come to mind include 'The Majesty of the Law' about a maker of illegal poteen who seals his own bargain with a policeman; 'Peasants' which deals with the theft of the funds of a temperance association; and 'In the Train' which I have selected for this collection. O'Connor, who was born Michael O'Donovan in Cork, survived a childhood of unrelenting poverty and actually received much of his education while in prison with some college graduates after they had all been captured along with other Republican fighters during the Civil War. Subsequently he became a librarian and then a writer and lecturer. O'Connor is particularly admired in America where the New Yorker *first published many of his stories including 'In the Train' (1936), in which a woman acquitted of poisoning her husband finds herself travelling home on the same train as the policemen involved in prosecuting her . . .*

'There!' said the sergeant's wife. 'You would hurry me.'

'I always like being in time for a train,' replied the sergeant, with the equability of one who has many times before explained the guiding principle of his existence.

'I'd have had heaps of time to buy the hat,' added his wife.

The sergeant sighed and opened his evening paper. His wife looked out on the dark platform, pitted with pale lights under which faces and faces passed, lit up and dimmed again. A uniformed lad strode up and down with a tray of periodicals and chocolates. Farther up the platform a drunken man was being seen off by his friends.

222

'I'm very fond of Michael O'Leary,' he shouted. 'He is the most sincere man I know.'

'I have no life,' sighed the sergeant's wife. 'No life at all. There isn't a soul to speak to; nothing to look at all day but bogs and mountains and rain—always rain! And the people! Well, we've had a fine sample of them, haven't we?'

The sergeant continued to read.

'Just for the few days it's been like heaven. Such interesting people! Oh, I thought Mr Boyle had a glorious face! And his voice— it went through me.'

The sergeant lowered his paper, took off his peaked cap, laid it on the seat beside him, and lit his pipe. He lit it in the old-fashioned way, ceremoniously, his eyes blinking pleasurably like a sleepy cat's in the match-flare. His wife scrutinised each face that passed and it was plain that for her life meant faces and people and things and nothing more.

'Oh, dear!' she said again. 'I simply have no existence. I was educated in a convent and play the piano; my father was a literary man, and yet I am compelled to associate with the lowest types of humanity. If it was even a decent town, but a village!'

'Ah,' said the sergeant, gapping his reply with anxious puffs, 'maybe with God's help we'll get a shift one of these days.' But he said it without conviction, and it was also plain that he was well-pleased with himself, with the prospect of returning home, with his pipe and his paper.

'Here are Magner and the others,' said his wife as four other policemen passed the barrier. 'I hope they'll have sense enough to let us alone . . . How do you do? How do you do? Had a nice time, boys?' she called with sudden animation, and her pale, sullen face became warm and vivacious. The policemen smiled and touched their caps but did not halt.

'They might have stopped to say good evening,' she added sharply, and her face sank into its old expression of boredom and dissatisfaction. 'I don't think I'll ask Delancey to tea again. The others make an attempt but, really, Delancey is hopeless. When I smile and say: "Guard Delancey, wouldn't you like to use the butter-knife?" he just scowls at me from under his shaggy brows and says without a moment's hesitation: "I would not".'

'Ah, Delancey is a poor slob,' the sergeant said affectionately.

'Oh, yes, but that's not enough, Jonathan. Slob or no slob, he should make an attempt. He's a young man; he should have a dinner jacket at least. What sort of life will he get if he won't even wear a dinner jacket?'

'He's easy, I'd say. He's after a farm in Waterford.'

'Oh, a farm! A farm! The wife is only an incidental, I suppose?'

'Well, now, from all I hear she's a damn nice little incidental.'

'Yes, I suppose many a nice little incidental came from a farm,' answered his wife, raising her pale brows. But the irony was lost on him.

'Indeed yes, indeed yes,' he said fervently.

'And here,' she added in biting tones, 'come our charming neighbours.'

Into the pale lamplight stepped a group of peasants. Not such as one sees near a capital but in the mountains and along the coasts. Gnarled, wild, with turbulent faces, their ill-cut clothes full of character, the women in pale brown shawls, the men wearing black sombreros and carrying big sticks, they swept in, ill at ease, laughing and shouting defiantly. And so much part of their natural environment were they that for a moment they seemed to create about themselves rocks and bushes, tarns, turfricks, and sea.

With a prim smile the sergeant's wife bowed to them through the open window.

'How do you do? How do you do?' she called. 'Had a nice time?'

At the same moment the train gave a jolt and there was a rush in which the excited peasants were carried away. Some minutes passed; the influx of passengers almost ceased, and a porter began to slam the doors. The drunken man's voice rose in a cry of exultation.

'You can't possibly beat O'Leary,' he declared. 'I'd lay down my life for Michael O'Leary.'

Then, just as the train was about to start, a young woman in a brown shawl rushed through the barrier. The shawl, which came low enough to hide her eyes, she held firmly across her mouth, leaving visible only a long thin nose with a hint of pale flesh at either side. Beneath the shawl she was carrying a large parcel.

She looked hastily around; a porter shouted to her and pushed her towards the nearest compartment, which happened to be that occupied by the sergeant and his wife. He had actually seized the handle of the door when the sergeant's wife sat up and screamed.

'Quick! Quick!' she cried. 'Look who it is! She's coming in. Jonathan! Jonathan!'

The sergeant rose with a look of alarm on his broad red face. The porter threw open the door, with his free hand grasping the woman's elbow. But when she laid eyes on the sergeant's startled face she stepped back, tore herself free and ran crazily up the platform. The engine shrieked; the porter slammed the door with a curse; somewhere another door opened and shut, and the row of watchers, frozen into effigies of farewell, now dark now bright, began to glide gently past the window, and the stale, smoky air was charged with the breath of open fields.

*   *   *

The four policemen spread themselves out in a separate compartment and lit cigarettes.

'Poor old Delancey!' Magner said with his reckless laugh. 'He's cracked on her all right.'

'Cracked on her,' agreed Fox. 'Did ye see the eye he gave her?'

Delancey smiled sheepishly. He was a tall, handsome, black-haired young man with the thick eyebrows described by the sergeant's wife. He was new to the force and suffered from a mixture of natural gentleness and country awkwardness.

'I am,' he said in his husky voice. 'The devil admire me, I never hated anyone yet, but I think I hate the living sight of her.'

'Oh now, oh now!' protested Magner.

'I do. I think the Almighty God must have put that one into the world with the one main object of persecuting me.'

'Well indeed,' said Foley, ''tis a mystery to me how the sergeant puts up with her. If any woman up and called me by an outlandish name like Jonathan when everyone knew my name was plain John I'd do fourteen days for her—by God, I would, and a calendar month.'

The four men were now launched on a favourite topic that held them for more than a hour. None of them liked the sergeant's wife and all had stories to tell against her. From these there emerged the fact that she was an incurable scandalmonger and mischiefmaker who couldn't keep quiet about her own business, much less about that of her neighbours. And while they talked the train dragged across a dark plain, the heart of Ireland, and in the moonless night tiny cottage-windows blew past like sparks from a fire, and a pale simulacrum of the lighted carriages leaped and frolicked over hedges and fields. Magner shut the window and the compartment began to fill with smoke.

'She'll never rest till she's out of Farranchreesht,' he said.

'That she mightn't!' groaned Delancey.

'How would you like the city yourself, Dan?' asked Magner.

'Man dear,' exclaimed Delancey with sudden brightness, 'I'd like it fine. There's great life in a city.'

'You're welcome to it,' said Foley, folding his hands across his paunch.

'Why so? What's wrong with it?'

'I'm better off where I am.'

'But the life!'

'Life be damned! What sort of life is it when you're always under someone's eye? Look at the poor devils in court.'

'True enough, true enough,' agreed Fox.

'Ah, yes, yes,' said Delancey, 'but the adventures they have!'

'What adventures?'

'There was a sergeant in court only yesterday telling me one thing that happened himself. 'Twas an old maid without a soul in the world that died in an old loft on the quays. The sergeant put a new man on duty outside the door while he went back to report, and all he had to do was kick the door and frighten off the rats.'

'That's enough, that's enough!' cried Foley.

'Yes, yes, but listen now, listen can't you?' cried Delancey. 'He was there ten minutes with a bit of candle when the door at the foot of the stairs began to open. "Who's there?" says he, getting a bit nervous. "Who's there I say?" No answer, and still the door kept opening. Then he gave a laugh. What was it only a old cat? "Puss, puss," says he, "come on up, puss." Thinking, you know, the old cat would be company. Then he gave another look and the hair stood up on his head. There was another bloody cat coming in. "Get out!" says he to scare them, and then another cat came in and then another, and in his fright he dropped the candle. The cats began to hiss and bawl and that robbed him of the last stitch of sense. He made down the stairs, and if he did he trod on a cat, and went down head over heels, and when he tried to grip something 'twas a cat he gripped, and he felt the claws tearing his face. He was out for three weeks after.'

'That's a bloody fine adventure,' said Foley with bitter restraint.

'Isn't it though?' Delancey said eagerly. 'You'd be a long time in

Farranchreesht before anything like that would happen you.'

'That's the thing about Farranchreesht, lad,' said Magner. ''Tis a great ease to be able to put on your cap and go for a drink any hour of the day or night.'

'Yes,' added Foley, 'and to know the worst case you're likely to have in ten years is a bit of a scrap about politics.'

'I don't know,' Delancey sighed dreamily. 'Chrisht, there's great charm about the Criminal Courts.'

'Damn the much they had for you when you were in the box,' growled Foley.

'I know, sure, I know,' admitted Delancey crestfallen. 'I was sweating.'

'Shutting your eyes you were,' said Magner, 'like a kid afraid he was going to get a box on the ear.'

'Still,' said Delancey, 'this sergeant I'm talking about, he said after a while you wouldn't mind that no more than if 'twas a card party. He said you'd talk back to the judge as man to man.'

'I dare say that's true,' agreed Magner.

There was silence in the smoky compartment that jolted and rocked on its way across Ireland, and the four occupants, each touched with that morning wit which afflicts no one so much as state witnesses, thought of how they'd speak to the judge now if only they had him before them as man to man. They looked up to see a fat red face behind the door, and a moment later it was dragged back.

'Is this my carriage, gentleman?' asked a meek and boozy voice.

'No, 'tisn't. Go on with you!' snapped Magner.

'I had as nice a carriage as ever was put on a railway train,' said the drunk, leaning in, 'a handsome carriage, and 'tis lost.'

'Try farther on,' suggested Delancey.

'Ye'll excuse me interrupting yeer conversation, gentleman.'

'That's all right, that's all right.'

'I'm very melancholic. My best friend, I parted him this very night, and 'tis unknown to anyone, only the Almighty and Merciful God (here the drunk reverently raised the bowler hat and let it slide down the back of his neck to the floor) if I'll ever lay eyes on him again in this world. Good night, gentlemen, and thanks, thanks for all yeer kindness.'

As the drunk slithered away up the corridor Delancey laughed. Fox, who had remained thoughtful, resumed the conversation where it had left off.

'Delancey wasn't the only one that was sweating,' he said.

'He was not,' agreed Foley. 'Even the sergeant was a bit shook.'

'He was very shook. When he caught up the poison mug to identify it he was shaking, and before he could put it down it danced a jig
on the table.'

'Ah, dear God, dear God,' sighed Delancey, 'what killed me most
entirely was the bloody old model of the house. I didn't mind anything else only the house. There it was, a living likeness, with the bit
of grass in front and the shutter hanging loose, and every time I
looked at it I was in the back lane in Farranchreesht, and then I'd
look up and see the lean fellow in the wig pointing his finger at me.'

'Well, thank God,' said Foley with simple devotion, 'this time
tomorrow I'll be in Ned Iver's back with a pint in my fist.'

Delancey shook his head, a dreamy smile playing upon his dark
face.

'I don't know,' he said. ''Tis a small place, Farranchreesht; a
small, mangy old place with no interest or advancement in it.' His
face lit up as the sergeant appeared in the corridor.

'Here's the sergeant now,' he said.

'He wasn't long getting tired of Julietta,' whispered Magner mali-
ciously.

The door was pushed back and the sergeant entered, loosening
the collar of his tunic. He fell into a corner seat, crossed his legs, and
accepted the cigarette which Delancey proffered.

'Well, lads,' he exclaimed. 'What about a jorum?'

'Isn't it remarkable?' said Foley. 'I was only just talking about it.'

'I have noted before now, Peter,' said the sergeant, 'that you and
me have what might be called a simultaneous thirst.'

*   *   *

The country folk were silent and exhausted. Kendillon drowsed now
and then, but he suffered from blood-pressure, and after a while his
breathing grew thicker and stronger till at last it exploded in a snort
and he started up, broad awake and angry. In the silence rain spluttered and tapped along the roof and the dark windowpanes
streamed with shining runnels of water that trickled to the floor.
Moll Mhor scowled, her lower lip thrust out. She was a great flop of
a woman with a big, coarse, powerful face. The other two women
whose eyes were closed had their brown shawls drawn tight about

their heads, but Moll's was round her shoulders and the gap above her breasts was filled with a blaze of scarlet.

'Aren't we home yet?' Kendillon asked crossly, starting awake after one of his drowsing fits.

Moll glowered at him.

'No, nor won't be. What scour is on you?'

'My little house,' moaned Kendillon.

'My little house,' mimicked Moll. ''Twasn't enough for you to board the windows and put barbed wire on the gate.'

''Tis all very well for you that have someone to mind yours for you,' he snarled.

One of the women laughed softly and turned a haggard virginal face within the cowl of her shawl.

''Tis that have me laughing,' she explained apologetically. 'Tim Dwyer this week past at the stirabout pot.'

'And making the beds,' chimed in the third woman.

'And washing the children's faces! Glory be to God, he'll be mad.'

'Ay,' said Moll, 'and his chickens running off with Thade Kendillon's roof.'

'My roof is it?' he asked.

'Yes.'

''Tis a good roof,' he said roughly. ''Tis a better roof than ever was seen over your head since the day you married.'

'Oh, Mary my mother!' sighed Moll, ''tis a great pity of me this three hours and I looking at the likes of you instead of my own fine bouncing man.'

''Tis a new thing to hear you praising Sean then,' said a woman.

'I wronged him,' Moll said contritely. 'I did so. I wronged him before God and the world.'

At this moment the drunken man pulled back the door of the compartment and looked from face to face with an expression of deepening melancholy.

'She's not here,' he said in disappointment.

'Who's not here, mister?' asked Moll with a wink at the others.

'I'm looking for my own carriage, ma'am,' said the drunk with melancholy dignity, 'and whatever the bloody hell they done with it, 'tis lost. The railways in this country are gone to hell.'

'Wisha, if that's all that's worrying you, wouldn't you sit here with me?' asked Moll. 'I'm here so long I'm forgetting what a real man looks like.'

'I would with great pleasure,' replied the drunk politely, 'but 'tisn't only the carriage. 'Tis my travelling-companion. I'm a lonely man; I parted my best friend this very night; I found one to console me, and then when I turned my back—God took her!'

And with a dramatic gesture he closed the door and continued on his way. The country folk sat up, blinking. The smoke of the men's pipes filled the compartment and the heavy air was laden with the smell of homespun and turf-smoke, the sweet pungent odour of which had penetrated every fibre of their clothes.

'Listen to the rain!' said one of the women. 'We'll have a wet walk home.'

''Twill be midnight before we're in,' said another.

'Ah, what matter sure when the whole country will be up? There'll be a lot of talking done in Farranchreesht tonight.'

'A lot of talking and no sleep.'

'Oh, Farranchreesht! Farranchreesht!' cried the young woman with the haggard face, the ravaged lineaments of which were suddenly transfigured. 'Farranchreesht and the sky over you, I wouldn't change places with the Queen of England tonight!'

And suddenly Farranchreesht, the bare bogland with the hump-backed mountain behind, the little white houses and the dark fortifications of turf that made it seem like the flame-blackened ruin of some mighty city, all was lit up in their minds. An old man siting in a corner, smoking a broken clay pipe, thumped his stick on the floor.

'Well now,' said Kendillon darkly, 'wasn't it great impudence in her to come back?'

'Wasn't it indeed?' echoed one of the women.

'I'd say she won't be there long,' he went on knowingly.

'You'll give her the hunt, I suppose?' asked Moll politely, too politely.

'If no one else do, I'll give her the hunt myself. What right have she in a decent place?'

'Oh, the hunt, the hunt,' agreed a woman. 'Sure, no one could ever darken her door again.'

'And what the hell did we tell all the lies for?' asked Moll with her teeth on edge to be at Kendillon. 'Thade Kendillon there swore black was white.'

'What else would I do, woman? There was never an informer in my family.'

'I'm surprised to hear it,' said Moll vindictively, but the old man thumped his stick three or four times for silence.

'We all told our story,' he said, 'and we told it well. And no one told it better than Moll. You'd think to hear her she believed it herself.'

'I declare to God I very nearly did,' she said with a wild laugh.

'I seen great changes in my time, great changes,' the old man said, shaking his head, 'and now I see a greater change still.'

A silence followed his words. There was profound respect in all their eyes. The old man coughed and spat.

'What change is that, Colm?' asked Moll.

'Did any of ye ever think the day would come when a woman in our parish would do the like of that?'

'Never, never.'

'But she might do it for land?'

'She might.'

'Or for money?'

'She might so.'

'She might indeed. When the hunger is money people kill for the money; when the hunger is land people kill for the land. But what are they killing for now? I tell ye, there's a great change coming. In the ease of the world people are asking more. When I was a boy in the barony if you killed a beast you made six pieces of it, one for yourself and the rest for the neighbours. The same if you made a catch of fish. And that's how it was with us from the beginning of time. But now look at the change! The people aren't as poor or as good or as generous or as strong.'

'Or as wild,' added Moll with a vicious glance to Kendillon. ''Tis in the men you'd mostly notice the change.'

The door opened and Magner, Delancey and the sergeant entered. Magner was already drunk.

'I was lonely without you, Moll,' he said. 'You're the biggest and brazenest and cleverest liar of the lot and you lost me my sergeant's stripes, but I'll forgive you everything if you'll give us one bar of the "Colleen Dhas Roo".'

*   *   *

'I'm a lonely man,' said the drunk. 'And I'm going back to a lonely habitation.

'My best friend,' he continued, 'I left behind me—Michael

O'Leary, the most sincere man I know. 'Tis a great pity you don't know Michael and a great pity Michael don't know you. But look at the misfortunate way things happen! I was looking for someone to console me, and the moment I turned my back you were gone.'

He placed his hand solemnly under the woman's chin and raised her face to the light. With the other hand he stroked her cheeks.

'You have a beautiful face,' he said reverently, 'a beautiful face. But what's more important, you have a beautiful soul. I look into your eyes and I see the beauty of your nature. Allow me one favour. Only one favour before we part.'

He bent and kissed her. Then he picked up his bowler which had fallen once more, put it on back to front, took his dispatch case and got out.

The woman sat on alone. Her shawl was thrown open and beneath it she wore a bright blue blouse. The carriage was cold, the night outside black and cheerless, and within her something had begun to contract that threatened to crush the very spark of life in her. She could no longer fight it off even when for the hundredth time she went over the scenes of the previous day; the endless hours in the dock, the wearisome questions and speeches she could not understand, and the long wait in the cells till the jury returned. She felt again the shiver of mortal anguish that went through her when the chief warder beckoned angrily from the stairs and the wardress, glancing hastily in a hand-mirror, pushed her forward. She saw the jury with their expressionless faces. She was standing there alone, in nervous twitches jerking back the shawl from her face to give herself air. She was trying to say a prayer but the words were being drowned in her mind by the thunder of nerves, crashing and bursting. She could feel one which had escaped dancing madly at the side of her mouth, but was powerless to recapture it.

'The verdict of the jury is that Helena Maguire is not guilty.' Which was it? Death or life? She could not say. 'Silence! Silence!' shouted the usher though no one had tried to say anything. 'Any other charge?' asked a weary voice. 'Release the prisoner.' 'Silence!' shouted the usher again. The chief warder opened the door of the dock and she began to run. When she reached the steps she stopped and looked back to see if she was being followed. A policeman held open a door and she found herself in an ill-lit, draughty stone corridor. She stood there, the old shawl about her face. The crowd began to emerge. The first was a tall girl with a rapt expression as though she were walking on air. When she saw the woman she halted, her hands went up in an instinctive gesture, as though to feel her, to caress her. It was that look of hers, that gait as of a sleepwalker that brought the woman to her senses . . .

But now the memory had no warmth in her mind, and the something within her continued to contract, smothering her with loneliness, shame, and fear. She began to mutter crazily to herself. The train, now almost empty, was stopping at every little wayside station. Now and again a blast from the Atlantic pushed at it as though trying to capsize it.

She looked up as the door slammed open and Moll came in, swinging her shawl behind her.

'They're all up the train. Wouldn't you come?'

'No, no, I couldn't.'

'Why couldn't you? Who are you minding? Is it Thade Kendillon?'

'No, no, I'll stop as I am.'

'Here, take a sup of this.' Moll fumbled in her shawl and produced a bottle of liquor as pale as water. 'Wait till I tell you what Magner said! That fellow is a limb of the devil. "Have you e'er a drop, Moll?" says he. "Maybe I have," says I. "What is it?" says he. "For God's sake, baptize it quick and call it whisky".'

The woman took the bottle and put it to her lips. She shivered as she drank.

''Tis a good drop,' said Moll approvingly.

Next moment there were loud voices in the corridor. Moll grabbed the bottle and hid it under her shawl. But it was only Magner, the sergeant, and Delancey. After them came the two countrywomen, giggling. Magner held out his hand.

'Helena,' he said, 'accept my congratulations.'

She took his hand, smiling awkwardly.

'We'll get you the next time though,' he added.

'Musha, what are you saying, mister?'

'Not a word. You're a clever woman, a remarkable woman, and I give you full credit for it. You threw dust in all our eyes.'

'Poison is supposed to be an easy thing to trace but it beat me to trace it,' said the sergeant, barely concealing his curiosity.

'Well, well, there's things they're saying about me!' she said with a nervous laugh.

'Tell him,' advised Magner. 'There's nothing he can do to you now. You're as safe as the judge himself. Last night when the jury came in with the verdict you could have stood there in the dock and said: "Ye're wrong. I did it. I got the stuff in such and such a place. I gave it to him because he was old and dirty and cantankerous and a miser. I did it and I'm proud of it." You could have said every word of that and they couldn't have laid a finger on you.'

'Indeed, what a thing I'd say!'

'Well, you could.'

'The law is truly a remarkable phenomenon,' said the sergeant, who was also rather squiffy. 'Here you are, sitting at your ease at the expense of the state, and for one simple word of a couple of letters you could be up in Mountjoy, waiting for the rope and the morning jaunt.'

The woman shuddered. The young woman with the ravaged face looked up.

''Twas the holy will of God,' she said.

''Twas all the bloody lies Moll Mhor told,' replied Magner.

''Twas the will of God.'

'There was many hanged in the wrong,' said the sergeant.

'Even so, even so, 'twas God's will.'

'You have a new blouse, Helena,' said the other woman in an envious tone.

'I seen it last in a shop on the quays.'

'How much was it?'

'Honour of God!' exclaimed Magner, looking at the woman in stupefaction. 'Is that all you had to think of? You should have been on your bended knees before the altar.'

'And sure I was,' she answered indignantly.

'Women!' exclaimed Magner with a gesture of despair. He winked at Moll and they retired to the next compartment. But the interior was reflected clearly in the corridor window, and the others could see the pale quivering image of the policeman lift the bottle to his lips and blow a long silent blast on it. The young woman who had spoken of the blouse laughed.

'There'll be one good day's work done on the head of the trial,' she said.

'How so?' asked the sergeant.

'Dan Canty will make a great brew of poteen while he have all yeer backs turned.'

'I'll get Dan Canty yet,' replied the sergeant stiffly.

'You will, the way you got Helena.'

'I'll get him yet,' he said as he consulted his watch. 'We'll be in in another quarter of an hour. 'Tis time we were all getting back to our respective compartments.'

Magner entered and the other policemen rose. The sergeant fastened his collar and buckled his belt. Magner swayed, holding the doorframe, a mawkish smile on his thin, handsome, dissipated face.

'Well, good night to you now, ma'am,' said the sergeant primly. 'I'm as glad for all our sakes things ended as they did.'

'Good night, Helena,' said Magner, bowing low and promptly tottering. 'There'll be one happy man in Farranchreesht tonight.'

'Come on, Joe,' protested the sergeant.

'One happy man,' Magner repeated obstinately. ''Tis his turn now.'

'You're drunk, man,' said Delancey.

'You wanted him,' Magner said heavily. 'Your people wouldn't let you have him but you have him now in spite of them all.'

'Do you mean Cady Driscoll?' hissed the woman with sudden anger, leaning towards Magner, the shawl tight about her head.

'Never mind who I mean. You have him.'

'He's no more to me now than the salt sea.'

The policemen went out first, the women followed, Moll Mhor laughing boisterously. The woman was left alone. Through the window she could see little cottages stepping down over wet and naked rocks to the water's edge. The flame of life had narrowed in her to a pinpoint, and she could only wonder at the force that had caught her up, mastered her and then thrown her aside.

'No more to me,' she repeated dully to her own image in the glass, 'no more to me than the salt sea.'

MAIDEN'S LEAP

Benedict Kiely

The strength of human emotions which run just beneath the surface of everyday life, frequently generating scandal and occasionally even crime and murder, is a theme that Benedict Kiely (1919-) has pursued in a number of his stories, especially those to be found in the collection, The State of Ireland *(1980). Born in County Tyrone during the Civil War, Kiely initially trained to be a priest but later abandoned this calling to study history and literature at University College, Dublin. His knowledge of both these subjects, and his understanding of human nature, are used to splendid effect in 'Maiden's Leap', a story which most suitably ends this section about crimes of passion . . .*

The civic guard, or policeman, on the doorstep was big, middle-aged, awkward, affable. Behind him was green sunlit lawn sloping down to a white horse-fence and a line of low shrubs. Beyond that the highway, not much travelled. Beyond the highway, the jetty, the moored boats, the restless lake-water reflecting the sunshine.

The civic guard was so affable that he took off his cap. He was bald, completely bald. Robert St Blaise Macmahon thought that by taking off his cap the civic guard had made himself a walking, or standing, comic comment on the comic rural constable, in the Thomas Hardy story, who wouldn't leave his house without his truncheon: because without his truncheon his going forth would not be official.

Robert St Blaise Macmahon felt like telling all that to the civic guard and imploring him, for the sake of the dignity of his office, to restore his cap to its legal place and so to protect his bald head from the sunshine which, for Ireland, was quite bright and direct. Almost like the sun of that autumn he had spent in the Grand Atlas, far from the tourists. Or the sun of that spring when he had submitted to the natural curiosity of a novelist, who was also a wealthy man and could afford such silly journeys, and gone all the way to the United States, not to see those sprawling vulgar cities, Good God sir no, nor all those chromium-plated barbarians who had made an industry out of writing boring books about those colossal bores, Yeats and Joyce, but to go to Georgia to see the Okefenokee Swamp which interested him because of those scared drooping melancholy birds, the white ibises, and because of the alligators. Any day in the year give him, in preference to Americans, alligators. It could be that he made the journey so as to be able at intervals to say that.

But if he talked like this to the bald guard on the ancestral doorstep the poor devil would simply gawk or smirk or both and say: Yes, Mr Macmahon. Of course, Mr Macmahon.

Very respectful, he would seem to be. For the Macmahons counted for something in the town. His father's father had as good as owned it.

The fellow's bald head was nastily ridiculously perspiring. Robert St Blaise Macmahon marked down that detail for his notebook. Henry James had so wisely said: Try to be one of those on whom nothing is lost.

Henry James had known it all. What a pity that he had to be born in the United States. But then, like the gentleman he was, he had had the good wit to run away from it all.

The bald perspiring cap-in-hand guard said: 'Excuse me, Mr Macmahon. Sorry to disturb you on such a heavenly morning and all. But I've come about the body, sir.'

Robert St Blaise Macmahon was fond of saying in certain circles in Dublin that he liked civic guards if they were young, fresh from the country, and pink-cheeked; and that he liked Christian Brothers in a comparable state of development. In fact he would argue, you came to a time of life when civic guards and Christian Brothers were, apart from the uniforms, indistinguishable. This he said merely to hear himself say it. He was much too fastidious for any fleshly contact with anybody, male or female. So, lightly, briefly, flittingly, trippingly, he now amused himself with looking ahead to what he would say on his next visit to town: Well if they had to send a guard they could have sent a young handsome one to enquire about the . . .

What the guard had just said now registered and with a considerable shock. The guard repeated: 'About the body, sir. I'm sorry, Mr

Macmahon, to disturb you.'

'What body? Whose body? What in heaven's name can you mean?'

'I know it's a fright, sir. Not what you would expect at all. The body in the bed, sir. Dead in the bed.'

'There is no body in my bed. Dead or alive. At least not while I'm up and about. I live here alone, with my housekeeper, Miss Hynes.'

'Yes. Mr Macmahon, sir. We know Miss Hynes well. Very highly respected lady, sir. She's below in the barracks at the moment in a terrible state of nervous prostration. The doctor's giving her a pill or an injection or something to soothe her. Then he'll be here directly.'

'Below in the barracks? But she went out to do the shopping.'

'Indeed yes, sir. But she slipped in to tell us, in passing, like, sir. Oh it's not serious or anything. Foul play is not suspected.'

'Foul what? Tell you what?'

'Well, sir.'

'Tell me, my good man.'

'She says, sir, there's man dead in her bed.'

'A dead man?'

'The very thing, Mr Macmahon.'

'In the bed of Miss Hynes, my housekeeper.'

'So she says, sir. Her very words.'

'What in the name of God is he doing there?'

'Hard to say, Mr Macmahon, what a dead man would be doing in a bed, I mean like in somebody else's bed.'

With a huge white linen handkerchief that he dragged, elongated, out of a pants pocket, and then spread before him like an enveloping cloud, the guard patiently mopped his perspiration: 'Damned hot today sir. The hottest summer, the paper says, in forty years.'

The high Georgian-Floridian sun shone straight down on wine-coloured swamp-water laving (it was archaic but yet the only word) the grotesque knobbly knees of giant cypress trees. The white sacred crook-billed birds perched gravely, high on grey curved branches above trailing Spanish moss, oh far away, so far away from this mean sniggering town and its rattling tongues. It was obvious, it was regettably obvious, that the guard was close to laughter.

'A dead man, guard, in the bed of Miss Hynes, my housekeeper, and housekeeper to my father and mother before me, and a distant relative of my own.'

'So she tells us, sir.'

'Scarcely a laughing matter, guard.'

'No, sir. Everything but, sir. It's just the heat, sir. Overcome by the heat. Hottest summer, the forecast says, in forty years.'

That hottest summer in forty years followed them, panting, across the black and red flagstones of the wide hallway. A fine mahogany staircase went up in easy spirals. Robert St Blaise Macmahon led the way around it, keeping to the ground floor. The guard placed his cap, open end up, on the hall stand, as reverently as if he were laying cruets on an altar, excusing himself, as he did so, as if the ample mahogany hall stand, mirrored and antlered, were also a Macmahon watching, or reflecting, him with disapproval. It was the first time he or his like ever had had opportunity or occasion to enter this house.

In the big kitchen, old-fashioned as to size, modern as to fittings, the hottest summer was a little assauged. The flagstones were replaced by light tiles, green and white, cool to the sight and the touch. She had always held on to that bedroom on the ground floor, beyond the kitchen, although upstairs the large house was more than half empty. She said she loved it because it had french windows that opened out to the garden. They did, too. They would also give easy access for visitors to the bedroom: a thought that had never occurred to him, not once over all these years.

Earlier that morning she had called to him from the kitchen to say that she was going shopping, and had made her discreet escape by way of those windows. They still lay wide open to the garden. She was a good gardener as she was a good housekeeper. She had, of course, help with the heavy work in both cases: girls from the town for the kitchen, a healthy young man for the garden. All three, or any, of them were due to arrive, embarrassingly, within the next hour. Could it be the young man for the garden, there, dead in the bed? No, at least, thank God, it wasn't her assistant gardener, a scape-grace of a fellow that might readily tempt a middle-aged woman. She hadn't stooped to the servants. She had that much Macmahon blood in her veins. This man was, or had been, a stranger, an older man by far than the young gardener. He was now as old as he would ever be. The hottest summer was heavy and odorous in the garden, and flower odours and insect sounds came to them in the room. The birds were silent. There was also the other odour: stale sweat, or dead passion, or just death? The guard sniffed. He said: He died sweating. He's well tucked in.

Only the head was visible: sparse grey hair, a few sad pimples on the scalp, a long purple nose, a comic Cyrano nose. Mouth and eyes were open. He had good teeth and brown eyes. He looked, simply, surprised, not yet accustomed to wherever he happened to find himself.

'Feel his heart, guard.'

'Oh dead as mutton, Mr Macmahon. Miss Hynes told no lie. Still, he couldn't die in a better place. In a bed, I mean.'

'Unhouselled, unappointed, unannealed.'

'Yes, sir,' the guard said, 'every bit of it.'

'I mean he died without the priest.'

With something amounting almost to wit—you encountered it in the most unexpected places—the guard said that taking into account the circumstances in which the deceased, God be merciful to him, had passed over, he could hardly have counted on the company of a resident chaplain. That remark could be adopted as one's own, improved upon, and employed on suitable occasions and in the right places, far from this town and it petty people.

'Death,' said the guard, 'is an odd fellow. There's no being up to him, Mr Macmahon. He can catch you unawares in the oddest places.'

This fellow, by heaven, was a philosopher. He was, for sure, one for the notebook.

'Quite true, guard. There was a very embarrassing case involving a president of the great French Republic. Found dead in his office. He had his hands in the young lady's hair. They had to cut the hair to set her free.'

'Do you tell me so, sir? A French president? 'Twouldn't be the present fellow, de Gaulle, with the long nose would be caught at capers like that.'

'There was a Hemingway story on a somewhat similar theme.'

'Of course, sir. You'd know about that, Mr Macmahon. I don't read much myself. But my eldest daughter that works for the public libraries tells me about your books.'

'And Dutch Schultz, the renowned American gangster, you know that he was shot dead while he was sitting, well in fact while he was sitting on the toilet.'

'A painful experience, Mr Macmahon. He must have been surprised beyond measure.'

Far away, from the highway, came the sound of an automobile.

'That', said the guard, 'could be the doctor or the ambulance.'

They waited in silence in the warm odorous room. The sound passed on and away: neither the doctor nor the ambulance.

'But that fellow in the bed, Mr Mamahon, I could tell you things about him, God rest him.'

'Do you mean to say you know him?'

'Of course, sir. It's my business to know people.'

'Try to be one of those on whom nothing is lost.'

'Quite so, sir, and odd that you should mention it. For that fellow in the bed, sir, do you know that once upon a time he lost two hundred hens?'

'Two hundred hens?'

'Chickens.'

'Well, even chickens. That was a lot of birds. Even sparrows, Or skylarks. He must have been the only man in Europe who ever did that.'

'In the world, I'd say, sir. And it happened so simple.'

'It's stuffy in here,' Robert said.

He led the way out to the garden. The sound of another automobile on the highway was not yet the doctor nor the ambulance. They walked along a red-sanded walk. She had had that mulch red sand brought all the way from Mullachdearg Strand in County Donegal. She loved the varied strands of Donegal: red, golden or snow-white. To right and left her roses flourished. She had a good way with roses, and with sweetpea, and even with sunflowers, those lusty brazen-faced giants.

'He was up in Dublin one day in a pub, and beside him at the counter the mournfullest man you ever saw. So the man that's gone, he was always a cheery type, said to the mournful fellow: "Brighten up, the sun's shining, life's not all that bad." The mournful one says: "If you were a poultry farmer with two hundred hens that wouldn't lay an egg, you'd hardly be singing songs".'

'The plot,' said Robert St Blaise Macmahon, 'thickens.'

"So," says your man that's inside there, "and at peace we may charitably hope, how much would you take for those hens?" "A shilling a hen." "Done," says he, and out with two hundred shillings and buys the hens. Then he hires a van and a boy to drive it, and off with him to transport the hens. You see, he knows a man here in this very town that will give him half-a-crown a hen, a profit of fifteen pounds sterling less the hire of the van. But the journey is long and stops plentiful at the wayside pubs, he always had a notorious drouth, and whatever happened nobody ever found out, but when he got to this town at two in the morning, the back doors of the van were swinging open.'

'The birds had flown.'

'Only an odd feather to be seen. And he had to pay the boy fifteen shillings to clean out the back of the van. They were never heard of again, the hens I mean. He will long be remembered for that.'

'If not for anything else.'

'His poor brother, too, sir. That was a sad case. Some families are, you might say, addicted to sudden death.'

'Did he die in a bed?'

'Worse, far worse, sir. He died on a lawnmower.'

'Guard,' said Robert, 'would you have a cup of tea? You should be writing books, instead of me.'

'I was never much given to tea, sir.'

'But in all the best detective stories the man from Scotland Yard always drinks a cup o' tea.'

'As I told you, sir, I don't read much. But if you had the tiniest drop of whisky to spare, I'd be grateful. It's a hot day and this uniform is a crucifixion.'

They left the garden by a wicket-gate that opened through a beech-hedge on to the front lawn. The sun's reflections shot up like lightning from the lake-water around the dancing boats. Three automobiles passed, but no doctor, no ambulance, appeared. Avoiding the silent odorous room they re-entered the house by the front door. In the dining-room Robert St Blaise Macmahon poured the whisky for the guard, and for himself: he needed it.

'Ice, guard?'

'No thank you sir. Although they say the Americans are hell for it. In everything, in tea, whisky, and so on.'

Two more automobiles passed. They listened and waited.

'You'd feel, sir, he was listening to us, like for a laugh, long nose and all. His brother was the champion gardener of all time. Better even than Miss Hynes herself, although her garden's a sight to see and a scent to smell.'

'He died on a lawnmower?'

'On his own lawn, sir. On one of those motor mowers. It blew up under him. He was burned to death. And you could easily say, sir, he couldn't have been at a more harmless occupation, or in a safer place.'

'You could indeed, guard. Why haven't I met you before this?'

'That's life, sir. Our paths never crossed. Only now for that poor fellow inside I wouldn't be here today at all.'

This time it had to be the doctor and the ambulance. The wheels came, scattering gravel, up the driveway.

'He was luckier than his brother, sir. He died in more comfort, in a bed. And in action, it seems. That's more than will be said for most of us.'

The doorbell chimed: three slow cathedral tones. That chime had been bought in Bruges where they knew about bells. The guard threw back what was left of his whisky. He said: 'You'll excuse me, Mr Macmahon. I'll go and put on my cap. We have work to do.'

When the guard, the doctor, the ambulance, the ambulance attendants, and the corpse had, all together, taken their departure, he sprayed the bedroom with Flit, sworn foe to the housefly. It was all he could think of. It certainly changed the odour. It drifted out even into the garden, and lingered there among the roses. The assistant gardener and the kitchen girls had not yet arrived. That meant that the news was out, and that they were delaying in the town to talk about it. What sort of insufferable idiot was that woman to put him in this way into the position of being talked about, even, in the local papers, written about, and then laughed at, by clods he had always regarded with a detached and humourous, yet godlike, eye?

He sat, for the sake of the experience, on the edge of the rumpled bed from which the long-nosed corpse had just been removed. But he felt nothing of any importance. He remembered that another of those American dons had written a book, which he had slashingly reviewed, about love and death in the American novel. To his right, beyond the open windows, was her bureau desk and bookcase: old black oak, as if in stubborn isolated contradiction to the prevalent mahogany. She had never lost the stiff pride that a poor relation wears as a mask when he or she can ride high above the more common servility. She was a high-rider. It was simply incomprehensible that she, who had always so rigidly kept herself to herself, should have had a weakness for a long-nosed man who seemed to have been little better than a figure of fun. Two hundred hens, indeed!

The drawers of the bureau-bookcase were sagging open, and in disorder, as if in panic she had been rooting through them for something that nobody could find. He had seldom seen the inside of her room but, from the little he had seen and from everything he knew of her, she was no woman for untidiness or unlocked drawers. Yet in spite of her panic she had not called for aid to him, her cousin-once-removed, her employer, her benefactor. She had always stiffly, and for twenty-five years kept him at a distance. Twenty-five years ago, in this room. She would have been eighteen, not six months escaped from the mountain valley she had been reared in, from which his parents had rescued her. He closes his eyes and, as best he can, his nose. He remembers. It is a Sunday afternoon and the house is empty except for the two of them.

He is alone in his room reading. He is reading about how Lucius Apuleius watches the servant-maid, Fotis, bending over the fire: Mincing of meats and making pottage for her master and mistresse, the Cupboard was all set with wines and I thought I smelled the savour of some dainty meats. Shee had about her middle a white and clean apron, and shee was girdled about her body under the paps with a swathell of red silk, and shee stirred the pot and turned the meat with her faire and white hands, in such sort that with stirring and turning the same, her loynes and hips did likewise move and shake, which was in my mind a comely sight to see.

Robert St Blaise Macmahon who, at sixteen, had never tasted wine except to nibble secretively at the altar-wine when he was an acolyte in the parish church, repeats over and over again the lovely luscious Elizabethan words of Adlington's translation from the silver Latin: We did renew our venery by drinking of wine.

For at sixteen he is wax, and crazy with curiosity.

Then he looks down into the garden and there she is bending down over a bed of flowers. She is tall, rather sallow-faced, a Spanish face in an oval of close, crisp, curling dark hair. He has already noticed the determination of her long lithe stride, the sway of her hips, the pendulum swish and swing of her bright tartan pleated skirt. For a girl from the back of the mountains she has a sense of style.

She has come to this house from the Gothic grandeur of a remote valley called Glenade. Flat-topped mountains, so steep that the highest few hundred feet are sheer rock-cliffs corrugated by torrents, surround it. One such cliff, fissured in some primeval cataclysm, falls away into a curved chasm, rises again into one cold pinnacle of rock. The place is known as the Maiden's Leap, and the story is that some woman out of myth—Goddess, female devil, what's the difference?—pursued by a savage and unwanted lover, ran along the ridge of the mountain, and when faced by the chasm leaped madly to save her virtue, and did. But she didn't leap far enough to save her beautiful frail body which was shattered on the rocks below. From which her pursurer may have derived a certain perverse satisfaction.

All through her girlhood her bedroom window has made a frame for that extraordinary view. Now, her parents dead, herself adopted into the house of rich relatives as a sort of servant-maid, assistant to the aged housekeeper and in due course to succeed her, she bends over a flower-bed as Fotis had bent over the fire: O Fotis how trimely you can stir the pot, and how finely, with shaking your buttocks, you can make pottage.

Now she is standing tall and straight snipping blossoms from a fence of sweetpea. Her body is clearly outlined against the multi-coloured fence. He watches. He thinks of Fotis. He says again: We did renew our venery with drinking of wine.

When he confronts her in this very room, and makes an awkward grab at her, her arms are laden with sweetpea. So he is able to plant one kiss on cold unresponding lips. The coldness, the lack of response in a bondswoman, surprises him. She bears not the slightest resemblance to Fotis. It was the done thing, wasn't it: the young master and the servant-maid? In the decent old days in Czarist Russia the great ladies in the landed houses used to give the maids to their sons to practise on.

The sweetpea blossoms, purple, red, pink, blue, flow rather than fall to the floor. Then she hits him with her open hand, one calm, deliberate, country clout that staggers him and leaves his ear red, swollen and singing for hours. She clearly does not understand the special duties of a young female servant. In wild Glenade they didn't read Turgenev or Saltykov-Schedrin. He is humiliatingly reminded that he is an unathletic young man, a pampered only child, and that she is a strong girl from a wild mountain valley. She says: Mind your manners, wee boy. Pick up those sweetpea or I'll tell your father and mother how they came to be on the floor.

He picks up the flowers. She is older than he is. She is also taller, and she has a hand like rock. He knows that she has already noticed that he is afraid of his father.

This room was not then a bedroom. It was a pantry with one

whole wall of it shelved for storing apples. He could still smell those apples, and the sweetpea. The conjoined smell of flower and fruit was stronger even than the smell of the insect-killing spray with which he had tried to banish the odour of death.

That stinging clout was her great leap, her defiance, her declaration of independence but, as the case of the Maiden of Glenade, it had only carried her halfways. To a cousin once-removed, who never anyway had cared enough to make a second attempt, she had demonstrated that she was no chattel. But she remained a dependent, a poor relation, a housekeeper doing the bidding of his parents until they died and, after her death, continuing to mind the house, grow the roses, the sweetpea and the sunflowers. The sense of style, the long lithe swinging stride, went for nothing, just because she hadn't jumped far enough to o'erleap the meandering withering enduring ways of a small provincial town. No man in the place could publicly be her equal. She was part Macmahon. So she had no man of her own, no place of her own. She had become part of the furniture of this house. She had no life of her own. Or so he had lightly thought.

He came and went and wrote his books, and heard her and spoke to her, but seldom really saw her except to notice that wrinkles, very faint and fine, had appeared on that Spanish face, on the strong-boned, glossy forehead, around the corners of the eyes. The crisp dark hair had touches of grey that she had simply not bothered to do anything about. She was a cypher, and a symbol in a frustrating land that had more than its share of ageing hopeless virgins. He closed his eyes and saw her as such when, in his writings, he touched satirically on that aspect of life in his pathetic country. Not that he did so any more often than he could help. For a London illustrated magazine he had once written about the country's low and late marriage rate, an article that had astounded all by its hard practicality. But as a general rule he preferred to think and to write about Stockholm or Paris or Naples or Athens, or African mountains, remote from everything. His travel books were more than travel books, and his novels really did show that travel broadened the mind. Or to think and write about the brightest gem in an America that man was doing so much to lay waste: the swamp that was no swamp but a wonderland out of a fantasy by George MacDonald, a Scottish writer whom nobody read any more, a fantasy about awaking some morning in your own bedroom, which is no longer a bedroom but the heart of the forest where every tree has its living spirit, genial or evil, evil or genial.

At that moment in his reverie the telephone rang. To the devil with it, he thought, let it ring. The enchanted swamp was all round him, the wine-coloured water just perceptibly moving, the rugged knees of the cypress trees, the white priestly birds curved brooding on high bare branches, the silence. Let it ring. It did, too. It rang and rang and refused to stop. So he walked ill-tempered to the table in the hallway where the telephone was, picked it up, silenced the ringing, heard the voice of the civic guard, and then noticed for the first conscious time the black book that he carried in his right hand.

The guard said: 'She's resting now. The sergeant's wife is looking after her.'

'Good. That's very good.'

It was a ledger-type book, eight inches by four, the pages ruled in blue, the margins in red. He must, unthinkingly, have picked it up out of the disorder in which her morning panic had left the bureau-bookcase. For the first time that panic seemed to him as comic: it wasn't every morning a maiden lady found a long-nosed lover, or something, cold between the covers. It was matter for a short story, or an episode in a novel: if it just hadn't damned well happened in his own house. What would Henry James have made of it? The art of fiction is in telling not what happened, but what should have happened. Or what should have happened somewhere else.

The guard was still talking into his left ear, telling him that the doctor said it was a clear case of heart failure. Oh, indeed it was: for the heart was a rare and undependable instrument. With his right hand he flicked at random through the black book, then, his eye caught by some words that seemed to mean something, he held the book flat, focused on those words until they were steady, and read. The hand-writing was thick-nibbed, black as coal, dogged, almost printing, deliberate as if the nib had bitten into the paper. He read: Here he comes down the stairs in the morning, his double jowl red and purple from the razor, his selfish mouth pursed as tight as Mick Clinton, the miser of Glenade, used to keep the woollen sock he stored his money in when he went to the market and the horsefair of Manorhamilton. Here he comes, the heavy tread of him in his good, brown hand-made shoes would shake the house if it wasn't as solid on its foundations as the Rock of Cashel. Old John Macmahon used to boast that his people built for eternity. Thud, thud, thud, the weight of his big flat feet. Here he comes, Georgeous Gussie, with his white linen shirt, he should have frills on his underpants, and his blue eyeshade to show to the world, as if there was anybody to bother looking at him except myself and the domestic help, that he's a writer. A writer, God help us. About what? Who reads him? It's just as well he had old John's plunder to live on.

The black letters stood out like basalt from the white, blue-and-red lined paper. Just one paragraph she wrote to just one page and, if the paragraph didn't fully fill the page, she made, above and below the paragraph, whorls and doodles and curlicues in inks of various colours, blue, red, green, violet. She was a lonely self-delighting artist. She was, she had been, for how long, oh merciful heavens, an observer, a writer.

The guard was saying: 'She said to the sergeant's wife that she's too shy to face you for the present.'

'Shy,' he said.

He looked at the black words. They were as distinct as that long-ago clout on the side of the head: the calloused hard hand of the mountainy girl reducing the pretensions of a shy, sensitive, effeminate youth.

He said: 'She has good reason to be shy. It is, perhaps, a good thing that she should, at least, be shy before her employer and distant relation.'

'It might be that, sir, she might mean not shy, but ashamed.'

'She has also good reason for being ashamed.'

'She says, Mr Macmahon, sir, that she might go away somewhere for a while.'

'Shouldn't she wait for the inquest and funeral? At any rate, she has her duties here in this house. She is, she must realise, paid in advance.'

So she would run, would she, and leave him to be the single object of the laughter of the mean people of this town? In a sweating panic he gripped the telephone as if he would crush it. There was an empty hungry feeling, by turns hot, by turns cold, just above his navel. He was betraying himself to that garrulous guard who would report to the town every word he said. It was almost as if the guard could read, if he could read, those damnable black words. He gripped the phone, slippy and sweaty as it was, gulped and steadied himself, breathed carefully, in out, in out, and was once again Robert St

Blaise Macmahon, a cultivated man whose education had commenced at the famous Benedictine school at Glenstal. After all, the Jesuits no longer were what once they had been, and James Joyce had passed that way to the discredit both of himself and the Jesuits.

'Let her rest then,' he said. 'I'll think over what she should do. I'll be busy all day, guard, so don't call me unless it's absolutely essential.'

He put down the telephone, wiped his sweating hand with a white linen handkerchief, monogrammed and ornamented with the form of a feather embroidered in red silk. It was meant to represent a quill pen and also to be a symbol of the soaring creative mind. That fancy handkerchief was, he considered, his one flamboyance. He wore, working, a blue eye-shade because there were times when lamplight, and even overbright daylight, strained his eyes. Any gentleman worthy of the name did, didn't he, wear hand-made shoes?

On the first page of the book she had pasted a square of bright yellow paper and in it printed in red ink: Paragraphs.

In smaller letters, in Indian black ink, and in an elegant italic script, she had written: Reflections on Robert the Riter.

The finally, in green ink, she had printed: By his Kaptivated Kuntry Kusin!!!

He was aghast at her frivolity. Nor did she need those three exclamation marks to underline her bitchiness, a withdrawn and secretive bitchiness, malevolent among the roses and the pots and pans, overflowing like bile, in black venomous ink. She couldn't have been long at this secret writing. The book was by no means full. She had skipped, and left empty pages here and there, at random as if she dipped her pen and viciously wrote wherever the book happened to open. There was no time sequence that he could discern. He read: He says he went all the way to the States to see a swamp. Just like him. Would he go all the way to Paris to see the sewers?

'But the base perfidy of that.'

He spoke aloud, not to himself but to her.

'You always pretended to be interested when I talked about the swamp. The shy wild deer that would come to the table to take the bit out of your fingers when you breakfasted in the open air, the racoon with the rings round its eyes, the alligators, the wine-coloured waters, the white birds, the white sand on the bed of the Suwannee River. You would sit, woman, wouldn't you, brown Spanish face inscrutable, listening, agreeing with me, oh yes, agreeing with me in words, but, meanly, all the time, thinking like this.'

Those brief words about that small portion of his dream-world had wounded him. But bravely he read more. The malice of this woman of the long-nosed chicken-losing lover must be fully explored. She was also, by heaven, a literary critic. She wrote: Does any novelist, nowadays, top-dress his chapters with quotations from other authors? There is one, but he writes thrillers and that's different. Flat-footed Robert the Riter, with his good tweeds and his brass-buttoned yellow waistcoat, has a hopelessly old-fashioned mind. His novels, with all those sophisticated nonentities going nowhere, read as if he was twisting life to suit his reading. But then what does Robert know about life? Mamma's boy, Little Lord Fauntleroy, always dressed in the best. He doesn't know one rose from another. But a novelist should know everything. He doesn't know the town he lives in. Nor the people in it. Quotations. Balderdash.

He found to his extreme humiliation that he was flushed with fury. The simplest thing to do would be to let her go away and stay away, and then find himself a housekeeper who wasn't a literary critic, a secret carping critic, a secret lover too, a Psyche, by Hercules, welcoming by night an invisible lover to her bed. Then death stops him, and daylight reveals him, makes him visible as a comic character with a long nose, and with a comic reputation, only, for mislaying two hundred hens, and with a brother, a great gardener, who had the absurd misfortune to be burned alive on his own lawn. Could comic people belong to a family addicted to sudden death? Somewhere in all this, there might be some time the germ of a story.

But couldn't she realise what those skilfully chosen quotations meant?

'Look now,' he said, 'what they did for George MacDonald. A procession of ideas, names, great presences, marching around the room you write in: Fletcher and Shelley, Novalis and Beddoes, Goethe and Coleridge, Sir John Suckling and Shakespeare, Lyly and Schiller, Heine and Schleiermacher and Cowley and Spenser and the Book of Judges and Jean Paul Richter and Cyril Tourneur and Sir Philip Sidney and Dekker and Chaucer and the Kabala.'

But, oh Mother Lilith, what was the use of debating thus with the shadow of a secretive woman who was now resting in the tender care of the sergeant's wife who was, twenty to one, relaying the uproarious news to every other wife in the town: Glory be, did you hear the fantasticality that happened up in Mr Robert St Blaise Macmahon's big house? Declare to God they'll never again be able to show their faces in public.

Even if she were with him, walking in this garden as he now was, and if he was foolish enough thus to argue with her, she would smile her sallow wrinkled smile, look sideways out of those dark-brown eyes and then go off alone to write in her black book: He forgot to mention the Twelve Apostles, the Clancy Brothers, and the Royal Inniskilling Fusiliers.

All her life she had resisted his efforts to make something out of her. Nor had she ever had the determination to rise and leap again, to leave him and the house and go away and make something out of herself.

He read: He's like the stuck-up high-falutin' women in that funny story by Somerville and Ross, he never leaves the house except to go to Paris. He doesn't see the life that's going on under his nose. He says there are no brothels in Dublin. But if Dublin had the best brothels in the long history of sin . . .

Do you know, now, that was not badly put. She has a certain felicity of phrase. But then she has some Macmahon blood in her, and the educational advantages that over the years this house has afforded her.

. . . long history of sin, he'd be afraid of his breeches to enter any of them. He says there are no chic women in Dublin. What would he do with a chic woman if I gave him one, wrapped in cellophane, for Valentine's Day? He says he doesn't know if the people he sees are ugly because they don't make love, or that they don't make love because they're ugly. He's the world's greatest living authority, isn't he, either on love or good looks?

On another page: To think, dear God, of that flat-footed bachelor who doesn't know one end of a woman from the other, daring to write an article attacking the mountainy farmers on their twenty pitiful acres of rocks, rushes, bogpools and dunghills, for not marrying young and raising large families. Not only does he not see the people around him, he doesn't even see himself. Himself and a crazy priest in America lamenting about late marriages and the vanishing Irish. A fine pair to run in harness. The safe, sworn celibate and the fraidy-cat bachelor.

And on yet another page: That time long ago, I clouted him when he made the pass, the only time, to my knowledge, he ever tried to prove himself a man. And he never came back for more. I couldn't very well tell him that the clout was not for what he was trying to do but for the stupid way he was trying to do it. A born bungler.

The doodles, whorls and curlicues wriggled like a snake-pit, black, blue, green, red, violet, before his angry eyes. That was enough. He would bring that black book down to the barracks, and throw it at her, and tell her never to darken his door again. His ears boomed with blood. He went into the dining-room, poured himself a double whisky, drank it slowly, breathing heavily, thinking. But no, there was a better way. Go down to the barracks, bring her back, lavish kindness on her, in silence suffer her to write in her book, then copy what she writes, reshape it, reproduce it, so that some day she would see it in print and be confounded for the jade and jezebel that she is.

With deliberate speed, majestic instancy, he walked from the dining-room to her bedroom, tossed the book on to her bed where she would see it on her return and know he had read it, and that her nastiness was uncovered. He had read enough of it, too much of it: because the diabolical effect of his reading was that he paused, with tingling irritation, to examine his tendency to think in quotations. Never again, thanks to her malice, would he do so, easily, automatically, and, so to speak, unthinkingly.

Coming back across the kitchen he found himself looking at his own feet, in fine hand-made shoes, his feet rising, moving forwards, settling again on the floor, fine flat feet. It was little benefit to see ourselves as others see us. That was, merciful God, another quotation. That mean woman would drive him mad. He needed a change: Dublin, Paris, Boppard on the Rhine—a little town that he loved in the off-season when it wasn't ravished by boat-loads of American women doing the Grand Tour. First, though, to get the Spanish maiden of wild Glenade back to her proper place among the roses and the pots and pans.

The guard answered the telephone. He said: 'She's still resting, Mr Macmahon, sir.'

'It's imperative that I speak to her. She can't just take this lying down.'

That, he immediately knew, was a stupid thing to say. On the wall before him, strong black letters formed, commenting on his stupidity.

There was a long silence. Then she spoke, almost whispered:

'Yes, Robert.'

'Hadn't you better get back to your place here?'

'Yes, Robert. But what is my place there?'

'You know what I mean. We must face this together. After all, you are half a Macmahon.'

'Half a Macmahon,' she said, 'is better than no bread.'

He was shocked to fury: 'This is nothing to be flippant about.'

'No, Robert.'

'Who was this man?'

'A friend of mine.'

'Do you tell me so? Do you invite all your friends to my house?'

'He was the only one.'

'Why didn't you marry him?'

'He had a wife and five children in Sudbury in England. Separated.'

'That does, I believe, constitute an impediment. But who or what was he?'

'It would be just like you, Robert, not even to know who he was. He lived in this town, It's a little town.'

'Should I have known him?'

'Shouldn't a novelist know everybody and everything?'

'I'm not an authority on roses.'

'You've been reading my book.'

She was too sharp for him. He tried another tack: "Why didn't you tell me you were having a love affair? After all, I am civilised."

'Of course you're civilised. The world knows that. But there didn't seem any necessity for telling you.'

'There must be so many things that you don't feel it is necessary to tell me.'

'You were never an easy person to talk to.'

'All your secret thoughts. Who could understand a devious woman? Far and from the farthest coasts . . .'

'There you go again. Quotations. The two-footed gramophone. What good would it do you if you did understand?'

'Two-footed,' he said. 'Flat-footed.'

He was very angry: 'You could have written it all out for me if you couldn't say it. All the thought hidden behind your brooding face. All the things you thought when you said nothing, or said something else.'

'You really have been reading my book. Prying.'

The silence could have lasted all of three minutes. He searched around for something that would hurt.

'Isn't it odd that a comic figure should belong to a family addicted to sudden death?'

'What on earth do you mean?'

Her voice was higher. Anger? Indignation?

'That nose,' he said. 'Cyrano. Toto the Clown. And I heard about the flight of the two hundred hens.'

Silence.

'And about the brother who was burned?'

'They were kindly men,' she said. 'And good to talk to. They had green fingers.'

It would have gratified him if he could have heard a sob.

'I'll drive down to collect you in an hour's time.'

'He loved me,' she said. 'I suppose I loved him. He was something, in a place like this.'

Silence.

'You're a cruel little boy,' she said. 'But just to amuse you, I'll give you another comic story. Once he worked in a dog kennels in Kent in England. The people who owned the kennels had an advertisement in the local paper. One sentence read like this: Bitches in heat will be personally conducted from the railway station by Mr Dominic Byrne.

'Dominic Byrne,' she said. 'That was his name. He treasured that clipping. He loved to laugh at himself. He died for love. That's more than most will ever do. There you are. Make what you can out of that story, you flat-footed bore.'

She replaced the telephone so quietly that for a few moments he listened, waiting for more, thinking of something suitable to say.

On good days, light, reflected from the lake, seemed to brighten every nook and corner of the little town. At the end of some old narrow winding cobbled laneway there would be a vision of lake-water bright as a polished mirror. It was a graceful greystone town, elegantly laid-out by some Frenchman hired by an eighteenth-century earl. The crystal river that fed the lake flowed through the town and gave space and scope for a tree-lined mall. But grace and dancing light could do little to mollify his irritation. This time, by the heavenly father, he would have it out with her, he would put her in her place, revenge himself for a long-ago affront and humiliation.

Body in the bed, indeed. Two hundred hens, indeed. Swamps and sewers, indeed. Bitches in heat, indeed. She did not have a leg to stand on. Rutting, and on his time, with a long-nosed yahoo.

The Byzantine church, with which the parish priest had recently done his damnedest to disfigure the town, struck his eyes with concentrated insult. Ignorant bloody peasants. The slick architects could sell them anything: Gothic, Byzantine, Romanesque, Igloo, Kraal, Modern Cubist. The faithful paid, and the pastor made the choice.

Who would ever have thought that a lawnmower could be a Viking funeral pyre?

The barracks, a square, grey house, made ugly by barred windows and notice-boards, was beside the church. The guard, capless, the neck of his uniform jacket open, his hands in his trouser pockets, stood in the doorway. He was still perspiring. The man would melt. There was a drop to his nose: snot or sweat or a subtle blend of both. Robert St Blaise Macmahon would never again make jokes about civic guards. He said: 'I've come for Miss Hynes.'

'Too late, Mr Macmahon, sir. The bird has flown.'

'She has what?'

'Gone, sir. Eloped. Stampeded. On the Dublin train. Ten minutes ago. I heard her whistle.'

'Whistle?'

'The train, sir.'

'But the funeral? The inquest?'

'Oh, his wife and children will bury him. We phoned them.'

'But the inquest?'

'Her affidavit will do the job. We'll just say he dropped while visiting your house to look at the roses.'

'That's almost the truth.'

'The whole truth and nothing but the truth is often a bitter dose, sir.'

'As I said, guard, you are a philosopher.'

He remembered too late that he hadn't said that, he had just thought it.

'Thank you kindly, sir. Would you chance a cup of tea, sir? Nothing better to cool one on a hot day. Not that I like tea myself. But in this weather, you know. The hottest day, the forecast says.'

Well, why not? He needed cooling. The bird had flown, sailing away from him, over the chasm, laughing triumphant eldritch laughter.

In the austere dayroom they sat on hard chairs and sipped tea.

'Nothing decent or drinkable here, sir, except a half-bottle of Sandeman's port.'

'No thank you, guard. No port. The tea will suffice.'

'Those are gallant shoes, sir, if you'll excuse me being so pass-remarkable. Hand-made jobs.'

'Yes, hand-made.'

'Costly, I'd say. But then they'd last for ever.'

'Quite true, guard.'

'He's coffined by now. The heat, you know.'

'Don't remind me.'

'Sorry, sir. But the facts of life are the facts of life. Making love one minute. In a coffin the next.'

'The facts of death, guard. Alone withouten any company.'

'True as you say, sir. He was a droll divil, poor Byrne, and he died droll.'

'Among the roses, guard.'

'It could happen to anyone, God help us. Neither the day nor the hour do we know. The oddest thing, now, happened once to the sergeant's brother that's a journalist in Dublin. This particular day he's due to travel to Limerick City to report on a flower show. But he misses the train. So he sends a telegram to ask a reporter from another newspaper to keep him a carbon. Then he adjourns to pass the day in the upstairs lounge bar of the Ulster House. Along comes the Holy Hour as they call it for jokes, when the pubs of Dublin close for a while in the early afternoon. To break up the morning boozing parties, you understand. There's nobody in the lounge except the sergeant's brother and a strange man. So the manager locks them in there to drink in peace and goes off to his lunch. And exactly halfways through the Holy Hour the stranger drops down dead. Angina. And there's me man that should be at a flower show in Limerick locked in on a licensed premises, the Ulster House, during an off or illegal hour, with a dead man that he doesn't know from Adam.'

'An interesting legal situation, guard.'

'Oh, it was squared, of course. The full truth about that couldn't be allowed out. It would be a black mark on the licence. The manager might lose his job.'

'People might even criticise the quality of the drink.'

'They might, sir. Some people can't be satisfied. Not that there was ever a bad drop sold in the Ulster House. Another cup, Mr Macmahon, sir.'

'Thank you, guard.'

'She'll come back, Mr Macmahon. Blood they say is thicker than water.'

'They do say that, do they? Yet somehow, in spite of what they say, I don't think she'll be back.'

On she went, leaping, flying, describing jaunty parabolas. He would, of course, have to send her money. She was entitled to something legally and he could well afford to be generous beyond what the law demanded.

'So the long-nosed lover died, guard, looking at the roses.'

'In a manner of speaking, sir.'

'Possibly the only man, guard, who ever had the privilege. Look thy last on all things lovely.'

But the guard was not aware of de la Mare.

'That's what we'll say, sir. It would be best for all. His wife and all. And no scandal.'

'Days of wine and roses, guard.'

'Yes, sir. Alas, that we have nothing here but that half-bottle of Sandeman's port. She was a great lady to grow roses, sir. That's how they met in the beginning, she told me. Over roses.'

4

THE DETECTIVES
Police and Private Investigators

THE LAW IS THE LAW

Liam O'Flaherty

That classic story of treachery and heroism, The Informer *by Liam O'Flaherty, which was published in 1925 and then made into an acclaimed movie by John Ford in 1935, has been described as 'a modern keystone in the history of crime writing'. It is often thought, mistakenly, to be the author's only excursion into crime writing, whereas elements of this may be found in another of his finest works,* Famine *(1937), and in several short stories including 'The Pedlar's Revenge', about the deadly feud between a tiny itinerant and Paddy Moynihan, 'the tallest, strongest man in living memory'; and 'The Law is the Law'. O'Flaherty (1896-1984), who was born on Inishmore, the largest of the Aran Islands, was educated for the priesthood but decided he did not have the vocation and for a time served in the Irish Guards. For a while he also took part in the Civil War in Ireland, but fearing arrest, he escaped to London where he started to write. Although he later spent a good deal of time travelling in America, Europe and Russia, Ireland was invariably the subject of his stories.*

'The Law is the Law' is a wonderfully evocative tale of administering justice to suit the circumstances, set on just the kind of island where Liam O'Flaherty grew up. And in Superintendent Corrigan, the hero and narrator of this case, we have an archetypal Irish detective—now, sadly, one can only wish that the author had written more stories about him.

I was Superintendent of Police in the district of Kilmorris. It is one of the most remote parts of Ireland, on the west coast. The inhabitants are all practically of pure Gaelic stock, and during the centuries of English occupation they retained most of their old customs. A very fine race of men, industrious, thrifty, extremely religious, and

261

proud to a fanatical degree. To illustrate this latter characteristic the case of Sean McKelvey seems to me worthy of record . . .

He lived on the small island of Inishcam, which is separated from the mainland by a narrow channel of about a quarter of a mile. Even so, this tiny channel renders the island an excellent headquarters for its principal industry, which is—or was, at least—the distilling of illicit whisky. We call it poitheen locally. Except for one narrow cove, the island is surrounded by rugged cliffs, so it was an easy matter for scouts to give warning when any of my men came from the mainland to search for the still. And the islanders went on merrily distilling through the first year of my service in the district, just as they had been doing for centuries. In the same way, when the spirits were ready for the market, they could sneak over to the mainland during the night in their currachs and dispose of their goods in safety. I was at my wits' end as to how to deal with the nuisance.

Ours is a democratic police force, and, as I understand it, the business of a good police officer is to preserve order in his district at the expense of as little coercion as possible. It was impossible to adopt rough measures with the 25 or 30 families on the island. There would be a rumpus on the mainland, followed by the usual protests to Dublin by people who are always looking for a chance to accuse the police force of tyrannical conduct. I decided the only thing to do was to tackle Sean McKelvey in person.

He was the chief man in Inishcam and was commonly called The King. Sometime during the eighties of the last century, a party of British military and police invaded the island in the hope of being able to collect some rent from the inhabitants, who had paid none for years. On the approach of the authorities, the inhabitants fled to the cliffs, leaving only the aged and the infants in the village. The officer in charge picked on one dignified old fellow as the most likely to be able to give him information and assistance in dealing with the others.

'Are you the head man of this island?' he asked.

The old man bowed, understanding no English.

Then the officer, to cover his defeat and to impress the natives with the power of Britain, delivered the old man a lecture on the futility of resisting British law and told him to have his islanders parade at the rent office with their rent within one month, or else their property would be impounded. Then he went away, and some newspaper reporter picked on the incident for a story, and the story

reached London, and presently there were scholars and other fad-
dists coming to the island to visit the last remaining Irish king. In
that way old McKelvey, Sean's grandfather, received the title, and
his descendants inherited it, and the islanders politely accepted the
situation, since it brought them revenue from summer visitors.

However, if a man is called King, even in fun, he develops a kingly
manner in course of time. Sean McKelvey, being the third of this
prosperous line of monarchs, was firmly convinced of his royal blood
and behaved as if he had divine right to rule over Inishcam. Many a
time he was heard to say on the mainland, when he came there on
business, that the police had no authority over him and that, if they
made any attempt to interfere with his person, he would die rather
than submit to the indignity. And the islanders believed him. So that
it can be easily understood it was a ticklish business putting an end
to his distillery.

*   *   *

I dressed in civilian clothes and got a man to row me over to the
island, on which I landed alone and unarmed, to beard The King in
his realm.

It was a fine summer morning, and when I jumped ashore on the
little sandy beach. I saw a crowd of the islanders lounging on a
broad, flat rock near the village, which stands above the beach. I
climbed the steep, rocky path, which was like the approach to a for-
tress. They all stared at me as I came to the rock, but nobody spoke.
They knew who I was and were not pleased to see me.

I will admit that I grew slightly uneasy, for the men on that island
are of tremendous physique, tall, slim, and as hard as whipcord. The
surroundings were even more menacing than the islanders themselves. Beyond the village there was some arable land, covered with
patches of rye and potatoes. Beyond that rose the mountains,
covered with heather and cut by deep, gloomy valleys. Fat chance
my men would have trying to find a still in that impassable wilderness.

'Good morning, men,' I said cheerfully. 'I have come to see The
King.'

A man nodded over his shoulder towards a house in the centre of
the village. It was a one-storied cottage like the rest, with a slate
roof, but it was longer, and its walls had a pink wash, whereas the

others were white-washed. Some flowers grew in the yard in front of it, beside a heap of lobster pots and nets that were hanging up to dry.

I strode towards the house. When I entered the yard, a man appeared in the doorway with his arms folded on his bosom. It was Sean McKelvey, The King of the island.

'You want to see me?' he said arrogantly.

He was about six feet in height and as straight as a rod. He was dressed only in his shirt and trousers, which were fastened at the waist by a red handkerchief. His shirt was open at the neck, and the sleeves were rolled up beyond his biceps, which were stiff, owing to his arms being folded. He was as muscular as a prizefighter in training, and as I glanced at his muscles I doubted the good sense of my plan. There was a fair stubble on his powerful jaws and upper lip, increasing the menacing expression of his arrogant countenance. His blue eyes seemed to bore through me, as they say in romances. In fact, he looked every inch a king, and I wished that he had chosen somebody else's district for his damned distilling, for his type is one I admire. But the law is the law and must be upheld.

'Yes,' I answered. 'I've come to see you, McKelvey.'

'As friend or foe?' he asked.

Affecting a calm which I did not feel, I took a cigarette from my case and tapped the end on the lid. The other men began to crowd around.

'Whichever way you like to take it,' I said.

'Well! That means you've come as an enemy,' said McKelvey.

'I suppose you know who I am,' I said.

'Troth, that I do,' said he. 'I know who ye are well enough but I don't give a toss rap for you or yer men. You have nothing against me. So I don't want you nosing about this island.'

'Oh! Yes, I have something against you, McKelvey.'

'What is it?'

'You make poitheen here.'

'I'm not saying that we do, but even if we do it has nothing to do with you.'

'I'm afraid it has. I am police officer of this district and I won't have you or anybody else poisoning the people with your rotten drink. That's what I came to see you about.'

'Well! You have your journey for nothing. I'm taking no orders from you, Mr Corrigan.'

'I'm not giving you orders, but if you had the courage of a man I'd like to make a bargain with you.'

His face darkened, and he leaned back slightly as if he were going to spring at me. He unfolded his arms, and his hands crept slowly down by his sides, the fingers doubling over the palms.

'What's that I heard you saying?' he whispered.

He came forward two paces slowly, just like an animal getting into position for a pounce. Even at that moment I had to admire the magnificent stance of the man. The other islanders behind me began to growl, and I knew that my bait had taken.

'If you had the courage of a man,' I repeated in a low, offensive sort of tone, 'I'd like to make a bargain with you.'

'And what makes you think,' drawled McKelvey, 'that I haven't the courage of a man?'

At that moment a young woman appeared in the doorway with a baby in her arms. She was a handsome woman with red hair, with a rather startled expression in her eyes.

'Sean,' she cried, 'what ails you?'

He wheeled around like a shot and barked at her: 'Go into the house, Mary.'

She obeyed instantly, and he turned back to face me.

'Speak what's in your mind,' he cried.

'It's like this, McKelvey,' I said casually. 'You and your still are a damn nuisance in my district. You call yourself King of this island, and I'm the local police officer whose business is to see that the law is observed. There isn't room for the two of us. Well! This is what I propose. I'm ready to fight you and let the winner have the sway. If you win, you can carry on with your still, and I give you my word of honour that I'll not interfere with you in the future. If I win, you'll come along with me to the police barracks and give a written guarantee that you'll break up your still and obey the law in the future. How does that strike you as a fair deal? I'm putting it to you as man to man. If you have the guts of a man you'll agree to it.'

For a few moments there was dead silence. The infant began to cry inside the house. And then McKelvey sighed deeply, swelled out his chest, and nodded. I noticed that the whites of his eyes had gone red and the veins of his neck stood out, as if they were going to burst with outraged anger.

'So help me God,' he muttered, 'I'm going to kill you for this if I have to swing for it.'

'Just a moment,' I said. 'I have come here alone. Are you going to give me fair play and are you going to agree to the bargain I proposed?'

I wanted to infuriate him as much as possible in order to give myself a better chance of beating him.

'Who the hell do ye think yer dealing with?' he roared. 'A rat like yourself or Sean McKelvey, the King of Inishcam?'

'Then it's a bargain,' I said.

'Put up your fists,' he roared.

'Give me time to strip,' I said, unbuttoning my coat.

As I took off my coat and waistcoat leisurely, he stood in front of me, shaking with anger and then he suddenly seemed to collect himself and master his rage. He bit his lip, and a queer, startled look came into his eyes. For all the world he looked at that moment like a wild animal of the African forest confronted by a hunter for the first time, awed and at the same time infuriated.

He stooped down and slipped off his shoes. Then he pulled his socks up over the ends of his trouser legs and rubbed some sand from the yard on his palms. By that time I was set for action.

'I'm ready now if you are,' I said.

'Then take your medicine.'

With that he drove with his right at my chin, and I ducked just in time to let it graze the right side of my head. Even so, it rocked me to my heels and it enabled me to judge the calibre of the man with whom I had to deal. I realised that my only chance was being able to avoid the sledge hammer that he carried in his right hand, until his frenzy exhausted him. Ducking and skipping about the yard, I kept teasing him in order to keep his rage at fever pitch.

'So you think you can fight, do you, McKelvey?' I sneered. 'You couldn't hit a haystack. I'm ashamed to fight you. It's like taking milk from a child. You'd better surrender before I do you damage. What's the use? Look at that. You thought it was my head and it was only the air. Man alive, who told you you could fight?'

And sure enough, although he had the strength and agility of a tiger, he was handicapped by knowing nothing about boxing. All he could do was to swing that terrifying right hand and trust to luck. Little by little he began to tire, and I was overjoyed to hear that telltale panting.

'Now for it,' I thought.

I waded into him and landed twice on his chin with all the power in my body behind each blow, but the only result was that I smashed two knuckles in my left hand. McKelvey swayed backwards and then for the first time swung his left hand wildly and met me straight on the chest. I went back four yards before I fell, all in a heap, conscious but at the same time convinced that my ribs had been smashed to splinters and that the breath had been driven from my body. A great roar went up from the islanders.

I turned over and waited on my hands and knees until I recovered a little and then struggled to my feet. Had McKelvey gone for me at once it would have been his show, but the fool was dancing around the yard like a wild Indian, boasting of his prowess.

'There's not a man in Ireland that I wouldn't do the same to,' he yelled. 'Aye, or ten men either. I'll take every peeler they have and break every bone in their bodies. I'm Sean McKelvey, King of Inishcam, and I dare them to lay a hand on me.'

And then he gave a wild yell that re-echoed through the mountains.

His men yelled in response, and somehow that pulled me together.

'Hold on there,' I said. 'You're not done with me yet, you windbag. Come and take it.'

Crouching, he came towards me, his underlip turned downwards.

'Is it more ye want, ye rat?' he muttered. 'Very well, then. Take that.'

Taking his time and no doubt thinking that, because I slouched and swayed a bit, I was easy prey, he swung his right at me once more. It was so slow coming that I countered it. I dived in and landed a beauty on the mark. He grunted and doubled up. Then I lashed out with a vengeance, having found his tender spot.

'Don't kill him,' screamed his wife, running out into the yard.

The child wailed in the house, and several women, who had gathered to see the fight, also began to scream. The men, however, standing in a sullen group, were silent and astonished. In every one of their faces I saw a look of utter astonishment, as I glanced around at them nervously, not at all certain that they were not going to fall on me for having dishonoured their king. Not a bit of it. They stood there gaping, obviously unable to understand how it had come to pass that their invincible chief was down in a heap on the ground.

By the time I had finished dressing, McKelvey had come to his senses. He got to his feet and looked at me with an expression I shall never forget. It was an expression of bitter hatred, and at the same time there was in his eyes the picture of a shame that had already eaten to his very soul. At that moment I wished from the bottom of my heart that the result had been different. I saw that I had mortally wounded the man.

'You took me unawares,' he said quietly. 'It wouldn't happen again in a thousand years, if we met hand to hand every day of that thousand years. I lost my temper. You are a cunning man. Now what do you want with me? You won. I'm not able to go on with it.' And his strange, wild, blue eyes were fixed on mine, boring through me. Never in my life have I felt more ashamed and sorry than at that moment.

'You'll have to surrender your still, McKelvey,' I said, 'and come with me just as you promised.'

He lowered his eyes to the ground and answered: 'I'll do that. Come on with me into the house.'

Then indeed a strange thing happened. When I had followed him into the house, he went down to the hearth, where a small fire was burning. He took a heather broom from a corner of the hearth and began to sweep ashes over the burning embers.

'What are you doing, Sean?' said his wife, who stood nearby with the infant.

He did not answer but continued to sweep the ashes over the embers until he had extinguished the flames and there was no more smoke coming from the pile. Then he dropped the broom and stood erect.

'Come now into the garden,' he said.

I followed him out through the back door into the garden that adjoined the house. There he handed me a pinch of earth and a twig which he tore from a briar bush, the ancient formula for surrendering legal possession of his house and grounds.

'But you can't do this,' I said.

He drew himself up and answered arrogantly: 'You won. You are now the master. Isn't that what you wanted to be?'

'But I only want your still. I don't want your house and land. Man alive, are you mad?'

'You'll get the still as well,' he said. 'You're not thinking I'd go back on me word?'

He beckoned me to follow him, and I did.

He was still in his stockinged feet and he moved as nimbly as a goat over the rough ground, leaping from rock to rock, at a brisk trot, so that I had great difficulty in keeping up with him. We circled a spur of the mountain that rose immediately behind the village and then climed from ledge to ledge along a precipitous path that brought my heart to my mouth, until finally we arrived in a ravine. About midway down the ravine, he turned suddenly to the left and when I reached him he was pulling loose rocks away from what proved to be the mouth of a cave. We entered the cave and moved in almost complete darkness along a narrow passage between two smooth walls, against which my shoulders brushed when I stumbled over the loose granite slivers that covered the floor.

I was now in an extremely nervous state. I wondered: Has he brought me here to kill me?

The thought was a natural one. For a man in his state, his pride deeply humbled at being knocked down in the presence of his people and then going through the ceremony of 'sod and twig', to kill his conqueror in an access of frenzy would be the most likely thing in the world. I remembered his terrible eyes and the unnatural cal'n of his bearing since he had risen after his fall.

At last I could not prevent myself from crying out to him, in a voice which must have disclosed the fear that was upon me, 'Where are you taking me, McKelvey?'

'We're nearly there,' he said quietly.

And then my fear vanished, and I felt ashamed of having suspected him.

Presently the cave grew lighter, and then we emerged from the narrow walls suddenly into an open space overlooking the sea. Here, to my astonishment, I found the distillery in full blast, attended by three men who looked at us in speechless astonishment. The still was set up in a natural chamber formed by an overhanging brow of the granite cliff, and there were full kegs stacked in a corner.

'Give your orders,' said McKelvey.

One of the men began to speak rapidly to McKelvey in Irish, using the dialect of the island which I did not understand, although I have a passable knowledge of the language. McKelvey answered the man with some heat, and then the other two men joined in the argument, until it ceased all of a sudden on a shout from McKelvey. Then again he turned to me.

'Give your orders,' he said.

'Well!' I said. 'I suppose the easiest way is to chuck them over the cliff. The rocks below will do the rest.'

'Very well,' he said.

He turned to the men and gave them orders in Irish. They proceeded to obey him with reluctance. I stood by until the last of the stuff had been dragged to the edge and hurled down the steep face of the cliff, to smash on the rocks 400 feet below.

'That's that,' I said. 'Now, let's go.'

We turned back into the cave, leaving the three men chattering and gesticulating wildly in the clearing. Not a word was spoken until we got back to the village. There I noticed that the whole population was gathered on the flat rock, talking excitedly in low voices. By the way they looked at us as we approached, I knew that McKelvey's reign was at an end.

I waited outside in the yard while he went indoors to dress. Then he appeared again, in his best clothes.

'Are you ready?' I said.

'If it's all the same to you,' he said, 'I won't go with you but I'll follow.'

'But why not come with me?' I said. 'I have a boat down here, and it can bring you back again.'

'Well!' he said. 'I swore that I'd never be taken to a police barracks or before a magistrate alive.'

'But this is not a case of going to a police barracks or a magistrate. This is a personal thing between you and myself.'

'All the same,' he said, 'the people wouldn't understand that. If I went with you now they'd say you took me prisoner.'

I stared at him in astonishment. How could he still stand on ceremony, after having made a complete surrender? Now that he was dressed and in spite of the stubble on his cheeks, he looked more a king than ever, and nobody would believe that it was the same man who had danced around like a wild Indian after having felled me. He looked so austere and dignified and magnificently handsome. But his eyes had lost their arrogance, and they had the bitter expression of a defeated man. There was no hatred in them, but they gave the harrowing picture of a sorrow that could not be cured.

'I understand that,' I said. 'Then I have your word for it that you'll come along later.'

'I give you my word,' he said proudly, 'and I would not break my word for the richest kingdom in the world.'

'I have no doubt of it,' I said.

I hurried away, anxious to get out of sight of those eyes. When I reached the office and told Sergeant Kelly what had happened he could hardly believe me.

'Just you wait,' I said. 'McKelvey will be here himself shortly.'

'He'll never come,' said Kelly. 'The man would rather eat his own children than put a foot in this office.'

'We'll see,' I said.

And true enough, about an hour later McKelvey marched into the office.

In the meantime I had drawn up a document, which he signed without reading. It was all very irregular but it was the only way I could deal with a difficult situation. After all, fine character and all that he was, he was a public menace, and I had to put a stop to his distilling some way or other.

'Is that all you want of me now, Mr Corrigan?' he asked when he had finished.

'No,' I said. 'I'd like to shake hands with one of the finest men I ever met.'

He looked at my outstretched hand and then looked me straight in the eyes and shook his head.

'Oh! Come on, man,' I said. 'Let's be friends. One of us had to win. I've taken a licking myself many a time and I daresay I'll take a good many more. Don't hold it against me. I was only trying to do my duty as best I could. After all, you were breaking the law, and I had to stop you.'

'I wasn't breaking my own law,' he said quietly

And with that he marched out of the room with his head in the air.

'Keep an eye on him, Kelly,' I said to the sergeant. I had an idea that he might begin to drink at one of the local public houses and then run amok before returning to his island. From past experience I knew that men of his type are extremely dangerous, once they lose their self-control with drink.

However, McKelvey did nothing of the kind. He marched down to the shore, staring straight in front of him, and rowed back to the island without speaking to a soul.

'Well! That's that,' I said to the sergeant. 'McKelvey'll give us no more trouble with his still.'

'I hope not,' said Kelly, 'but I have me doubts.'

My own doubts were of a somewhat different kind. I was afraid that I had done the man a mortal injury and many a time during the following week I cursed the fate that had destined me to be a police officer, and one with a conscience at that. Had the man been a mean and treacherous scoundrel I should have had no compunction about overthrowing him; but he was, on the contrary, a splendid type that is of immense value to any community.

*   *   *

On the ninth day afterwards his wife called at my hotel while I was having lunch. I went out to see her. She looked ill and terribly worried. She had obviously been weeping quite recently.

'I'm Mrs McKelvey from Inishcam,' she said. 'I came to see you about my husband.'

'You look ill,' I said. 'Won't you sit down? Could I get you a drink of some sort?'

'No, Mr Corrigan,' she said gently, 'it's nothing like that I want. But wouldn't you come over and do something for Sean? He's been terrible since that day you came to the island, and I'm greatly afraid that he'll never rise again from his bed unless you can stop the people from thinking he was taken.'

'How do you mean?' I said.

'Well! It's how the people said that you took him, which you know well, sir, is a lie. And it broke his heart that they should say that about him. He took to his bed and he won't take bite or sup. He'll die that way. I know he will, for he's that proud.'

That was just what I feared. I told her to return at once to her home and that I would come over early in the afternoon.

'For God's sake, sir,' she said, 'don't let him know that I came to see you. That would kill him altogether.'

'Don't be afraid, Mrs McKelvey,' I said. 'I'll see to that.'

After she had gone, I did some hard thinking and finally hit upon a plan which, I felt sure, would succeed with the type of man that McKelvey was. This time I crossed over to the island in uniform, in accordance with the idea I had in mind. There were some people down on the beach, taking a catch of fish from the currachs that had just landed. I noticed that they touched their hats to me and bid me good day, quite unlike their conduct on the previous visit, when they scowled at me in silence. Presumably they had transferred their allegiance to the man who had defeated their king. Most of them followed me up to McKelvey's house and stood around the yard when I entered.

'God save all here,' I said.

'You too, sir,' said Mrs McKelvey, who was alone in the kitchen. As she spoke she put her fingers to her lips, as a sign that I was to say nothing about her visit to my hotel.

I nodded and inquired: 'Is McKelvey at home?'

'He's in the room, sir, in bed,' she said. 'Won't you go on in?'

I thanked her and entered the bedroom, where I found McKelvey lying on his back in the bed, his arms folded on his bosom, his head propped up high by pillows. His face was very pale, and his eyes looked sunken. I strode over to the bed, an angry scowl on my face.

'So this is your idea of keeping your word, McKelvey,' I said with a sneer. 'You are the man that wouldn't break his word for the richest kingdom in the world. What the devil do you mean by it? Are you making fun of me?'

I spoke as loudly as possible, so that the islanders outside could hear. McKelvey did not move for some moments. Then he sat bolt upright in bed and the colour came back to his pale cheeks. His eyes flashed with their old fire. He roared at his wife.

'Give me my clothes, Mary,' he cried. 'Leave the room, you. I'll talk to you on my feet and I'll talk to you outside my door, for I'll not commit murder on my hearth.'

I left the house and waited while he dressed. I could hear the people murmuring behind me in the yard and wondered what was going to be the outcome of infuriating this man, who was very likely by now out of his senses. However, as he came towards me, tightening his red handkerchief around his waist, dressed exactly as he had been the day I fought him, I could see that he was in his proper senses.

'Now you can say what you have to say,' he cried. 'And this time, I'm warning ye, it's going to be a fight to the finish.'

'I don't want to fight you, McKelvey,' I said. 'This time I have come here as a police officer to make a complaint. Nine days ago you came to my office of your own free will and gave a guarantee, as King of this island of Inishcam, that you were going to prevent your islanders from manufacturing spirits and selling them illegally on the mainland, which is my territory. Is that true or is it not?'

He stared at me and then he said in a loud voice: 'It is true.'

'It is also true that you are King of this island, is it not?'

'It is true,' he cried in a still louder voice.

'Well! Then, why don't you act up to your promise?'

'In what way have I broken it?'

'I have received information that one of your men has been to the mainland within the last few days, trying to buy another still to replace the old one we threw over the cliff.'

I had, of course, received no such information but I had a shrewd idea that something of the kind might have been afoot. In any case, it had the desired effect.

McKelvey thrust out his chest and cried: 'There may have been one of my men on the mainland looking for a still, but if he lands with it on this island I'll break every bone in his body. I've been sick for the past week but from now on I'm on my feet, and you may take your gospel oath that what I say I'll do will be done.'

'Well! In that case,' I said in a humble tone, 'I'm very sorry to have spoken so roughly, Mr McKelvey. I apologise. I can only beg your pardon.'

'You have it and welcome, Mr Corrigan,' he said, his face beaming with a great joy. 'And now, sir, I'm going to take that hand I refused before, if ye do me the honour.'

We shook hands, and I believe that I never have felt so happy in my life as when I grasped the hand of that magnificent man. Nor did I ever afterwards, during my service in the district, have the least trouble with poitheen-making on Inishcam.

THE VANISHING DIAMONDS

M. McDonnell Bodkin

Ireland's first serial detective was Paul Beck, nicknamed the 'Rule of Thumb Detective', created by Matthias McDonnell Bodkin, QC (1850-1933), a barrister from County Clare who later became a judge and for a time served as the Irish Nationalist MP for North Roscommon. Like his modern counterpart, John Mortimer, Bodkin found his relaxation from the law in writing detective stories. In 1898 he had the idea of creating a sleuth who was the direct opposite of Sherlock Holmes—then enjoying enormous success in the Strand Magazine— *and conceived Paul Beck who claimed to be not very bright. 'I just go by the rule of thumb,' he declared in his first case, 'and muddle and puzzle out my cases as best I can.' Looking more like a respectable retired milkman than a detective, Beck became very popular with readers in Ireland and in England where Bodkin's stories were reprinted in* Pearson's Magazine *as direct competition to Holmes. Considering the popularity of Paul Beck during these years, it remains a mystery to detective story aficionados why the stories about him are so little known. It may have something to do with the fact that Bodkin (like Sir Arthur Conan Doyle) considered his detective stories 'inferior work'—although the only one of his other books which was remembered at the time of his death was his volume of memoirs,* Recollections of an Irish Judge, *published in 1914!*

In 'The Vanishing Diamonds' Paul Beck tackles a case similar to those that confronted the analytical Sherlock Holmes, but without any of the Baker Street sleuth's romanticism, merely a little common sense and good fortune. Someday, perhaps, His Honour Judge Bodkin may be given the accolade he deserves as a unique contributor to the development of the modern detective story.

She was as bright as a butterfly in a flower garden, and as restless, quivering down to her fingertips with impatient excitement. That big room in the big house in Upper Belgrave Street was no bad notion of the flower garden.

There were just a few square yards of clear space where she sat alone—on a couch made for two—patting the soft carpet with a restless little foot. The rest of the room was filled with long tables, and oval tables, and round tables, all crowded with the pretty trifles and trinkets that ladies love. It seemed as if half a dozen of the smartest jewellers and fancy shops of Regent Street had emptied their show windows into the room. The tables were aglow with the gleam of gold and silver and the glitter of jewels, and the bright tints of rich silk and painted fans, and rare and dainty porcelain.

For Lilian Ray was to marry Sydney Harcourt in a week, and there was not a more popular couple in London. Her sweet face and winning ways had taken the heart of society by storm; and all the world knew that warm-hearted, hot-headed Harcourt was going hop, step, and jump to the devil when she caught and held him. So everybody was pleased, and said it was a perfect match, and for the last three weeks the wedding presents came pouring into the big house in Upper Belgrave Street, and flooded the front drawing-room. Lilian was impatient, but it was the impatience of delight.

No wonder she was excited, for her lover was coming, and with him were coming the famous Harcourt diamonds, which had been the delight and admiration and envy of fashionable London for half a century. The jewels had gone from the bank, where they had lain in darkness and safety for a dozen years, to the glittering shop of Mr Ophir, of Bond Street. For the setting was very old, and the vigilance of the tiny silver points that guarded the priceless morsels of bright stone had to be looked to, and a brand-new case was ordered to set the precious sparklers off to the best advantage.

A sudden knock at the door starts her again to the window, the cobweb silk flying behind. But she turns away petulantly like a spoiled child.

'Only another travelling bag,' she says; 'that makes seven—two with gold fittings. I wonder if this has gold fittings. I have set them all there in a row with their mouths open, and their gold or silver teeth grinning. There is not room for another one. I wonder do people think that ——'

The sentence was never finished, for at this moment a hansom cab came sharply round the corner in full view of the window. She caught one glimpe of an eager young face and a flat parcel, then she dropped back into her couch, panting a little. There came a second knock, and a foot on the stairs mounting three steps at a spring. She heard it, and knew it, but sat quite still. Another moment and he was in the room. Her eyes welcomed him, though her lips pouted.

'You are ten minutes before your time, sir,' she said, 'and I am terribly busy. What have you got there?'

'Oh! you little sly-boots. You know you have been longing for me and the diamonds, especially the diamonds, for the last hour. I've a great mind to carry them off again.'

He dropped into the seat beside her and his right arm stole round her waist, while he held the jewel-case away in his left hand. She blushed and laughed, and slipping from his encircling arm, made a dash for the diamonds. But he was too quick for her. He leaped to his feet and held the case aloft. Straining to the utmost of her tip-toes she could just reach one hand to his elbow; she placed the other among his brown curls, making ready for a leap. Her face was close to his and quite undefended. What happened was, under the circumstances, inevitable.

'Oh!' she exclaimed in quite a natural tone of surprise.

'Payment in advance,' he retorted, as the precious case came down to her desiring hands; 'overpayment, I confess, but then I am ready to give change to any amount.'

But she fled from him, with her treasure, to the couch. 'Now to be sensible for one short moment, if you can, and hand me the scissors out of that lady's companion there beside the photograph frame on the table.'

The jewel-case was done up in whitey-brown paper with strong cord and sealed with broad patches of red sealing-wax. Quite excitedly she cut through the string, leaving the seals unbroken, and let paper and twine and wax go down in a heap on the carpet together.

There emerged from the inner wrapping of soft, white tissue-paper the jewel-case in its new coat of light brown morocco with the monogram L. H. in neat gold letters on it. She gave a little cry of pleasure as her eyes fell on the lettering which proclaimed the jewels her very own, and he, sitting close beside, watching lovingly as one watches a pretty child at play, made believe to snatch it from her fingers. But she held it tight. Like a bather on the water's brim, she paused for one tantalising moment, drew a deep breath to make ready for the coming cry of rapture, and opened the case.

It was empty!

The slope of the raised centre of violet velvet was just ruffled a little, like a bed that had been slept in. That was all.

She looked suddenly in his eyes, half amused, half accusingly, for she thought he had played her some trick. His face was grave and startled.

'What does it mean, Syd? Are you playing with me?' But she knew from his face he was quite serious even while she asked.

'I cannot make it out, Lil,' he said, in an altered voice. 'I cannot make it out at all. I brought the case just as it was from Mr Ophir's. He told me he had put the diamonds in and sealed it up with his own hands. See, you have not even broken the seals,' and he mechanically picked up the litter of paper and twine from the floor. 'No one touched it since except myself and you, and the diamonds are gone. Old Ophir would no more dream of playing such a trick than an archbishop. Still it must be either that or—— But that is too absurd. He's as respectable as the Bank of England, and nearly as rich. It beats me, Lily. Why, the old boy warned me as he gave me the precious parcel. "We cannot be too careful, Mr Harcourt," he said. "There is twenty thousand pounds in that little parcel; let no hand touch it except your own." And I did not, of course; yet the diamonds have vanished, through case and paper and seals, into space.'

He stared ruefully at the expanse of violet velvet.

'The first thing is to see Mr Ophir,' he said.

'Oh, don't leave me, Syd.'

'Well to write him then. There must be some ridiculous mistake somewhere. Perhaps he gave me the wrong case. He would never— No, that's too absurd. Perhaps someone substituted the empty case when he looked aside for a moment. It may be necessary to employ a detective. I'll tell him so at once. Can I write a line anywhere?'

'There are half a dozen writing-cases there in a row on that table.'

She sat him down to a pretty mother-of-pearl and tortoise-shell affair, with violet scented ink in the silver-mounted bottles.

Then Harcourt showed a quick impatience, quite unlike his usual sunny manner, which Lilian thought nothing could disturb.

'Do get a fellow some decent ink, Lil,' he said, pettishly. 'I cannot write to an old don like Ophir with this stuff.'

She slipped from the room like a shadow and was back again

almost in a moment. When she returned she found him on the couch nervously fingering the fragments of paper, twine, and sealing-wax.

'I cannot make it out at all,' he muttered. 'They seem to have vanished into thin air. However, old Ophir will be able to help us if anyone can.'

He growled a bit at the dainty feminine pen and paper and then began:

'DEAR MR. OPHIR,—A most extraordinary thing has happened. I took the case you gave me, as you gave it to me, straight to Miss Ray, Belgrave Street, and opened it without breaking the seals, by cutting the strings in her presence. The diamonds were gone. There must be some mistake somewhere. Perhaps you may be able to clear up the mystery. If you suspect dishonesty, engage a detective at once. The driver will wait for a reply.

'Yours in haste,
'SYDNEY HARCOURT.'

He ran downstairs himself to hail a cab to take the note. A smart hansom with a smart driver on the box was crawling up the street. He dashed across with sudden alacrity, like a startled trout in a stream, when Harcourt raised his hand, almost taking the feet off a sturdy mendicant who was standing in front of the door.

'Here, my man. Take this to Mr Ophir's, in Bond Street. The address is on the envelope. Wait for an answer—double fare if you look sharp.'

The driver took the letter, touched his hat, and was off like a shot.

Harcourt threw the grumbling beggar a shilling and slammed the door. If he had waited just one second, he would have seen the beggar go off almost as quickly as the hansom, and disappear round the corner.

'Oh, Sydney, do cheer up a little,' pleaded Lily, transformed from tease to comforter. 'They will come all right. If they don't, I won't mind in the least, and your father is too fond of you, and of me, I think, too, to be really angry. It wasn't your fault, anyway.'

'Well, you see how it is, Lil; the infernal things were lost out of my hands. They were a mighty big prize for anyone to get hold of, and I have been going the pace a bit before I met you, my darling, and many people think I have outrun the bailiff. So there is sure to be malicious whispering and tattling, and people may say—no, I cannot tell you what they may say, and what is more, I don't care a— dash. You can never say or think or look anything but what's kind, and I would not have a pucker in that pretty brow or a tear in your blue eyes for all the diamonds that ever came out of Golconda. The diamonds may go hang. "Here's metal more attractive".'

Wonderful is Love's Lethe. In five minutes the diamonds had vanished from their memory as completely as they had vanished from the case. The sound and sight of a cab whirling to the door brought them suddenly back to the work-a-day world.

A footman entered, bearing in the very centre of a silver salver a visiting card slightly soiled. Harcourt took it.

Mr Paul Beck,
Private Detective.

'What is he like, Tomlinson?'

'Stout party in grey, sir. Don't seem particular bright.'

'Well, show him up.'

'Who can he be? What can he want?' muttered Harcourt to himself uneasily when the footman disappeared. 'There was no time to get to Ophir and back, much less to find a detective. I cannot make it out.'

'Oh, he came to the door like a whirlwind, and you know we never know how time goes when we are talking of——'

'Mr Paul Beck,' said the discreet footman, opening the door with a flourish.

Mr Paul Beck did not require much showing up apparently. He slipped furtively into the room, keeping his back as much as possible to the light, as if secrecy had grown a habit with him. He was a stout, strongly built man in dark grey tweed, suggesting rather the notion of a respectable retired milkman than a detective. His face was ruddy, and fringed with reddish brown whiskers, and his light brown hair curled like a water dog's. There was a chronic look of mild surprise in his wide-open blue eyes, and his smile was innocent as a child's.

Just as he entered, Lilian thought she noticed one quick, keen glance at where the empty jewel-case lay on the table and the tangle of paper and twine under it. But before she could be sure, the expression vanished from his eyes like a transparency when the light goes out.

Harcourt knew the man by reputation as one of the cleverest detectives in London—a man who had puzzled out mysteries where even the famous Mr Murdock Rose had failed—but looking at him now he could hardly believe the reputation was deserved.

'Mr Beck,' he said, 'will you take a chair? You come, I presume about——'

'About those diamonds,' said Mr Beck abruptly, without making any motion to sit down. 'I was fortunately with Mr Ophir when your note came. He asked me to take charge of the case. Your cabman lost no time, and here I am.'

'He told you the facts.'

'Very briefly.

'And you think——'

'I don't think. I am quite sure I know where and how to lay my hands on the diamonds.'

He spoke confidently. Lilian thought she saw the trace of a smile on the innocent-looking mouth, and a futile attempt to wink.

'I am delighted you think so,' said Harcourt; 'I am exceedingly anxious about the matter. Did Mr Ophir suggest——'

'Nothing,' broke in Mr Beck again. 'I didn't want his suggestions. Time is of importance, not talk. We are running on a hot scent; we must not give it time to cool. Is that the jewel-case?'

'Yes,' said Harcourt, taking it up and opening it; 'just as it came, empty.'

Mr Beck abruptly closed it again and put it in his pocket.

'That's the paper and twine that was around it, I suppose?'

Harcourt nodded. Mr Beck picked it up carefully and put it in the other pocket.

'You will observe,' said Harcourt, 'that the seal is not broken. The string was cut by Miss Ray. But when——'

'I must wish you good-day, Mr Harcourt,' said the unceremonious detective. 'Good-day, miss.'

'Have you finished your investigation already?' said Harcourt in surprise. 'Surely you cannot have already found a clue?'

'I have found all I wanted and expected. I see my way pretty plainly to lay my hands on the thief. When I have more news to tell I'll write. Good-day for the present.'

He was manifestly eager to be off on his mission. Almost before Harcourt could reply he was out of the room and down the stairs. He opened the door for himself, and the hansom which he had kept waiting whirled him away at headlong speed.

He had not disappeared five minutes down one side of the street when another hansom, driven at the same rapid pace, came tearing up the other. Lilian and Sydney had not got well over their surprise at his abrupt departure when a second knock came to the door, and Tomlinson entered again with a salver and a card—a clean one this time—

Mr Paul Beck,
Private Detective.

Harcourt started.

'The same man, Tomlinson?'

'The same, sir; leastways he seems a very absent-minded gentleman. "Anyone been here for the last ten minutes?" he said, breathless-like, when I opened the door. "You was, sir," I said, "not five minutes ago." "Oh, was I?" says he, with a queer kind of a laugh, "that's quick and no mistake. Am I here now?" "Of course you are, sir," I said, looking at him hard, but he seemed no way in liquor; "there you are and there you stand." "Oh, I mean did I go away at all?" "Fast as a hansom could carry you, sir," I said, humouring him; for he was as serious as a judge, and seemed quite put out to hear he had gone away in a hansom. "That's bad, that's bad," he said; "ten minutes late. Well, young man, there is no help for it. Take this card to Mr Harcourt." Shall I show him up, sir?'

'Of course.'

'What can it mean?' cried Lilian. 'Surely he cannot have found them in five minutes?'

'Perhaps so,' said Harcourt. 'He has probably found some clue, anyhow. His sober chaff of poor Tomlinson in the hall looks as if he were in good humour about something. Gad, I didn't think the old chap had so much fun in him!'

'Mr Paul Beck, sir.'

There was a slight, indescribable change in the manner of Mr Beck as he now entered the room. He was less furtive and less abrupt in his movements, and he seemed no longer anxious to keep his back to the light.

'You are back again very soon, Mr Beck,' said Harcourt. 'Have you got a clue?'

'I wish I had come five minutes sooner,' said Mr Beck, his voice quite changed. 'I'm afraid I have lost a clue. I have lost *the* clue in fact, and I must set about to finding it. Where is the jewel-case?'

'Why, I gave it to you not ten minutes ago.'

'To me?' began Mr Beck, and then stopped himself with a queer smile that was half a grimace. 'Oh, yes, you gave it to me. Well, and what did I do with it?'

'I don't understand you in the least.'

'Well, you need not understand me. But you can answer me.'

'Mr Beck, you will excuse me, but this is no time for bad jokes.'

'Mr Harcourt, you will learn later on that the joke in this business is not of my making, and I hope to make the joker pay for it. Meanwhile, I come from Mr Ophir.'

'You said that before.'

'Did I? Well, I say it again. I come from Mr Ophir commissioned to find those diamonds, and I ask you, as civilly as may be, what has been done with the case?'

'What you yourself have done with it?'

'Well, what I myself have done with it, if you like.'

Harcourt reddened with anger at this cool audacity, and Lilian suddenly interposed.

'You put it in your pocket, Mr Beck, and carried it away.'

'Was I in a hurry, miss?'

'You were in a great hurry."

'Was I dressed as I am now?'

'Exactly.'

'And looked the same?'

'Precisely.'

'Figure and face the same?'

'Well, yes. I thought you were more made up than you are now.'

'Made up! What do you mean, miss?'

'Well, Mr Beck, I thought you had been beautifying yourself. There was a trace of rouge on your cheeks.'

'And I kept my back to the light, I warrant.'

'Your memory is wonderful.'

Mr Beck chuckled, and Harcourt broke in angrily—

'Don't you think we've had enough of this foolery, sir?'

'More than enough,' said Mr Beck, calmly. 'I have the honour to wish you a very good morning, Mr Harcourt, and to you miss.' There was a touch of admiration in his voice as he addressed Miss Lilian.

'Oh, Syd!' she cried, as the door closed behind him, 'isn't it just thrilling! There never was such a mixed-up mystery. I do wonder which is the right Mr Beck.'

'Which! What in the world do you mean? I was dizzy enough without that. Of course they are both the right Mr Beck, or the wrong Mr Beck, whichever you please. They are both the same Mr Beck anyhow.'

*   *   *

Meanwhile Mr Beck is driving as fast as a hansom can carry him back to Mr Ophir's establishment, in Bond Street.

He found the eminent jeweller in his little glass citadel at the back of his glittering warehouse. A thrill of excitement disturbed his usual stately dignity.

'Well?' he said, when Mr Beck stepped into the little glass room, closing the door carefully behind him.

'Well,' responded the detective, 'I think I have got a clue. I can make a fair guess who has the diamonds.'

'Mr Harcourt was rather a wild young man before this engagement,' said Mr Ophir, smiling an embarrassed tentative smile.

'Who made the new case for you?' said Mr Beck, changing the subject with unceremonious abruptness.

'Hem—ah—Mr Smithson, one of the most competent and reliable men in the trade. He has done all our work for the last twenty years. It was a very finely finished case indeed.'

'Who brought it here?'

'One of Mr Smithson's workmen.'

'I think you told me this man saw you put the diamonds into the case, and seal them up for Mr Harcourt?'

'Yes. He was standing only a few yards off at the time. There were two of my own men standing close by also, if you would care to examine them. Brown, will you kindly tell Mr Carton and Mr Cuison to step this way for a moment?'

'Never mind,' said Mr Beck, with a sharp authority in his voice. 'Thank you, Mr Ophir, I don't want to see them just yet. But I will trouble you for Mr Smithson's address, if you please. I have an idea his man would be useful, if we could lay our hands on him.'

'I don't think so, Mr Beck; I don't think so at all. He was quite a common person. My own men will be much more satisfactory witnesses. Besides, you may have some trouble in finding him. Though of that, of course, I know nothing whatever.'

The detective looked at him curiously for a moment. He had grown quite flushed and excited.

'Many thanks for your advice, Mr Ophir,' he said quietly; 'but I think I will take my own way.'

Twenty minutes afterwards the indefatigable Mr Beck was at Mr Smithson's workshop cross-examining the proprietor; but nothing came of it. The man who brought the case to Mr Ophir's establishment was the man who made it. He was the best workman that Mr Smithson ever had, though he only had him for ten days. His name was Mulligan. It sounded Irish, Mr Smithson imagined, and he spoke like the man in Mr Boucicault's play *The Slaughraun*. But whether he was Irish or Dutch, he was a right good workman. Of that Mr Smithson was quite certain. He seemed hard up, and offered himself for very moderate wages. But before he was half an hour in the place he showed what he could do. So when the order came in for a case for the Harcourt diamonds Mr Smithson set him on the job. He worked all day, took the case home with him, and brought it back the next morning finished.

'I never saw a job done as well or so quick before,' concluded Mr Smithson out of breath.

'But how did he manage at home. You surely did not let him take the diamonds home with him?'

'Bless you,' cried Mr Smithson briskly, with a look of surprise at the great detective's innocent, imperturbale face, 'he never saw the diamonds, and never will.'

'Then how did he make the case to fit them?'

'We had a model—the old case.'

'Have you got it still?'

For the first time there was a gleam of interest on Mr Beck's face as he asked the question.

'Yes, I think it is somewhere about. Excuse me for a moment.'

He returned with a rubbed and faded jewel-case covered with what had once been dark green morocco. Inside, the white velvet had grown yellow with age.

'That was our model, Mr Beck. You see in the raised centre a place for the great star. The necklet ran round this slope.'

'I see,' said Mr Beck, and for a quiet man he managed to get a lot of meaning into those two simple words. Then, after a pause: 'You can let me have this old case, I suppose?'

'Certainly. Mr Ophir's instructions are sufficient.'

'By the way, Mr Smithson,' he said, carelessly, 'did Mr Mulligan—I think you said that was his name—say anything about Mr

Ophir?'

'Well, now, Mr Beck, now that you mention it, he did. When he came first he asked me did I not do work for Mr Ophir, and seemed anxious about it, I thought. He was very strong in his praise of Mr Ophir. He said he thought he could get a recommendation from him if I wanted it, but I didn't. His work was recommendation enough for me. That's my was of doing business.'

Mr Beck put the case in his coat-tail pocket, and moved towards the door. He paused on the threshold.

'Good day, Mr Smithson,' said Mr Beck. 'Mr Mulligan did not turn up in the afternoon, I suppose?'

'Now how did you guess that, Mr Beck. He did not. I gave him something extra for the way the thing was done and I fear he may have been indulging. But how did you guess it?'

'From something Mr Ophir said to me,' replied Mr Beck.

'But he is coming back in the morning. I have promised him double wages. You see, I took him as it were on trial first. He will be here at eight o'clock tomorrow. I can give you his address if you want him meanwhile.'

'Thanks. I fear it would not be of much use to me. I fancy I will find him when I want him, perhaps before you do. Good day again, Mr Smithson. By the way, I would not advise you to count too securely on Mr Mulligan's return tomorrow morning.'

Mr Beck had dismissed his hansom when he went into Mr Smithson's. He was only a few streets from the Strand, and he now walked very slowly in that direction, almost getting run over at the crossing between New Oxford Street and Tottenham Court Road, so absorbed was he in a brown study.

'He's my man,' he said to himself. 'He must help whether he likes it or not. It won't be the first time he has given me a lift, though never before in such a big thing as this. By George, he is a clever one! The devil himself is a dunce in comparison. What a success he would be if he had joined our profession, though I suppose he thinks he is better off as he is. I doubt it though. He would be the first detective of the century. Well, no one can say I'm jealous. If he helps me to unravel this business I'll take care he gets his share of the credit.'

Mr Beck laughed to himself as if he had made rather a good joke, and stopped abruptly as he glanced at a church clock.

'Four o'clock,' he muttered. 'How fast the day has gone by! Four is his hour, and I have no time to lose. I suppose I'll find him at the old spot;' and he set off at a double-quick pace, five miles an hour at least, without appearance of effort, in the direction of Simpson's restaurant in the Strand.

Just a word about the man he was going to meet. M. Grabeau was at this time the cleverest and most popular drawing-room entertainer in London. He was a somewhat shy man, and could neither sing nor talk much in public. But for all that he was a marvellous mimic and ventriloquist, a quick-change artist, but above all, a conjuror. He could maneuvre a pack of cards as a captain has company. They were animated and intelligent beings in his hands, obedient to his word of command.

In the construction and manufacture of mechanical tricks and toys he was possessed of a skill and ingenuity almost beyond belief. He had himself devised and constructed, with Mr Edison's permission, a doll, with a phonograph in her interior, which imitated nature with almost absolute perfection, and sang 'Home, Sweet Home,' not merely with the voice, but with the manner and gesture of one of the most popular singers on the concert stage. Indeed, there were malicious persons (rivals, for the most part) who insisted that the voice and gesture of the imitation singer were less wooden than the real.

Mr Beck had met M. Grabeau at some of those social functions where the introduction of a detective, either as a footman or a musician, had been thought a prudent precaution, and the acquaintance between them had ripened into companionship, if not friendship. Mr Beck's profession had an intense attraction for the Frenchman, who knew all Gaboriau's novels by heart.

'They are so clevaire,' he would say, with much gesticulation, to the stolid Mr Beck; 'they are too clevaire. The tangle in the commencement is superb. But what you call the unravel is not so good; the knots do not come undone so——'

Then he would hold up a string tied in a very kink of hard knots, and show it a moment later clean and smooth. It was one of his tricks.

'But the life of the detective, the real detective you will observe, it is charming. It is beyond the hunt of the fox. It is the hunt of the man. The clevaire man who runs, and what you call doubles, and hides and fights too, sometime. It is glorious; it is fine.'

'Going to waste,' Mr Beck would mutter disconsolately after one of these interviews, when the Frenchman would spy out and pick up an almost invisible clue. 'Going to waste. He would make one of the best detectives in the service, and he fiddles away his time at play-acting and trinket-selling and money-making.' So Mr Beck would shake his head over this melancholy instance of misplaced genius.

Naturally, when Mr Beck got tangled over the vanishing-diamond puzzle, he was anxious to consult his friend, M. Grabeau.

'I hope he's here,' said Mr Beck to himself, as he entered Simpson's restaurant.

One look round relieved his mind on that score. M. Grabeau was there at his accustomed place at a corner table, at his accustomed dinner—a plate of roast beef underdone. For M. Grabeau affected English dishes and English cookery, and liked the honest, substantial fare of Simpson's.

A stout, good-humoured man was M. Grabeau, with a quick eye, a close-cropped, shiny black head, blue eyes, and a smooth, cream-coloured face.

He noticed Mr Beck the moment he entered the room, and put down the evening paper on which a moment before he was intent.

'Hullo!' he cried out, pleasantly, 'that is you? *Bon-soir*, Monsieur Beck. I hope that you carry yourself well?'

It was noticeable about M. Grabeau that, though he could mimic any voice perfectly, when he spoke as M. Grabeau he spoke with a strong French accent, and interlarded his sentences with scraps of French.

Mr Beck nodded, hung up his hat, and seated himself.

'Boiled mutton,' he said to the waiter, 'and a pint of stout.'

'The fact is, monsieur,' he went on in much the same tone, when the waiter whisked away to execute his order, 'I wanted a word with you.'

'Ah-hah! I know,' said the other, vivaciously. 'It's the Harcourt diamonds that have come to you, is it not? The wonderful diamonds of which one talked all the evening at the Harcourt reception. They have disappeared, and his lordship has employed M. Beck, the great detective. I thought you would come to me. It's all here,' and he handed him across the table the *Westminster*, with his finger on a prominent paragraph headed in big, black letters:

THE VANISHING DIAMONDS

Mr Beck read it through carefully.

Quite a sensation has been created in fashionable London by the sudden disappearance—it would, perhaps, be premature to say robbery—of the famous 'Harcourt Heirloom,' perhaps, after the Crown Jewels, the most famous and valuable diamonds in London. Our representative learned from the eminent jeweller, Mr Ophir, of Bond Street, that he had with his own hands this morning put the jewels into a case, sealed up the parcel and handed it to the Hon. Mr Sydney Harcourt. Mr Harcourt, on the other hand, states that when the case was opened in his presence by his *fiancée*, Miss Ray—for whom the jewels were meant as a wedding present—it was empty. If Mr Ophir and the Hon. Sydney Harcourt both speak the truth— and we have no reason to doubt either, or both—the diamonds must have vanished through the case and brown paper in the hansom cab *en route* between Bond Street and Upper Belgrave Street. We need not say that in position and respectability Mr Ophir stands at the very head of his business, and the Hon. Sydney Harcourt, though he ran loose for awhile on the racecourse, contracted no serious pecuniary obligations of which the world knows; and his rank, character, and position should protect him from even the smallest taint of suspicion. All these circumstances, of course, heighten the mystery. We understand that the famous detective, Mr Beck, at the instance of Mr Ophir, called later on at Upper Belgrave Street. He has a clue as a matter of course. A clue is one of those things that no well-regulated detective is ever without.

M. Grabeau watched Mr Beck eagerly, reading his face as he read the paper.

'Well,' he asked impatiently, when Mr Beck at length came to an end, 'it is all right there?'

'Pretty accurate for a newspaper reporter!'

'And you have got the clue—you, the famous detective.'

There was sometimes the faintest suggestion of contempt, a vague hint at a sneer, in M. Grabeau's tone as he talked to Mr Beck, which Mr Beck never appeared to resent or even notice in the least.

'Well, yes, monsieur, I think I have a bit of a clue. But I came to hear your notion of the business. I have an idea that you are the man to put me on the right track. It would not be the first time, you know.'

Monsieur beamed at the rough compliment. 'You must first tell me all—everything.'

Mr Beck told him all—everything—with admirable candor, not forgetting the doubling of his own character at Belgrave Street.

'Well,' he said at last, 'what do you think, monsieur?'

'Mr Ophir,' said M. Grabeau shortly, and closed his mouth sharply with a snap like a trap.

'No,' cried Mr Beck, in a tone of surprise and admiration. 'You don't say so! You don't think, then, there is any truth in the hint in the paper that young Harcourt himself made away with the stones to pay some gambling debts?'

'No, my friend, believe me. He of them knows nothing more than he has said. It was not what you call the worth of his while. His father, he is rich; his lady, she is beautiful. I have seen her. Respectable Mr Ophir gives to him the jewels. The risk is too great, even if he have debts, which is not proved.'

'But how did Mr Ophir get them out of the case?'

'He did not even put them in.'

'I thought I told you that three people saw him put them in—two of his own men and the messenger, a Mr Mulligan, who came from the casemaker.'

'That messenger—you have seen him then?'

'Well, no. He had not come back to his place of employment when I called.'

'And he will never come. He has vanished. Mr Ophir perhaps could tell where he has vanished, but he will not tell you, believe it well.'

'But the other two men saw the jewels packed. There were two others besides the messenger.'

'*Hélas!* my great detective, are you not a little—I will not say stupid—a little innocent today? You will not think harm of Mr Ophir. *Très bien.* But that which you object, it is so simple. Give me for a moment your watch and chain.'

He leaned across the table, and as if by magic Mr Beck's watch and chain were in his hands—a heavy gold watch with a heavy gold chain that fitted to the waistcoat buttonhole with a gold bar.

'Now observe; this will be our case.' With rapid, dexterous fingers he fashioned the copy of the *Westminster Gazette* into the semblance of a jewel-case with a closely fitting lid. He opened the box wide, put the watch and chain in, so that Mr Beck could see it plainly inside, and closed the lid with two fingers only.

'There was no deception.'

He pushed the box across the tablecloth to Mr Beck, who opened it and found it empty. The wide eyes and bland smile of the detective expressed his astonishment.

'But where has it gone to?' he cried.

'Behold, it is there,' said M. Grabeau, tapping him on the capacious waistcoat.

The watch was comfortably back in Mr Beck's waistcoat pocket, for which, by the way, it was a pretty tight fit, and the gold bar of the chain was again securely fastened in his waistcoat buttonhole.

'I could have sworn I saw you put it into the case and leave it there.'

'*Eh bien!* So could the men of this M. Ophir of whom you speak. I put it in your pocket, he put it in his own. Behold all the difference. His plan was, oh! so much easier.'

'But, monsieur, M. Ophir has the name of a most decent and respectable man.'

M. Grabeau snapped his fingers in contemptuous anger. 'This man,' he said, 'I know him, I have had what you call shufflings—dealings—with him. He is cold, but he is cunning. He called me—me, Alphonse Grabeau—one cheat. Now I, Alphonse Grabeau, call him, M. Ophir, one thief, and I will prove it. He has stolen the diamonds. I will help you, my friend, to run him up.'

'I am much obliged, monsieur. I rather thought from the first you could give me a lift in this case. Where can I see you tomorrow if I have anything to say to you?'

'I will be in my leetle establishment until two hours of the afternoon. At four I will be here at my dinner. In the evening I will be in the saloon of the Duke of Doubleditch. At any time I will be glad to talk to you of this case—of this M. Ophir, the thief. But you must be punctual, for I am a man of the minute.'

'Quite sure you are going to the Duke's in the evening?'

'It is equally certain as a musket.'

'Oh, very well, if I don't see you at the shop I will see you at dinner.'

M. Grabeau drained the last drops of his glass of whisky-and-water, picked up his cane and hat and gloves.

Mr Beck rose at the same moment.

'Good evening, monsieur,' he said admiringly, 'I must shake hands with if you if it was to be the last time. I always thought you were almighty clever, but I never rightly knew how clever you are until tonight. It is a thundering pity that——'

'What?' asked M. Grabeau sharply, for Mr Beck paused in the very middle of his sentence.

'That you are not one of us; that your talents didn't get fair play and full scope in the right direction.'

M. Grabeau beamed at the compliment, and went out beaming.

Mr Beck called for a second helping of boiled mutton, and ate it slowly. His face and manner were more vacuous than ever.

Something of special importance must plainly have detained Mr Beck, for it was a quarter past two next day when he walked with a quick, swinging step up to the 'leetle establishment' of M. Grabeau, in Wardour Street. He paused for one moment before the window where all sorts of ingenious and precious knickknacks and trifles were temptingly arranged, then walked into the shop.

There was a young man of about nineteen years alone behind the counter; a young man with a long nose, very fleshy at the top, and an unwholesome complexion, and a pair of beady black eyes.

'Good day, Jacob,' said Mr Beck. 'Master out?'

'Just gone a quarter of an hour ago.'

'Coming back?'

'Not this evening.'

'Oh, well, I'll see him later on. By the way, Jacob, that's a new thing you have got. The coral necklet and brooch there in the window. Will you let me have a peep at it?'

Jacob took the case from the window and set it on the counter. The set was a fine specimen of carved coral linked with fine gold, in a case of faded brown morocco and dingy white velvet that looked as old as themselves.

Mr Beck inspected the trinkets carefully for a full five minutes with intent admiration, turning the case round several times to get a better view. He seemed much interested in a smear of what looked like damp gum on the edge of the leather.

'What's the damage, Jacob?' he asked at last.

'Not for sale, sir. Master cautioned me four different times— not for sale, no matter what price I might be offered. Not likely to be tempted much, I should say; there is not half a sovereign's worth of gold in the lot.'

'Ah!' said Mr Beck meditatively, Then persuasively: 'Well, it is not so much the red affairs I want as the box they are in. My aunt desired me to get her one for a brooch and necklace she picked up cheap at a sale, and this would about do. You were not forbidden to sell the box, were you, Jacob? It doesn't seem to fit these things as if it were made for them, does it?'

'It fits them most beautifully, Mr Beck. But there, don't go. I Don't say I won't sell it to oblige a friend of the master, if I get a fair price for it.'

'What do you call a fair price?'

'What would you say to a soverign now?'

Mr Beck said nothing to a sovereign. He said nothing at all. But he produced the coin in question from his waistcoat pocket and placed it on the counter, turned the contents of the case out in a jingling heap, put the case itself in his pocket, and walked out of the shop.

Mr Beck let himself in with a latchkey, and walked noiselessly upstairs to his own pretty little sitting-room on the drawing-room floor. He took the old case from his pocket and set it beside another old case—the one he got from Mr Smithson—on the round table in the centre of the room. There were flowers on the table, and Mr Beck sniffed their fragrance approvingly; he seemed on this particular afternoon to be pleased with everything.

The two cases were alike, though not identical in form; he opened them. Inside, the shape was almost precisely the same. Mr Beck gave a short assenting nod at them, as if he was nodding approval of something he had just said himself. Then he walked to the door, closed it softly, and turned the key in the lock. Anyone with an eye to the keyhole—such an eye as Sam Weller graphically described in the witness-box—might have seen Mr Beck drop into an easy-chair with one of the two cases in his hand, turning it slowly round and round with that look, puzzled yet confident, which so many people wore when that delightful problem 'Pigs in Clover' was the rage.

A little later anyone with an ear to the keyhole might have heard Mr Beck draw a deep breath of relief, and chuckle quietly to himself; then, if the ear was preternaturally acute, might have heard him lock something in his own pet patent-safe which stood in a neat overcoat of mahogany in a corner of the room.

*　　　*　　　*

'Oh! how can people be so mean?' cried Lilian Ray, in a voice that quivered with indignation.

She was standing in the middle of her own drawing-room, and the tattered fragments of the 'extra special' edition of the *Evening Talebearer* fluttered round her like a pink snowstorm. She stamped on the bits of paper with angry little feet.

'Easy, Lil, easy!' cried Harcourt from the sofa where he sat, a gloomy look on his handsome face. 'Take it quietly, my pet. It's the nature of the beasts. Besides, it's true enough—most of it. I have been as they say, "a wild young scamp." "No one knows the amount of my debts"—because there aren't any. "Mr Ophir is a gentleman of unimpeachable respectability." "This is a most unpleasant mystery for the Hon. Sydney Harcourt." There's no denying that's true, anyway.'

'I wonder at you, Syd—you, a great strong man, to sit there quietly and hear such things said!' She turned on him sharply, her blue eyes very bright behind the unshed tears.

'But I haven't heard them, Lil.'

'Oh, well, you know what I mean. Why don't you stamp this thing out, and teach those vile slanderers a lesson they would never forget? Why don't you go straight to their low den, wherever it is, and—and—oh, how I wish I were a man!'

'Glad you're not, Lil, for my sake,' he answered, in a tone that brought the quick blood to her cheek.

She ran to him impetuously, and played with his curls as she bent caressingly over him. 'My poor boy, I am so sorry to see you worried.'

A sharp knock came to the door, and Lilian was sitting on the sofa, and at the extreme end of it, panting a little, when the footman entered.

'Mr Beck, sir,' said the footman.

'Show him in. What does the fellow want now, I wonder?'

'I won't detain you a moment, Mr Harcourt,' said the inperturbable Mr Beck, walking quietly into the room.

'Oh, I beg your pardon, Mr Beck,' stammered Harcourt. 'I did not know; that is to say, I was engaged.'

'So I see, sir,' said Mr Beck drily. 'But I think the young lady will spare a moment or two for what I have to say and to show.'

'You have a clue, then?'

'Well, yes, I think I may say I have a clue.'

He took from his coat-tail pocket the old jewel-case which he had purchased for a sovereign, and set it on the table, pushing aside some costly trifles to make place for it.

'You see this, miss. Is it at all like the case that came with the diamonds?'

'The case that came without the diamonds you mean, Mr Beck,' said Lilian smiling. 'It is just like it in shape, but the other was quite new and shining.'

'That is a detail, miss. A clever hand could make that little change from new to old in half an hour. Now will you kindly open it?'

As Lilian opened it she thrilled with the sudden unreasonable notion that the diamonds might be inside. But it was quite empty; faded and empty.

'The inside is just the same, too,' she said, 'only this is so faded. Anything else, Mr Beck?'

'Would you oblige me by taking the case in your hands for one moment. No, don't close it. Now will you kindly put your thumb here, and your other thumb here in the opposite side?'

Mr Beck guided the slender little thumbs to their places while Harcourt looked on in amazement.

'Now, miss, kindly squeeze both together.'

Lilian gave a quick, sharp gasp of delight and surprise. For suddenly, as if by magic, there blazed on the slope of faded velvet a great circle of flashing diamonds with a star of surpassing splendour in the centre.

'Oh! oh! oh!' she cried breathlessly. 'They are too beautiful for anyone! Oh, Syd,' turning to her lover with eyes brighter than the jewels, 'did you ever see anything so beautiful? They dazzle my eyes and my mind together. I cannot look at them any longer,' and she closed the case with a snap, and turning to the placid detective: 'Oh, how clever you were to find them, Mr Beck; wasn't he, Syd? Do tell us how and where and when you managed it?'

She so bubbled over with delight and admiration and gratitude that even the detective was captivated. He beamed like a full moon and bowed with the easy grace of a bear.

'Will you open the case again, miss,' was all he said. She raised the lid and was struck dumb with blank amazement.

The case was empty.

'A trick case,' said Harcourt, after a pause.

'Just so, sir, that's the whole story, in three words. About as neat a bit of work as ever came out of human hands. No wonder. Twenty thousand pounds, more or less, was the price the maker wanted for it. The closing of the case works the spring, as you see, sir. That's the notion of it, and not a bad notion either.'

'And the diamonds are safe inside,' cried Lilian; 'they were there all the time, and I have only to squeeze with my thumbs and they will come out again. It's wonderful! Wonderful! I declare I like the case as much as the jewels. I hope the maker will be well paid, Mr Beck.'

'He'll be well paid, miss, never you fear,' said Mr Beck, a little grimly, 'though not perhaps in the coin he expected.'

'But however did you find it out? You must be most wonderfully clever. I suppose you have worked up some marvellous system that nobody can understand but yourself.'

Mr Beck actually blushed under this shower of compliments.

'A little common sense, miss, that's all. I have no more system than the hound that gets on the fox's scent and keeps on it. I just go by the rule of thumb, and muddle and puzzle out my cases as best I can.'

'When did you guess the diamonds were in the case?' said Harcourt.

'I guessed it, sir, when I saw Mr Ophir, and I was sure of it when I saw you. You see how it is, sir; if Mr Ophir put the diamonds into the case and no one took them out, it stood to reason they were still there—whatever might be the appearance to the contrary!'

'It sounds quite simple,' murmured Lilian, 'when you are told it.'

'Of course, when I found my double had been for the case, it made certainty doubly certain.'

'Your double! Then you were right, Lilian; there were two Mr Becks.'

'Of course; I am always right.'

'Might I ask, sir,' continued Harcourt, 'which you are?'

'He's the second Mr Beck, of course, Syd. How can you be so silly? But I want to know where is the first Mr Beck, the man with the beautiful hands?'

'The first Mr Beck, miss, otherwise Mulligan, otherwise Monsieur Grabeau, is in jail at present, awaiting his trial. He was arrested this afternoon by appointment at Simpson's restaurant by the second Mr Beck.'

JUSTICE EVADED

Dorothea Conyers

Mervyn Henderson, 'the human bloodhound' of this story by Dorothea Conyers (1873-1949) was clearly modelled on Sherlock Holmes, although with a nice acknowledgement to Conan Doyle's profession his author describes him as 'a struggling young doctor who in time has become a great detective.' Like Holmes, he has been university educated, is fiercely intellectual and smokes strong cigars. Conversely, he nurses a passion for his cousin, Joan, that must have raised the eyebrows of many readers in the 1920s! The author, who was born in Limerick, made her name with a series of novels about Irish life, including The Waiting of Moya *(1921) and* The Toll of the Black Lake *(1922). It was in 1926, after consulting a private detective in Dublin to investigate a family scandal, that she had the inspiration for Mervyn Henderson and introduced him in a short story called 'The Fair-Haired Companion'. In this case, the resourceful private investigator was able to rescue an heiress from the clutches of her scheming uncle who was trying to poison her and claim her inheritance.*

In later adventures such as 'The Pitmaston Duchess', 'Chase-Me-Charlie' and 'The Murder on the Dover Train', Mervyn Henderson outwitted a jewel thief, a criminal mastermind who turned out to be a girl, and solved the mystery of a murder victim who had changed his identity. However, for me the most ingenious of his cases is 'Justice Evaded', which begins as a simple case of suicide and turns into something far more sinister, during the course of which the great detective's character—like that of Sherlock Holmes—is revealed to have its darker side, too . . .

'Strange cases.' The great detective tapped his long fingers against the arm of his chair. 'H'm, yes, I've known a few.'

The light fell on his face. A tracker of men, clear-eyed, thin mobile mouth, firm chin; a human sleuth, relentless and, men said, without heart—but a flicker of humour in lips and eyes denied this rumour.

'Tell us of one—the strangest you have ever known.'

Joan Henderson, the detective's cousin, leant forward. A tall girl, with a face not unlike that of Henderson. Clearly cut, full of power. But her mouth was passionate and wistful, her eyes gentle. Henderson was unmarried, and it was whispered that he loved his cousin, and that she would have none of him.

She rose now, lighting a cigarette. Her soft silver-flecked dress caught the light, glittering.

'Tell us one,' she said, 'in which you showed *mercy*.'

Henderson laughed. 'Shall I tell you of the Croft Danly case, when I tracked a hunted woman down, of the case of the foreign prince's emeralds, of—or'—he looked strangely at the girl—'of a case where a detective lied and evaded justice?'

'Yes, tell us that,' she said quietly. 'It might be interesting.'

We were sitting round a piled-up fire. Outside, a north-east wind howled across the chilled earth, and plasters of snow, or rather of fierce hail, dashed against the windows. There were three men, friends of Henderson's, and Joan, his cousin, in her blue and silver gown.

'Well'—he filled his pipe slowly—'I'll tell you a story. How shall I begin? Long years ago—yes, that will do.' He spoke with the ease of the born raconteur.

'Long years ago two young fellows were educated together. One called Mervyn Henderson, a lean, imaginative boy, who dreamt instead of working; the other—we'll call him Fred Crighton, though that was not his name. They were chums at Harrow—always together. Fred, quick and bright, would help the dreamer with his books, save him from many ratings; then they went on to Oxford, and grew fonder of each other. Fred was a big, merry fellow, sensitive as a child; romantic, passionate, a contrast to quiet Henderson, who was afraid of women and despised romance.'

Joan sighed sharply.

'Oxford, glorious and merry, passed; the friends were separated. Fred took up a situation at'—Henderson hesitated—'at Cross Minster, a rambling old town; he went there as a solicitor to some works. Henderson found his dreams fogged by prescriptions, by measles, and broken heads. You see, I started life as a doctor, but I dreamt on, attended criminal trials, studied the methods of thieves and murderers, deduced and surmised and finally, fascinated, burnt my boats and started my sleuth-hound's work.

'My chance came. Some of you may recall the murder at Wye Croft, the brutal slaughtering of a young and popular man, the complete lack of motive and the helplessness of the police. I followed the case breathlessly. Then, one day, I walked to Scotland Yard and asked boldly for a high official, who saw me when I sent in a pencilled note. I was confronted by a big, burly man, keen-eyed and obstinate-looking; a second man stood waiting.

'What was this, had I got any information?

'I put my cards on the table. I had no information, but I believed that I, if given a free hand, could bring the Wye Croft murderer to the gallows.

'"And your solution?" the big man snapped.

'"That, sir, when you employ me, even temporarily."

'They fired me out, but they came to see me and let me try. And in a week we arrested the murdered man's cousin, and, hang it, he shot himself.'

'But this,' Joan Henderson raised her eyebrows, 'is not a story of a detective's humanity.'

'No, I am merely telling you of my start. Then came the Silverview diamond episode, and I was taken on as a 'tec.

'Success has dogged me. I seem to possess the nose of a human bloodhound. "Send for Henderson," is the cry now when a man has to be trailed.'

'Ooh,' Joan shivered.

'Well, now to my story.' His eyes sought Joan's and the others all knew that he was telling it to her.

'Even detectives take holidays. June passed in silver sunshine across London, and just as July commenced to heat his furnaces I had a letter from Fred. He wrote in low spirits. He was doing well from a financial point of view, prospering—had even come into a substantial legacy, but he was miserable. Would I come down and spend a month with him? There was golf, the sea three miles away, fresh air and rest.

'I accepted gladly. I had just got through a difficult case and won for the side of justice.' Joan shivered. 'So I wired, packed my bag and left Euston on a hot, still morning. The train rushed through the still green country, how far I will not say. I changed to a branch line and ran into Cross Minster at half-past four. I had not seen Fred for three years.

'At first sight he looked his old self; big, jolly, clear-eyed, but as he steered his two-seater through the pack of station cabs, I saw deep lines round his lips, and the set look of trouble in his eyes. Lines on the face are a study of mine, and have often helped me—those of worry, ill-humour, fear.'

Henderson laughed. 'I must not ride my hobbies. We motored through a wide main street, past old-fashioned inns and modern shops, to the edge of the quiet old town. Fred's house was a dream. A rambling mass of angles and gables, set in a jewelled garden; an orchard and fields at the back, even a little stream, a mere thread of silver water then, creeping through the orchard, and widening to a still sunken pool in the garden.

'"This was part of my legacy," he explained. "My aunt lived here. I came to Cross Minister to be with her."

'It was all rest to a jaded man. The tang of the sea sharpened the air, the scent of mignonette, sweet peas and roses drenched it. We ate fresh trout, chickens, green peas and strawberries, and sat on a verandah afterwards smoking in what ought to have been blissful peace. It was to me. I was not there to force confidence, but I could see Fred looking drearily into the dusk, sighing to himself when he was silent.

'He spoke of his own accord at last.

'"You're wondering what's up with me, Mervyn. It's a case of a woman who is being murdered——"

'"Ah-h!" I sat up. No rest then, but a fresh case.

'"No, old man; not by the means you know of, but there are other methods. Perhaps you'll understand them when you see what is breaking my heart, Mervyn."

'"A big, gentle heart to break." I touched his arm.

'"Thanks, old chap. Well, until tomorrow—I am on holidays too, so we can laze the days through."

'Morning came crisply. I faced the west, rising in rosy flush behind a beech-tree—it was never too hot down there. And I had an ambrosial breakfast, eaten near an open french window, fresh, pink sweet peas decking our little table.

'Then we motored to the sea, swam far out, and came back blissfully hungry.

'"I'll take you to the Dennisons'," Fred said. "Dennison is Neil Armour, the author, who writes turgid love tales, cakes of fluffy dough, spiced by dukes and earls and their amours, which sell as they don't deserve to."

'I had seen the books at stations; but never read any.

'"He'll try to pick your great brain for copy. Come along."

'We walked back towards the town, then turned to the right down a quiet suburban road. It was only a couple of hundred yards from Fred's house.

'Oaklawn was a great imposing villa—brick-red, ornate, unlovable; its flower-beds a flare of brilliancy, its greenhouses glittering in the sunlight. Then the owner called to us from a window shaded by green sunblinds—a long window, opening into a handsomely furnished study, books lining the walls. A knee-hole writing-desk set close to the window, a deep, luxurious couch placed in the centre of the room. The author closed his ink-bottle ostentatiously, laid down a sheet of manuscript, and welcomed us. The click of a typewriter sounded from an adjoining room. Fred introduced me.

'"Just finishing a chapter in *Lady Guinevere's Dilemma*," Dennison said pompously. "It's running through the *Moon*, and I've been lazy about it. Correct that, Miss Smith." He rang a bell and handed the neatly written sheets to a thin, capable-looking girl who admired her employer.

'"You don't go over it yourself?" I said.

'"I don't need to.' Neil Dennison was tall and stout, his florid good looks getting clouded by good living, his hard eyes sunken, his full, sensual mouth cruel when he was not smiling. There was a certain shrewd cleverness about him, and a look of cunning tenacity which I did not like. I often come across the type—and caught them.

'"They wear me out for short stories and so on," he said. "Very glad to meet you, Mr Henderson. We've heard of you even in our backwater here. You've some interesting experiences hidden away, I expect. You'll stay for tea, of course. Denys!" he called. "Denys, Fred's here."

'Denys must be the serpent in this paradise. I made up my mind to dislike her, but when she came in—well, I changed the determination. Denys, the wife, was a tall girl with chestnut hair and deep-blue eyes. Her mouth, made for laughter, drooped ominously. She was quiet; to use an old expression bred to her finger-tips.

'This was the woman who was being murdered. And Fred looked

at her with open admiration.

'We sat outside in the shade of a cedar. It took me a bare half-hour to fathom the case.

'She was being murdered by words. Neil Dennison contradicted her, ridiculed everything she said, and always with an air of bonhomie, as if he was trying to keep his patience with some half-witted child. Faugh! He was a windbag filled by pride, his own hand ever working the bellows.

'I praised the air of the place, absently.

'"Yes, it's glorious. I yearn for the simple life, for food out-of-doors, but Denys won't have it, so we waste sunlit hours in a stuffy dining-room."

'"The servants would have to carry everything out," she said timidly.

'"I could keep an extra servant," he said arrogantly. "A Ganymede to minister."

'"To Jove," I put in slyly.

'And he liked it, laughed as if delighted.

'"By gad! yes—just so. Now Denys does not know who Ganymede is. Never reads a book, do you, Denys?"

'"Sometimes," she answered, her hands trembling as she lifted the teapot.

'So it went on. Heckling, bullying, until I, a mere stranger, could have slain the big, good-looking author; and Fred, my friend, loved the ground the girl walked on.

'"Denys, go and ask McKenzie if he has any nectarines ready," Dennison commanded. "Take Fred with you." Dennison lighted a fat, black cigar. I could see his eyes gleam happily as the two walked away.

'"So delighted to meet you," he said to me. "Brain cries for brother brain. Young fellows worship beauty," his evil lip curled. "We two can *talk*." His speech was as full of italics as his books.

'The brute was hinting openly that his wife had no brains. I chewed a cigarette into damp ruins.

'"And now tell me something of *your* work—of your marvellous methods. They call you the human bloodhound."

'"And—what would *you* call the book," I said, with open rudeness.

'Bless you, his hide was far too thick.

'"Ah, you are quick. You would love, of course, to provide *me* with copy. What an interest for you. Yes, I want to hear something thrilling, suitable for a serial and film work. Of course, you are a merciless lot. Do you ever feel inclined to let a man off?"

'"Not often. He who sheddeth man's blood—But he who slays a woman, what of him?"

'"Oh, no one decent would. Come, spin me a yarn. I can take notes."

'I can see him now, the bombastic windbag, waiting for me to commence, his coarse face creased by a smile. And then I saw that the smile was not for me, but for a pair lingering by the rose-trees, and for a woman handing a little scented bud to a man.

'I smiled then. He wanted brains. Mine were at his diposal, and he might not like them.

'So I told him a tale. Invented it, of a medieval castle, a secret chamber, changed babies, a faithless wife, slow murder by poison. Stale melodramatic stuff, and he drank it in—down to a suicide and a trite solution.

'"Oh, fine!" he rolled out. "Now you'll be pleased, for I'll send you a copy of the book. I can put you in as a typical 'tec."

'"And what," I inquired grimly. "is your idea of a typical 'tec?"

'"Oh!" he waved his big hands. "Narrowed eyes, a mobile mouth, ostentatious cleverness, you know. Shall we have a game of bridge?—it acts as a sedative to me."

'It was certainly no sedative to his partner. He played badly, declared rashly, grumbled throughout and abused Denys. I say abused, but it was clever spite used with the skill of custom. Then, to my surprise, we were asked to stay for dinner.

'This marked the commencement of days spent at Oaklawn. And the brains which the windbag had asked for fathomed the reason.

'For the big bluff man possessed a friend—a vapid, brassy-haired girl, brilliantly pretty. I saw them together in the evenings in his two-seater. It was easy to piece the puzzle together. Madge Pearson, the publican's daughter, was playing for the matrimonial stakes. Neil was infatuated, desiring her fiercely. He wanted to divorce his wife. Unfortunately for him, Denys dreaded scandal, and he could not gather any evidence against her.

'Yes, I had never before seen a woman's soul slowly slain. She bore it so nobly, her head high, her tortured eyes brave, as her health broke, and she walked and talked with Fred as a friend but nothing more. She would not go out motoring with him, or up to

London, as Dennison urged. She stood firm in the circle drawn by her own convictions.

'Well, I must not be verbose. I took a hand and spoke to Fred. I told him he must leave the town. What would Denys do? Bear misery more easily, I said, when she was not looking at happiness through a barred door. I laid the facts before him and he understood. So he settled things quietly, booked his passage for Australia, and would leave a friend to make or mar the business.

'He had finished all his arrangements on a certain Wednesday, and we were to dine at Oaklawn that night.

'Dennison was writing when we arrived, pouring out the turgid words which delighted housemaids and lonely women. He called to me, and as I came in a loose sheet fluttered to the floor. I picked it up.

'"See me slaving," he burst out. "I have rewritten a *whole* sentence; I did not think it was quite touching enough. My soul cries for real sentiment—they harry me, Henderson—harry me; this chapter is overdue. Hi! Miss Smith, get on with the script. I have to write with my own hands. I cannot dictate."

'"Sensational?" I queried.

'"Yes; the public likes mustard and moonlight. I want change. I'm tired now; I'll just wash the ink off."

'"Yes." I read the written sentence and smiled a little.

'Oh, it was a miserable dinner. He caled Denys a bad housekeeper; he scolded the maid who waited, knowing that his wife liked the girl; he abused the dishes. But he got his desert over the raspberries, when Fred announced his intended departure.

'Denys took it quietly, it was no news to her. But the mask fell from Dennison's face, and he looked the monster which he was, as he fumed and raged.

'"It could not be. You can't go, Fred, *unless* you are taking a companion," he leered. Denys went white. "Rubbish. Give it up."

'The big brute saw his plans crumbling to pieces; his desire put away from him. And he was not brave enough to take ordinary methods.

'His hairy hands fumbled on the table-cloth, his eyes were savage.

'"I have business in Australia." Fred's voice was quietly firm. "I must go."

'This Dennison possessed imagination. He fell into troubled thought, planning some scheme, weaving it as he wove his brute plots. The night was dull and gloomy. Dennison tried to send Fred and Denys into the garden, but the woman could not face saying good-bye to her one solace, and refused to go. So we played bridge in silence. Dennison was quiet for once, immersed in thought.

'"Mervyn!" Fred gripped my arm as we walked home. "I'm leaving her to *hell*—I can't stand it. That pure soul, that sensitive heart, tortured hour by hour."

'"Better that, than that his plan should succeed. Some women would be compensated by love, she is a Puritan and disgrace would kill her. Servants' evidence, twisted episodes; those brave eyes of hers fixed on the judge as she denied, proudly, uselessly. You are just in time. He is not ready—this injured husband."

'"I'd kill him first!" Fred shouted. "Shoot him."

'A passer-by started, and looked round.

'"It's old Jones," said Fred. "I've frightened him."

'"Be careful," I warned, "that devil is not beaten yet. No farewells, boy. We'll spend tomorrow by the sea—you and I."

'We drove off in the morning and got through the day. As we came back we passed Dennison's two-seater turning into the station. A dark, clean-shaven man was seated in it.

'"Why, that's Fluter," I said. "The big, heart specialist. I came across him in the Grey case. H'm, costs money to drag him from London. Can Dennison be ill? Author's breakdown?"

'"He'll die of apoplexy when he is eighty," said Fred grimly. "It—it—— Oh, it could not be Denys."

'The telephone rang at nine. Fred's man answered it.

'"Mr Dennison, sir, wants Mr Crighton to come over at once—it is important."

'"Don't go," I begged. "Don't—it's some trap."

'But he went as a nail flies to a magnet, and I put on a pair of tennis shoes and ran after him.

'Dennison was in his library, sitting at the table. He called to Fred, who entered by the open french window. I crept close and listened.

'"Fred—Fred," the big man whispered. "It's awful. Denys—Denys is *dying*."

'"What!" Fred screamed.

'"Hush! No noise. Fluter has pronounced it hopeless—a matter of hours."

'"You fiend—you've killed her," Fred stormed. "Murdered her, you devil. You shall answer, you shall pay for it."

'"Hush! They can hear you."

'A bell whirred, and Miss Smith ran in—she must have heard.

'"Go to bed, Miss Smith; we do not wish to be disturbed. Now, now, Fred; keep quiet. Don't bluster. Denys wants to see you before she dies. Oh, I'm not blind—*I* know how it is between you. And you shall see her privately for ten minutes."

'"Oh, God!— oh, God!" moaned Fred.

'A chain rattled. The maid was fastening the front door.

'"But I want no breath of scandal on *her* name. Not yet—when they are in bed. The nurse is a stranger; I shall call her out of the room. I'll run up now."

'Dennison slipped from the room. I could see Fred huddled in his chair, stunned, horrified.

'"The nurse says you must wait for twenty minutes. Denys is drowsy; then go straight to her room, the first on the right. I am doing my best for you, but I must protect her name."

'"I would rather wait outside than breathe the air you poison." Fred got up. "And afterwards," he thundered, "you shall pay."

'"Yes—I'll whistle softly for you. I feel for you Fred."

'Fred staggered into the dusk, away to the road outside. Dennison sat on alone in the lighted room; he moved to a deep couch. And I saw him laugh and rub his hands together. I knew then. He had caught his birds. I saw through his melodramatic penny-dreadful plot.

'The house was quiet. Then the stillness was broken by the sound of a woman sobbing at a window.

'Now'—Henderson bent forward—'from this point I shall tell the story as if I had been an onlooker, and call myself the London detective. You asked for the strangest case I ever handled—I think that this is it.

'The detective slipped from his hiding-place and hurried back to his friend's house. He feared that Fred had gone for his revolver, but there was no one about; the man sitting up in the kitchen said that he had heard his master run up to his study and out again. The 'phone whirred—the detective answered the call.

'"Oh, who's speaking?—Mr Henderson? Come at once, Mr Dennison's murdered. Mr Crighton has shot him. Come, come! I've 'phoned the police. Hurry." Miss Smith's voice rang shrilly. The detective went back to Oaklawn at racing pace.

'As he slipped across the grass he saw Smith, the typist, lifting something in her hands.

'It was too true. Dennison was crumpled up on the sofa, a revolver on the floor beside him, his mouth slack, the grey pallor of death on his harsh features. Smith, the typist, was bending over him.

'"I found him," she shot out firecely. "I 'phoned for you. I heard him and Crighton quarrelling, yelling—then the shot. Mrs Dennison fainted when we told her."

'"Touch nothing," ordered the detective. "Yes, he is dead, shot through the heart." He bent over the corpse. A tiny piece of paper lay on the chest and was stained by the blood which had welled from the wound.

'"Leave the room, Miss Smith. You may disturb some finger-prints. Have you touched anything?"

'"I lifted the revolver," she faltered, "to look at it."

'So the London man, the sleuth-hound, stood alone with the dead. The little automatic lay on the floor. The case was black—black as ink. Fred had been 'phoned for, seen coming to the house; Smith had overheard the quarrel; old Jones had heard the boy rave out a threat—the detective was bound to bring the criminal to justice, to see the vengeance of the law fall on his one dear friend. Oh, Fred, Fred!—so palpably guilty.'

'"You did not do it," breathed Joan.

'"I—was merely the detective." He waited; steps sounded, a quiet-looking inspector and two policemen hurried in.

'"Oh, you are here, Mr Henderson. We are lucky to have your help. Miss Smith informed us that she heard Mr Crighton and the deceased quarrelling violently half an hour ago, then, hearing a shot, she ran down, then——"

'Fred Crighton came slowly to the window.

'"Dennison, can I—now?" he said tonelessly. "Why—my God! My God!"

'"Better take care what you say, sir," snapped the Inspector sharply. "You were overheard quarrelling with the deceased."

'"He's dead—too late," was Fred's reply. "Can I see her?"

'He took no notice of the dead man.

'Then Denys Dennison walked into the room—pale but composed, and Fred sprang between her and what lay on the deep couch.

'"Go back—don't look!" he cried. "Where is your nurse?"

'"I am not ill," she said coldly. "Move aside, Fred."

'"Not ill?" Fred staggered. "He said——"

'The detective watched the local men whispering together, nodding sage heads.

'I met Fred's eyes—the diabolical plot was bare to him now. Dennison would have taken him to Denys's room when everyone was asleep, and then roused the house. Denys was not ill—Fred's story would have been swept aside and the much-needed divorce would have been gained.

'"The doctor," said Inspector Hughes, as a car drove up.

'Nothing to say—death was apparent.

'"Mr Crighton," Hughes cleared his throat. "We regret, but——"

'"A moment." The London detective bent over the dead man— the face changed and his eyes grew full of tense excitement.

'"Doctor, Inspector—look *here*!"

'He held out the scrap of blood-stained paper and read aloud:

"So I must leave. Life is too hard for me. No one knows of the disease which ravages in my veins. I cannot face it. My last love to my wife, and good-bye all. A shot is cleanest.—N.

'"He shot himself?" Denys moved forward. "Why should he? He was not ill. Dr Fluter came here today, but I understood nothing was wrong. He would never do it—never," she screamed, and she looked at Fred, terror in her eyes. She swayed.

'"Doctor, see to the living," said the detective sharply. "Get Mrs Dennison to bed. I say this is conclusive, but we'll search the room— and you, Crighton."

'There were no finger-prints. Miss Smith had moved the revolver; nothing save the blood on the man's coat and the mark of tennis shoes on the gravel. "Mine," the detective explained quietly.

'Well, there was an inquest. Fred Crighton gave his evidence. He could not say why Mr Dennison had pretended that Mrs Dennison was dying, why he had made up such a story. But the Coroner, worthy man, touched his own bald forehead significantly.

'Yes, they had quarrelled. Mr Dennison had not, in his, witness's, opinion, been good to Mrs Dennison, and as he was leaving for Australia they had had words—hot ones.

'Why was he carrying a revolver?

'"I went back to fetch it." Fred was quite direct. "I meant to shoot him, for he had, as I thought, killed his wife. But there was no need for me to do it. He wanted to blacken his wife. But there was no need for me to do it. He wanted to blacken his wife's fair name."

'The twelve good men and true knew Dennison and knew of his fair flame in the town, and they exchanged glances and pursed their moral lips.

'Dr Fluter deposed to being called down urgently—there was nothing wrong with Mr Dennison, yet the man seemed to think that he was very ill. Oh, suicide while of unsound mind and very little regret or sympathy; only the thin typist looked at us venomously.

'Fred married the lady in six months' time, and they were very happy.'

'But Mr Dennison did not shoot himself—you saved Fred?' Joan leaned forward.

'Yes, you asked for a case in which I showed mercy. I put the revolver where it lay—I put that scrap of his own writing on his breast. It was the piece of MS which I had picked up. He was a wild beast, better dead—and that scrap of paper helped me greatly.'

'But,' Joan frowned, 'the typist must have noticed that neither the revolver nor the the paper was there when she found the body. It doesn't fit.'

'It does, for *they were there* when I left the garden and ran back to look for Fred. Vermin are best out of the way, and you see—it was her life or his. I shot him myself. My gun makes very little noise. I set the stage and slipped away. That is the exact truth.'

Henderson leaned back in his chair, and his cousin Joan crossed over to him.

'So you are human,' she said softly.

'Yes, very,' he answered.

Her hand fell on his shoulder, and we left them alone.

'Women are strange creatures,' Joan remarked. 'If true, Mervyn is a murderer—but of course he made it up.'

'I don't bet,' said one man, 'but I'd lay a thousand to ten on the story being a true one.'

EAST WIND

Freeman Wills Crofts

Freeman Wills Crofts (1879-1957) is listed as one of the 'big five' of the Golden Age of Detective Fiction, and for years his work was as highly acclaimed and popular as that of Agatha Christie, Dorothy L. Sayers, H. C. Bailey and R. Austin Freeman. He also created the first really significant police detective, Inspector Joseph French—at a time when all other crime novels featured private investigators or amateur detectives—and was the first writer in the genre regularly to use the step-by-step methods of police routine. Major achievements indeed for a man whose career had been that of an engineer with the Irish railways, until in 1919 poor health confined him to bed. Indeed, he wrote his first detective story merely to amuse himself. Crofts was born in Dublin and it was thanks to an uncle, who was the chief engineer of the Belfast and Northern Counties Railway, that he got a job as a junior construction engineer, rising in time to the position of chief assistant engineer for the entire line. The Cask, his first story, was hailed as a classic, selling more than 100,000 copies over the next two decades. The success of this book and those that soon followed enabled him to devote himself wholeheartedly to writing crime fiction, introducing the ostensibly ordinary but still suave Inspector French— known as 'Soapy Joe' because of his skill at handling witnesses of all kinds—in 1924 in Inspector French's Greatest Case.

Because of his years working on the Irish railways, trains not surprisingly feature in a number of Freeman Wills Crofts' best stories— including 'East Wind' in which Inspector French, on what he hopes will be a relaxing journey, finds himself in the midst of a hold-up and double killing . . .

Inspector Joseph French of the CID had handled in his time a great diversity of cases. Of these, some were remarkable for their dramatic setting, some for the terrible nature of the crimes revealed, and some for the brilliant logical analysis by which the inspector reached his result. The case which had its beginning on the famous 10.30 a.m. Cornish Riviera Limited Express belonged to none of these categories. In it French was shown, not as the abstract reasoner triumphantly reaching the solution of some baffling problem, but as the practical man of affairs, the organiser using with skill and promptitude the great machine of the British police force.

It was towards the end of May and French had been working for several weeks on an intricate case of forgery in South London. He was tired of Town and longed to get out of it. When therefore it became necessary for him to interview an old lag who was doing a stretch in Princetown, he was delighted. A breath of the air of Dartmoor would come as a pleasant change from the drab and sordid Lambeth streets.

It was with pleasurable anticipation that he drove to Paddington and took his seat in the train. He had a good deal of work to do before he reached the prison, and as soon as the express settled down into its stride, he got out his papers and began. For some hours he read and noted, then with a sigh of relief he bundled the documents back into his bag and turned his attention to the scenery.

They had just passed Exeter and were running down the river opposite Exmouth. The previous night had been wet, but now the sky had cleared and the sun was shining. Everything had been washed by the rain and looked fresh and springlike. The sea, when they reached it, was calm and vividly blue and contrasted strikingly with the red cliffs and pillars of Dawlish and Teignmouth.

They turned up the estuary of the Teign and ran through Newton Abbot. From here to Plymouth French thought the country less interesting and he turned to a novel which he had thrust into his bag. For a few minutes he read, then he heard a whistle and the brakes began to grind on the wheels.

There was no halt scheduled hereabouts, the train running without a stop from London to Plymouth. Repairing the line or blocked by some other train, French thought. Since he had done that job on the Southern near Whitness French rather fancied himself as a railway expert.

The speed decreased and presently they stopped at a small station; Greenbridge, he saw the name was. With a slight feeling of displeasure he was about to apply himself again to his book when he heard a faint report, and another, and another.

Three distant fog signals, he supposed, and as he knew this was an emergency danger signal, he lowered the window and looked out. He was at the platform side and down the platform he saw a sight which brought him to his feet in the twinkling of an eye.

A hold-up was in progress. Some four carriages down the train a door was open and opposite it stood a man, a big stout fellow in grey with a white mask on his face and a pistol in his raised hand. With it he covered the passengers, none of whom was to be seen, but the guard had alighted and was standing opposite his van, his arms raised above his head.

As French reached the platform, two men stepped out of the compartment with the open door. One, medium-sized and dressed in a fawn coat and hat, was also wearing a mask and brandishing a pistol. The other, of about the same height, was without arms or mask, and even at that distance French could sense an eager haste in his movements. The three, the two armed men and the eager one, ran quickly out of the station and immediately the sound of a rapidly accelerating car came from the road.

French dashed to the exit, but the vehicle had disappeared before he reached it. Then he ran back to the compartment from which the men had descended, and which was now surrounded by an excited crowd of passengers. French pushed his way to the front.

In the compartment lay two men in the uniform of prison warders. One was obviously dead, shot through the forehead; the other was hunched up in a corner, apparently unconscious, but with no visible injury.

'I'm a police officer from Scotland Yard,' French shouted. 'I'll take charge here.' He pointed to a couple of the passengers who were crowding round. 'Will you gentlemen search the train quickly for a doctor. You others, close the compartment and let no one in except to attend to the man in the corner. Where is there a telephone, guard?'

The moment French had seen the warders' uniforms, he knew what had taken place. Though it was not his business, he happened to be aware that a prisoner was being conveyed to Dartmoor by the train. He was a man named Jeremy Sandes, and French was interested in him because he was one of his own captures.

The crime for which Sandes had been taken was the theft of Lady Ormsby-Keats' jewels from her country house of Dutton Manor, situated about a mile from Epsom. With forged testimonials he had got a job as footman. This gave him his opportunity. It was suspected that Sandes was only one of a gang and that before capture he had managed to pass on his takings to his accomplices, though neither of these assumptions could be proved. At all events not a single pennyworth of the £17,000 odd of jewellery he had stolen had been recovered.

French's inspiring example galvanised the passengers into activity. A doctor was speedily found, and while he was attending to the warder, French and the guard and some of the passengers ran towards the station buildings. The station was little more than a halt, but there was a general waiting-room and a tiny ticket office. Of these, the office was locked. French rattled at the door. 'Anybody there?' he shouted.

For answer a dismal groan came from within. French and the guard threw themselves on the door, but it was strongly made and resisted their efforts.

'The seat,' French pointed.

On the platform was a heavy wooden seat. Willing hands quickly raised it, and using it as a battering ram, swung it back and brought its end crashing against the door. With the tearing sound of splintering wood the keeper gave way and the door swung open.

In the little office was a single chair and on the chair sat a man in porter's uniform. He was securely gagged with a cloth and bound to the chair with a rope. A few seconds only sufficed to release him. Beyond the possibility of apoplexy from suppressed fury, he seemed none the worse for his experience.

'The big man came in with a mask on his face,' he spluttered indignantly, 'and before I could move I found myself looking into the wrong end of a gun. Then the second man came in and I was tied up before you could say knife.'

'Anyone else about the station?' French asked sharply.

'Yes, there's the signalman. They must have tied him up too, else they couldn't have stopped the train.'

The signal-box was at the end of the platform to the rear and the little party hurried down. It was as the porter suggested. The signalman was seated on a stool, bound and gagged, but uninjured.

He had, he said, been sitting in his box, when he noticed two men pacing the other end of the platform, as if measuring. They disappeared, then a few minutes later they suddenly rushed up the box steps and covered him with their guns. He could do nothing and was at once gagged and bound. He had already accepted the express and pulled off the signals, and the men at once threw the latter to danger. They waited till the departure came through for the express, acknowledged the signal correctly, and then cut the block and telephone wires. When the train appeared and was slowing down they pulled off the home signal, leaving the distant and starter at danger. This was correct railway practice and showed that they knew what they were doing. Then they hurried down to the platform, and were ostensibly reading a time bill with their backs to the line when the train came in. Thanks to their skilful operation of the signals, it pulled up as if it had been timed to stop. They evidently knew where the prisoner was, for they had been waiting opposite his compartment and opened its door without hesitation.

French heard the story in the briefest outline and then asked for a description of the men. But he could get nothing of value. Between the speed with which everything had happened and the masks which had been worn, only a blurred picture of their assailants had been left in the railwaymen's minds.

He ran back to the train, and holding up his hand for silence, asked if anyone had noticed any peculiarity about the men by which they might be recognised. For a moment there was no reply, then a lady in the compartment adjoining that of the tragedy came forward.

She had been in the window and had had plenty of time to observe the big man who had kept guard on the platform. She could not of course see his face, but she was able to describe his clothes. These were quite ordinary except for one point. On the toe of his rather elegant black shoe were three small spots of mud forming the angles of a tiny equilateral triangle.

This was the only clue French could get, but it was of an entirely satisfactory nature. If the big man did not notice the marks and rub them off, they might well lead to his undoing.

French turned again to the railwaymen, asking urgently where was the nearest telephone. The wires in the signal-box being cut, the porter advised application to Farmer Goodbody, who lived three hundred yards up the road. It would be quicker, he said, than travelling on by the train to the next station.

In three minutes French was knocking at the farmer's door and in another two he was speaking to the superintendent in Exeter. He had been extremely quick in his enquiries and not more than ten minutes had elapsed since the crime. The fugitives could not have gone more than seven or eight miles at the most, and prompt action should enable a police ring to be thrown round the area before they could get clear. French however asked that they should not be arrested, but only shadowed.

He was able to supply very fair descriptions of the trio. About the prisoner, Jeremy Sandes, he could give complete information. He had worked at his description so often that he remembered it in detail. As to the others, he knew their height and build, and there was that priceless point about the three spots of mud.

The information was passed to Exeter, Plymouth, Okehampton and other centres, as well as to the Yard. Arrangements were made about the bodies of the dead warders and then French rang up the nearest village for a car and was driven into Newton Abbot. There he was fortunate enough to find a train just about to start for Exeter. Forty minutes later he reached police headquarters in the city. Superintendent Hambrook was an old friend and received him with effusion.

'We've done what you said, inspector,' he went on. 'As far as we have men to do it, all roads have been blocked in a circle from here through Crediton, Okehampton, Tavistock and Plymouth, and we are having the Exmouth ferry and all ports in the area watched. That circle is about twenty to twenty-five miles radius as the crow flies and it would take the parties thirty or forty minutes to reach it. With luck we'll get them. But, French, are you sure you're right in not arresting them? If you lose them now they mayn't be easy to get again.'

'I know, super, but I think it's worth the risk. What do you suppose this escape was organised for?'

Hambrook closed his right eye. 'The swag?' he suggested.

French nodded. 'That's it. They'd never have committed a murder just to help their pal. This Sandes had hidden the stuff and the others were left. Now they're going to make him fork up.'

'And you want to let him find it?'

'He's the only one who can.'

'It's an idea,' the super admitted doubtfully. 'But I don't know. If it were my case I think I'd go for the bird in the hand.'

French's reply was interrupted by a strident ring on the super's telephone bell. Hambrook picked up the receiver, handing a second to French.

'Constable Cunningham speaking from the London bypass, Exeter. I think we've identified the big man and the prisoner, Sandes. They're driving towards London in a Daimler limousine Number AZQ 9999. If we're right, they've changed their clothes. The big man is wearing a dark coat and hat, but when we had him out we saw the three spots of mud on his left toe. The driver answers the description of Sandes, though his face has been darkened and he's wearing chauffeur's uniform. The big man gave the name Mr Oliver Hawke, diamond merchant, of 767B Hatton Garden and St Austell's, Grabfield Road, Hampstead. They stopped at once and were quite civil. They said they were coming from the Burlington Hotel in Plymouth and going home. We let them go and Constable Emerson is following them on the motorbike. The tyres are newish Dunlops.'

French was highly delighted. 'If they're being civil and answering questions it means they've fixed up an alibi and feel safe about it.' He rubbed his hands. 'A diamond merchant! The best fence in the world!'

Hambrook agreed and French went on. 'I bet you anything you like Hawke's going home as he says. If so, we'll get him there, and Sandes too. Ring up ahead, will you, super? If he's making for Town we'll call off the pursuit.'

While Hambrook was telephoning French had been studying a time-table. 'There's an express at 5.42,' he said. 'If they go towards London I'll take it. I confess I'd like to be in Hampstead to see them arrive. Just get the Plymouth men to look up that hotel, will you, super?'

The Burlington reported that Mr Hawke and his chauffeur had stayed there for the past two nights and had left for London that day about noon. They had taken lunch with them and said they would eat it in the car *en route*.

'There's the alibi emerging already,' French declared. 'Why did they take so long between Plymouth and Exeter? Because they stopped for lunch. Why were they not seen at any hotel? Because they took it in the car. Quite. Now the Yard, like a good fellow.'

To headquarters French reported what had happened, asking if a Mr Hawke lived and moved and had his being at the addresses given, and if so, what was this gentleman like in appearance? In a short time there was a reply which showed that the man in the car had given his real name.

French rose. 'I'll just get that train if I look slippy,' he said. 'Well, super, glad to have seen you again. If your people come on that other ruffian, I'd shadow him also. We think there's still another of them in the gang and we may as well have a shot for the lot.'

As French sat thinking over the affair in the up express he saw that there definitely must have been another confederate. The two men at Greenbridge had known in which compartment the prisoner was travelling. Now it was impossible that they could have evolved this information out of their inner consciousnesses. It must therefore have been sent to them, and there was only one way in which it could have been obtained. Someone had watched the man and his escort entraining at Paddington. French wondered could he trace a trunk call or a telegram from Paddington shortly after 10.30 that morning.

At Taunton, their first stop, French sent wires in veiled language to the Yard and the Exeter super, asking the former to find out if such a message had been sent, and the latter if Hawke had called anywhere to receive it. Then feeling he had done his duty by the case for the moment, he went to the dining-car for a long-delayed meal.

At nine o'clock French stepped down on to the platform at Paddington and fifteen minutes later was at the Yard. There he found his colleague Inspector Tanner waiting for him.

'I've been handling this stuff of yours,' said Tanner. 'Your friends are coming up nicely. They were seen passing through Chard, Shaftesbury, Salisbury, Andover and Basingstoke. They dined at Basingstoke and left there half an hour ago. They should be in Hampstead between ten and eleven. We'll go out and see them arrive.'

'Get anything about Hawke's business?'

'Small one-man show. Doesn't seem to be much going on. Yet Hawke must be well-to-do, judging by the house he lives in. I went to the office to ask for him. The clerk made no bones about it. Mr Hawke was down at Plymouth on business, but was coming up today and would be available tomorrow.'

'I thought that part of it would be all right.'

'What about arresting him now, French?' Tanner went on earnestly. 'If we find him in the company of Sandes we have him; he can't put up any kind of defence. Once we let them separate we'll find the case a darned sight harder to prove.'

'And what about the swag?' French returned. 'No, we'll take the risk. And there's another point you've missed. As you know, we believe there are four men in the gang. Now we want them all. If we arrest Hawke and Sandes tonight, we may lose the other two. No, let's watch them: we may get the lot. By the way, did you find out anything about that message from Paddington?'

'Yes, we've got something there.' Tanner drew a scrap of paper from his pocket. With eagerness French read it. 'Quotation required Exodus chapter six verse four.' 'It was sent at 10.40 from the telegraph office at Paddington,' Tanner went on, 'to "Anderton, Post Restante, Plymouth". It was called for at 11.45 by a man resembling Hawke. Does that give you any light?'

French nodded delightedly. 'I should just think it does!' he declared with enthusiasm. 'You see it of course? The sixth carriage from the engine and the fourth compartment. That's what the men were measuring on the platform at Greenbridge. If those post-office people in Plymouth can swear to Hawke, that'll come in handy.'

'Pretty sure to, I should think.' Tanner glanced anxiously at the clock. 'Your friends should have been past Blackwater before now. It's only fifteen miles from Basingstoke and they've left nearly forty minutes.' He picked up his telephone and asked for Blackwater. 'No sign,' he said presently. 'I don't like this, French. Have they turned aside?'

French was already examining a large-scale road map.

'Reading or Farnham are the obvious places north and south,' he answered, 'but there are endless roads in between. Give a general call over that area, Tanner.'

Tanner did so as quickly as he could and they settled down to wait. As the minutes passed French became more anxious than he cared to show. Had he overreached himself? If so, and if these two got away, it would be a pretty serious thing for him. Yet, he told himself, they *couldn't* get away.

Once again the telephone bell rang. 'Blackwater at last,' said Tanner with relief. Then his expression changed. 'Oh, you have? Good man, sergeant! Splendid! I'll wait for his report.' He rang off.

'Blackwater reports that when they didn't turn up he sent a man out on a motorbike to look for them and he's found them parked up a side road near Basingstoke. He's watching them and will keep us advised what happens.'

'What's that for on earth?' French queried.

Tanner shook his head and once more they settled down to wait. And wait they did, endlessly and with growing mystification. Twice at intervals of an hour the constable rang up on an accommdating householder's telephone to say that the men were still sitting in the stationary car, but the third message, when it came at half-past twelve, showed that the halt was over.

'Speaking from Farnham,' the constable reported. 'About twelve they started and ran here and have gone on towards Guildford. I've asked the Guildford men to have a look out and ring you.'

'Guildford!' French exclaimed anxiously. 'What in Hades are they going there for?' He glanced at Tanner. On his face was imprinted the same anxiety.

Once again the bell rang. 'They've been seen,' Tanner reported. 'They passed through Guildford four minutes ago in the Leatherhead direction. The Guildford men have already rung up Leatherhead.'

Suddenly French started. Leatherhead! Leatherhead was near Epsom. Not more than three or four miles between them. With a rising excitement he wondered if he could guess their destination.

In a moment his mind was made up. He would stake everything on this idea of his. He spoke quickly to Tanner.

Tanner swore. 'You can go at once,' he answered with equal speed. 'The cars are waiting to go to Hampstead. I'll be here if you want anything.'

A moment later French was racing down the corridor to the courtyard. There, with Sergeant Carter and a number of plain-clothes men, were two police cars.

'Come on, men,' French shouted. 'Tumble in. Hard as you can lick to Epsom.' Ten seconds later the cars glided out on to the Embankment and turned south over Westminster Bridge.

French had done many a race by car, but seldom had he made such going as on the present occasion. Traffic in the streets was at a low ebb and they took full advantage of it. They gave way to nothing, slinging across the fronts of trams and causing other motorists to jam on their brakes and complain to the nearest policemen. Twice disaster was avoided by a hair's breadth, and again and again only profound skill saved a spill. So, leaving behind them a trail of indignant and exasperated drivers, they rushed on through the streets.

Presently they left Town behind them and still further increased their speed. The edge of the road became a quivering line in the light of their headlamps and their tyres roared on the asphalt surface. The needles of their speedometers rose and rose till for one brief moment on a down-grade straight they touched 65. Their horns were seldom silent, and more than once as they took curves French thanked his stars the road was not greasy.

At Epsom they swung quickly in to the police station. A sergeant was waiting on the footpath.

'Your car went through seven minutes ago,' he said quickly: 'towards Burgh Heath.'

This news practically confirmed French's idea. Dutton Manor lay about a mile out along the Burgh Heath road.

'Good,' he cried with a feeling of relief. 'After it, drivers.'

Once again their tyres roared over the smooth road. A mile slipped away in a few seconds.

'Steady,' said French presently. 'Stop before you get to that corner.'

Round the corner was a straight upon which the Manor front and back drives debouched. As the cars came to a stand French leaped out and ran forward with his torch, followed by his men. They passed round the corner and reached the straight. No car lights were visible ahead.

This however was scarcely to be expected and they raced on, keeping for the sake of silence along the grass verge. Presently they came to the front entrance.

With his torch held vertically so as not to betray their presence, French made a hurried examination of the drive. It was surfaced with gravel and the recent rain had softened it. He could have sworn that no car had passed over it recently. Calling softly to his followers, he hurried on along the road.

From his investigation at the time of the robbery French knew every inch of the little domain. The back drive was a hundred yards farther along the road and this was his new objective.

When he shone his torch on to the ground at its entrance he gave a grunt of satisfaction. There entering the drive were fresh tyre marks, fairly new Dunlops. Good for the Exeter constable's observation!

More cautiously they hurried up the drive, the men moving with speed and silence. There was no moon, but the stars gave a certain light. A wind had been blowing earlier, but it died down and now everything was still. Suddenly French thought he heard a voice. A touch passed down the line and all instantly became rigid.

Yes, people were moving a short distance ahead and speaking in low tones. French crept stealthily forward.

'. . . stopped us at Exeter,' he heard a man say in low tones, 'but they didn't suspect anything and we passed through all right. How did you manage, Taylor?'

'I garaged the car at Newton Abbot and came by train,' returned another voice. 'I reached Paddington at 6.55, got your 'phone from Basingstoke, picked up Gould and came on here. What's it all about, Hawke?'

'The swag. Sandes had hidden it here. I thought we ought all to be here in case——'

The speaker must have turned away, for French lost the remainder of the sentence. Crouching back into the hedge, he could now see four figures moving like shadows in front of him. They were entering the drive from a field, obviously after hiding their car. As they turned towards the house, French and his men dropped in behind.

To say that French was delighted would convey no impression of his state of mind. From the first he had felt that only hope of the recovery of the swag could account for the rescue of Sandes. Now his ideas and his actions had been abundantly justified. A little more patience and a little more care and both men and jewels would be his! Something more than a triumph, this! Out of what had seemed defeat he would snatch an overwhelming victory!

The two parties were now silently creeping up the drive with a hundred feet or more between them. Surely, French thought the quarry would not go near the yard, where there were dogs and where the chauffeur slept? No, they were turning aside. They left the drive through the small gate which led to the side of the house, and began to work forward over a grass sward containing flower-beds and a fountain. Here in the open French's little band had to drop back to avoid being seen, but on reaching some clumps of shrubs they closed up again.

French was growing more and more surprised. It was beginning to look as if the others were meditating an attack on the house itself. They were certainly moving on to the very walls. Then suddenly French saw where they were going. Just in front of them was a loggia. He knew it well. It was a biggish area, some fifty feet by twenty, and was roofed and bounded by the house on two sides, but save for pillars, was open on the third and fourth. On it gave a passage from the main hall, as well as french windows from the principal reception-room, while a short flight of stone steps led down to the terrace. These steps were in the centre of the longer open side, which faced southwest. The short open side faced southeast. These sides were edged with a stone balustrade and every few feet were pedestals bearing large stone vases, each containing a laurestinus.

French's heart beat more rapidly. The end, whatever it might be, was upon them. He wondered if he were about to witness house-breaking. The french windows would be just the place to try, but as he knew them to be fitted with burglar alarms, he did not think the attempt would succeed. Well, if Hawke & Co. gave back, believing they had aroused the household, he and his men would be ready for them.

Slowly and silently the four men crept up the stone steps to the loggia, and as they disappeared within, French and his followers slipped up against the wall at each side of the steps. The floor was some four feet high, and standing on the grass, the watchers could see in between the stone balusters. Contrary to French's expectation the quarry did not approach the french windows. Instead they moved like shadows over to the north-east corner, where the shorter open side joined the wall of the house. French, slipping round the corner, crept along the outside of that short side till he came opposite where they had congregated. They had turned a torch on the floor, which gave a faint light in all directions.

'All quiet.' The whisper came from the man who had been referred to as Hawke. 'Now, Sandes.'

A shadow detached itself from the group and came forward towards French, who shrank down beneath the floor-level. "'Ere in this 'ere vase,' he heard in a Cockney whisper. 'It were the nearest place outside the 'ouse I could find and because of the east wind no one sits in this 'ere corner.'

Slowly French raised his head. With a thrill of excitement which he would have died rather than admit, he watched the man put his hand over the edge of the vase and feel about. Then the man gave a sudden grunt, snatched the torch from Hawke, and shone it into the basin. Finally, throwing all caution to the winds, he began to grope wildly. The others had closed in round him.

'Well,' said Hawke, and there was a sharp tenseness in his voice. 'Where is it?'

From Sandes there came a sort of dreadful strangled cry. Then as if reckless from fury and disappointment he swore a lurid oath. 'It's not there!' he cried aloud. 'It's gone! Someone 'as taken it!'

'Silence, you fool,' Hawke hissed. He snatched the torch from Sandes and gazed into the vase. 'You——liar!' he went on, and his voice, low as it was, cut like a knife. 'This soil where you haven't disturbed it hasn't been moved for months! It's grown green scum. See, you others.'

The other two men looked and cursed in low tones.

'Now see, you,' Hawke went on, still hissing venomously like an angry snake. 'You tell us where that stuff is inside ten seconds or this knife goes into your heart. You thought you'd do us out of our shares so that you could have it all when you got out of quod, and now you think you can put us off with fairy tales! I suspected this and that's why I brought these others.' He raised his hand, which held a long pointed knife. 'You won't escape, Sandes, and we'll all be responsible for your death. Now where is it? I'll give you till I count ten. Hold him, you others.'

French wondered if he should take a hand. He believed Hawke was in earnest and he couldn't stand there and see murder done. Then he realised that Hawke would delay in the hope of learning the truth. And as he himself was quite as anxious as the others to hear what Sandes had to say, he also waited, his heart thumping from the suspense.

'One!' Hawke paused, then went on slowly: 'Two! Three! Hold his mouth, will you!' French saw the little knot bunch together. Hawke raised the knife and began to press the point against the little man's breast. Suddenly the prisoner began to struggle violently. Hawke withdrew the knife.

'We're not bluffing,' he whispered in that voice of steel. "If we don't get our shares this knife goes into your heart. I've counted to three.' Again he paused. 'Four!' And again. 'Five!' And again. 'Six!' Then came another voice. 'Try him with the knife again, guv'nor,' said the man who had not previously spoken.

'No, no, no!' came in a muffled scream. 'I've told you the truth, I swear I 'ave. I 'id it there.' He swore by all his gods. ' If you kill me I can't tell you no more!'

'Hold him again,' said Hawke inexorably, once more raising the knife.

French felt he couldn't stand this any more. He believed Sandes. He recognised the ring of truth as well as of desperate despairing fear in his voice. The man had, French felt sure, hidden the stuff there in that vase and—someone else had got it and was sitting tight. Perhaps a gardener or one of the servants . . . He began edging round the wall to the steps.

He had formed his men for the assault and they were about to rush up the steps to take the others by surprise, when there came a terrible scream from above followed by Hawke's savage voice: 'That's torn it, you——fools! Why couldn't you hold his mouth as I said? We may run for it now! Bring him along!'

Dispensing with any further attempt to preserve silence, the three men dashed across the loggia, dragging the fourth with them. So headlong was their flight that they did not see the waiting constables till they were at the steps. Then arose a terrible outcry. 'The cops!' yelled Hawke with a furious oath. 'Leave Sandes and get away over the balustrade!' As he shouted he doubled back, fumbling desperately in his pocket. French, flashing out his torch, rushed forward, followed by his men. As Hawke drew a pistol French closed with him.

Now the loggia became a nightmare of whirling bodies, of groans and curses, of thuds and—a couple of times—of pistol-shots. The torches had been knocked down and had gone out and no one could see what he was doing. Everyone clung to whoever he could feel, but he had no idea who he was holding. Three of the policemen found themselves struggling together, and it was a couple of minutes before they discovered it and went to their companions' help. Then French touched a torch with his foot and managed to pick it up. With the light the end came quickly. There were eight police to three criminals, for Sandes was too much overcome to take any part in the *mêlée*.

'Take them along to the cars, Carter,' French panted.

Presently, handcuffed, the four men were led off, while French remained behind to assuage the fears of those in the Manor.

Next morning French walked up to have a look at the scene of the combat. With Sergeant Carter he stood in the centre of the loggia and looked around.

'Do you see anything interesting?' he said presently, and when the sergeant had failed to give the required reaction, he went on: 'That corner where Sandes said he hid the stuff gets the east wind. You remember he said he chose it because for that reason no one sat there. And yet I notice that the plants there are finer and more healthy than those on the sheltered south side. Does that suggest anything to you? Ah, it does, does it? Then let us see.'

He walked over to the poorest of the plants, which looked indeed as if it had been scorched by wind. In the vase he began to dig with his penknife.

'Ah,' he said in accents of deepest satisfaction. 'What have we here? I think this is Sandes's little lot!'

It was a lucky deduction. In a parcel were the whole of the jewels, and an enquiry from the head gardener showed that only the week before he had changed the vases round, so as to get the poorer shrubs out of the east wind.

At the trial only Hawke and Taylor could be proved guilty of murder, the sending of the telegram not being held to cover compliance with all that had been done at Greenbridge. The first two were executed and the others spent many years in retreat from their normal haunts. In gratitude for French's work Lady Ormsby-Keats contributed £500 to police charities, so for a twofold reason French felt his efforts had not been wasted.

CHAILEY'S FOLLY

L. A. G. Strong

*Irish advocate John Rogan is another quietly effective man of the law
who has seen crime from both sides, defending men and women who
are as likely to be innocent as guilty. Created by L. A. G. Strong
(1896-1958), the Anglo-Irish novelist and short story writer who is
also famous for hsi biographies of John McCormack and James
Joyce, the advocate is a man whose help is sometimes called upon in
situations where the law is yet to be broken. In 'Chailey's Folly'
Rogan finds himself up against a master of fraud who is planning to
use a gang of criminals in a major coup. He is also another of those
figures in crime fiction about whom readers would like to read a great
deal more . . .*

The buzzing ceased, and the Governor's voice sounded clear again
over the 'phone.

'It is true then, that you're coming to the moor for a holiday?'

'Yes. For a holiday.'

John Rogan put a slight emphasis on the last word; and smiled to
himself to hear the other pause.

'I thought perhaps you might like to give me a little assistance.'

'It's only a short holiday, you know,' protested Rogan. 'However,
I shall, of course, find time to come and see you.'

'I should hope so.' The Governor paused again. 'As a matter of
fact, I want you to see someone else.'

'Oh?'

'It's that infernal Chailey, Rogan. He's becoming a positive nuisance. Positive menace to law and order. Confoundedly awkward
position, for me.'

'For you, Evershed? But how?'

The voice at the other end was understood to mutter something about 'a laughing-stock'.

'You've a good deal of influence over the fellow, haven't you?' it went on.

Rogan laughed.

'I don't know that unsuccessfully defending a man gives him any great confidence in one,' he replied. 'If I'd got him off, now, there might have been some chance—   —'

'If you'd got him off he wouldn't be where he is,' snapped the other. 'I wish to the Lord you had. You'd have saved me a deal of worry.'

'What's this, what's this! The Governor of one of His Majesty's prisons wishing that a guilty man had defeated the ends of justice? Well, well, Evershed, I'm surprised at you.'

'Go on. Be humorous,' came the disconsolate voice. 'Will you see the chap, or won't you?'

'Certainly. I'm all curiosity. I intended to pay him my respects, in any case. But I still can't understand why you don't simply get rid of him.'

'Can't, man. No power. He's not actually breaking the law.'

'Oh, come. Don't tell me. There are ways of working these little matters.'

'I'd be glad to hear of 'em, then. We have our legal advisers, you know. The point may not have occurred to you.'

Rogan smiled again. He was enjoying himself.

'I know. Huckworthy is one of them, isn't he? I had the privilege of—er—appearing on the opposite side to him a short while ago.'

'Getting too big for your boots, aren't you?'

'You'd better be polite to me, or I shan't come.'

'Oh, go to hell.'

'Thanks.'

'You will come, then?'

'If only to congratulate my old client.'

There was an abrupt sound from the other end. Rogan, well pleased, put the receiver softly back in its place, and sat down by the fire to consider.

So Mortimer Chailey's mad whim was taking effect, after all! What a man! Brilliant, dangerous, his brilliance and danger much lessened by an almost insane pride which would never let him forget a slight or an injury. It was this revengefulness which had led to his downfall. A system of fraud so vast, so simple, and so perfectly screened that it must have run on undetected for years, was revealed owing to Chailey's personal spite against a colleague. The colleague, in a deal so small that Chailey could have written off a hundred like it, had got the better of him.

Chailey, his pride stung, pursued the man: attention was drawn to the affairs of his company; and a petty, insensate lawsuit led to the arrest of the prosecutor, Mortimer Chailey, world-famous financier, on a colossal charge of fraud. The arrest shook the City. Chailey out of custody, and free to act, might conceivably save the situation, or at least reduce the losses. Chailey convicted could mean one thing only—the ruin of hundreds. The law, however, can take no cognisance of such matters. Once its machinery is set going, the process cannot be delayed. Chailey, even if he had had no means of his own, could have commanded an almost unlimited sum from the City for his defence: but he had enough to spare.

Then came his first set-back. Eminent advocates, despite the celebrity of the case, seemed far from anxious to undertake it. The closer they looked into it, the less anxious they were: since it appeared that the prosecution were going to have matters all their own way. Moreover, the attitude of Chailey himself, as soon as he heard of their hesitation, did nothing to win them over. It was not till a week had passed that his harassed solicitor came to inform him that they had at last secured an advocate—one John Rogan—who expressed himself willing to conduct the defence.

'Rogan! Rogan! Who the hell's Rogan! I tell you, I want the best that money can buy.'

There was a long scene, but at last the cornered man consented to see his counsel. After two minutes, he realised that he had met his match.

'Look here, Mr Chailey,' the Irishman interrupted him, holding up a large hand. 'There's not the least use in going on like that. We're neither of us here for our health. You want to get off—for obvious reasons. I want to get you off, for my own sake, not for yours. It so happens that the same result will suit us both. Now: tell me what you like.'

Well, thought Rogan, leaning back and looking at the ceiling, I didn't get him off. No man alive could have done that. But I got him off three of the charges, and I made my name, for good and all.

He might have gone on that, strangely enough, he and Chailey had won each a real respect for the other. Chailey admired the advocate's frankness and independence of mind: Rogan admired the other's skill, and understood, even if he could not agree with, his passionate conviction that he had committed no crime, and that society had done him a mortal injury. Chailey believed, and half made Rogan believe, that despite the crookedness of his start he could have brought off his bluff with immense profit, and made a fortune for all who had trusted him.

He was a bad prisoner. Not a single day's remission did he earn, but served the full bitter five years. And then—well, now came the Governor's trouble.

*   *   *

'Put me down here, will you?'

The car stopped at the edge of a little wood, and Rogan, pulling up his coat collar, stepped out into the narrow moorland lane. Tiny trickles of water, gleaming in the headlights, ran between the stones of the road: the pine trees, looming above, were heavy with moisture, and every breath of air brought down a shower of drops.

The driver, after a puzzled look at Rogan, went on downhill to a place where he could turn. Rogan, who had purposely overshot his mark, walked sharply up the hill till he came to a gate. Turning in, he stood shivering, until he heard the car pass on its homeward way.

Then he emerged again into the lane. Ten minutes' walking brought him to his goal. There was a moon behind the mist, and it showed up, clearly enough, the long rectangular building with the stone courtyard and the extraordinary high stone gateway. Grimacing to himself Rogan passed under its shadow, crossed the yard, and tugged vigorously at an old iron bell-pull. At once, there broke out in the still dark house a hideous clangour, a jangling of alarm bells that took half a minute to subside into resentful, rusty silence. Then came heavy steps, and the sound of bolts and chains.

Rogan clicked his tongue.

'Really,' he said under his breath, 'it's too childish.'

The door swung open, and he stepped into a dark hall, lit only by a diminutive candle at the far end. Wriggling out of his coat, he essayed to hand it to the form in the gloom behind him.

'Pass forward.'

There was no authority in the voice. It sounded hollow, unconvinced.

'Oh, all right. Anything you like.'

Rogan walked forward in the direction of the candle. Before he reached it a door opened, framing in brilliant light a figure which he at once recognised as that of his one-time client, Mortimer Chailey. At the same moment his hat and coat were whipped away from behind with an almost alarming suddenness.

'Ah, Mr Rogan! What a pleasure to entertain you here. It is indeed good for you to honour us with your company.'

'Us?'

Rogan, still dazzled by the light, his hand being cordially shaken, was drawn into the room, and the door closed behind him.

'Yes. These gentlemen, who are staying with me, will all be delighted to make your acquaintance.'

He steered the bewildered Rogan round, to confront a company of six or seven grinning old lags, all like their host, dressed in convict clothes. They sat about the room in deep leather chairs, or lolled on sofas, smoking cigars.

Rogan bowed.

'Delighted. But—' He turned to his host: 'I am sorry. I didn't realise it was a fancy dress evening.'

Chailey's face changed.

'What we choose to wear is our own affair,' he said.

'Certainly. Certainly. I commend you. A pleasing asceticism. You are accustoming yourselves to the pleasures of civilised life gradually, lest they go to your heads. Besides—so economical.'

'Look here,' said Chailey harshly, 'you have come at your own request. What for, God knows; but the least you can do is to keep a civil tongue in your head.'

'My dear Chailey, I'm sorry. But I really think you ought to have warned me, so that I could have procured suitable apparel.'

'You have no right to wear this uniform,' cried Chailey. 'Society has not injured you. You are not the victim of its hypocrisy and narrow-mindedness. Look at the man—' He turned to the others. 'Look at the man who would like to have put on our uniform for a joke.'

'No joke, Chailey,' cut in Rogan quickly, before they could answer. 'And, even if society has not injured me, as you put it, I have often done my best for those whom it has.'

'That's right, governor,' came a voice from the back of the room. 'Always for the defence, John Rogan.'

'That's right.'

'So he is.'

An approving murmur ran round the company. Taking advantage of it, Rogan crossed to the fireplace, and stood warming himself.

'Gentlemen,' he said, 'I am your guest tonight, and by my own desire. Let us forget everything but that.'

'Right.'

Chailey, giving his lean shoulders a shake, went over to a side table.

'Have a drink?'

'Thanks.'

The atmosphere was quiet, but still a little strained, when a man in warder's uniform flung open the door.

'Dinner is served, gentlemen,' he announced.

Of all the meals John Rogan ate in his life, that dinner was the strangest. Eight men in broad arrows, and himself in full evening dress, were waited upon by uniformed warders. At least—not quite. At his first sight of them, Rogan's heart leaped: for it seemed that here was an instant solution of Evershed's trouble. It is against the law for any person to wear His Majesty's uniform who is not entitled to do so. A closer look, however, dashed his hopes. The uniforms were almost identical, but not quite. Chailey had been too cunning.

The warders, at first disconcerted that an outsider should see their degradation, seemed speedily to forget, and relapsed to an accustomed servility that was even more horrible to Rogan than their first sickly smiles. The conversation seldom strayed far from its spiritual homes, the Old Bailey, and the Court of Criminal Appeal: but all, save Chailey and a young dark-haired man, whose eyebrows met thickly above his nose, seemed to take their convictions as a matter of course, and their present situation as a joke.

Chailey, supported by an occasional fierce monosyllable from the young man, remained morose. Rogan was glad when the meal was at an end, and he found himself at last closeted with Chailey in the latter's study. There, the spectacle of his host lolling in broad arrows in a deep leather armchair seemed more bizarre than ever.

For some time they talked of neutral matters, the City, the state of business, and Rogan's career. Then Chailey asked the question which had been trembling on his tongue all the time.

'Well,' he said, 'what do you think of my house and retinue, eh?'

Rogan knocked the ash off his cigar before replying.

'I was afraid you were going to ask me that,' he said.

The other's face darkened.

'Indeed?'

'If you really want to know what I think——'

'That's why I asked you.'

'Childish, my dear Chailey. Nursery games. I simply can't understand,' he went on quickly, giving the other no chance to interrupt, 'how a man of your intelligence can behave in such an infantile fashion. I should have thought your pride would stop you, if nothing else.'

'Pride?' choked the other. 'My pride——?'

'If I had taken a toss, I'm damned if I'd advertise to all the world how sore I felt.'

Chailey controlled himself.

'Would you have the goodness to explain what you mean?'

'Why, man, you're making yourself a perfect laughing-stock. You've simply gone to pieces. Instead of determining to get your own back in a reasonable, manly way, you skulk down here, afraid to face the world——'

'WHAT!'

'What else can you call it? You skulk down here, king of your fancy dress castle, like a little boy who's been put in the corner and won't come out when his time's up, trying to pretend he's enjoyed it. Good heavens, what a come-down! Charabancs coming and pulling up to laugh at Chailey's Folly! That's what it's called—Chailey's Folly. You think they come to admire, to marvel at your daring. Man, they come to laugh at you! The rude, sulky little boy, sticking out his tongue!'

Rogan, who had been leaning back, addressing the ceiling, out of the corner of his eye saw Chailey spring from his chair. For a moment he thought his host would strike him. Turning round, as if in innocent surprise, he saw Chailey's face livid with anger. Then a sneer came over it.

'Very clever, Mr John Rogan! Very clever indeed! But not quite clever enough. I'm not to be bluffed quite so easily.' He rubbed his forehead and managed to laugh. 'You've given something away, my dear Rogan. Now I know that I'm getting a bit of my own back. Our dear friend Governor Evershed wouldn't have sent for you to come and bait me here if he wasn't anxious to get rid of me. Oh, no, Mr Rogan. I'm not so easily disposed of as that.' He pulled out a silk handkerchief, and mopped his face with it. 'You very nearly made me lose my temper. I congratulate you.'

Rogan laughed.

'I thought you were rising rather easily. Living in a place like this must be bad for one's sense of humour. No, but seriously, Chailey: you'd much better clear out. You're doing no good here. No harm, either, except to yourself. I've always given you good advice, haven't I?'

'Yes. And you've been well paid for it.'

'Well, now I'm going to give you a bit gratis: the best I've ever given you. Drop all this nonsense, and come back to town.'

'I'll pay for your advice when I want it,' said Chailey, with a pale grin. 'I only value what costs me something.'

'Well, I'll give you the same advice professionally, if you prefer it.'

'Shut up, man. You've said enough, and more than enough. Have another drink.'

Rogan shrugged his shoulders and smiled.

'As you please,' he said. 'You'll wish you had taken my advice, all the same. You haven't a chance with Evershed. He'll get rid of you, double quick.'

'He can't,' flashed the other. 'I'm doing no wrong.'

'What about your servants?'

'I pay tax for them—*and* their liveries.'

'How did you get the poor devils?'

'Bribed 'em when I was in, and blackmailed 'em when I came out.'

'I thought as much. You're an attractive character, Chailey.'

'Bah! Jackals like that—I've no compunction. They chose me instead of their excellent master. They go on serving me. That's all.'

'You'll be nobbled, Chailey, and that right soon,' declared Rogan, sitting up and holding out his glass. 'You can't go on running a place like this, in open mockery of His Majesty's prison and in defiance of all law and order. You're a scandal to the neighbourhood, and you'll be nobbled. I'll be sorry to see it, but——'

'Oh, no, you won't—a virtuous pillar of society like you.'

'Oh, yes, I will. I'm always sorry to see a clever man make a fool of himself.'

'I think it's time we joined the rest and had a little music,' said Chailey drily. 'One of our company is very talented. His rendering of the celebrated ballad of "Samuel Hall" is a pleasure to hear.

Perhaps you don't know it?'

'Oh,' replied Rogan, with a grim smile, heaving himself out of his chair, 'I know it all right.'

*   *   *

One evening, nearly a fortnight after the events last related, when a dense mist lay thick upon the moor, the denizens of Chailey's were startled by the sudden clanging of the bell, followed by an agonised rat-tat upon the massive front door. Before they had time to exchange surprised glances the clamour broke out afresh. Their babble of comment was stilled by the appearance of Chailey.

'Open on the chain, Richards,' he commanded and followed the ex-warder down the passage, keeping well out of sight in the darkness.

The bolts shot back, the door opened a foot, and jarred on the heavy chain.

'What d'you want?' snarled the ex-warder, as fiercely as he could, buoyed up by Chailey's presence close behind him.

'Let me in, for God's sake,' gasped a voice. 'They're after me. They'll get me. Oh, let me in!'

'*Who* are after you?'

Chailey shot forward, elbowing Richards roughly out of the way.

'All of them—from the prison. The mist—I made a bolt——'

Chailey uttered a startled exclamation.

'Are they on your track now?'

'I don't know. I don't know. Oh, for God's sake let me in.'

There was a pause.

'Oh, for God's sake! Won't you——'

'Never fear. I'll let you in.'

Chailey undid the chain, and a figure plunged in almost on top of him and fell to the floor.

'Here—a light, you fool.'

Richards ran back and returned with a torch, which he flashed on the recumbent form.

'A young 'un, eh?'

Taking his arm Chailey helped the fugitive roughly to his feet. The light showed a well-bred, sensitive face, now pale and haggard.

'Here. What about those hands?'

The keen eye of Chailey had at once noted that the young man's hands showed no sign of hard labour.

'I know. I only came up with the batch on Monday. I couldn't stick it. Look——'

He pointed to a row of newly formed blisters just above the palm.

'Only just come, eh!' Chailey's eyes were blazing. He turned to Richards. 'We'll get him away. God, what a score! Escapes after two days! Don't you worry,' he added quickly. 'We'll get you away. For the moment—a hiding place.'

'What about the bloodhounds, governor?' doubtfully asked the ex-warder. 'They'll track him here.'

'Buzzacott can fix that,' cried Chailey. 'He's done it before. With aniseed. We need only fix it a couple of hundred yards from the house. They'll never find him. Here—Buzzacott!' He turned and hurried back to the living-room—only to find it empty. Custom was too strong for the guests of Mortimer Chailey. When in doubt they hid.

Reassured, they all emerged like snails after rain; but before Chailey and the chuckling expert could get to work an even more imperative thundering at the door sent all back into hiding again. The financier, obliged to answer the door himself, was confronted by a small army of prison officials, come to search for an escaped convict whom, presently to the extreme prejudice of the aforesaid Mortimer Chailey, they found and apprehended. Mortimer Chailey they also apprehended; but before he was led away the Governor of the prison arrived on the scene, and expressed a wish to interview him. Chailey at first refused, but was at last persuaded to accede to the Governor's request. The two went off together to Chailey's study.

*　　*　　*

H.M. Prison, Highmoor,
March 2nd, 19—.

My dear Rogan,

You may be interested to hear, if your nephew has not already told you his part in the business, that, upon reflection, I decided to act on your very irregular suggestion. I got into touch with your nephew, and had him out to stay with me till a suitable occasion arose for trying out your plan. As you know, when one doesn't want them, there are mists here every day in the week. When one does, one has to wait a fortnight.

However, last night there came a real mist, thick as could be wished. We motored your nephew as close as we dared, for the mist was so thick he'd have got lost if he'd tried to find the place for himself: and he ran up and down the hill till he was half-dead. He doesn't do things by halves, that young man. He insisted on breaking stones for an hour and a half yesterday morning to roughen his hands. Said they'd be the first things Chailey and Co. would look at, if they were at all suspicious. I doubt if that repertory theatre will hold him for long.

Anyway, he staggered off, and presently we heard him raising hell's delight at Chailey's door. For a while it seemed they weren't going to let him in; but they did at last, and we settled down to wait. We gave them twenty minutes, and then stormed the place. Chailey himself had to let us in: his precious crew of gaolbirds were all hiding under the beds. We found young Noel—with a little assistance from himself—most cunningly hidden. In fact, but for his help we mightn't have found him yet.

Acting on my instructions, they handcuffed Chailey and made a few remarks on the subject of the sentence given for harbouring fugitives from justice, and the sort of time likely to be enjoyed by those who had endeavoured to make prison officials ridiculous, etc., etc. He was pretty green by the time I came along. When I thought it had sunk in enough I made them bring him along to his study, and there I gave him his chance. You should have seen his face! Upon my word, I was half-sorry for the brute myself.

'You ring *that* bell,' he said, and I rang it; and a warder came in and unlocked his handcuffs. Then he sat down at his desk and wrote me an undertaking to leave his rotten place in twenty-four hours, and take his gang of toughs with him.

He's been as good as his word. The last car load of them passed through the village half an hour ago.

Well, Rogan, I can't deny I'm grateful to you: though, as you know, I didn't half like the means adopted to get rid of the fellow. Still, it's good to be rid of him. Needless to say, he knows nothing of your share in the matter——

Rogan broke off and cocked an eye at the ceiling.

'I bet he guessed,' he said to himself, and smiled, knowing the pride of Mortimer Chailey to be such that never, never, by so much as a gesture, would he betray the knowledge that his mind had been read, and the right trap set to catch him.

'Well,' continued Rogan, picking up the letter again, 'I'll keep out of his way, and he'll keep out of mine, and that will please both of us.'

He looked at the end of the letter and burst into a laugh.

'Really, you know,' he said, 'they're very much alike.'

MURDER IN REPOSE

Peter Tremayne

'Murder in Repose' introduces a unique detective—a member of the Church adept at solving crimes, one Sister Fidelma whom the author has described as 'a kind of seventh-century Irish Perry Mason'. She is, in fact, both a religieuse and a qualified advocate practising in the Ireland of the Celtic 'Golden Age' when the Church, with its saints and scholars, held sway and the country was governed by the ancient and sophisticated native Brehon Law system. Created by Peter Berresford Ellis (1943-) under his pen-name, Peter Tremayne, the stories draw on his extensive knowledge of Celtic history and culture which he has already revealed in several highly acclaimed works of non-fiction. Tremayne is also the creator of the urbane city detective Inspector Lehane of the Dublin Metropolitan South Division, who appeared in the novel Angelus! (1985) and several short stories.

The red-headed, youthful and attractive Sister Fidelma is a quite unique figure whose patient unravelling of a 'whodunnit' in the Brehon court draws on the same rich vein of medieval folklore exploited by Ellis Peters and Umberto Eco. It is good to know that she is shortly to make her debut in a full length novel in which she joins forces with a Saxon monk to solve a murder during the famous Synod of Whitby.

'There is no question of Brother Fergal's guilt in this crime,' said the Brehon with assurance. 'He clearly murdered the girl.'

He was a stocky man, this chief judge of the clan of the Eóghanacht of Cashel. His round, lugubrious face was betrayed by a pair of bright, sharp eyes. His slow-speaking meticulous manner disguised a mind that was sharp and decisive. Here was a man who, as his profession demanded, looked at life carefully and weighed the evidence before making a decision. And he was no one's fool.

Sister Fidelma, tall, green-eyed, stood before the Brehon with

337

hands folded demurely in front of her. Her robes and hood, from under which wisps of rebellious red hair stuck out, scarcely disguised her youthfulness nor her feminine attractiveness. The Brehon had placed her age in her mid-twenties. He noticed that her stance was one of controlled agitation, of someone used to movement and action in life. The habit of a religieuse did not suit her at all.

'The Abbess has assured me that Brother Fergal is no more capable of taking life than a rabbit is capable of flying through the air.'

The Brehon of the Eóghanacht of Cashel sighed. He made little effort to conceal his irritation at the young woman's contradiction.

'Nevertheless, sister, the evidence is plain. The man Fergal was found in his *bothán*, the cabin he had rebuilt, on the slopes of Cnocgorm. He was asleep. By his side was the body of the girl, Barrdub. She had been stabbed to death. There was blood on Fergal's hands and on his robes. When he was awakened, he claimed that he had no knowledge of anything. That is a weak defence.'

Sister Fidelma bowed her head, as if acknowledging the logic of the Brehon's statement.

'What were the circumstances of the finding of the body of the girl Barrdub?'

'Barrdub's brother, Congal, had been worried. The girl, it seems, had been smitten with a passion for this Brother Fergal. He is a handsome young man, it must be admitted. That night, according to Congal, his sister went out and did not return. Early in the morning, Congal came to me and asked me to accompnay him to Fergal's *bothán* to confront them. Barrdub is not yet at the age of choice, you understand, and Congal stands as her guardian in law for they have no other relatives living. Together we found Fergal and the body of Barrdub as I have described.'

Sister Fidelma compressed her lips. The evidence was, indeed, damning.

'The hearing will be at noon tomorrow,' the Brehon went on. 'Brother Fergal must give account to the law for no one can stand above the jurisdiction of the Brehons, either priest or druid.'

Sister Fidelma smiled thinly.

'Thanks be to the holy Patrick that it is two centuries since the druids of Ireland accepted the teachings of the Saviour of this world.'

The Brehon returned her smile.

'Yet they say that many who live in the mountains or in remote fastnesses still practise the old ways; that there are many whom the teachings of Christ have not won from the worship of The Dagda and the ancient gods of Ireland. We have such a one even here, in our territory. Erca is a hermit who also lives on the slopes of Cnocgorm and claims to practise the old ways.'

Sister Fidelma shrugged indifferently.

'I am not here to proselytise.'

The Brehon was examining her carefully now.

'What precisely is your role in this affair, sister? Do you simply represent the Abbey which, I understand, now stands in place of Brother Fergal's *fine* or family? Remember, in law, the *fine* must ensure that the penalties are provided when judgement is given by the court.'

'I am aware of the law, Brehon of the Eóghanacht,' replied Sister Fidelma. 'The Abbess has sent me to this place in the capacity of a *dálaighe*; an advocate to plead before the court on behalf of Brother Fergal.'

The Brehon raised an eyebrow, slightly surprised. When the girl had come to him, he had assumed that she was simply one of Brother Fergal's religious community who had come to find out why he had been arrested and charged with murder.

'The law requires that all advocates must be qualified to plead before the *Dál*.'

Sister Fidelma drew herself up, a little annoyed at the patronage in the man's voice, at his arrogant assumption.

'I am qualified. I studied law under the great Brehon Morann of Tara.'

Once again the Brehon barely concealed his surprise. That the young girl before him could be qualified in the law of Éireann was astonishing in his eyes. He was about to open his mouth when the girl pre-empted his question by reaching within her robes and passing him an inscribed vellum. The Brehon read quickly, eyes rounded, hesitated and passed it back. His glance was now respectful, his voice slightly awed.

'It states that you are a qualified *Anruth*.'

To have qualified to the level of *Anruth* one had to have studied at a monastic or bardic school for between seven to nine years. The *Anruth* was only one degree below the highest qualification, the *Ollamh*, or professor, who could sit as an equal with kings. The

Anruth had to be knowledgeable in poetry, literature, law and medicine, speaking and writing with authority on all things and being eloquent in debate.

'I was with the Brehon Morann for eight years,' Fidelma replied.

'Your right to act as advocate before the court is recognised, Sister Fidelma.'

The young religieuse smiled.

'In that case, I call upon my right to speak with the accused and then with the witnesses.'

'Very well. But there can be only one plea before the court. The evidence is too damning to say other than that Brother Fergal is guilty of the murder of Barrdub.'

Brother Fergal was, as the Brehon said, a handsome young man no more than five and twenty years of age. He wore a bewildered expression on his pale features. The brown eyes were wide, the auburn hair was tousled. He looked like a young man awakened from sleep to find himself in a world he did not recognise. He rose awkwardly as Sister Fidelma entered the cell, coughing nervously.

The burly jailer closed the door behind her but stood outside.

'The grace of God to you, Brother Fergal,' she greeted.

'And of God and Mary to you, sister,' responded the young religieux automatically. His voice was slightly breathless and wheezy.

'I am Fidelma sent from the Abbey to act as your advocate.'

A bitter expression passed over the face of the young man.

'What good will that do? The Brehon has already judged me guilty.'

'And are you?'

Fidelma seated herself on a stool which, apart from the rough straw pallaisse, was the only furniture in the cell, and gazed up at the young monk.

'By the Holy Virgin, I am not!' The cry was immediate, angry and despairing at the same time. The young man punctuated his response with a paroxysm of coughing.

'Be seated, brother,' said Fidelma solicitously. 'The cell is cold and you must take care of your cough.'

The young man contrived to shrug indifferently.

'I have suffered from asthma for several years now, sister. I ease it by inhaling the odours of the burning leaves of *stramóiniam* or taking a little herbal drink before I retire at night. Alas, such a luxury is denied me here.'

'I will speak to the Brehon about it,' Fidelma assured him. 'He is not a harsh man. Perhaps we can find some leaves and seeds of the *stramóiniam* and have them sent into you.'

'I would be grateful.'

After a little while, Fidelma reminded the young man that she awaited his story.

Reluctantly, the young man squatted on the pallaisse and coughed again.

'Little to tell. The Abbess sent me to the clan of Eóghanacht of Cashel, to preach and administer to them, four weeks ago. I came here and rebuilt a deserted cell on the blue hill of Cnoc-gorm. For a while all went well. True that in this part of Éireann, two hundred years after the blessed saint Patrick converted our people, I have found some whose hearts and souls have not been won over for Christ. That was a great sadness to me . . .'

'I have heard that there is one here who still follows the old ways of the druids,' Fidelma commented encouragingly when the young man paused and faltered in his thoughts.

'The hermit Erca? Yes. He dwells on Cnoc-gorm, too. He hates all Christians.'

'Does he now?' mused Fidelma. 'But tell me, what of the events of the night of the murder?'

Brother Fergal grimaced expressively.

'All I remember is that I returned to my cell at dusk. I was exhausted for I had walked sixteen miles that day, taking the Word of Christ to the shepherds in the mountains. I felt a soreness on my chest and so I heated and drank my herbal potion. It did me good for I slept soundly. The next thing I knew was being shaken awake to find the Brehon standing over me and Congal with him. Congal was screaming that I had killed his sister. There was blood on my hands and clothes. Then I saw, in my cell, the poor, blooded body of the girl, Barrdub.'

He started coughing again. Fidelma watched the face of the young religieux intently. There was no guile there. The eyes were puzzled yet honest.

'That is all?' she pressed when he had drawn breath.

'You asked me what I knew of the events of the night of the murder. That is all.'

Fidelma bit her lip. It sounded an implausible story.

'You were not disturbed at all? You heard nothing? You went to sleep and knew nothing until the Brehon and Congal woke you, when you saw blood on your clothes and the body of the dead girl in your cabin?'

The young man moaned softly, placing his face in his hands.

'I know nothing else,' he insisted. 'It is fantastic, I know, but it is the truth.'

'Do you admit that you knew the girl, Barrdub?'

'Of course. In the time I was here, I knew everyone of the clan of Eóghanacht.'

'And what of Barrdub? How well did you know her?'

'She came to religious service regularly and once or twice came to help me when I was rebuilding my *bothán*. But so did many others from the village here.'

'You had no special relationship with Barrdub?'

Priests, monks and nuns of the Celtic Church could enter into marriage provided such unions were blessed by a bishop or the congregation of the Abbey.

'I had no relationship with Barrdub other than as pastor to one of his flock. Besides, the girl is not yet of the age of choice.'

'You know that Congal is claiming that Barrdub was in love with you and that you had encouraged this? The argument of the prosecution will be that she came to you that night and for some reason you rejected her and when she would not leave you, you killed her. It will be argued that her love became an embarrassment to you.'

The young monk looked outraged.

'But I did not! I only knew the girl slightly and nothing passed between us. Why . . . why, the girl is also betrothed, as I recall, to someone in the village. I can't remember his name. I can assure you that there was nothing between the girl and me.'

Fidelma nodded slowly and rose.

'Very well, Brother Fergal. If you have nothing else to tell me . . .?'

The young man looked up at her with large, pleading eyes.

'What will become of me?'

'I will plead for you,' she consented. 'But I have little so far to present to the court in your defence.'

'Then if I am found guilty?'

'You know the law of the land. If you are adjudged guilty of homicide then you must pay the honour-price of the girl, the *eric*, to her next of kin. The girl, I understand, was a free person, the daughter of a member of the clan assembly. The *eric* fine stands at forty-five milch cows plus four milch cows as the fee to the Brehon.'

'But I have no wealth. It was given up when I decided to serve Christ and took a vow of poverty.'

'You will also know that your family becomes responsible for the fine.'

'But my only family is the Abbey, our order of brothers and sisters in Christ.'

Fidelma grimaced.

'Exactly so. The Abbess has to decide whether she will pay your *eric* fine on behalf of our order. And the greater trial for your immortal soul will be heard under her jurisdiction. If you are judged guilty of killing Barrdub then not only must you make atonement to the civil court but, as a member of the religieux, you must make atonement to Christ.'

'What if the Abbess refuses to pay the *eric* fine . . .?' whispered Fergal, his breath becoming laboured again.

'It would be unusual for her to refuse,' Fidelma assured him. 'In some exceptional circumstances she can do so. It is the right of the Abbess to renounce you if your crime is so heinous. You can be expelled from the Abbey. If so, you can be handed over by the Brehon to the victim's family to be disposed of, to treat as a slave or punish in any way thought fitting to compensate them. That is the law. But it will not come to that. The Abbess cannot believe that you killed this girl.'

'Before God, I am innocent!' sobbed the young man.

Fidelma strode with the Brehon up the winding path to the tree-sheltered nook on Cnoc-gorm where Fergal had refurbished an old *bothán* for use as his cell. The Brehon led the way to the building which was constructed of inter-laid stones without mortar.

'This is where you found Brother Fergal and the dead girl, Barrdub?' asked Fidelma, as they paused outside the door.

'It is,' acknowledged the Brehon. 'Though the girl's body has been removed. I cannot see what use it will be to your advocacy to view this place.'

Fidelma simply smiled and went in under the lintel.

The room was small and dark, almost like the cell in which she had left Fergal, except that the *bothán* was dry whereas the cell was damp. There was a wooden cot, a table and chair, a crucifix and some other items of furnishing. Fidelma sniffed, catching a bitter-sweet aromatic smell which permeated from the small hearth. The smell was of burnt leaves of *stramóiniam*.

The Brehon had entered behind her.

'Has anything been removed apart from the girl's body and the person of Brother Fergal?' Fidelma asked as her eye travelled to a wooden vessel on the table.

'As you see, nothing has been touched. Brother Fergal was in the bed, there, and the girl lay by the hearth. Only the girl's body and the person of Brother Fergal have been removed. Nothing else has been removed as nothing else was of consequence.'

'No other objects?'

'None.'

Fidelma went to the table, took up the wooden vessel and sniffed at it. There was a trace of liquid left and she dipped her finger in it and placed it, sniffing as she did so, against her lips. She grimaced at the taste and frowned.

'As Brehon, how do you account for the fact that, if Brother Fergal is guilty, it would follow he killed Barrdub and then went to bed, leaving her body here, and slept peacefully until morning? Surely a person who killed would have first done their best to hide the body and remove all trace of the crime lest anyone arrive and discover it?'

The round-faced Brehon nodded and smiled.

'That had already occurred to me, Sister Fidelma. But I am a simple judge. I have to deal with the facts. My concern is the evidence. It is not in my training to consider why a man should behave in the way he does. My interest is only to know that he does behave in such a manner.'

Fidelma sighed, set down the vessel and looked round again before leaving the cell.

Outside she paused, noticing a dark smear on one of the upright stone pillars framing the doorway. It was a little over shoulder height.

'Barrdub's blood, I presume?'

'Perhaps made as my men were carrying the body out,' agreed the Brehon uninterestedly.

Fidelma gazed at the smear a moment more before turning to examine the surroundings of the *bothán* which was protected by a bank of trees to one side, bending before the winds which whipped across the hill, while bracken grew thickly all around. The main path to the *bothán*, which led down to the village, was narrow and well-trodden. An even narrower path ascended farther up the hill behind the building while a third track meandered away to the right across the hillside. The paths were certainly used more than occasionally.

'Where do they lead?'

The Brehon frowned, slightly surprised at her question.

'The way up the hill will eventually bring you to the dwelling of the hermit, Erca. The path across the hillside is one of many that goes wherever you will. It is even an alternative route to the village.'

'I would see this Erca,' Fidelma decided.

The Brehon frowned, went to say something and then shrugged.

Erca was everything Fidelma had expected.

A thin, dirty man, clad in a single threadbare wollen cloak; he had wild, matted hair and staring eyes, and he showered abuse on them as they approached his smoking fire.

'Christians!' he spat. 'Out of my sight with your foreign god. Would you profane the sacred territory of The Dagda, father of all gods?'

The Brehon frowned angrily but Fidelma smiled gently and continued to approach.

'Peace to you, brother.'

'I am not your brother!' snarled the man.

'We are all brothers and sisters, Erca, under the one God who is above us all, whichever name we call Him by. I mean you no harm.'

'Harm, is it? I would see the gods of the Dé Danaan rise up from the *sidhe* and drive all followers of the foreign god out of this land as they did with the evil Fomorii the times of the great mists.'

'So you hate Christians?'

'I hate Christians.'

'You hate Brother Fergal?'

'This land could not set boundaries to my hatred of all Christians.'

'You would harm Brother Fergal, if you could?'

The man cracked his thumb at her.

'That to Fergal and all his kind!'

Fidelma seemed unperturbed. She nodded towards the cooking pot which sat atop the man's smoking fire.

'You are boiling herbs. You must be knowledgeable of the local herbs.'

Erca sneered.

'I am trained in the ancient ways. When your mad Patrick drove our priests from the Hill of Slane and forced our people to turn to his Christ, he could not destroy our knowledge.'

'I see you have a pile of pale brown roots, there. What herb is that?'

Erca frowned curiously at her a moment.

'That is *lus mór na coille.*'

'Ah, deadly nightshade,' Fidelma acknowledged. 'And those leaves with the white points next to them?'

'Those of the leaves of the *muing*, or poison hemlock.'

'And they grow on this hill?'

Erca made an impatient gesture of affirmation.

'Peace to you, then, brother Erca,' Fidelma ended the conversation abruptly, and she turned away down the hill leaving the bewildered Erca behind. The perplexed Brehon trotted after her.

'No peace to you, Christian,' came Erca's wild call behind them as the hermit collected his thoughts. 'No peace until all worshippers of foreign gods are driven from the land of Éireann!'

Fidelma said nothing as she made her way down the hillside back to Fergal's *bothán*. As she reached it, she darted inside and then re-emerged a moment or two later carrying the wooden vessel.

'I shall need this in my presentation. Will you take it into your custody?'

'What line are you following, sister?' frowned the Brehon as he accepted the vessel and they continued on to the village. 'For a moment I thought you might be suggesting that Erca is somehow involved in this matter.'

Fidelma smiled but did not answer the question.

'I would now like to see the brother of Barrdub. What was his name? Congal?'

They found the brother of Barrdub in a poor dwelling by the river bank, a *bothán* of rotting wood. The Brehon had made some preparation as they walked to Congal's cabin.

'Congal's father was once the hostel keeper for the Eóghanacht of Cashel, a man held in high honour, and a spokesman at the clan assembly. Congal was not the man his father was. Congal was always a dreamer. When his father died, he squandered away what could have been his so that he and his sister were reduced to living in this *bothán* and Congal forced to hire himself to work for other members of the clan rather than run his own cattle.'

Congal was a dark, brooding person with fathomless grey eyes as deep and angry as the sea on a stormy winter's day.

'If you have come to defend the murderer of my sister, I will answer no questions!' he told Fidelma belligerently, his thin, bloodless lips set firm.

The Brehon sighed in annoyance.

'Congal, you will obey the law. It is the right of the *dálaighe*, the advocate, to ask you questions and your duty to reply truthfully.'

Sister Fidelma motioned the man to be seated but he would not.

'Did you ever take *stramóiniam* to Brother Fergan?' she opened.

Congal blinked at the unexpectedness of her question.

'No,' he replied. 'He purchased his asthma medication from Iland the herbalist.'

'Good. Now I have heard how you discovered the body of your sister. Before you confirm the Brehon's account of that discovery, I want you to tell me what made you seek your sister in Brother Fergal's *bothán* when you knew her to be missing?'

Congal grimaced.

'Because Barrdub was enamoured of the man. He mesmerised her and used her.'

'Mesmerised? Why do you say this?'

Congal's voice was harsh.

'I knew my sister, did I not? Since Fergal came to this village, Barrdub mooned after the man like a sick cow after a farmer, always making excuses to go to visit him and help him rebuild the priest's *bothán*. It was disgusting.'

'Why disgusting?' the Brehon chimed in, suddenly interested. 'If she would have Fergal, or he would have her, there was nothing to prevent her save she have your consent or had reached the age of choice. You know as well as I do that all servants of Christ have the ancient right to marry the partner of their choice, even to an abbot or abbess?'

'It was disgusting because she was betrothed to Rimid,' Congal insisted.

'Yet before Fergal arrived here,' the Brehon observed wryly, 'you objected to Rimid as husband for Barrdub.'

Congal flushed.

'Why did you object to Rimid?' interposed Fidelma.

'Because . . .'

'Becaue he could not afford the full bride-price,' offered the Brehon before the man could reply. 'Isn't that so?'

'The *tinnscra* is as old as Éireann. No one marries without an offering of dowry to compensate the family of the bride,' Congal said stubbornly.

'And you were Barrdub's only family?' asked Fidelma.

'She kept my house. With her gone, I have no one else. It is right that I be compensated according to our ancient law.'

'Presumably, you raised this same objection over her liaison with Fergal? As a religieux he was not able to supply a *tinnscra*.'

Congal said sullenly: 'There was no question of that. He had no thought of marriage. He was using my sister and when she went to him seeking marriage, he killed her.'

'That remains to be proved,' Fidelma responded. 'Who else knew about the affair between your sister and Fergal?'

'No one,' Congal said promptly. 'My sister only admitted it to me with great unwillingness.'

'So you kept it to yourself? Are you sure no one else knew. What of Rimid?'

Congal hesitated, his eyes downcast.

'Yes,' he answered reluctantly. 'Rimid knew.'

'I will see this Rimid next,' Fidelma told the Brehon. She turned to leave and then hesitated, pausing to examine bunches of dried flowers and plants hung on the wall by the fireplace.

'What herb is this?'

Congal frowned at her for a moment.

'I have no knowledge of such things. Barrdub gathered all our herbs for cooking.'

Outside the Brehon cast a long puzzled look at Fidelma.

'You are greatly interested in herbs, sister,' he observed.

Fidelma nodded.

'Did you know that Brother Fergal suffers from asthma and that he is in the habit of inhaling the fumes of the burning leaves of *stramóiniam* or drinking an infusion of similar herbs each night to ease his chest?'

The Brehon shrugged.

'Some people are so afflicted,' he conceded, perplexed at her comment. 'Is it important?'

'Where will we find Rimid?'

'He may he at his work at this hour,' the Brehon sighed.

Fidelma raised an eyebrow.

'I was under the impression that Rimid did not work because Congal intimated that he was in no position to pay the *tinnscra*.'

The Brehon smiled broadly.

'Congal objected to the fact that Rimid could not pay the *full* bride-price. Rimid is not a man of wealth but he is a freeman of the clan and, unlike Congal, can sit in the clan assembly.'

'Congal cannot? He is so poor?'

'As you saw. A self-inflicted poverty. He has great schemes but they all come to nothing for he dreams of marvellous ways to gain respect and advancement in the clan but his expectations always exceed his means. He often has to rely on the generosity of the clan to feed himself. It makes him bitter.'

'And Barrdub? Was she bitter also?'

'No. Her hope was to escape her brother's poverty through marriage.'

'She must have been disappointed when Congal refused Rimid's offer of marriage.'

'This was so. I thought she might wait until she reached the *aimsir togu*, the age of consent, when she would be a woman and with full right of choice. Then I thought she would marry with Rimid. When she reached the age where she could decide, there would be no question of Congal being able to demand a bride-price. I think Rimid shared that belief. He was bitter when he learnt that Barrdub was throwing herself at Brother Fergal.'

'Was he now?' mused Fidelma. 'Well, let us go and speak with this Rimid. You say he might be at his work? Where would that be?'

The Brehon sighed.

'He might be at the *bothán* of Iland, the herbalist.'

Fidelma halted and stared at the Brehon in astonishment.

'Is Rimid a herbalist?'

The Brehon shook his head.

'No, no. He is not a professional man. He is employed by the herbalist to go abroad each day and gather the herbs and flowers wanted for the preparations.'

Rimid's face was full of bitter hatred. He was a flushed-faced, excitable youth, scarcely beyond the age of choice.

'Yes. I loved Barrdub. I loved her and she betrayed me. I might have won her back, but for this man, Fergal. I will kill him.'

The Brehon sniffed disdainfully.

'It is not your right, Rimid. The law will punish and seek compensation.'

'Yet if I meet him on the highway, I will slay him with as little compunction as I will a vermin.'

'Your hatred is great, Rimid, because you feel that he stole Barrdub from you,' interposed Fidelma. 'That is understandable. Did you also hate Barrdub?'

Rimid's eyes widened.

'Hate? No! I loved her.'

'Yet you say that she betrayed you, deserted your love for Brother Fergal. You must have been angry with her . . . angry enough . . .'

Fidelma let her voice trail off purposely.

Rimid blinked.

'Never! I would never harm her.'

'In spite of your hate? And did you also hate Congal?'

'Why hate Congal?' Rimid seemed puzzled.

'But he also denied you Barrdub by refusing your offer of a *tinnscra* which he thought was not sufficient.'

Rimid shrugged.

'I disliked Congal, yes. But Barrdub was only six months away from the *aimsir togu*, the age of choice, and she promised that when that time came we would marry without her brother's approval.'

'Did Congal know this?'

Rimid shrugged. 'I do not know. It is likely that Barrdub told him.'

'How did he accept it?'

'There was nothing he could do . . . but then Brother Fergal came along.'

'But Fergal did not have a *tinnscra* to offer. He is one of our order and took a vow of poverty.'

'Congal says there was no question of marriage. Fergal just mesmerised and played with the affections of Barrdub until she became too troublesome to him.'

'Mesmerised?' Fidelma frowned. 'An interesting choice of word, Rimid.'

'It is true.'

'Did you rebuke Barrdub about her relationship?'

Rimid hesitated and shook his head.

'I was blind. I did not know what was going on behind my back until the day before the murder.'

'How did you find out?'

'Congal told me. I met him on the road that evening with anger in his face. Barrdub had told him that day.'

'And when did you know about her death?'

'I was going to Fergal's *bothán* that morning to have it out with him when I met the Brehon and Congal on the path and they told me of Barrdub's death. Two men were carrying Barrdub's body on a litter and Fergal had been arrested for the crime.'

Fidelma glanced quickly to the Brehon for confirmation and he nodded.

'How long have you been a herb gatherer, Rimid?' Fidelma suddenly asked.

'Since I was a boy,' the man replied, hestitating slightly at her abrupt turn of tack.

'Did you, or Iland the herbalist, supply herbs to Brother Fergal?'

'I did not, but I knew that Iland did. I gather herbs for Iland. Fergal suffered from want of breath and took herbs for the condition.'

'Was that well known?'

'Many knew,' replied Rimid.

'Barrdub knew?'

'Yes. She mentioned it to me once when we were at religious service.'

'Congal? Did he know?'

Rimid shrugged. 'Many knew. I do not know who specifically did or who did not.'

Fidelma paused and then smiled.

'I am finished.' She turned to the Brehon. 'I am now prepared to plead before the court tomorrow.'

Most of the clan of the Eóghanacht of Cashel were assembled in the great hall of the chieftain. The chieftain, Eóghan himself, sat on the right-hand side of the Brehon, who would sit in judgement. It was law and courtesy to consult with the chieftain of the clan when judgement was made.

Brother Fergal stood before the Brehon and the chieftain, a thickset and muscular clansman at his shoulder, with sword and shield, to keep order. Fergal was placed before a small waist-high wooden bar which was known as the *cos-na-dála*, the foot of the court, from which all accused before the *Dál*, or court, had to plead.

To the right of this was a small platform which had been erected for the prosecution's advocate or *dálaighe*; a thin, sharp-faced man. To the left, on a similar platform, sat Sister Fidelma, hands demurely folded in her lap, yet her clear green eyes missing nothing. The witnesses had been summoned and the *Dál* was crowded with the men and women of the clan, for never in the memory of the village had a member of the religieux been charged with the heinous crime of murder.

The Brehon, calling for silence, asked Brother Fergal if he accepted Sister Fidelma as his advocate for it was, according to ancient law, Fergal's right to conduct his own defence. Brother Fergal shook his head and indicated that Sister Fidelma would speak for him.

The prosecution then delivered his case in the manner which the Brehon had already advised Sister Fidelma.

There was a murmur of expectation as Sister Fidelma finally rose to address the Brehon.

'Brother Fergal is innocent of this crime,' she began in a loud compelling tone.

There was silence among the people.

'Do you dispute the evidence?' asked the Brehon, smiling slightly now. 'Remember, I went with Congal and discovered Barrdub's body lying in Brother Fergal's *bothán* with Fergal asleep on his bed. I saw the blood on his clothes.'

'I do not dispute that,' Fidelma assured him. 'But that in itself is no proof of the act of murder. The events as the prosecution describes them are not in contention, only the manner of their interpretation.'

Rimid let out an angry protest from the well of the court.

'Fergal is a murderer! She only seeks to protect one of her own!'

The Brehon gestured him to silence.

'Continue with your defence, Sister Fidelma.'

'Brother Fergal suffers from asthma. He is known to take herbal remedies to relieve his condition. This was known to several people. That night he returned to his *bothán* exhausted. He usually lit a fire of *stramóiniam* leaves and inhaled them before bed. But sometimes, when he was too exhausted, took a drink of an infusion of similar herbs.'

Brother Fergal was staring at her.

'Fergal, did you inhale or drink the herbs that night?'

'I was too tired to sit up and prepare the inhalation. I always kept a kettle with an infusion of herbs ready. So I merely heated and drank a measure.'

'And you knew no more until the morning?'

'Nothing until I was awakened by the Brehon and Congal,' agreed the monk.

'You slept soundly. Is that usual?'

Brother Fergal hesitated, frowning as if he had not considered the matter before.

'Unusual. My chest often troubles me so that I wake in the early hours and must ease it with more of the infusion.'

'Quite so. You slept unusually soundly. So soundly that someone could enter your *bothán* without disturbing you? As, indeed, did the Brehon and Congal. You had to be shaken awake by both of them or you would not have known of their presence.'

The court was quiet and the Brehon was looking at her with curiosity.

'What are you suggesting, Sister Fidelma?'

'I suggest nothing. I present evidence. I took a wooden vessel from Brother Fergal's *bothán* in your presence and gave it to you as evidence.'

The Brehon nodded and indicated the wooden vessel on the table before him.

'This is so. There is the bowl.'

'Is this the vessel from which you drank, Fergal?'

The monk examined the vessel and nodded.

'It is mine. There is my name scratched on its surface. It is the vessel from which I drank.'

'There remains some liquid at the bottom of the vessel and I tasted it. It was not an infusion of *stramóiniam*.'

'What then?' demanded the Brehon.

'To please the court, we could call Iland, the herbalist, to examine it and give his opinion. But the court knows that I am an *Anruth* and qualified in the knowledge of herbs.'

'The court accepts your knowledge, Sister Fidelma,' replied the Brehon impatiently.

Fidelma bowed her head.

'It contains the remains of an infusion of *lus mór na coille* together with *muing*.'

'For those not acquainted with herbs, explain what these are,' instructed the Brehon, frowning.

'Certainly. The *lus mór na coille*, which we call deadly nightshade, is a powerful sedative inducing sleep, while *muing*, or poison hemlock, if taken in large doses can produce paralysis. Any person knowledgeable about herbs will tell you this. By drinking this infusion, Brother Fergal was effectively drugged. He slept the sleep of one dead and was oblivious to everything. It was lucky that he was aroused at all. It may well be that whoever provided him with the potion did not expect him to ever awake. Brother Fergal would simply have been found dead, next to Barrdub. The conclusion would have been that he killed her and then took this poisonous mixture in an act of remorse.'

She paused at the disturbance which her words provoked. Brother Fergal stood staring at her with a shocked, pale face.

The Brehon, calling for silence, then addressed himself to Fidelma.

'Are you saying that Barrdub was killed in Fergal's *bothán* while he slept and he did not know it?'

'No. I am saying that the person who drugged Fergal, killed Barrdub elsewhere and carried her body to the *bothán*, leaving it inside. That person then rubbed some of her blood on Fergal's hands and clothes while he lay in his drugged slumber. Having created the scene, that person then departed. The murderer made several errors. He left the tell-tale evidence of the drinking vessel in which were the remains of the drugs. And he left Barrdub's blood smeared on the side of the door when he carried her body into the *bothán*.'

'I recall you showing me that strain,' the Brehon intervened. 'At the time I pointed out that it was probably caused when we removed the body.'

'Not so. The stain was at shoulder height. When you removed the body, it is reported that your men placed it on a litter. Two men would have carried the litter.'

The Brehon nodded confirmation.

'The highest the litter, with the body, could be carried in comfort would be at waist height. But the stain was at shoulder height. Therefore, the stain was not caused when the body was removed from the *bothán* but when it was carried in. The murderer, being one person, had to carry the body on his own. The easiest method to carry such a dead weight is on the shoulders. The stain was made at shoulder height when the body was carried inside by the murderer.'

'Your argument is plausible,' conceded the Brehon. 'But not conclusive.'

'Then let me put this before the court. Your argument is that Brother Fergal stabbed Barrdub to death in a mad frenzy. Then, exhausted, too exhausted to take the body out of his *bothán* to conceal the murder, he fell asleep on his bed and was found the next morning.'

'That is as the prosecution contends.'

'Where then is the weapon?'

'What?' The word came slowly from the mouth of the Brehon, a growing doubt appearing in his eyes.

'You made no mention of a weapon, the knife by which Barrdub was stabbed to death. If you did not take it when you found Fergal that morning, it must have still been there. I searched the *bothán*. I found no weapon. Brother Fergal carries no such knife.'

The Brehon bit his lip.

'It is true, no weapon was found.'

'Yet a weapon must exist with Barrdub's blood upon it.'

'Fergal could have hidden it,' countered the Brehon, realising his fault for not instigating the search before.

'Why? Why hide the weapon when he was too exhausted to hide the body?'

'Your arguments are possible explanations. Yet if Fergal did not murder Barrdub, who did?' Before she could answer, the Brehon's eyes lit up. 'Ah, so that is why you were interested in the hermit Erca's herbs? Do you contend that he did this? That he did it to harm Fergal? We all know that he hates every Christian.'

Fidelma shook her head emphatically.

'Erca hates all Christians, but he did not do this. He simply confirmed my suspicion that I had tasted two powerful drugs which could be easily obtained in the vicinity. A deeper motive lies behind this murder than simply a hatred of Christians.'

She turned and caught Rimid's pale face. The man's lips were trembling.

'She is trying to lay the blame on me!' he cried.

The Brehon also was looking at Rimid with deep suspicion. He demanded: 'Was not your hatred of Fergal great? You said as much to us yesterday.'

'I did not do it. I loved Barrdub . . . I . . .' Rimid sprang to his feet and began to fight his way out of the great hall.

'Seize him!' cried the Brehon. Two clansmen moved forward.

But Fidelma had turned to the Brehon with shaking head.

'No, let him go. It was not Rimid.'

The Brehon frowned. Rimid, caught between the two clansmen, halted his struggles and glanced back in bewilderment.

'Who then?' the Brehon demanded in exasperation.

'Barrdub was murdered by Congal.'

There was a gasp.

'A lie! The bitch lies!' Congal had leapt to his feet in the great hall, his face pale, his hands clasped into fists.

'Congal murdered his own sister?' The Brehon was incredulous. 'But why?'

'For one of the oldest motives of all. For gain.'

'But, Barrdub had no property. What gain is in this deed?'

Sister Fidelma sighed sadly.

'Congal was an impecunious man. His father had held a good position within the clan and Congal, if all went well, could have expected no less. But things were never well for Congal. He was capricious, undependable. He preferred to dream and make great plans which always went awry. He was reduced, with his sister, to living in a poor wood and mud *bothán*, hiring out his labour to his neighbours who were better off than he was. They pitied him. That made him bitter. All this was common knowledge. You, Brehon, told me as much.

'Rimid and Barrdub were in love with each other. Rimid was not possessed of great wealth. He survived as most of us do, content to earn his living. But when Rimid went to ask Congal's approval to marry Barrdub, who was not yet at the age of consent, Congal refused. Why? Because Congal did not care for his sister's happiness. He cared for wealth. He demanded the full bride-price or *tinnscra* due for the daughter of a free hostel keeper of the tribe, even though both his sister and he had long fallen from that social position.'

'Yet that was his right in law,' interposed the Brehon.

'A right, truly. But sometimes rights can be a form of injustice,' replied Fidelma.

'Carry on.'

'Rimid could not afford the full *tinnscra*. Barrdub was indignant and made it clear to her brother that when she reached the age of consent, when she had free and equal choice, she would go with Rimid anyway. Her brother would not profit from any *tinnscra* then.'

Sister Fidelma paused a moment to gather her thoughts.

'Congal has conceived the idea that his only hope to alleviate his poverty and become respectable in the tribe was to get his hands on twenty milch cows which a prospective husband would pay for the full *tinnscra* or bride-price. Then a new idea came into his mind. A fantastic idea. Why settle for twenty milch cows for the bride-price? If his sister was slain, the murderer or his family would have to pay compensation and that compensation was set in law at no less than forty-five milch cows, the foundation of a respectable herd and one which would make him a person of position in the tribe. But he would have to ensure that the person charged with the crime could pay such a sum.

'Then Brother Fergal appears. It is true that an individual monk is not wealthy. However, it is the law that members of the *fine* or family of a person unable to pay the *eric* or compensation become responsible for the payment to the victim's family. It is well known that the Abbey stands in place of a family. If a member of the Abbey is found guilty of a crime, then the Abbey would be expected to pay the *eric*. Congal reasoned that the Abbey could well afford the forty-five milch cows that would be the compensation. Poor Barrdub's fate was then sealed.

'Congal knew of Fergal's ailment and means of medication. He prepared the potion, threw out Fergal's usual mixture and substituted his own drugged brew. He reasoned that Fergal would not check the contents of his kettle before he heated the herbal drink. Then Congal saw Rimid and prepared the way further by telling him that Barrdub was smitten by Fergal, that they were in love. Finally, Congal went to find Barrdub and the rest we already know.

'He killed her, carried her into Fergal's *bothán* as soon as the monk had dropped into his deep sleep, and left her there, smearing Fergal's hands and clothes with her blood. His two major mistakes were not leaving the murder weapon at the scene and not destroying the traces of the herbs in Fergal's bowl.'

She turned to where Congal was standing, his face white, his mouth working.

'There stands your contemptible killer. He murdered his own sister for a herd of cows.'

With a shriek, Congal drew a knife and leapt towards Sister

Fidelma. People scattered left and right before his frenzied figure.

Just before he reached her, the dark figure of a man intercepted him and struck him full in the face. It was Rimid. Congal collapsed senseless to the ground. As Rimid made to move forward, Fidelma reached forward and laid her slender hand on his shoulder.

'Revenge is no justice, Rimid. If we demand vengeance for every evil done against us, we will be guilty of greater evil. Let the court deal with him.'

Rimid hesitated.

'He has no means of paying adequate compensation to those he has wronged,' he protested.

Fidelma smiled softly.

'He has a soul, Rimid. He attempted to wrong a member of the family of the Abbey. The Abbey will demand compensation; the compensation will be his soul which will be given to God for disposal.'

'You will have him killed? Dispatched to God in the Otherworld?'

She shook her head gently.

'God will take him when the time is ordained. No, he will come to serve at the Abbey and, hopefully, find repentance in the service.'

After Brother Fergal had been absolved and Congal taken to be held for his trial, Fidelma walked to the door of the great hall with the Brehon.

'How did you suspect Congal?' asked the man.

'A man who lies once, will lie again.'

'In what lie did you discover him?'

'He claimed he knew nothing about herbs but he knew soon enough what the herb *stramóiniam* is used for and that Brother Fergal took it regularly. The rest was a mixture of elementary deduction and bluff for it might have been hard to prove conclusively without Congal's admittance of guilt.'

'You are an excellent advocate, Sister Fidelma,' observed the Brehon.

'To present a clever and polished argument is no great art. To perceive and understand the truth is a better gift.' She paused at the door and smiled at the judge. 'Peace with you, Brehon of the Eóghanacht of Cashel.' Then she was gone, striding away along the dusty road towards the distant Abbey.

MUGGING IN HARCOURT STREET

Cathal Ó Sándair

Undoubtedly the most popular detective in the Irish language is Réics Carlo—Rex Carlo—whose racy and colourful cases told by Cathal Ó Sándair (1922-) have been delighting generations of readers since the early 1940s. Specifically created by Cathal as an 'Irish Sexton Blake', the resourceful private investigator made his debut in 1942 in a thriller called NaMarbh a d' Fhill *(Return of the Dead). This story, and its successors, quickly established Carlo as the favourite reading matter for youngsters who should have been busy with their inspirational studies, as well as many adults who enjoyed a fast-paced thriller in their own language. The author, Cathal Ó Sándair, who had an English father and an Irish mother, grew up in Dublin and entered the Civil Service. In his spare time, however, he devoted himself to writing and was just 22 when he published the first Réics Carlo novel. Since then he has written more than 160 books, of which about 50 have featured his detective hero. At the height of Carlo's fame in the 1950s, the books were selling more than 100,000 copies per title—an enormous sale for a book in Irish. The 'Irish Sexton Blake' still has a large following today, and this short story, which Cathal has chosen especially for my anthology, is the first to be published in English and will, I am sure, not be the last. (It first appeared in* Feasta *magazine in 1982 and has been translated by Séamas Ó Coileáin.) The tense events of the 'Mugging in Harcourt Street' are typical of a Rex Carlo battle against crime and provide an ideal finale to the book.*

The time: end of the day, nightfall. The place: Harcourt Street, Dublin 2—a street of high office blocks, hotels and flats. Busy in the daytime. But a lonely, eerie glen when the dark clouds of bitter night press down like a roof over buildings which have witnessed the times of Victoria, Edward, George, the Free State, the Republic . . .

To any other pedestrian, the stooped, shrunken man walking slow and wearily that night would have appeared to be in his sixties: a pensioner most likely.

'Assault and battery,' he was thinking, 'that's the danger, the constant danger to old people in our cities and towns.'

There was another term: it was from America that we got both the term and the terror: 'mugging' . . . *mugail* in the language our ancestors have spoken since before the death of Christ: an ugly word for a terrible and ugly deed.

The fragile, bent man glanced around intently . . . Dark, lonely lanes on one side: danger there, without a doubt. People would say that it wasn't wise at all for the old to be out walking so late at night. So late? Well, doubtless that depends on your age.

'How often have muggings occurred—assault and battery—in this district for some time now?' the stooped walker asked himself.

There were reports in the news every week about such shameful events. The district was earning itself an unhealthy reputation. The man's expression became grave and dissatisfied: he didn't like it. He didn't like it at all. For a long time it had been a respectable, friendly place. But were barbarous, menacing villains to be allowed to dissipate the good name, like a puff of mist, like the river's foam?

The suit of clothes the man was wearing was smart, new, and expensive. A pensioner, one might say, retired from a generous company—from Dublin Corporation, from the Civil Service, or from the brewery up at James Gate . . . A reasonably good pension, the opportunity for a man to retain his dignity after the years of work: to be warm, comfortable and dry. A pound or two, or three even, always in his purse. In brief, the answer to a mugger's prayer.

The man went ahead nervously. It wasn't nice, not right or fitting that elderly citizens should be nervous like that in Dublin, capital city of *Banba na n-ainnir n-órchiabh*, in the year of Our Lord one thousand nine hundred and seventy nine. New York—fair enough: no sensible person there is out on his own when day is done. Wasn't it there that the diabolic, unnatural phenomenon of our times, mugging, was first reported?

'I don't think it's far from me now,' said the walker with surprising stoicism.

'*Que sera, sera*' . . . whatever will be, will be . . . well, what can't be cured must be endured, as they say. But most certainly whoever coined that old saying wasn't thinking of assault!

Was this the night when the walker would be ambushed? The same savages, who would think nothing of leaving an old person in the gutter, his life's blood flowing profusely from a gash in his head . . . would be content with a couple of pounds—the price of a bottle of wine, a packet of cigarettes . . . Was even hanging too good for them?

At any rate, the fateful moment was approaching the pedestrian in Harcourt Street. At that very moment, two young scoundrels were in Hatch Street, making for Harcourt Street; young, active and strong, two without pity or compassion. Two more villainous-looking people, you would not meet in a day's journey . . . nor in a night's journey.

'We've got to get some money, Nicky,' said Billy to his companion, 'some way or other. We haven't a cigarette between us, nor the price of a bottle.'

Nicky sniggered. 'We've never yet been left without a way, lad.'

'The usual way, of course!' said Billy.

'There's a fool born every minute,' said Nicky. 'Especially an old fool, with more money than sense.'

'Very nice too,' said his partner.

Turning into Harcourt Street, their eyes fell on a pedestrian under the street lamp on the other side of the road . . . a hunched man making his way slowly along the pavement. Nicky and Billy glanced at each other. Nicky nodded at his fellow conspirator. No need to speak. A nod was enough for the practised. Birds of a feather, they thought as one.

They waited a second or two till it was quite safe to cross the road Quickly they made for the other side. There were twenty yards between the young scoundrels and their prey.

He must have seen them crossing towards him out of the corner of his eye. It was clear that he was getting worried: he tried to quicken his pace. But he was pathetically weak. The little extra speed was nothing to his pursuers. The lone walker knew that very well, too.

Even worse: the street was more deserted than usual. There wasn't even much traffic to be seen. The fragile, stooped man was passing a piece of ground on which a large new building was going up, walls of boards and scaffolding along the way. It would be here, he thought, that the attack would take place, the assault and battery

. . . the mugging. He heard the footsteps clearly, closer, more urgent. That would be the ground where . . . a . . . Oh God, he wouldn't think of such a thing . . .

As for Nicky and Billy, they were in their element. It would be so simple . . . so quick. Like taking sweets from a child. It was clear from the appearance of the man ahead of them that he was not down to his last pound.

There was no justice in the world . . . and this kind of old codger was wealthy without being able to enjoy it. Well, Nicky and Billy would soon be living it up with what he had. They changed their pace and broke into a run, bearing down hotfoot on the walker.

Nicky ran past him, turned round, and spread his arms out to bar the pensioner's way. Billy stayed behind him thrusting out at him, throwing him against the board wall. The stooped fellow fell back and the boards supported him.

'W-what do you want?' he said, trembling. Nicky grabbed a fistful of lapel of their victim's overcoat. The old man sensed the foul odour of his assailant in his face.

'Everything you've got, grandad!' threatened Nicky through his teeth. 'Do you hear . . . everything . . . watch . . . money, down to the last penny.'

He gave a glancing blow to the pensioner's face and released his grip.

'Start fishing . . . deep in your pockets!' said Nicky roughly. 'We haven't got all night.'

'If I give . . . you—you won't hurt me?' pleaded the fragile hunched man.

The pair burst into derisive laughter.

'Money, cigarettes, watch . . . hurry up, you old fool!' said Billy.

The fellow took hold of his purse and offered it nervously to Nicky, who tore it out of his hand, looked inside, and let out a groan of displeasure.

'A few paltry coins, you simpleton, what good are they?'

To underline what he said, he punched his fist into the captive chest.

'Yeah, the bank notes!' repeated Billy, and clouted him hard on the ear.

Then they drew the man backwards and forwards between them, leaving him no time to fall.

'Quickly, the money!' ordered Nicky.

'A-all right . . .' said the man hoarsely. 'I've got a wallet . . . but give me room to get it out of the inside pocket of my suit . . .'

Billy smiled. 'That's the kind of talk we want to hear . . . Give him room, Nicky.'

As the pair of them moved back a few inches, something quite surprising happened. In a way, it was more like a miracle. It was as if the pensioner had suddenly grown taller, broader, stronger. When he moved his arms, they were like a windmill. They flew out and grabbed the pair, and threw them together, heavily, noisily. Then, in the twinkling of an eye, it was the two of them who were against the board wall with the ex-captive on the outside. Nicky and Billy tried to recover, but it was futile. Boxing, karate . . . judo; the fellow used every trick in the book. A thrust, a poke, a heavy blow . . . crash, thump, wallop . . . slap, bang, thud . . . a hurricane of clouts and blows fell on the two of them, drawing blood from the nose, the ear, the temple.

'Mercy!' cried Billy.

'Murder!' bellowed Nicky.

The fellow never let up, he never stopped nor stayed until the pair were laid low . . . knocked senseless . . . Then, he slapped his hands together, as if to wipe the dust from them, stooped to pick his wallet up from the ground, and went back down the street with an agile gait . . . without a trace of weakness or old age. . .

The guards found the pair later.

'W-we've been mugged!' said Nicky.

'It was dreadful, outrageous!' said Billy. 'We didn't stand a chance.'

But the guards knew the pair of them from of old, though they had never been able to connect them with serious crime. The guards considered that the treacherous had reaped their own reward.

A little before that, the one responsible for the havoc had reached a house in Harcourt Street . . . taken a key from his pocket and gone inside.

There was a brass plate on one of the door columns. On it was written:

REX CARLO
PRIVATE INVESTIGATOR

SOLUTION TO
A STUDY IN WHITE

by Nicholas Blake

The Inspector arrested the Guard for the wilful murder of Arthur J. Kilmington.

Kilmington's pocket had been picked by Inez Blake, when she pretended to faint at 8:25, and his gold watch was at once passed by her to her accomplice, Macdonald. Now Kilmington was constantly consulting his watch. It is inconceivable, if he was not killed till after 9 p.m., that he should not have missed the watch and made a scene. This point was clinched by the First-class passenger who had said that a man, answering to the description of Kilmington, had asked him the time at 8:50: if it had really been Kilmington, he would certainly, before inquiring the time of anyone else, have first tried to consult his own watch, found it gone, and reported the theft. The fact that Kilmington neither reported the loss to the Guard, nor returned to his original compartment to look for the watch, proves he must have been murdered *before he became aware of the loss*—i.e., shortly after he left the compartment at 8:27. But the Guard claimed to have spoken to Kilmington at 9 p.m. Therefore the Guard was lying. And why should he lie, except to create an alibi for himself? This is clue Number One.

The Guard claimed to have talked with Kilmington at 9 p.m. Now, at 8:55 the blizzard had diminished to a light snowfall, which soon afterwards ceased. When Stansfield discovered the body, it was buried under snow. Therefore Kilmington must have been murdered *while the blizzard was still raging*—i.e., some time before 9 p.m. Therefore the Guard was lying when he said Kilmington was alive at 9 p.m. This is Clue Number Two.

Henry Stansfield, who was investigating on behalf of the Cos-

364

mopolitan Insurance Company the loss of the Countess of Axminster's emeralds, reconstructed the crime as follows:

Motive: The Guard's wife had been gravely ill before Christmas: then, just about the time of the train robbery, he had got her the best surgeon in Glasgow and put her in a nursing home (evidence of engine-driver: Clue Number Three). A Guard's pay does not usually run to such expensive treatment: it seemed likely, therefore, that the man, driven desperate by his wife's need, had agreed to take part in the robbery in return for a substantial bribe. What part did he play? During the investigation the Guard had stated that he had left his van for five minutes, while the train was climbing the last section of Shap Bank, and on his return found the mail-bags missing. But Kilmington, who was travelling on his train, had found the Guard's van locked at this point, and now (evidence of Mrs. Grant: Clue Number Four) declared his intention of reporting the Guard. The latter knew that Kilmington's report would contradict his own evidence and thus convict him of complicity in the crime, since he had locked the van for a few minutes to throw out the mail-bags himself, and pretended to Kilmington that he had been asleep (evidence of Kilmington himself) when the latter knocked at the door. So Kilmington had to be silenced.

Stansfield already had Percy Dukes under suspicion as the organiser of the robbery. During the journey Dukes gave himself away three times. First, although it had not been mentioned in the papers, he betrayed knowledge of the point on the line where the bags had been thrown out. Second, though the loss of the emeralds had been also kept out of the Press, Dukes knew it was an emerald *necklace* which had been stolen: Stansfield had laid a trap for him by calling it a bracelet, but later in conversation Dukes referred to the 'necklace'. Third, his great discomposure at the (false) statement by Stansfield that the emeralds were worth £25,000 was the reaction of a criminal who believes he has been badly gypped by the fence to whom he has sold them. Dukes was now planning a second train robbery, and meant to compel the Guard to act as accomplice again. Inez Blake's evidence (Clue Number Five) of hearing him say,'You're going to help us again, chum,' etc., clearly pointed to the Guard's complicity in the previous robbery: it was almost certainly the Guard to whom she had heard Dukes say this, for only a railway servant would have known about the existence of a platelayers' hut up the line, and made an appointment to meet Dukes there;

moreover, if Dukes had talked about his plans for the next robbery, on the train itself, to anyone *but* a railway servant suspicion would have been incurred should they have been seen talking together.

Method: At 8:27 Kilmington goes into the Guard's van. He threatens to report the Guard, though he is quite unaware of the dire consequences this would entail for the latter. The Guard, probably on the pretext of showing him the route to the village, gets Kilmington out of the train, walks him away from the lighted area, stuns him (the bruise was a light one and did not reveal itself in Stansfield's brief examination of the body), carries him to the spot where Stansfield found the body, packs mouth and nostrils tight with snow. Then, instead of leaving well alone, the Guard decides to create an alibi for himself. He takes his victim's hat returns to the train, puts on his own dark, off-duty overcoat, finds a solitary passenger asleep, masquerades as Kilmington enquiring the time, and strengthens the impression by saying he'd walk to the village if the relief engine did not turn up in five minutes, then returns to the body and throws down the hat beside it (Stansfield found the hat only lightly covered with snow, as compared with the body: Clue Number Six). Moreover, the passenger noticed that the inquirer was wearing blue trousers (Clue Number Seven). The Guard's regulation suit was blue; but Dukes' suit was grey, and Macdonald's a loud check—therefore, the masquerader could not have been either of them.

The time is now 8:55. The Guard decides to reinforce his alibi by going to intercept the returning fireman. He takes a short cut from the body to the platelayer's hut. The track he now makes, compared with the beaten trail towards the village, is much more lightly filled in with snow when Stansfield finds it (Clue Number Eight): therefore, it must have been made some time after the murder, and could not incriminate Percy Dukes. The Guard meets the fireman just after 8:55. They walk back to the train. The Guard is taken aside by Dukes, who has gone out for his 'airing', and the conversation overheard by Inez Blake takes place. The Guard tells Dukes he will meet him presently in the platelayers' hut: this is aimed to incriminate Dukes, should the murder by any chance be discovered, for Dukes would find it difficult to explain why he should have sat alone in a cold hut for half an hour just around the time when Kilmington was presumably murdered only one hundred and fifty yards away. The Guard now goes along to the engine and stays there chatting with the crew for some forty minutes. His alibi is thus established for the period from 8:55 to 9:40 p.m. His plan might well have succeeded, but for three unlucky factors he could not possibly have taken into account—Stansfield's presence on the train, the blizzard stopping soon after 9 p.m., and the theft of Arthur J. Kilmington's watch.

ACKNOWLEDGEMENTS

The editor would especially like to thank the following for their help in assembling this collection: Peter Berresford Ellis, W.O.G. Lofts, Brian Cleeve, William Trevor and Séamas Ó Coileáin. He and the publishers are also grateful to the following authors, publishers and agents for permission to reprint copyright stories: Random Century Publishers Ltd for 'Events at Drimaghleen' by William Trevor, 'Telling' by Elizabeth Bowen, 'Murder at Cobbler's Hulk' by Sean O'Faolain and 'In the Train' by Frank O'Connor; *Irish Times* for 'The Informers' by Brendan Behan; Davis Publications Ltd for 'A Study in White' by Nicholas Blake; Express Newspapers for 'Rats' by Rearden Connor and 'The Glass Panel' by Eimar O'Duffy; Mills & Boon Ltd for 'A Lunatic at Large' by George A. Birmingham and 'Justice Evaded' by Dorothea Conyers; HarperCollins Publishing Group for 'The Sting' by Flann O'Brien, 'Girl of my Dreams' by Peter Cheyney and 'East Wind' by Freeman Wills Croft; Brian Cleeve for his story 'Foxer'; A.P. Watt Literary Agency for 'Two Bottles of Relish' by Lord Dunsany and 'All in the Way You Look at It' by Edmund Crispin; Victor Gollancz Ltd for 'Maiden's Leap' by Benedict Kiely and 'The Law is the Law' by Liam O'Flaherty; Peters, Fraser & Dunlop for 'Chailey's Folly' by L.A.G. Strong; A.M. Heath & Co for 'Murder in Repose' by Peter Tremayne; and Cathal Ó Sándair for his story 'Mugging in Harcourt Street'.